"With her trademark narrative intimacy, Finkbeiner returns to the world of Pearl Spence, a heroine already beloved by readers of *A Cup of Dust*. Finkbeiner's Depression-era canvas is replete with historical authenticity and colored by a voice both erudite and accessible. This coming-of-age story pairs its winsome heroine with a cast of salt-of-the-earth characters who will be welcomed by readers of Harper Lee and Julie Cantrell.

"With a stoic look at faith and resilience in a time of famine, *A Trail of Crumbs* is a perfect modern-day parable—destined to inspire, challenge, and beguile any who step into its fully realized world."
—Rachel McMillan, author of *A Lesson in Love and Murder*

"Susie Finkbeiner takes us right into the heart of the devastating years of the Great Depression. Pearl's story could have been my own grandmother's. It's as though I tapped into a piece of my own history that I didn't know was missing. *A Trail of Crumbs* is a beautiful, heart-wrenching tale of grief, suffering, love, and the enduring hope that comes from piecing a family back together. This was one of those books I didn't want to end."
—Kelli Stuart, author of *Like a River from Its Course*

Praise for *A Cup of Dust*

"This is a suspenseful page-turner, intricately plotted and bursting with meticulously drawn characters who jump from the page. [Pearl's] voice isn't one you'll soon forget."
—*RT Book Reviews*

"Riveting. An achingly beautiful tale told with a singularly fresh and original voice. This sepia-toned story swept me into the Dust Bowl and brought me face-to-face with both haunting trials and the resilient people who overcame them. Absolutely mesmerizing. Susie Finkbeiner is an author to watch!"
—Jocelyn Green, award-winning author

D0954199

Also by Susie Finkbeiner

Paint Chips
My Mother's Chamomile

Pearl Spence Novels
A Cup of Dust: A Novel of the Dust Bowl
A Trail of Crumbs: A Novel of the Great Depression
A Song of Home: A Novel of the Swing Era

A TRAIL *of* CRUMBS

A Novel of the Great Depression

SUSIE FINKBEINER

Kregel
Publications

A Trail of Crumbs: A Novel of the Great Depression
© 2017 by Susie Finkbeiner

Published by Kregel Publications, a division of Kregel, Inc.,
2450 Oak Industrial Dr. NE, Grand Rapids, MI 49505.

Published in association with the literary agency of Credo
Communications, LLC, Grand Rapids, Michigan,
www.credocommunications.net.

ISBN 978-0-8254-4446-3

Printed in the United States of America

17 18 19 20 21 22 23 24 25 26 / 5 4 3 2 1

In memory of
Wendy Gingrich

ACKNOWLEDGMENTS

Writing this novel was a battle against self-doubt and a monstrously cruel inner voice. But I survived it and so did Pearl, and it's all to the credit of those I am honored to call my good friends.

Alexis De Weese, Amelia Rhodes, and Darron Schoeder: Thanks for the texts, the emails, the phone calls. You three reminded me to breathe and I am forever grateful.

Jocelyn Green: Thank you for understanding the madness which is novel writing and teaching me how much stronger our voices are when we sing together.

Ann Byle: I'll never forget how you refused to let me give up on this novel, on Pearl, and most of all on myself. Thank you.

Janyre Tromp: Your unending enthusiasm for this novel served as fuel on the tougher days. Your edits broadened the story, making it richer and more beautiful.

Dawn Anderson: Your honesty is what transformed this novel and made it the story it needed to be. Your belief in my abilities spurred me on. I'm a better writer because of you.

Steve Barclift: You have the gift of writing the most encouraging emails I've ever received. They make me want to live up to your opinion of me. Thank you.

Jim Kregel: When I sat beside you to sign the contract for this book, you told me you were praying for me. I cannot tell you how grateful I am for your prayers.

Elise, Austin, and Timmy: You three ate more than your share of pizza and mac 'n' cheese as I wrote this novel. Thank you for understanding and being quick to forgive your quirky mama. I love you!

Jeff: Thanks for never swerving in your love for me. You make this life so much fun and I love you more than coffee and chocolate.

And, finally, to my heavenly Father: For all the times I struggled or strayed, You kept Your eyes on me, waiting for me to come back to You. You left a trail for me to follow, helping me find my way. And when I did return, You came running. I never want to forget how it feels to come home to You.

CHAPTER ONE

Red River, Oklahoma
Palm Sunday, April 14, 1935

If a girl could go blind from too bright a sky, I would have gazed upward anyhow, burning the sight right out of my eyes. Far as I could remember, there'd never been a day so calm and blue, without a whisper of wind. Of all the things I could've done with that Sunday afternoon, all I wanted was to sit on the porch and let the sunshine warm my skin.

I believed it would have been a sin to stay inside when God had sent us such fine weather. According to Pastor Ezra Anderson, sin was the reason we'd gotten into the dusty mess we were in. The way I saw it, that day was God's way of letting us know He wasn't mad at us anymore.

Just maybe He'd seen fit to forgive us.

My older sister, Beanie, sat beside me on the porch, her eyes clamped tight against the sunshine like she didn't want it getting in. Every now and again she made one of her little grunting sounds that came from the back of her throat. I'd grown used to the noises Beanie made, and they didn't bother me like they did other people.

Thing was, most folks didn't understand Beanie on account she wasn't like anybody else in Red River. She wasn't smart like most people because she was born not breathing. Some people in town didn't seem to know it was wrong to say nasty things about a person just because they were different. They'd say my sister was an idiot or stupid or any number of other cruel things. Seemed to me they were the ones lacking in brains, to say something so hurtful.

Meemaw, though, never listened to what those folks said. She'd told me Beanie was just the way God wanted her and that no soul on earth had the right to question it.

Meemaw had always known just what to say to make me feel better. I wondered if she wasn't hobbling around heaven, spreading her wisdom and sweet smiles the same way she'd done on earth. I sure did miss her.

"I wanna hear a story," Beanie said, opening one of her lids and eye-balling me.

"You do?" I asked, giving her a half smile.

She grunted her yes.

"Then go on and get my book off the shelf." I nodded at the open front door. "I'll read something to you."

"Don't wanna go in."

"Well, I don't either." I sighed.

Some days I got tired of having to take care of her so much. She could do about anything for herself. Problem was, she was stubborn as an old mule. When she got in her mind that she didn't want to do a thing, there was no way of convincing her otherwise. She'd stay put until I gave up. I usually just shook my head and did for her on account it wound up being easier in the end.

"I wanna hear a story," she repeated in case I'd forgotten what she said.

"How about I just tell it to you?" I asked. "Which one you want?"

"The girl and the boy and the forest."

"You never remember their names, do you?" I asked.

She closed her eye again and shook her head.

"Hansel and Gretel," I told her. "That the one?"

She gave me an "uh-huh."

Silly smile on her face, she scooted on her backside so that she could lean against the slats under the porch railing. Tipping her head, she let the sun shine full on her face. Her wild dark hair fuzzed around her like a shadowy halo.

"All right," I started. "There was once a boy and a girl named Hansel and Gretel. They lived deep in the dark woods with their father and mother."

"She weren't their real mama," Beanie said. "Their real one was dead."

"That's right. They had a stepmother."

"A wicked one," she said. "She ain't nice."

Beanie opened her eyes just a slit and peeked at me a second before closing them again.

I thought of Mama, how she wasn't my real mother. How she and Daddy had taken me in as their own, never treating me any different from Beanie. Mama loved me like I'd come from her.

My real mother had left me right after I was born. My mother, Winnie—best-kept secret in all the history of Red River. Much as I didn't like to, I thought of her most days even if just a little. And when she did come to mind, it was her with glassy eyes and bleeding body, the life gushing out all over me.

That was hardly more than a month ago. I hoped after a while the memory of her getting shot and killed the way she did would fade away. I hoped that enough sunny days might work to do just that.

Beanie made another of her noises, pulling me out of the bad memory and back to that sunshine-soaked porch.

"Nope," I said, sitting up straighter. "She wasn't nice. That stepmother was real mean and selfish. When they ran out of food, she got even meaner."

Turning, I saw Mama in the side yard, where she shook out a rug, Oklahoma dust clouding up from it, showing like gold in the sun. She caught me watching her and smiled.

"Well," I went on. "That stepmother got the idea to send the children away."

"Out in the woods," Beanie added.

"But Hansel, he was a smart boy. He'd been listening and came up with a plan all his own."

"He took him a piece of bread." Beanie swatted at a bug that got too close to her face.

"He got that bread and broke it all to bits. As he and Gretel followed behind their father into the dark woods, he dropped pieces of it behind them, leaving a trail of crumbs so they could find their way back home."

"They never went home," Beanie said. "Once you go, you can't never get back."

Shifting, she turned her face toward town and opened her eyes. Her overgrown eyebrows twitched up and down, and she rubbed at her nose with the back of her hand.

"What do you mean?" I asked.

She acted like she hadn't heard me even though I knew well enough she had. Wiping her hand on the skirt of her dress she closed her eyes again.

"I don't wanna hear no more," she said.

I watched as she leaned her head on the slats again. After a minute she started on her snoring I knew to be fake. Sometimes she'd do that, pretend to be asleep, so I'd leave her alone.

On her lap she held her hand in a fist, the dirt-under-the-nails fingers tucked tight into her palm. I put my hand over it, covering it.

"I love you," I said.

I meant it.

She opened her hand enough to hold my fingers just for a moment. She squeezed them before she went back to her pretend snoring.

Out back of our house, Millard had set up his horseshoes. He'd been mayor of Red River long as anybody could remember. He said he was born mayor, which I knew wasn't true. He'd been born in Virginia. I never did remind him of that fact on account of it wasn't my place to.

Ladies didn't contradict old men, that was what Mama'd taught me. And they didn't say somebody was old, either.

I tried being as much a lady as I could for Mama's sake. I did. But it sure wasn't easy.

"Now, you gotta hold that shoe just like this," Millard said, lifting his hand in front of him so Ray could see. "That's fine. Just like that."

Ray Jones stood, nodding at Millard. He was eleven and a half, a whole year older than me, but didn't mind being my best friend. Really, he was about the only one left in town to be friends with. Still, if there'd been a whole truckload of kids in Red River, I would've picked Ray over all of them any old day.

He'd been staying with us since his old dugout had gotten flattened by a month of dusters. Meemaw'd always told me to see how all things worked together for the good of those who loved God. I supposed if there was any good from all the dust, having Ray around was it.

"Now, swing back before you give it a toss." Millard showed him what he meant, then threw the old rusted horseshoe toward the stake in the ground. It clanked, hitting the goal and circling round it before thumping on the dirt. "Just like that. Nothin' to it."

Ray stuck his tongue out the side of his mouth and wrinkled up his forehead, eyes trained on that old stake.

I shimmied myself up on the back porch, watching him and Millard play.

Ray's father never would've taken the time to teach him how to play a game like that. Mr. Jones had been too busy pouring whiskey down his throat and wandering all over creation doing who knew what. He'd say he was looking for work, but we all knew better than that. When he was at home, he'd spend his time whupping Ray and Mrs. Jones for something or other. But he couldn't hurt them anymore. He was dead, Mr. Jones was, and by his own doing. I wondered if Ray was haunted by seeing his father hanging like he had.

I hoped not.

The good thing that came out of Mr. Jones killing himself was that it left room for Daddy and Millard to show Ray all the man things he ought to learn. Still, I didn't think it took all the sting out of it.

It sure was an awful thing, losing your pa, no matter how nasty he'd been.

Their game done, Ray slumped his shoulders. He'd never liked losing much. But the way Millard made sure to shake his hand and smile, I knew Ray wouldn't be too sore about it.

"You're learnin'," Millard said, rubbing Ray's head so the tan hair stuck to the sweat on his forehead. "Pretty soon you'll be better than me, I bet."

"My, my," Daddy said, stepping out the back door. He hopped off the porch and made his way to Millard. "What've we got here?"

"Thought it's as good a day as any for horseshoes," Millard answered, taking off his hat and wiping at his head with a bandana. "How about you try and beat me at a game."

"I'd like nothing better." Daddy rubbed his hands together. "It's been a couple years."

"Don't worry." Millard nodded his head at him. "I'll go easy on ya."

Daddy stooped and picked up one of the shoes off the ground, giving it a toss. He missed the stake by a good foot.

"Well, I might have to give you a lesson, too," Millard said, laughing.

Ray came toward me, his hands shoved in his overall pockets and his bare feet shuffling through the dust.

"Wanna go for a walk?" he asked.

I shrugged, not wanting to say that Mama didn't want me wandering around. She'd kept a close eye on me ever since Eddie DuPre had taken me and kept me hidden away in a cellar. With all the nightmares I'd had since then, I didn't mind being watched so close.

"Come on," Ray said.

"I don't know." I crossed my arms.

"You think your ma'll say no?" he asked.

I shrugged again.

"Can't hurt to ask, can it?"

I shook my head.

"You too scared?" Ray asked, but not in a mean way. And not in a way that tried to make me feel small. "You don't gotta be scared no more, Pearl."

I couldn't look at him just then, so I turned toward the empty part of the yard where Mama'd once had a garden. It had long been lost to the drought and the dust like everything else that'd once been green and living. Life didn't seem to stand much of a chance anymore there in No Man's Land.

"I'm not scared," I whispered. It was a lie, and I figured he knew it.

"I promise I won't let nothin' happen to you," he said. "You trust me?"

I did and I told him so.

"Sheriff, sir?" Ray called out, turning toward Daddy. "Can Pearl go for a walk with me?"

"Go ahead," Daddy said, not turning from the game. "Just don't wander off too far, hear? We'll be having supper in a little bit."

"Yes, sir."

Daddy tossed and missed again, making Millard laugh so hard his head tilted back and his face pointed to the sky. The sound of his laughter made me think the dry days were over after all, and that good days were coming.

His laughter stole away some of my fear. Not all of it, but enough.

Pastor had told us that morning in church that God's wrath was spent. He'd said we weren't going to be punished anymore for our transgressions. The wage had been paid and the blessings were on the way. I didn't put much stock in his words, if I were honest.

Millard, though, he could've said that elephants could fly all the way to the stars or that horny toads could talk and I'd have believed every word of it.

"Come on," Ray said, nudging me with his elbow.

I slid off the porch and chased after him at an almost run from the back yard.

"Ray," Daddy called after us. "You take care of my girl, will ya?"

"Yes, sir," Ray hollered back, looking over his shoulder.

We circled around to the front of the house. There Beanie still sat, her head against the slats of the porch. But when I saw her just then, her eyes were open wide as they could get, and she seemed to be breathing in the air like she was catching some kind of a scent.

I swallowed hard, pushing down the scared feeling that bubbled up in me. And I tried to tell myself that nothing bad would happen. Not that day, at least. All I had to do was look up at the blue sky to prove it was true.

Mama hadn't pulled my hair back that day, so it fluttered behind me, long and blond and wild. Months before I might have broken into a gallop, pretending my hair was a horse's mane and my feet hooves. But that was before, and I didn't make believe anymore, not like I used to, at least. Those days were gone.

Still, running alongside Ray with my hair loose felt good. I thought we could have gone on like that forever, the land wide-open as the sky. It was as if the whole world had changed while we slept the night before. The air even smelled different, like fresh-washed clothes. I wondered if that wasn't the way spring had always smelled in the days before the dust had come. If it had, I'd forgotten.

Down the center of the road, Ray and I slowed. I hadn't taken off my shoes, and they'd gotten full of grit. I took a second to dump them out. He waited for me.

Standing up straight, I thought about Jesus coming into the town of Jerusalem and wondered if it'd been springtime there that day. Pastor'd gone on and on that morning in church about Palm Sunday, not saying anything about what the weather might've been like. I did hope it had been sunny and warm that day as Jesus rode along on the donkey.

Just then the street running through Red River was empty of people. I figured, though, if Jesus came to town they would come on out of their shacks or dugouts or from where some stayed in the Hooverville. They'd come from miles, happy enough to greet Him. There weren't too many still around, but enough folks for a good welcome.

I didn't know that Jesus would pick a donkey to ride into Red River. Maybe He'd come on an old, squeaky bicycle. Folks in town wouldn't have palm branches to wave for Him like they'd had in old Jerusalem. Nothing green had grown in Oklahoma in about forever, but they'd wave their hands and say "howdy," which I thought Jesus would like just fine. Since they were at it, that "howdy" would work for a "hosanna."

Once Jesus was in town, He wouldn't go straight to see Pastor just like He didn't seek out the scribes and Pharisees. Instead, I figured, He'd take His time shaking hands and slapping backs that belonged to the regular old folks in Cimarron County.

I just hoped He wouldn't find us the kind to wave our howdies on Sunday only to turn tail on Him by Friday.

Before I knew it, we were well past town and weaving around behind Pastor's house. Once we got by their backyard fence, Ray stopped and dropped down to peep through a hole in the wood. He waved for me to come beside him. I looked around me to be sure nobody saw before I kneeled and took a peek for myself.

"What is it?" I asked, quiet as I could, trying to find a gap in the fence.

Ray shushed me and pulled me closer to him where there was a space to look through. Closing one eye, I focused my sight through the space in the crumbling wood. There on the other side of the fence was Pastor's wife. Most people called her Mad Mabel on account she was loony in the head.

Mad Mabel scared me something awful, even though Daddy said more than once that she wouldn't hurt a fly. But I'd seen the snakes she'd killed and set to dry on the fence line to try and bring the rain. If that didn't give a body the willies, I didn't know what would.

She stood at the back of the yard, Mad Mabel did, spinning in circles, a dingy rag in her hand that she waved up and down and all around. The dress she had on seemed like it had been fine long ago. Lace hung wilted off the yellowed fabric. When she turned her back toward us, I could see the buttons lined up from top to bottom. Years before, those buttons maybe had a shimmer to them. But just like most other things, they'd got the shine rubbed right out of them.

Mad Mabel'd only managed to get a couple of those buttons through the holes, though, keeping her pale, mole-spotted flesh open to the day.

The way the dress hung loose made me think she'd been a good deal bigger when she'd first worn it. She'd withered over the years, I imagined. I could see just about every bone in her spine and that made me feel embarrassed on her behalf.

"What's she doing?" I whispered, glancing at Ray.

"Don't know," he answered before putting his finger to his lips, hushing me again.

We watched her strange dancing for a few minutes. It seemed something that wasn't for us to see, but we didn't move away or cover our eyes. I wondered if it wasn't something she did just for herself, maybe for God even.

I made to get up to leave, but Ray grabbed hold of my arm, keeping me next to him.

Pastor called from inside the small house, his voice thinner than I was used to it sounding. Mad Mabel didn't seem to hear him. She just kept on spinning and waving her rag, her eyes closed.

He stepped out of the house, his suspenders hanging off the waist of his trousers, making them hang on his slender hips. The good shirt he'd worn to preach in that morning was unbuttoned all the way, showing his sweat-stained undershirt. Everything about him drooped, hung, sagged.

"Mabel, what in tarnation are you doin'?" He put his hands on his hips. "Come on in and take off that dress. You're fixin' to spoil it."

There wasn't a hint of authority in his words. Just weakness. Exhaustion. Plum wore out.

Mad Mabel didn't obey him. What she did was raise her voice, singing some tune I couldn't place. The words didn't make sense, like she was making them up as she went along. She went to swinging that rag even more wild in the air. Her dress slipped off one of her shoulders and she didn't bother to push it back up, like she didn't even notice.

Ray raced me to the old Watson ranch. I didn't know why I even tried catching him. He'd always been faster than me by a mile. Still, I pumped my legs, not caring how my skirt flipped up on my thighs or how my shoes rubbed against the backs of my heels. I'd not felt that free in months. It was worth a blister or two.

Yards ahead of me he dropped in the dirt of what used to be the Watsons' front yard. I made it to him, huffing and puffing, trying to catch a breath.

"What took you so long?" he asked, winking up at me.

I kicked dust on his feet. He laughed and put out his hand.

"Help me up," he said.

"Nuh-uh." I stepped back and crossed my arms, jutting out one of my hips like Mama often did. "Get your own self up, ya lazy dog."

He did just that, but not before tossing a handful of dirt at me. I shoved him, almost knocking him back to the ground. We never meant any harm.

I knew he could've hurt me if he'd wanted to. But it wasn't in him, much as it could have been, the way his father'd mistreated him.

"Come on," he said, nodding at the Watsons' house.

I followed him to the porch that wrapped all the way around both sides of the ranch house. I remembered Mrs. Watson'd kept rocking chairs on that porch back in the day when they still lived there. Mama'd sit in one, sipping sweet tea and chatting with Mrs. Watson about whatever it was women had to say when times were good.

We'd been invited to eat supper there many times. I'd made chase with their boys around the ranch, playing pirate ship on their porch on days when Mama and Mrs. Watson were inside putting up cans of food for winter.

It would've surprised me if Ray and his family ever got an invitation to so much as step inside that place. Rich people didn't like to rub shoulders so much with poor folk. Not in the long-gone days of plenty, at least.

The Watsons' house had stood empty more than a year. That was how long it'd been since that family had packed up their things, even tying the rocking chairs to the side of the truck, and rumbled away from Red River.

They'd lost everything, that was what Daddy told me. Their crop failed, their stock died out, and the bank came calling in their debts.

Same old story all over Cimarron County. All of Oklahoma, too.

Only thing that land was good for anymore was rounding up the plague of jackrabbits for the slaughter.

On the day they'd left, Mrs. Watson had promised Mama she'd write, let us know where they ended up and if they were all right. Far as I knew, Mama had never gotten that letter.

"Ray, you think you'll ever leave?" I asked.

"You mean Red River?" He turned toward the house, tugging at a loose nail in the porch.

"Yeah," I answered.

"Don't rightly know." Not getting the nail to budge, he gave up and put both hands in his overall pockets. "Guess it matters what my ma wants to do."

"I hope you don't," I said. "Leave, I mean."

He nodded and scratched at his chin.

"If my ma wants to go West, I gotta go, too," he said. "Can't stay here all my life. Ain't nothin' for me to do but go, I reckon."

I held myself against a shiver that traveled up my skin. Seemed the day was getting colder.

"I'd miss you," I said.

He squinted at me, giving me his most crooked smile. "Course you would."

Ray Jones always did know how to make me laugh.

I shoved him, and he tried to run from me. In our chasing I got all turned around so I was looking in the direction of home.

My smile dropped hard as a brick along with any hope in the blue-sky day. My shiver turned to a shudder. Fear froze me all the way to the soles of my feet.

"Ray," I said.

He was still laughing and kicked a toe-full of dirt on my shoes. "You're gonna miss me so bad."

"No, Ray." My voice was full of panting breath and shaky quakes. "It's coming."

"What're you talkin' about?"

I lifted my hand and pointed, not knowing what words to use so he'd know what I saw. "It's coming."

He turned and was quiet, seeing what headed our way.

Birds came flying over our heads, moving fast along the pushing wind. So strong that wind blew, they hardly had to flap a wing. They didn't squawk or twitter or scream even. No time for alarm. Only time to flee.

It was coming.

Needle pricks of flying sand stung my arms, my legs, my face. It worked its way into my eyes and my nose. When I opened my mouth it stippled on my tongue. My ears filled up with the angry, hateful roaring as darkness itself came rolling across the fields.

It was coming.

CHAPTER TWO

Pastor liked to preach about the wrath of God flattening the old Bible cities of Sodom and Gomorrah. His eyes would take on a certain kind of wild glow when he talked about the sulfur raining down on the sinners. He'd say how Lot and his family escaped the blazing anger of God by the skin of their teeth. I wondered if Pastor wasn't disappointed that they got away.

"But Lot's wife, in her unfaithfulness, turned to look back," he'd roar. "And for her godless doubt, she got turned into a pillar of salt. Praise God!"

Red River was no Sodom, and Cimarron County no Gomorrah. Still Pastor'd told us the dust storms were the weight of God's punishing hand for our sin.

Like Lot's wife, I couldn't keep from turning to see the rolling punishment headed our way. I didn't turn to salt, but the weight of fear fell heavy on me anyhow, making me like to crumble to nothing.

Taller than any building, wider than the whole Panhandle of Oklahoma, darker than any night I'd ever seen, the full fury of dust rushed toward Ray and me. Thick, evil-black earth moved across the land, picking up what was left loose and working it into its crushing, rolling, sideways cyclone.

Above it, the sky stayed bright as God's promise to never destroy the earth with floodwater again.

He never did promise not to destroy it with dirt, though.

Ashes to ashes. Dust to dust.

"We gotta get down in the cellar," Ray hollered at me, grabbing hold of my wrist.

"No," I yelled, wishing he knew how I'd rather die than go underground. "I want to go home."

"Storm's gonna hit there first." He tugged me, making me turn around toward him. "We'll be safe if we get in that cellar. Come on."

I yanked my hand from him.

"We'd get buried," I screamed.

Turning to see the storm once more, I saw an outline of somebody running ahead of the roller. Wild hair stood up all over her head; her dress was blown this way and that, showing her legs all the way up to her underthings. I tried to get to her, to fight my way against the force of wind. I stumbled and fell. Stumbled and fell. I screamed in frustration that I was not so strong as the storm.

"Beanie," I hollered, hoping she'd hear me over the roaring wind.

She stopped and I struggled to see her face, unable to keep my eyes open too long for the stinging dust. Lifting her arms, Beanie turned away from me, reaching for the swirling dirt like she hoped to hold it back, to keep it from getting to me. The sun seemed to work with her, breaking through the pelting dust with small beams that glowed every color I could imagine.

"Come on," Ray yelled, his voice cracking.

Thick and hazy the air moved around Beanie, moved around me. Again I tried to get to her, and again I got knocked down. She somehow stood firm in the charging wind.

"Beanie," I screamed over and over again. I crawled, my hands and knees sinking into the shifting sands beneath me. No matter how I tried I couldn't get close enough.

Then the dust overtook her.

She was gone. Swallowed up. I couldn't see so much as her outline or her shadow. It had come on so quick, the roller. Squinting, I tried to find her, but all I could see was black and tan and gray. Even though I knew it couldn't help, I kept calling out for her.

It didn't take long for the storm to take me, too. It gobbled me up, chewing on my flesh with the stones and scraps of sharp things that flew around in its cycle.

All I could think to do was fall to the ground and curl into a ball, holding my face in my hands. I screamed with my mouth closed. I screamed for terror and for anger and for the feeling that I'd never be found.

I prayed and prayed.

Save Beanie. Save Beanie. Save Beanie.

Every inch of dust that fell over me pushed me down, down, down. I feared soon I'd end up underground.

"I wanna go home," I whimpered. "I want my mama. I want my mama now."

Lost in the wind, lost in the storm. Hidden from help by the inky-thick sky.

Nobody's gonna find you here.

Eddie's ghost howled along on the wind.

Ain't nobody comin' lookin' for you.

But Beanie, she'd come. She must've known the storm was brewing. Probably smelled it on the air. She'd always felt them before anybody else.

Beanie had come.

She's a idiot, ain't she?

But she had known to come, that I'd needed her. She'd figured that much out.

Nobody's gonna find you here.

Daddy would. And Mama'd sit, wringing her hands with worry.

They ain't your real family. They don't love you.

They did love me, I knew that much.

Nah, they just feel sorry for you. Pity ain't love.

Rage blended with my fear, pulling a savage shriek from me. I tried with all my mental strength to remind myself that Eddie was dead. He had a bullet in his head and he was dead, never to bother me again. Dead and gone. Still, his memory haunted, pulsing against me like the shredding storm.

You're never gonna make it back, his voice whispered on the wind.

The black cloud of dirt rolled over me, pulling at me, trying to make me join its turning, churning path.

Pushing my hands against my head even harder, I held myself tight.

I was as good as lost.

I walked into Meemaw's bedroom. It was a waking dream and I knew it. Still it seemed as real as anything else. And better by miles than hearing Eddie's haunting.

Mama stood by the bed. A sheet covered the lump that I knew to be Meemaw's lifeless body. Touching the crisp white cotton, Mama asked if I wanted to feel the cold skin.

I made a sound from the back of my throat, wanting to say no, but afraid if I opened my mouth I'd let in too much dirt.

Snaps of static popped blue in the air when Mama pulled the sheet up, sparking bright and cracking loud. Meemaw's eyes jolted open.

"Good morning, Mother," Mama said.

Loose and shaky, Meemaw's head rolled to one side so she could face me. Her mouth opened once, twice, again before any noise came out. The jaws creaked like a thirsty hinge. A small moaning escaped, sticking in her throat like a warped door getting forced open.

"The Lord is near," she rasped, her eyes piercing through the haze in the room. "He sees you. He knows where you're at. All you gotta do is be still."

Her eyelids snapped shut and her head creaked back to the way it was before. The sheet dropped gentle over her face.

"She's at rest," Mama said.

Outside Meemaw's window, the black swirl of dust raged.

My name. I heard my name hollered through the still-roaring wind. The voice wasn't a dream, or a haunting either. My name. It was real. The voice belonged to Ray. It drew nearer and nearer until I felt hands groping, landing on my back.

"Ray?" I said, dust rushing into my open mouth.

"Where's Beanie?" he asked.

I tried to tell him I didn't know, but all I managed was a choking cough.

"We'll find her," he said. "We will."

My name again. A deeper voice called it out. And another voice, deeper still. Daddy and Millard. I let Ray yell to them. He kept his arms around me and I was glad to be held down so I wouldn't get lost again.

They called back and forth to each other. Back and forth. Eventually Daddy and Millard got closer until we huddled together, the four of us. I grabbed onto Daddy, my arms holding him tight as I could, and I had no intention of letting go.

"I got bandanas," Daddy said, feeling in the dark to tie one around my face, covering my mouth and nose. His knot pulled at my hair, tangling it with the fabric, but I didn't care. "Ray, I got one for you, too."

"Beanie came," I said. "She's gone."

"She ain't too far off," Ray added. "Over to your right, I think."

"She was coming for us." I started crying and I didn't think my words made a lick of sense. "She knew."

"All right," Daddy said. "It's gonna be all right, darlin'. She'll find her way back to us."

"What if she doesn't?" I asked.

Nobody answered.

"We'd best get 'em home," Millard said.

"Would you take them?" Daddy asked.

"Course I will."

"Can't you come?" Panic rose from deep in my guts. "Daddy, please?"

"I gotta find your sister."

"I'll stay," I said. "I can help."

"Darlin', you'll be helping me by getting home to your mama. She's real worried." His voice was stern. Not mad, but serious. I knew I'd best mind, much as I didn't want to leave him there. "Go on home with Millard, hear?"

I didn't answer him because my crying clamped my throat shut.

Ray put both his hands on my shoulders, and I took Millard by a couple of his fingers. We walked the direction I imagined was the way home. Three blind mice walking one after the other, leaving Daddy and Beanie behind.

If I shook all the way down to my fingers Millard didn't say anything about it. He did, though, rub his rough-padded thumb against the back of my hand now and then and say, "Gettin' closer. We're findin' our way just fine."

Daddy's voice, calling for Beanie, got fainter and fainter the more we made strides away from them.

"Now, no matter what, don't you touch that barbed wire," Millard said, turning his head toward us. "See it?"

The dark was thinning, even if the dust still thickened the air. I turned and looked at the wire Millard pointed at. It was a small comfort that I could see, even if it wasn't very much.

"Don't want ya to get shocked. Don't know if it still would, but it ain't worth the chance," he went on.

Over the years of dust, I'd gotten my share of pokes from the charge the storms caused. Daddy'd tried explaining it to me one time, but it seemed like nothing more than an awful sort of magic to me. The kind of magic used by evil queens to change crops into dust, blue days into inky nights, and barbed wire into blazing threads of fire.

As we walked on, the haze cleared inch by inch. We moved slowly, step after step after step, for what seemed like the remainder of eternity. The more we walked, the clearer the air got.

Out of the corner of my eye I spied a lump on top of a pile of dirt. It jerked and flicked its feathers and beak. Brown wings tried to move, tried to get the body set to fly off. The most it could manage, though, was a frantic, scared flapping.

Letting go of Millard's hand, I leaned over to look at the bird. Feathers the color of earth were rumpled, full of dust. I could see, even through my sore and scratched eyes, it was nothing but a sparrow.

"Come on," Ray said, tapping my shoulder. "Let's keep on."

"It's hurt." I reached out one finger to touch the bird. It made a scratchy, squeaking sound and struggled away from my hand.

"Looks like it's got a broke wing," Millard said, squatting on his haunches beside me. "Probably got downed in the storm. I imagine there's lots of critters took a beatin'."

"We gotta help it," I said, hearing the begging in my own voice.

"Don't know what we can do." Millard made his voice quiet and gentle. "It's more scared of us than anything just now. Might do it more hurt if we tried pickin' it up."

"I don't wanna leave it here alone." I tried touching it again. Millard wrapped his fingers around my wrist, staying my hand. "Please, Millard. I don't wanna let it die. Not here."

"Ain't nothin' else we can do, much as I wish there was." He spoke right to me. The tenderness in his eyes made me want to cry. "We gotta keep movin'. I gotta get you outta this dust. All right, darlin'?"

I didn't have any fight left in me to tell him no. The three of us moved along, staying clear of the fence that might give us a jolt and shuffling our way in the direction of home.

I sure hated to leave that bird to die alone in that pile of dust.

It was hard to know how long we walked. With each step I knew for sure I couldn't take another. Millard felt me falling behind. He told me to hold him around the neck, and he hefted me up into his arms, carrying me like I weighed nothing at all.

For an old man, he was sure strong.

I didn't tell him so much, of course.

By the time we reached the main street of Red River, we could see well enough to know where we were. It was an awful sight, how that one storm dumped a whole world-full of dust right down on top of us.

I rested my head against Millard's chest, closing my eyes so I wouldn't have to see more than I needed to. All I could think about was the dust covering over Beanie and fearing she was so buried nobody'd ever find her.

After a little while more, Millard let out a sigh, and I did hope it was a relieved one.

"We made it," he whispered. "You're home."

I opened my lids, but I couldn't see for the flood that blurred my eyes.

He put me down on the front porch before he opened the door.

"Thank God!" Mama cried. "Thank God."

She rushed to me, putting her hands all over me, checking me from head to toe. She examined every sore and bump and gash. She pushed the hair from my face and kissed both my cheeks and used her thumbs to wipe away my tears.

"Are you all right?" she asked, her voice shaking.

I wasn't sure I had a good answer for her question so I didn't say anything.

"And you, Ray?" she said, putting her hand out for him. "Okay?"

"Yes, ma'am," he answered.

"And Beanie? Tom?" She looked at the door. "Where's your sister and daddy?"

"Tom's out lookin' for her," Millard answered.

"She wasn't with you?" Mama asked, looking right at me and touching her fingertips to her mouth.

I shook my head. "She came looking for us," I told her.

Ray told Mama as best he could what'd happened.

"Lord God." Mama pulled me to her.

❁

Millard had gone back out to help Daddy. Mama'd given him a lantern and a flashlight and a thermos of water.

It was all she could do to keep Ray in the house. He worried so about his mother.

"She's probably just fine," Mama said. "I'll bet she's just worrying about you something awful."

"I gotta see she's all right," he said.

"In the morning," Mama said. "Wait until morning."

"But—"

"Ray. Please don't go." Mama put her hand on his cheek. "Stay."

He did as she said but I knew he wasn't happy about it.

Mama walked me up to my room, where she had me undress all the way. She rubbed ointment on the sores and blisters that covered me all over. I was embarrassed, her seeing me naked like that. But the medicine soothed and I didn't argue. She had me sip a little water. The whole time she kept the place in between her eyebrows tensed and wrinkled.

She lowered a nightie over my head and lifted my blanket. Inches of dust slid off to the floor. I climbed onto my bed and she tucked me in under the sheet and the blanket, fretting that I'd be cold. I told her I'd be all right. I flipped over my pillow and then put my head down.

Quick as could be I was sinking into sleep, deep and warm.

Beanie stood ahead of me in the swirl of dust and sunshine. Greens and blues and yellows streaked the blacks and tans of sand. It looked like a pinwheel with my sister as the unmoving center.

No matter how hard I ran, I couldn't reach her. Even if I screamed with all my might I couldn't get her to hear me.

The dust cloud danced around her, spinning, hypnotizing. It gathered her into itself, wrapping all around her. An arm of dirt and rock reached out and knocked me to the ground, forcing all the wind out of me.

It wanted Beanie for itself.

By the time I managed to get up and find her, she was on a mound of earth, jerking and flapping her arms. When I reached for her, she screeched, fighting to get away from me.

I woke in the dark. Feeling for Beanie, I touched nothing but flat sheet, empty space. Grit against the bedclothes.

I sat up and put my feet on the floor. Bare toes wiggled in the soft-as-flour dirt. It seemed strange to me, how the storms rolled in both the grit and the fine dust.

Standing, I made my way to the window and pushed aside the curtain. It might as well have been glass painted black for all I could see. The lack of light felt like a vice tightening around me.

But a flickering caught my eye and I turned toward it, to my bedroom door. I heard the scraping of a chair on the dining-room floor.

Slow as I could, I made my way down the steps, a sandpaper burning stinging in my chest with every deep breath.

Daddy sat at the table, a cigarette between his fingers. It wasn't lit, and I didn't think he realized that, the way he stared at the tabletop. His eyes were red and I thought they must've been sore.

"Daddy?" I said.

"It's still nighttime, darlin'," he answered, putting the cold cigarette to his lips. Getting no smoke he tossed it on the table. "Go on back to bed."

"Where's Beanie?" I asked.

Lifting his head, he moved his mouth like he had a whole world of words to say to me, but not the sound to make them come out. He covered over his mouth with one of his hands like he wanted to catch whatever he might say before it could make any noise.

For the first time in my life, I saw fear in his eyes. I couldn't look at him anymore.

Turning, I went to the living room where Ray lay sleeping on the davenport. His eyes twitched under closed lids. Other than that, he didn't move.

From Mama and Daddy's room I heard crying. It was Mama, I knew it. I went to the door. It wasn't closed all the way so I pushed it open. The hinges whined and Mama looked up at me, her eyes squinted and her hands held together like she was begging for something.

She didn't tell me to go away, and she didn't stand up from the edge of the bed. I stood in front of her but didn't take another step into the room.

A black cloth covered the mirror Mama had hanging on the bedroom wall.

It's something we do, she'd told me months before after Meemaw'd died.

I wanted to tear that cloth down, to throw it outside. Let it get buried deep under the dust. But I didn't because Mama whimpered and drew my attention.

She'd put her folded hands against her forehead and rocked back and forth, her mouth pulled out of shape and wailing mourning spilling out from it.

There on the bed was my sister. Her hair spread out on the pillow, wild curls knotted and full of dirt. Her hair, I could stare at her hair and not know. I didn't want to know.

I took a step into the room, not breathing. And then I tried to have faith that it would be all right. I made myself look.

Beanie's face was tinged blue, her body rigid.

"No, no, no," I whispered, shaking my head. "No."

Mama reached for me, but I stepped away, pulling my hands to my chest, still shaking my head and telling Mama no.

Beanie Jean, born blue as a violet. God had seen fit to breathe life into her then. Why wouldn't He do it again?

I wondered if it was a magic that could only be done once.

I backed out of the room, ramming into the doorjamb. I kept going backward, into the living room, stumbling on my own two feet and falling to the floor.

I pushed myself on my behind all the way until I ran into the wall clear to the other side of the living room. Right next to me was the bookcase. There, sticking out just an inch, was my fairy-tale book.

I wanna hear a story, Beanie'd said not too many hours before. She'd had plenty breath then. She was breathing in and out without any problem, her skin the right color. Her eyes alive.

Pulling that book off the shelf, I put it on my lap, opening the cover. I turned through the pages, not seeing a single thing on any of them, just flipping, flipping, flipping.

I took hold of the pages and tore them, one after another. Rip and rip and rip. The paper hissed as I pulled. The paper cut into my hands, slicing the skin in thin marks that would sting later, just not then.

All I felt was hollowed out, and it surprised me how that feeling hurt.

Surrounded by the shreds of my book, I curled up on the floor, letting grief lull me to sleep, my hands bleeding and my heart pounding.

CHAPTER THREE

Mama's face hovered over mine. She spoke to me, I knew, because her lips moved. The sound coming out of her mouth didn't make a bit of sense to me, though. She put her hand on my forehead and it felt like it weighed a hundred pounds for how it made my head ache. Keeping her eyes locked with mine she pressed her lips closed tight and her forehead wrinkled all the way to her hair.

Something was wrong.

Daddy came near and spoke, too. He was fresh shaved and had pomade in his hair, making it look slick. He had on a black tie and Mama wore her black dress, the one she saved for funerals.

Who had died? I couldn't remember. Not Meemaw. That had been before. I opened my mouth to ask, but all that came out was a cough that curled me up into a tight ball. If I hadn't known any better, I would've thought a thousand knives had somehow gotten inside me, stabbing and slicing.

I tried to pull in breath, but there wasn't room enough inside me to hold it. I was burning from the inside out.

Once the wheezing fit was over Mama dabbed at my face with a cool cloth and Daddy pulled the blanket back up over my body.

Too hot. Too cold. Not even close to just right.

I closed my eyes against the ache in my body, against the light that seared through my eyes. Whoever it was that was dead I didn't want to remember just then. Maybe never.

All I wanted to do was sleep.

When Meemaw was alive she'd sometimes let me help her pour elixir into a spoon before she'd swallow it down. That medicine gave off a smell that made me think it could strip the paint clean off Daddy's truck.

That same sharp smell filled my nostrils before the bitter taste of a thick syrup slid into my mouth and inched down my throat. It made me gag, made me open my eyes wide. A man stood over me, one I'd never seen before. He had glasses that were just about to fall off the tip of his nose and hair that I couldn't tell if it was yellow or white.

"Hello there," he said, his voice not sounding like Oklahoma. "How are you feeling?"

"Plain awful," I whispered, my voice sounding like something out of a nightmare.

His heavy hand rested on my forehead then patted my cheek. Feeling under my jaw, he pushed on tender spots of my neck that made me flinch.

"I'm sorry if that hurt you," he said. He fitted a tool into his ears, placing a cold metal disk on my chest. "Can you take a good breath for me?"

I did my best, but all I could do was gasp a little sip of air. Even that made me cough. He frowned, watching as I tried to catch my breath. It made me feel bad that I couldn't do as he wanted. I hadn't tried to upset him.

"Okay, okay," he said, his voice soft. "Take it easy. Slow . . . slow . . . easy."

Once the fit passed he turned and shook his head. "She can't stay here," he said.

That was when I saw Mama standing behind him. At his words she covered her mouth and cried.

Daddy carried me out to his truck. "Easy does it," he said when he lifted me into the seat. Mama climbed in next to me and had me rest my head on her shoulder.

He got in on his side and started the truck, sadness in his eyes. I wanted to ask where they were taking me and I wanted to know if they'd ever let me come back.

Before I could ask, though, I got to coughing so hard I folded in two. Mama shushed me, rubbing my back, but it didn't ease the fit.

Eyes tearing up I clenched my fists so hard I thought my nails would break right through the skin of my palms. I heard a crack in my side and cried out. It felt like somebody'd stuck me with a red-hot poker.

I was dying for sure.

I dreamed that Daddy and I walked through dark woods. Watercolor paintings of trees stood tall on every side of us, their green canopies shadowing everything below.

"Where are we going?" I asked.

Daddy just kept right on walking.

I touched the pocket of my dress. Something was inside it. Slipping my hand in I felt a piece of crusty bread. I broke it to bits, dropping the crumbs on the ground behind me.

"Daddy," I called. "Where are you taking me?"

"Your mama wanted me to take you back where you belong," he answered, not turning around.

"Where's that?"

He didn't answer.

We tramped on for a good many minutes, the crumbs not running out no matter how many of them I scattered. But when I looked behind me, I saw they'd gone. Birds swooped and dived to peck them from the ground. I'd never find my way without those crumbs.

"Are we lost?" I asked.

"I'm not," Daddy answered.

We came to the end of the path. At our feet were cellar doors painted red. Without pulling them open or gazing down into that hole, I knew what was at the bottom of the steps. Winnie's and Eddie's bodies torn by bullets, and their blood soaking into the dirt.

"You gotta go live with your real family now," Daddy said. "We can't keep you with us anymore."

He reached down and pulled up one of the doors, and red light glowed out.

"Go on," he told me.

I fell in. Down and down and down I went, feeling like I'd never reach the bottom, hoping with all my heart I wouldn't. Spinning, I felt dizzy and was sure I'd get sick.

Before I hit the blood-muddied dirt floor, my body jerked, pushing me out of the dream.

White. That was what I saw when I first woke. White sheet under me, white sheet on top. A white curtain hung from ceiling to floor. White woman wearing white all over and even with white hair like a cloud on her head.

"Would you look who's up," she said.

Her words sounded crisp, clipped, and white.

A cough raged through my chest. It felt red. What came out of my mouth splattered brown, spoiling the white sheet.

"It's all right, darlin'," Daddy said, his smell not of cigarettes and coffee like I was used to. Instead it was flat, his scent dusty. "Just be strong, hear?"

His heavy arm rested across my chest, holding me to the bed.

A different kind of pain burned through me, coming from my side. Tears streamed down my face and into my ears. Gurgling noises came from somewhere deep in me.

"Help me," I whispered. "Daddy, please."

"Can't you do more for the pain?" Daddy asked, turning his head to look at somebody. "She's feeling this."

"We gave her ether," a voice next to me said. "She should't have any pain."

"But she does." Daddy growled a cuss. Then he held me firmer and looked right into my eyes. "I'm sorry, Pearlie. I am. They gotta do it."

A woman leaned her face over mine and pressed a cloth over my nose and mouth, smothering me. I would've fought her off if my arms were free. But Daddy was holding me down, letting them kill me.

"There now," she said. "That should be better."

She lifted the cloth and it seemed a whole other world clicked into place in my mind. It came with a taste like nothing else I'd ever had in my mouth, like paint. Smacking my lips I tried working up a spit, but I was dry as a bone.

Numb eased through every part of me, causing me to float above myself just an inch or two. It was as if a cloud of cotton had been packed all around me.

"I think we got it," a voice said. It sounded an awful lot like singing.

I'd said the sinner's prayer when I was nine years old. That was how I knew I'd go to heaven should I die.

Meemaw'd sat beside me on the edge of my bed and helped me find the words to say, asking Jesus to take up a home in my heart.

Seemed I would've felt different for saying those words. That I'd have felt holy and set apart. What I expected was magic, like the breaking of a curse.

But all I felt that day was regular, same-old, unchanged.

I'd asked Meemaw if it took. I asked if I might've done it wrong.

She smiled and covered my hand with hers. Blue veins made lines like a map under her see-through skin.

"There ain't a wrong way to give yourself to Jesus, darlin'," she said. "Besides, it ain't the prayer that saves you."

"What is it then?" I asked.

"It's Him," she told me. "He's the One does the leadin' home."

If I was going to die, I knew I'd go to heaven. I wanted Jesus to hold my hand. I'd follow Him to those pearly gates and maybe we'd both smile to think about my name being Pearl.

"Come on in," He'd say.

I'd do as He said, still holding onto His hand. Holding on as long as He'd let me.

I thought sure I was going to die.

I wasn't scared.

He'd show me the way home.

Cool water touched my lips, easing me awake. A sip slid down my throat, soothing the raw ache. I thought maybe I'd died already. That water felt better than anything ever had.

But when I opened my eyes I saw Mama's face real close to mine. She cradled my head. Tired smile and dark-ringed eyes, she still was the most beautiful woman I'd ever known.

"Am I still alive?" I asked her, my voice small as a mite.

She nodded and gave me another sip of water.

"Just a little more," she said. "Can't have too much all at once."

Lowering my head back onto the pillow, she leaned over and kissed my forehead. I tried stretching and felt a tug from my side. I touched my ribs, finding a tube coming out of my skin.

"Don't pull on it," Mama said. "It's gotta stay another day or two."

She took my hand, brought it to her lips and gave it a kiss.

"What's it for?" I asked.

"That tube's getting all the gunk out." She put my hand down and pulled the blanket up over me. "Get some sleep now, darlin'."

Mama smiled again. How I wished there was even a little happiness behind it.

When I woke, my eyes snapped open, the light above my bed glaring on my face. My body ached. Not a sick ache, though, but one from staying in bed too long. I pulled my legs up making mountains with my knees under the blanket.

If I'd had the strength I would've got up and run laps around my bed until they let me loose outside. As it was, moving my legs even so much as an inch was tiring enough.

The woman with the cloud hair stepped to the side of my bed and tilted her head at me. She did have a sweet smile, one that I thought was a dose of medicine all its own.

"How's about we get you setting up a spell?" she said, wrapping her hand around the back of my neck. "And how's about something to eat?"

I felt of my side where the tube had been. All that was there was a bandage under my cotton nightie.

"Doc Clem took that mean old tube out last night. Sure did the trick though, that tube did." Lifting me with one hand, she fussed with the pillows behind me with the other. "You're a brave girl. You know that?"

She didn't wait for my answer. "Now, I'm gonna have you set up against these pillows. When you're wore out, you can lie down again. All right?"

I nodded, letting her ease me against the soft pillows.

For the first time, I got a good look at all that was around me. Sheets hanging from clothes lines formed makeshift walls around my bed. Beyond the hanging walls I heard someone cough and somebody else moan. Shoes clicked and clomped and clacked across the hard floor. Voices murmured.

"You know where you're at?" the nurse asked.

"No, ma'am," I whispered, the words scrubbing against the inside of my throat.

"You ever been to Boise City before?"

I told her I had, a couple times.

"Welcome back, then." She put her arms up like she was fixing to give me a tour. "This here's George Washington High School. You're in the gymnasium. We got so many folks coming through with the dust pneumonia we up and run outta space at the hospital. That's why we're here. We got everything a normal hospital would. Even got the Red Cross helping out. You imagine that?"

I shook my head.

"Like I said, we got lots here with the dust pneumonia. Just like you've got." She went about straightening the sheets at the foot of the bed. "Not all the patients are doing so good as you, though."

"Where's my mama?" I asked.

"Well, she's getting her a little rest," the nurse answered. Her kind face dropped to sadness. "It's been a hard few weeks for her."

"And my daddy?"

"Getting a bite to eat." She wrote a note on a clipboard. "He's hardly taken a meal all this time. He's been so worried about you."

"Is he all right?"

"I think he will be over time," she said. "It's a hard thing on a parent, losing one child. And with the other one sick like you are, that just adds more fear to the grief."

Beanie. On Mama's bed. Her hair fanned out. Blue faced. Not breathing. Gone. I remembered it all just then and the grief flooded, sure to drown me.

How could I have forgotten a thing like that?

I curled on one side, burying my face into the pillow and soaking it with my crying. It didn't matter that I wasn't supposed to get worked up or that I started a coughing fit that hacked through me like a dust storm was caught up inside my chest.

The nurse in white tried all she could to calm me, to ease my pain.

All I wanted right then was my mama.

❖

Nighttime in my space of the makeshift hospital was dark and lonely. All the white that glowed too bright during the day turned to gray with shadows creeping behind the hanging sheets. Every noise echoed off the cold gymnasium walls, sounding more frightening than just a cough or whisper.

I stirred, trying to get comfortable. It turned out to be a tall order. No matter how I rolled, my body ached. Earlier that day they'd let me get up and walk on loose-as-noodles legs. It only took a handful of steps before I was out of breath and falling down tired.

Doc Clem had said it would take awhile for me to build up my strength again. I didn't think I could wait a minute more to be back to myself.

It took me some doing but I did get myself sitting up on that bed with my legs folded under me.

In a chair pulled close by, Daddy sat with his head tipped back and his mouth open. A light snore rattled in his throat. He had at least two days of stubble on his chin and I wondered if he wasn't fixing to grow himself a full beard.

A newspaper lay across his lap. Tilting my head I read the words printed big on the top of the page. It read, "DUST BOWL VICTIMS PRAY FOR OKLAHOMA RAIN."

If they'd asked me, that wasn't news. We'd been praying for rain the last five years or so. But they hadn't asked me. Nobody ever did.

Daddy started and righted his head. Blinking heavily, he looked at me and smiled. It was the first one in days that seemed real.

"You get up all by yourself?" he asked.

I told him I had.

"That's good, darlin'. Real good." He rubbed at his eyes with the meat of his hands. "You sleep all right?"

I nodded.

"When can I go home?" I asked. I was plenty sick of being cooped up in that hospital and I sure was ready to see something, anything, other than those cotton walls.

Daddy folded the newspaper and tossed it to the foot of the bed.

"Daddy?"

"What's that?" he asked.

"Can I go home soon?"

"Well." He rubbed at his prickly face with one of his hands. "That's something I gotta tell you."

Worry crept up from my insides, settling in the spot between my eyebrows.

"Now, Doc says you're well enough that you could go home tomorrow sometime," he said. "But he's worried about you staying in Oklahoma."

"Why?"

"He says we've gotta get you somewhere without all this dust. Says he's worried you'll just get full up of it again if you stay here."

"I won't go outside," I said, hearing the begging in my own voice. "I promise. And I'll wear a mask every day. All the time if you want me to."

"Darlin', that won't be enough." He turned his eyes down, not looking at me. "You can't stay. It could kill you, Pearl."

All I could picture was him putting me on a train to travel off to the unknown all by myself. I'd rather drown in dirt than leave him. I wished he knew that.

"I managed to get a call through to my cousin. His name's Gus. You remember me talking about him, don't you?" he asked.

"Yes, sir."

"He lives all the way up in Michigan. You know where that is?" Daddy leaned forward. "Now, Gus said he'd be happy to have us come up there. Said he'd help me get a job up there if I want. And he told me there's plenty of houses for rent, with yards even. We could find a place there."

"We'd all go?" I asked.

"Course." He put my hand between both of his. "I wouldn't think of sending you off by yourself. That wouldn't do."

The corners of my eyes pricked with tears of relief.

"You're my girl," he said. "Nothing could ever pull me away from you, darlin'."

Daddy helped me lie back down, making sure my head rested on the pillow in a comfortable way. I had to bite the inside of my cheek to keep from crying.

"You all right?" he asked, using his knuckle to dry under my eye.

I nodded and then shook my head, unsure which answer was more true.

"What is it?" he asked. "What's bothering you?"

"What's gonna happen to Ray?"

"I don't know." He sighed. "All I know is I gotta get you someplace safe. And quick."

Much as I didn't want to, I broke. I cried all the way until sleep came and pulled me under.

I floated, dreamless, along the top of sleep, still hearing the nighttime sounds of the dark, makeshift hospital.

CHAPTER FOUR

Mama would've had me swear on the Bible to sit still if she could've. But, seeing as she couldn't find it in any of the boxes Daddy'd already packed, she made me swear on her hand, which she said was just as strong a promise as God making Abraham a great nation and Moses getting the Israelites to the Promised Land.

I solemnly swore that I'd keep my backside on the davenport and not move so much as an inch no matter what. And that I'd keep the mask over my nose and mouth at all times. So help me God.

We'd gotten home from the hospital in Boise City just the night before and Mama'd hardly let me roll over in bed without fussing over how it would wear me out. She worried something awful about me getting sick again.

"I can't be watching you," she said, standing at the table and wrapping her good water glasses in pieces of newsprint. "Doc Clem said you've gotta rest. I agree with him, so don't you give me that look, missy. I don't need you getting worn-out. And straighten up that mask, would ya?"

I stayed put like she'd said to, wishing I had something to do besides watch her and Daddy rush around, getting things put in crates and boxes.

It wouldn't have hurt my feelings if Ray thought to come by to talk to me. I hadn't seen him since the big storm, the day we lost Beanie. I feared he'd stay away and we'd leave and I would never get to talk to him again.

Good-byes were hard, I knew that much. But leaving would only sting worse if I didn't get to see him one last time.

Millard had been there all day long, helping Daddy and trying to keep

Mama smiling. She fretted over if her dishes would survive the trip or if we'd have some place to sleep along the way. She even worried that she didn't have anything good to feed Millard for all his work getting us packed.

"All I've got is beans and bread now with the store closed like it is," she said, wringing her hands. "And I can't even heat them up. Tom packed all my pots and pans already."

"Don't you fuss over me," Millard told her. "Beans and bread's never killed me before. Don't think it's like to today."

The hurt of missing him had already set in and we hadn't even left yet.

Mama scooted me off to bed before it was even dark. I tried to argue, but Mama would have none of it.

"You're not all the way healed up yet, not even close. It's gonna take awhile," she said, pulling my by the hand to the stairs. "If I had my way I wouldn't have you going up and down these steps, even. They take too much out of you."

"I'm all right, Mama," I said. "I feel fine."

She gave me a sideways look that told me she didn't believe me for a minute. Mama always had a way of knowing when I was speaking lies.

"We've got a big day tomorrow." She'd gotten me up in my bedroom and helped me out of my dress and into a fresh nightie. "I need you to get a good night's sleep."

Mama's big day was us driving away from home, leaving Red River and all of Oklahoma behind. I didn't think I'd have minded if Jesus decided to come down and rapture us up to heaven before the sun rose on Mama's big day.

She helped me get into bed and pulled the covers up tight under my chin. I wasn't cold, but I was tired so I didn't fight her.

"Now, how about you say your prayers," she said, sitting on the edge of my bed.

I recited a prayer she and Meemaw'd taught me when I was smaller, skipping the if-I-die-before-I-wake part. I didn't want to upset Mama.

Besides, it seemed a hard thing to have in a child's prayer. Real hard.

Before I finished the prayer I peeked to see if she had her eyes closed.

She did not. Instead, she was turned at the waist, looking into the closet. The door stood open showing Beanie's dresses still hanging there, forgotten in all the packing. I imagined her box of treasured things was on the shelf, untouched. My sister hadn't owned a single thing of value to anybody but herself. She liked keeping whatever she found in the old, left-behind shacks after folks moved away. Tarnished spoons and torn hankies and maybe even a broken pencil. She'd see them and they'd find a home in her pockets and under the bed or in the dresser.

Beanie had a way of seeing treasures in what most folks saw as flawed and worthless.

My *amen* got choked up in my throat.

Mama kept staring at those old dresses of my sister's. She'd made every one of them, mended them whenever Beanie got them snagged or ripped. I wondered if they still smelled like my sister, those dresses, the way the pillow next to me did.

If loss had a color it was tan. Flat and dull and smelling like must.

"Go on to sleep, Pearl," Mama said, her voice thin and far away. "I have faith everything's gonna be all right."

I closed my eyes, hoping sleep would come fast and hoping I wouldn't carry that sadness over with me to my dreams. If I could've wished for something right then, I'd have left the sorry feeling in that closet and closed the door.

"There's nothing to be sorry about, darlin'," Mama whispered.

I thought she must've read my mind. She was wrong, though. There was plenty to be sorry for. It heaped up in my heart and spilled over with no hope of stopping. I knew I'd be sorry about losing Beanie in that dust storm for as long as I lived.

It wasn't morning yet, I knew that much, still I was awake with no hope of falling back to sleep. Some kind of noise woke me. I heard it again. A knocking.

Using the bed frame, I pulled myself to standing and held onto it until I got settled on my feet. Somehow I made it to the bedroom door with no problem. Running my hand along the wall I made it to the top of the stairs and lowered myself to sit, already winded from those few steps.

I couldn't see him, but I knew it was Daddy that was up and answering the knock at the door. His cigarette smoke filled the house, tendrils of it reaching me on the stairs, tempting me to fall into a terrible coughing fit.

"Luella," he said.

It was Ray's mother.

"I know it's late," she said.

"It's all right," Daddy told her. "Come on in."

Shuffling footsteps and then the door closed.

"I'm sorry to wake you," Mrs. Jones said.

"I was up." Daddy cleared his throat. "I can get Mary out of bed if you need her."

"No. Don't wake her."

"Well . . ."

"I come to talk to you."

"Have a seat then," Daddy said. "I'll try and find where Mary packed the coffee."

"I won't stay long. Don't fix nothin'."

"All right."

"I heard about a job," she said. "Over in Arkansas."

Daddy mm-hmmed.

"A family that way needs somebody to come do housework, watch their kids." Mrs. Jones kept her voice quiet, calm. "My sister wrote me about it. Guess it pays good, that job."

"Sounds fine," Daddy said. "You need money to get over there?"

She didn't tell him yes or no. What she did was sigh so loud it sounded like it came all the way from her toes.

"Problem is I can't take Ray with me," she said. "That family don't want nobody with kids."

"What are you asking for, Luella?"

She didn't say anything right away and I wondered if she ever would, long as she waited before answering him.

"Take him with you to wherever y'all are goin'," she said. "Please."

"Luella . . ."

"I'll send money once I get some saved up," she said. "If he's any trouble I'd come get him."

"He's a good boy. He's never been any trouble," Daddy told her. "Can't imagine it's in him."

"He can't have a good life with me," she said. "I can't give him nothin'."

"I don't think that's true," Daddy told her.

"Will you take him?"

Daddy made a sound like he was pushing air out his nose. "I don't know, Luella," he said. "Don't you understand the boy needs you?"

"He don't," she said.

"Why don't you come with us?" Daddy asked. "We'd help you get on your feet up there. You know Mary'd be glad to have you."

"I can't do that, Tom."

"What'll you tell Ray?"

"That he'll be going with you. That I'll come get him when I can."

"Will you?" Daddy asked. "Will you come get him?"

She didn't answer and that told enough.

I imagined Daddy standing in front of her, his arms crossed, and her, stoop shouldered and staring at the floor, her fingers pushed tight against her lips.

"We'll take him," Daddy said after a long quiet spell. "You got an address where you'll be?"

She told him she did and I heard the scratching of lead against paper.

"Ray ain't good at writin'," she said. "He don't gotta write if he don't want to."

"He'll want to, Luella."

"Could be."

"Take this," Daddy said. "It's not much, but it should help buy a train ticket or something."

"I can't take no more from you."

"It's all right, Luella."

The next thing I heard was the door opening and closing. Mrs. Jones was gone.

I always thought I'd be happy to have her leave Ray for us to keep. But just then all I could think on was how it would break his heart.

I'd gotten myself stuck there on the steps, my legs too weak to push me up and my arms too tired to pull on the railing. Daddy found me there and shook his head, climbing up the stairs to rescue me.

"How long you been there?" he asked.

I shrugged.

"Long enough to hear Mrs. Jones?"

"Yes, sir."

"Well, you don't gotta tell Ray what you heard her say, hear?"

I told him I'd keep it to myself.

Daddy picked me up and carried me to my bedroom. He was careful to keep my feet from knocking against the doorframe as he walked through it. Daddy always was careful with me.

"If I was a betting man I'd put money on Mrs. Jones coming to get Ray before three months is gone," he said. "That's what I'm hoping for at least. For his sake."

"You think he'll cry?"

"He might. But he won't do it in front of you."

I knew Daddy was right about that.

"How long will it take to get to Michigan?" I asked. "Will it take a month?"

"Nah," he said, lowering me into my bed. "Maybe a handful of days if nothing goes wrong. Lord, do I hope nothing goes wrong."

"Do you think I'll like it there?"

"Can't imagine you wouldn't." He covered me up. "Gus said it's real nice this time of year at his place. Plenty of things growing and blooming. Said he's got a heifer about to calve, too."

"You think he'd let me pet it?"

"Maybe."

"Will we get a place of our own?" I asked.

"After a little while."

"Can we have a garden?"

"I do believe we can," he said. "Your mama will look real pretty in a garden all her own. She won't even have to water it."

"She won't?"

"Nope. It rains there plenty." He squatted down next to me. "Everywhere you look is greener than anything you've ever seen before. Fields full of crop far as you can see. Late summer you can pick a fat tomato for your supper with an ear of corn to go along with it."

"Is there a school there?"

"Course there is. I'll bet it's a fine one, too."

"Will Ray go to school?"

"Sure he will."

"He can't read," I said.

"Then your mama will teach him." He smiled at me. "I'm getting you all riled up, aren't I? You best get some sleep."

I nestled into my bed, feeling tired enough to sleep another few hours. Daddy put his hand on my head.

"Things'll be good there," he said. "Do you believe that?"

I did and I told him so.

I couldn't see how anything could go wrong in such a beautiful place.

CHAPTER FIVE

I tried picturing it in my mind, how it would be on the day we left Red River.

I imagined us putting the last few things on the truck, moving slow and not saying much of anything. We'd put some of Beanie's things in a box, one Mama didn't know about just then. A box we'd show her later on when she was some healed up from the stab of losing her.

After we'd finished loading up, Daddy would give me a wink and reach for Mama, putting his kiss on her temple. He'd tell Ray to come on, too. Ray would feel strange about sharing in that family moment until Daddy put a hand on his back and called him "son."

Mama would make sure to let him know he was one of us now.

She'd let a tear or two drop from her eyes when she took one last look through the house to be sure she'd gotten everything. It had been her home as long as she'd been married to Daddy. She'd made it a good place for us to live.

I'd take Mama's hand so she'd know I felt it too, the leaving. We'd stand together, the four of us, taking our time in the last minute or so before stepping outside.

Once we did walk out, I'd try not to look at the house too close for fear I'd never be able to leave it. That place was all I'd ever known.

"Well, I guess we oughta," Daddy would say, turning toward the truck.

Ray would climb up in the back, settling in for the ride. I'd let him be there by himself for a bit. Men needed to be alone in moments of sadness, I knew that much.

Nodding, Daddy would open the passenger side door and take my hand, helping me climb in. I'd shimmy over to the middle of the seat and wait for Mama to slide in beside me. She wouldn't right away, though. She'd be caught up in Daddy's arms, the two of them giving one another a little comfort. Daddy'd whisper something into her ear and kiss her hair the way he did sometimes. I'd ache right along with them, but I'd keep it to myself so they wouldn't worry about me more than they already did.

"At least there's still us," Mama would say, leaning back to look full into Daddy's face. "We'll be all right. You'll see."

Daddy would make sure Mama got up into her seat and that the skirt of her dress was all tucked up under her so it wouldn't get slammed in the door. He'd take his time getting around to his side, stopping to check a few things on the truck to be sure it would run without any problems. He'd see to Ray, asking if he was all right.

Ray'd tell him he was. Daddy wouldn't believe him, not all the way, but he wouldn't push him. He'd know Ray was going through a real hard time, leaving his mother like he was.

"Here," Mama would say, pushing up against me. "Rest your head on my shoulder a spell."

I would, and she'd hum a little song to help me relax the way she had when I was real small and upset about something or other.

I imagined Daddy getting in on the other side of me and turning over the truck engine. When he eased the truck away from the house I would turn and look out the back window. It was my own way of telling home good-bye.

The truck would run smooth over the road leading out of Red River. Smooth and quiet.

The only person out and about that day would be Mad Mabel. The orange and red sunrise would glow on her wilted wedding dress and she'd stand out front of the church, blowing kisses at us as we drove away.

❈

On the morning of the day we left Red River, Mama was sore at Daddy. I knew by the way she didn't meet his eyes and how she'd hardly said so much as boo to him since breakfast.

He tried, Daddy did, to get her to smile. Used all his tricks like calling her sugar and cracking a joke. Not a one of his attempts worked. Seemed to just make her more and more upset.

When I asked her why she was angry, she sighed and told me just to keep still on the davenport. I knew I remained under the don't-move-an-inch Bible promise of the day before. I could've sworn that if I had to sit on my behind any more it would flatten out just like a flapjack. I wondered what Doc Clem would say about a thing like that.

Right around midmorning Mama and Daddy came down the steps, one after the other, arms loaded with quilts and pillows, both of them red-faced. I didn't think it was from all the rushing around.

"We can't take the davenport," Daddy told her for the tenth time that morning. "We don't have room."

"You haven't tried." She made her voice hard as a rock, like she did when she wanted to get her way.

"Where are we gonna put Ray if we've got that big old thing in the back?"

"Maybe you should've thought about that."

He stopped beside the table and turned to her. "Mary, we will make him feel welcome."

"But what'll we sit on once we get there?" She dumped her pile of linens on the table. "We're already leaving so much."

"Gus said he's got plenty to let us have once we get a place."

"Did he say he's got a davenport for us?"

Daddy sighed and hung his head.

"We can't take it, Mary," he said. "That's it."

"I'm not leaving without it." She stomped her foot and crossed her arms.

"I thought you couldn't wait to get out of Red River." He shook his head at her. "I seem to remember you saying you'd kill yourself if we didn't move. You remember that?"

"And you refused to budge," she said, her voice icy. "And we lost our daughter because you wanted to stick it out. Darn near lost Pearl, too. Now I get to be the stubborn one. I'm not going anywhere without this davenport."

"Have it your way." Daddy turned toward the front door. "But when I pull that truck away from the house, that sofa is not going to be on it."

She let out a frustrated howl.

They went on back and forth like that, neither of them like to win. So I shattered my promise to stay put and got myself up off that old, lumpy davenport Mama held so dear and made my way, slow and steady, out the front door and closed it behind me.

Neither of them seemed to notice.

Standing on the porch I looked out over what I could see of Red River. It'd turned more ghost town than anything with plenty of memories left to haunt.

Still, I had enough good recollections that might've given me cause to smile on any other occasion. Some day I'd need them to soothe the ache I'd feel for the place. I didn't believe anything could ever feel like home again.

If I'd even had one ounce of strength in my legs I would've wandered around all by my lonesome. Cupped my hands to see in the windows of the empty shops along the main street, tiptoed through the alleyways. Visited the abandoned sharecropper's cabins and the overflowing Hooverville, looking one last time at the folks living there and their slapped-together shacks.

If I hadn't been so weak I would have sifted the red Oklahoma dirt through my fingers, feeling the land I'd most likely never see again.

It would be my so-long to a whole lot of ruin.

Ray would've gone with me if I'd asked him, but that sort of wandering needed doing alone. It wasn't just the lame legs that kept me on the porch. It was fear that held me there. That fear was newer in me than the desire to wander. It'd been born the day Eddie DuPre hopped off the train and it grew after the black storm barreled down on us, sucking Beanie's life away.

So I just sat down on the porch, my elbows resting on my knees and hands holding up my chin, a mask covering the better part of my face. I never would've admitted it, but I was feeling sorry for myself something awful.

Millard came around the side of the house and hefted a toolbox into the back of the truck. He was one to whistle while he worked unless he had a plug of chaw in his lip. When he did whistle, he'd waggle his eyebrows up and down. Most days it would've made me laugh. Not that day, though.

I didn't think anything could cheer me up, not just then at least.

"How long you been sittin' there?" he asked, seeing me out the corner of his eye.

I shrugged.

"You not feelin' good?" He took a couple steps toward me.

"I'm all right," I answered. "This mask is awful. Wish I could tear it right off."

"Don't it work?"

"I don't know. Maybe."

"That's fine."

Pointing his finger, he told me to make room for him on the step. I did and he sat beside me. Fishing around in his pocket, he pulled out a pink candy and put it in my hand.

"I found them in Boise City when I was up there," he told me.

"Thank you." I pulled the mask away from my face a bit and popped the sweet into my mouth. It worked up a good spit and soothed my sore throat.

"You remember my comin' up to see you?"

I told him I didn't.

"Didn't figure. You was in and out, up and down. I was sure worried about you. We all were." He put a piece of the candy in his own cheek. "I come a couple times to sit with you."

"I'm sorry I don't remember," I said.

"Nah. Don't bother me none. Wasn't there to be remembered." He put an arm around my shoulders. "Some of the best things we do ain't remembered by anybody but God."

I wondered if he'd got that line from Meemaw. It sure did sound like something she would've said.

"Can't you come with us?" I asked. "We've got plenty of room."

He licked at his lips and blinked a couple times. "Wish I could."

"You could eat all the tomatoes you want," I said. "And Mama could make you a blueberry pie whenever you had a taste for one."

"Wouldn't that be somethin'!"

"Daddy said it's green as anything you could ever imagine." I took his chin in my hand, turning his face so he'd look right at me. "Millard, please come with us."

"Pearlie, I can't," he whispered. "My place is here."

I dropped my head so it rested on his chest and bawled my eyes out. He held me close, letting me cry as long as I needed to.

"Old men like me have a hard time leavin' a place they've known most their life. No other place'd be home for me. That's all there is to it, darlin'." He put his hand on the back of my head. "I sure am sorry, Pearlie."

What I wanted to say was that it wouldn't have to be home, Michigan wouldn't. It wouldn't be for me, either. But it could be a place where he'd be happy anyway. Happy along with us. With me. I wanted to tell him I'd even call him "grandpa" if he wanted. But all that came out was my sobbing.

"You'll write me, will you?" he asked, his voice thick like it was in the days after Meemaw died. "Tell me about all the trouble you and Ray're gettin' into up there. I'm sure you'll find plenty."

I nodded, my cheek rubbing against his soft flannel shirt.

"Tell me about that new school and all you're learnin'."

"Yes, sir."

"And, if you think of it, grab up a handful of grass and stick it in one of them letters you send me," he said. "It's been so long since I seen somethin' green."

I promised I'd do just that.

❀

Everything we were taking was packed into the truck. The davenport sat where it always had, right under the big window in the living room. Mama stood beside it, feeling of the upholstery, whispering about what a shame it was to leave such a fine piece of furniture behind.

I decided I'd best not point out the worn spots on it or how one of the springs liked to poke up at folks' behinds. Being quiet was a good idea right then.

Daddy stood in the doorway, rubbing his hands together. He bit at his lip and let his eyes wander around the living room. He nodded and made a noise like he was clearing his throat.

It was time.

Ray went out first, followed by Millard and Daddy. I made my way around the room, running my finger along the wall, steering around the davenport and Meemaw's rocking chair, walking my fingers over the top of the table. All of it we were leaving behind. I thought if we ever did come back, it would be waiting for us.

Mama'd gone to the kitchen, checking the cupboards one last time. Finding nothing, she slammed the last one shut. It hit so hard, the door bounced open, barely missing her head.

She said a cuss and slapped at the counter, holding on for dear life. Then she started sobbing, making the same horrified sounds from the night Beanie died.

It didn't go on long, her crying. When it'd passed, she used the collar of her dress to wipe her face dry. Holding herself steady, she turned and took in a couple shaky breaths.

Seeing me, she reached out, taking my hand. Her fingers were cold.

"It's all right," she told me.

She left the cupboard hanging open.

Daddy double-checked everything he and Millard had packed on the truck, making sure nothing was like to blow off or crush Ray if we went over a bump. The rest of us stood together, not saying a word, watching him work. I wondered if we'd stand there in front of the house for hours, no one ready to pile in and drive away from Red River and Millard.

Every few minutes Ray looked over his shoulder toward the sharecropper cabins. No matter how much he checked, his mother didn't come. I wondered if he hoped she'd change her mind and pack up to go along with us. Or if he wished she'd come to take him to Arkansas along with her.

The least she could do, I thought, was to see him off.

But she didn't come. I knew from the pit of my heart she never would.

"Ray?" Daddy went to him, putting a hand on his shoulder. "You wanna drive past on our way?"

"No, sir." Ray shook his head and stood a little taller like he had his pride to think of. "We already said our good-byes," he said, hardly louder than a whisper.

"You'll see her again soon," Daddy told him. "I have faith she'll stick by her word. She will find her way to you one of these days."

Ray nodded and turned away from all of us. I didn't watch him. I knew how he hated for anybody to see him cry.

"Guess we'd better get going," Daddy said. "If I don't now I might lose my nerve."

Mama was the first to go to Millard. They shared a couple words and a quick hug before she stepped aside.

Millard went to Ray and stood beside him a minute, keeping quiet the way men did. When Ray turned to him, Millard took his hand and gave it a firm shake.

"I'll sure miss you, son," he said. "I'm real proud of you. You're a good man."

"Thank you, sir," Ray said.

"You'll need to watch after Pearl for me," Millard told him. "You keep her smilin', will ya?"

Ray promised.

I was sure grateful for it.

It was my turn next and I didn't know that I had the courage to leave him behind. He came, stooping down to face me before giving me a kiss on the cheek.

I started crying again and he rubbed my back. "It's all right, darlin'," he whispered.

Closing my eyes I remembered when Daddy got me out of Eddie's cellar, how Millard had taken me in his arms.

I got her, he had said. *It's all right.*

"I love you," I said, my voice so quiet.

I hoped he'd heard it. It was the first time I'd told him and I wanted to be sure he understood.

"I love you, too," he told me back. When he wrapped his arms around me, he whispered in my ear. "If you ever need me—I mean really, really need me bad—you give me the word and I'll get on a train. I'd do that for you, Pearl."

I nodded.

"I'd do it for you," he said again.

Millard Young had never gone back on a single one of his promises. Not even once.

Daddy climbed into the truck beside me. His hands shook and he wiped the palms against his thighs. He kept his face forward, eyes open wide. His mustache wiggled as he bit at his upper lip. As hard as he held onto the steering wheel I thought he was like to snap it into a hundred pieces.

"Ready?" he asked, not turning to look at Mama or me.

"Just go," Mama said, looking out the window.

He started the engine and waved at Millard one last time before pulling away. Turning, I watched Millard waving back, his big hand in the air. He got smaller and smaller and I kept my eyes on him until Daddy turned off the main street of Red River toward the road that would take us away from home.

Not one of us said so much as a word for a long time. There wasn't anything to say.

"I ever tell you about the last time Jed Bozell came to town?" Daddy asked after we crossed the line outside of Cimarron County.

He'd been telling me stories about Jed Bozell and his traveling show as long as I could remember. I never did know if the stories were true or not. It didn't matter so much, though. I just liked it when Daddy got to storytelling, tall as the tales might be.

"Now, Jed and his show came around town every year, always in the summer." Daddy tapped the steering wheel with the heel of his hand. "Folks would save up nickels and dimes to see whatever attractions he brought with him. It was a different show every time."

I already knew that much, but didn't say anything to interrupt him.

"Guess I must've been seventeen that last time. School had been out a full month and I'd been working alongside Millard in the courthouse."

"What job did you do?" I asked.

"Oh, a little bit of everything. Anything that needed doing," Daddy answered. "My pa died the winter before and I had to make money any way I could to take care of Meemaw."

In my whole life I could only remember a handful of times when Daddy mentioned his father. Mama didn't talk about her folks much, either. I did know they were dead like Daddy's pa was. I wondered if we'd stop talking about Beanie, too, after a while. Seemed the way of things.

"Anyhow, I could hear the commotion of Jed's men setting up for the show all day long. Couldn't hardly work for the distraction." Daddy glanced at me. "Problem was, I knew Meemaw would have supper waiting when I got done working. You know how she hated to serve a meal cold."

I nodded.

"Well, I got out of the courthouse and decided I'd just take a quick look-see."

"What did he have in the show?"

"Little bit of everything. Sure did go all out on that trip. He had this kangaroo that'd box anybody if they'd pay a dime."

"Why'd anybody pay for that?" I asked.

"Darlin', a man'll pay about any price to prove he's stronger than a goofy-looking creature like that."

"Did the kangaroo ever win?"

"Every single match. That kangaroo had a nasty uppercut."

"Tom . . ." Mama said. "Don't fill her head—"

"And he brought the world's stinkiest pig." Daddy made a hooting noise. "We couldn't get the smell of that thing out of town for a full month."

"What did it smell like?" I asked.

"It's not polite to say." He winked at me. "Now, Jed had set up a grandstand at the far end of the grounds. I made my way to see what was going on there, forgetting all about Meemaw and supper. By the time I did remember I was stuck in the middle of a crowd pushing me forward toward the stage."

"How did you get out?"

"I'll get to that." He cleared his throat. "Well, there on the stage was Jed Bozell himself. Turns out he wasn't just the ringmaster, he was also a performer. Bozell the Amazing Pretzel Man."

Mama sighed and shook her head.

"I never would've thought it, but old Jed was sure flexible. He bent and twisted himself into all kinds of knots. Didn't know how he did it. Never did figure it out, either," Daddy went on. "He pulled his legs over his head and folded in half. Then he stood on his hands and reached his feet up behind him to play a piano."

"How'd he play it?"

"With his toes." Daddy waggled his eyebrows at me. "Played a little Beethoven if I remember right."

"Mama," I asked, "did you see him, too?"

"Can't say I did," Mama answered, not turning her face from the side window.

"Well, I remember seeing your mama there." He let out a whistle. "Boy, was she ever pretty in her yellow dress with her hair all loose around her shoulders. Almost spent as much time watching her as I did old Jed."

Most days, when Daddy said a thing like that Mama would blush. She'd smile and turn her eyes to her lap in a way that made her look real pretty. That day, though, she didn't blush. She just turned her shoulder so her back was to Daddy and me and she kept her face toward the window like she didn't want to miss anything as we passed it by.

It was like she'd stuffed her ears with cotton and didn't hear a word Daddy said. I thought about telling her she was being rude, ignoring Daddy after he'd paid her such a nice compliment, but I didn't want to be accused of being a sass mouth just then. I kept my trap shut.

"Halfway through Jed's pretzel show I started smelling the carnival food. Buttered corn and fried dough and . . . goodness, everything you can imagine. It made my stomach rumble." He wiped at his mouth like he was drooling. "That's when I remembered Meemaw was waiting supper for me. I thought I was in for a whole world of trouble."

"Did you get home in time?"

"Nah. Never did. When I looked to my right I saw Meemaw standing there, her eyes wide and staring at Jed Bozell."

"Meemaw told me Jed Bozell wasn't real," I told him.

"Course she'd say that. She didn't want you to know she was smitten with him just like all the other ladies in town."

"Mama, were you smitten with Jed Bozell?" I asked.

She just snorted and gave me a look that told me she thought it was all ridiculous.

"No. Your mama never had eyes for anybody but me," Daddy said.

"Not that you know of." She gave him the same look she'd just given me.

"Maybe," he said. "But I'm the one who got ya in the end, sugar."

He winked at her and gave her a crooked smile. She repaid him with a roll of the eyes that irked the dickens out of me.

"What did Jed Bozell do next?" I asked, not wanting Daddy to stop his storytelling.

"Well, he got himself all untangled and stood up tall in front of us." Daddy tipped the brim of his hat back and scratched at his hairline. "And he told us he was done. He wasn't coming around to perform anymore."

I leaned forward, waiting for Daddy to say that Jed Bozell disappeared in a puff of smoke or took off his mask to reveal that, really, he was an ape in disguise. Every one of Daddy's stories about Jed Bozell ended with something silly, something impossible.

"Then what?" I asked.

"The crowd gasped. A couple women cried even. It was hard news to hear."

"Why did he quit?"

"Said the traveling got him feeling lost. Like he didn't have a place in the world."

Daddy stopped talking and I knew the story was over. Just like that. He drove past a man standing by the side of the road. The man waved and Daddy waved back. It was an Oklahoma thing to do, waving at folks or tipping hats at them whether we knew them or not.

I rested my head on the back of the seat and closed my eyes, picturing Jed Bozell as I'd always imagined him. Long and lanky, with wild hair and big feet. He wandered, moving in circles and zigzags and going one way only to turn and go back the way he'd come. Lost.

Then I imagined him on the path to a nice house. A good one. One with a door painted yellow. He opened the door and a big smile spread all the way across his face before he stepped inside, closing the door behind him.

CHAPTER SIX

We drove until dark that first day. We made it deep into the middle of Kansas—that was what Daddy told me, at least. Seemed more like the middle of nowhere to me. Either that or the middle of No Man's Land, Oklahoma. It didn't look one bit different from where we'd come from. All around us was dust, dust, and another helping of dust for good measure.

I didn't tell Mama or Daddy how disappointed I was in Kansas. I'd at least expected something green, maybe even a tree or two. And I had thought I'd have felt different being in another state.

How I felt just then was buried in dust I couldn't seem to get out from under. I worried we'd get all the way to Michigan just to discover that the whole United States of America had gotten ruined by the dirt.

I said a short prayer to God, asking that He wouldn't let it be so. Besides, I thought if I had to wear that mask one more moment I'd go batty.

Daddy pulled over to the side of the road, saying we'd camp out there for the night. He and Ray unloaded a couple bedrolls and got a fire going. I imagined getting to sleep out under the stars right beside the flickering flames. I wouldn't even need a bedroll. I'd have been happy just to be right on the ground.

Laying on my back, I would have gazed up at the sparkling stars, letting the moon glow white on my face. It was a clear night and I knew if I'd had the chance I would be sure to see at least one shooting star. I knew just what I would've wished for but wouldn't tell a single soul for fear it wouldn't come true.

The warmth of the fire would glow all the way down one side of me, making me lay comfortable and sleep easy. There would be no sound but the crackling flames and the lullaby of a far-off coyote.

I blinked away the thought, though. Mama never would have allowed any of that. As it was, she worried about the dust settling back into my lungs even there in the truck. She handed me a plate of food and told me to shut the door while I ate it inside all by myself.

"It's just too dusty here, darlin'," she told me.

I hated to admit she was right.

Mama filled the morning chill with the smells of bitter coffee and toasting bread. More than once she told us she was sorry she didn't have anything better to offer by way of breakfast.

"I thought we'd come across a store by now," she said.

"We should sooner rather than later," Daddy told her, leaning over a map he'd spread out on the hood of the truck. "We'll just keep our eyes open."

"Wish I'd had more to bring along." She sighed, pouring coffee into a couple tin cups. "All I've got is some beans and a couple loaves of bread."

"We'll make do." Daddy took the cup she offered him and blew over it, making the steam curl up from the coffee. "You're doing a fine job, honey. You are."

She turned her head from him, holding her cup of coffee but not drinking from it. Her cheeks were bright red from working over the fire. When she lifted the cup to her lips, she pulled it away quick like she might get sick. Dumping her coffee onto the ground, she put her hand on her chest, fingers spread wide.

"You all right, Mama?" I asked.

She nodded her head. "Just not feeling so good is all. It'll pass."

We finished eating our bread and Daddy stomped out the fire. It left a black pockmark in the earth and smoldered for more than a couple minutes before dying out all the way. Mama told me not to get too close to it for fear I'd get a coughing fit from breathing in the smoke.

Even feeling sick she took to fretting over me.

I didn't think she'd ever get over being so worried about me. I pictured myself a full-grown woman still wearing that wicked mask over my face on account Mama'd give me a sour look and sigh if I didn't.

"Go on, now," she said to me. "Get back in the truck. And don't even think about taking that mask off."

Much as I didn't want to, I obeyed Mama. But when my back was to her I made a sour face of my own.

Daddy filled the driving time by singing a song or two. His voice was a deep one, not smooth exactly, but still nice enough. Mama didn't join in even when he asked her to.

"I'm too tired, Tom," was all she said.

Her refusal didn't stop him from going into a slow and low song, one that made me sleepy to hear it. I rested my head on his shoulder, letting myself drift off to sleep and hoping he'd just keep right on singing until I woke up. I thought his voice would keep me in good dreams as I slept.

I woke when the truck slowed. Seemed I'd only slept a couple minutes, but from the crick in my neck I wondered if it wasn't a whole lot longer. When I lifted my head off his arm Daddy leaned forward over the wheel. Something ahead of us had caught his eye. I squinted to see what it was.

Pulled off to the side of the road was a big truck, loaded high with mattresses and household things like pots and pans.

"Looks like they got themselves a flat," Daddy whispered, steering us to a spot on the shoulder of the road.

Two men squatted beside the big truck, looking at a tire that more resembled a black puddle than anything. They both glanced at us when Daddy turned off the engine.

"I'm gonna check it out," he told Mama. "Just wait here."

Daddy went to the men who stood when he neared. They shook hands before going back to inspecting the tire. They didn't say much, those three. One thing I'd learned about men was that they didn't need too many words between them. Instead they'd nod and scratch at chins or spit. That seemed all the talking they needed to do.

Off to the side, farther from the road and in the shade of a tall fence, sat a couple women and three small kids. They had a blanket spread out under them like they were having a picnic. Only there wasn't any basket of food.

Daddy walked around the back of our truck. I heard the clanking of his toolbox and him telling Ray a thing or two. Mama opened her door and got out.

"What can I do?" she asked as Daddy came around, toolbox in hand.

"Well, we have to get her jacked up so we can get another tire on," he said. "Might take some time."

"That's all right." Mama turned her head toward the women and kids. "Did you ask when they last had something to eat?"

"Sure did. Knew you'd ask." Daddy took in a deep breath. "Fella said it's been a good day or two."

"Have Ray get a fire going. I'll fix them something," she said. "Won't be fancy. But if they don't mind beans and bread, I'm happy to warm them up."

"You sure you're up to it?" Daddy asked in a whisper.

"I'm fine, Tom."

"I don't want you overdoing—"

"I said I'm fine."

Without saying so much as another word they both got moving. In no time Mama set up a makeshift kitchen. Ray and I unloaded every single can of beans she'd packed for the trip like she'd asked us to and she poured more than a couple of them into her pot to warm.

"Hand me that wooden spoon, please," she said to me. "Then sit down and rest, hear?"

I did as she said and watched her stir the beans, watched the rich sauce bubble and pop as they cooked.

"Mama?" I said to her real soft, making sure nobody else could hear me. "What if we don't find a store later on? What'll we eat?"

"I won't have you worrying about that." She didn't look up at me, just kept on stirring. "I reckon they're much hungrier than we are. We'll make out all right. Always do."

She tapped the spoon against the edge of the pot and stood straight, stretching her back.

"Just be sure you don't say anything to them about it, hear?" She gave me her most serious face. "I don't want them feeling ashamed."

"Yes, ma'am."

"You never do know when you might be entertaining angels," she said.

That was something I remembered Meemaw saying whenever the hobos would come knocking on the back door for a couple slices of bread. She never turned one of them away. Mama didn't either.

I looked at the women, still sitting on the spread-out blanket with the kids. I'd never seen an angel aside from the ones in my picture Bible. Those angels had long, gleaming robes and fluffy yellow hair. Halos ringed round their heads and they looked stone-cold serious.

Seemed to me, if angels came to earth hoping to test the kindness of humans, they wouldn't come dressed in white and with their wings hanging out for all creation to see.

No, I figured they'd come in everyday clothes, maybe with a little dirt under their fingernails. Their hair would be greasy and their shoes'd have a hole or two in the soles, if they had any at all. And they'd get themselves stranded in the middle of Kansas, waiting to see who might come along to patch a tire or offer a half gallon of gasoline to fill up a dried-out tank. And they'd see who might entertain them with a plate of runny beans and a cup of hot coffee.

I went back to the truck where my things were kept in a small carpetbag. Inside was the package with the rest of Millard's pink mints. He'd sent them along with me, knowing how much I liked them. I'd planned on saving those candies for when we crossed into Michigan as a surprise for Ray. I took them all out, putting them, bag and all, into my dress pocket.

When they finished with their beans, I gave that bag of candy to the ladies, saying they were for the children. One of the kids, a little girl with a dirty face, said thank you so nice I couldn't help but smile.

She giggled when she popped one in her mouth. I didn't think I'd ever heard anything in all my life that sounded so like an angel.

That night Mama said I could sit out by the fire with Daddy for a couple minutes before bed. I curled up beside him, his arm holding me near. I couldn't take my eyes off the tongues of flame as they licked the little bits of wood Ray fed them. The heat was almost too much on my face, but I didn't want to move away from it.

"Daddy," I whispered.

"Hm?"

"Are we rich?"

"No, darlin'. The Rockefellers are rich," he answered. "We're doing all right, though."

"Are we poor?"

"Almost. But we do fine, I guess."

"Those folks today, they're poor, aren't they?"

He told me they were. Said they were real poor, indeed.

"Why does God make some people rich and some people poor?"

He shifted a little so he could see into my face.

"That's a big question, isn't it?" He pinched his lips together the way he often did when he was thinking real hard. "I don't know as God makes anybody rich or poor. I think that's just how life is."

"Then why doesn't He make it so everybody's got equal?"

"Well, I don't know the answer to that," he said. "But what I do know is that sometimes He uses the rich to help the poor. And every once in a while He lets the poor help the rich."

"How do the poor help the rich?" I asked, scrunching my nose.

"By giving them a chance to be kind."

Daddy helped me up to my feet and told me I best get to sleep. He held the door of the truck until I got all the way inside and told me and Mama to sleep well.

She didn't even look at him.

Mama settled down next to me on the seat of the truck and I pretended to fall asleep. She kept her arm draped over me like she meant to protect me. That was how I fell asleep, drawn up close to her and feeling her slow, deep breathing. Her body warmed me and I felt safe.

I woke in the middle of the night. Mama was sat up and had my head in her lap. She held something in one hand. With the other, she covered her mouth, catching her sobs. I thought she was trying not to wake me.

"Mama?" I asked, pushing myself up so I was closer to her.

She turned from me, putting her face into a shadow.

"You all right, Mama?"

Even though she didn't answer me, I knew she wasn't okay.

I put my arms around her, my face against her stomach that tensed with each bout of crying. Like she'd done so many times for me, I told her it was going to be all right.

After a bit she caught her breath and calmed a little. I kissed her cheek and tried looking in her eyes. She stayed in that shadow, though.

"Why don't you lay back down?" I asked. "Get some rest?"

She did and I reached for the blanket that'd fallen off us, putting it over her.

That was when I saw what she had in her hand. It was a picture of Beanie. I asked if I could see it and she nodded, handing it to me. I put it in a beam of moonlight that shined on the dashboard.

It was a photo of my sister from before I was even born. Beanie was so small, her cheeks so round. She had on a dress with puffy sleeves. I wondered if I'd ever worn that dress once I got big enough. In the picture, she sat on a swing, holding the two ropes on either side of her. Daddy stood behind her and I imagined he was pushing her. He had his usual happy smile on.

As for Beanie, she didn't look at the camera and she didn't smile. She had her eyes trained on something off to the side.

Just looking at that old photograph caused an ache to spread all the way through me. Missing Beanie felt like a deep burning that wouldn't ever go out no matter how much water I tried tossing over it.

I knew very well that the Bible was full of stories of folks dying and then coming back to life. There was a little girl and a couple grown men, even a lady named Dorcas. Meemaw'd told me they'd all been dead, and even in the tomb. But by the power of almighty God they rose up and took fresh air into their lungs. She'd told me there were even a couple of them that wanted lunch soon as they could ask for it.

But that was the Bible and I wasn't living in those times. No amount of begging God was bringing my sister back to me.

I cried myself back to sleep, that picture of Beanie pinched between my fingers.

CHAPTER SEVEN

Every mile took us away from the land of tan and dust to a land of green and grass. Trees spread their arms wide, bright leaves fluttering from their fingertips. Fields full of growing crops on either side of us passed in a blur of emerald as we sped by.

I'd long since lost track of where we were, but I did know one thing— we were a world away from Oklahoma.

Mama told me I could take off my mask and I breathed easy for the first in a good long time. The air was so clean, so fresh, I could already tell it was healing me with every breath. I wished so hard that I could've talked Mama into letting me ride in back with Ray. I didn't dare ask, though. I knew she'd just tell me no.

I held that old mask on my lap for at least half an hour, fidgeting with the strap and feeling the weight of it. I thought of all the times Pastor said the dust was a curse, the wage of our sin. The way he'd made it sound most every Sunday of my memory was that God had sent the storms to break us to nothing so we'd have nothing left to turn to but God.

I hated that Pastor was right. The dusters had broke us. We had lost so much.

Picking up that mask, I held it close to my face. It was the last of the curse.

"I'd sure like to throw this thing out the window," I whispered.

"What's that, darlin'?" Daddy asked.

"I said I wanna throw this old mask out the window."

"You best keep it," Mama told me. "Just in case."

I couldn't think what might happen that would make me need that dumb old thing ever again. I sure didn't want to keep hold of it. Mama took it from me, holding it on her own lap as if she couldn't think of letting it go again.

Leaning my head back against the seat, I paid attention to every smooth and sweet intake of air until I fell asleep.

Hours passed with me hovering between shallow sleep and hazy waking. If any dreams came, I wasn't aware of them. Mama and Daddy spoke seldom, but when they did it was in hushed tones so as not to wake me. I listened, keeping my eyes closed so they didn't know I could hear.

"You feeling better?" Daddy asked.

"A little," she answered. "It comes in waves."

"You think you're getting sick?"

"I don't know," she said, her voice sounding dull, flat. "It feels more like being sad."

"I know it. I do." His voice got softer. "Is there anything I can do?"

"I don't know," she said again.

She shuffled in her seat and I peeked to see her body turned so she was facing the window once again. I couldn't tell if she was crying, but her shoulders did go up and down, up and down with slow and deep breaths.

Seemed to be awful hard work trying to fight off the sadness.

I was in one of those places between alert and snoozing when Daddy shook my shoulder. Blinking my eyes, I saw his face close to mine.

"You awake?" he asked. "You've gotta see this."

Rubbing at my eyes, I slid off the seat of the truck and put my feet down in grass so tall it tickled my bare legs. First thing I did was work off my shoes and socks so I could wiggle my toes in the cool blades.

Remembering my promise to Millard, I bent over and tugged out a handful of it. Holding it to my nose I breathed in the fresh scent of it. If green had a smell that was it.

"What are you doing?" Daddy asked, a laugh in his voice.

"I promised Millard I'd send him some." I held my hand to Daddy and grinned. "Can I?"

"Well, you promised. I suppose you'd better." Daddy put his hand out and put it on my elbow, pulling me away from the truck. "But I didn't wake you up just to show you grass. Come on."

I let him lead me to the front of the truck and lifted my eyes to see when he told me to look. In my surprise I dropped all of Millard's grass. It didn't matter. I figured there was plenty more where that came from.

"Is it real?" I asked.

"Sure it is," Daddy told me.

I had never seen so much water in all my life. Wide and long and beautiful it rolled, lazy and brown. The damp air filled me all the way up, soothing me like a balm. I wanted to put my feet and hands and head—all of me—into that water. Seemed it would feel like a miracle to let it soak up into my bone-dry skin.

"Is it the ocean?" I asked, only managing a whisper.

"Nah. Just the Mississippi River." Daddy stood behind me and rested both hands on my shoulders. "Big, isn't she?"

Mama stood to the right of me, her hands held to her chest and it rising and falling. Ray was on the other side of her, a step or two ahead. He let his mouth hang wide open.

"Can we go in?" he asked, bending down and folding his pant legs up.

"I don't think we better. It's deeper than you might think," Daddy answered. "We can go to the edge, though."

We did, Mama staying put by the truck, calling after us to be careful and not to fall in. Daddy kept me steady so I wouldn't stumble. I didn't tell him I could manage on my own on account it was real gentlemanly of him to help me.

We didn't go too close, really. Just near enough to watch the river travel like a slow-poke turtle moseying along a path. I didn't think I could ever tire of looking at it moving along. I only wished I could collect a little of it in a bottle to send back home to Millard. He sure would have liked that, I knew it.

"What state are we in now?" I asked.

"Missouri," Ray answered.

"That's right." Daddy nodded.

I didn't have to so much as look at Ray to know he stood taller just then.

"See that bridge over there?" Daddy asked, pointing. "We gotta cross over that. Then we'll be in Illinois."

Closing my eyes I tried to think of where that was on the big map of Daddy's. I couldn't picture it, though. All I could do was listen to the splashing of water.

I'd never once in my life heard anything like it.

Mama spread a blanket on the ground so we could have ourselves a little picnic up by the truck. I found I was so hungry, I almost ate as much as Ray. The dried meat and slices of cheese Mama had gotten at the store earlier in the day tasted as good as anything ever had.

Daddy finished eating and lit himself a cigarette, resting his elbow on his bent knee. The ribbon of smoke danced into the warm Missouri air. If I'd had a camera I would've made a picture of him just like that. How he looked was content, nearly happy.

"You know," Daddy said, nodding at the river. "It runs all the way out to the ocean."

"If I had me a boat I'd go all up and down it," Ray said. He was laying on his stomach and watching the river. "I'd just live on that old boat. Bet there's good fish for eatin' in there."

"Guess you're right about that," Daddy said.

"I could live the rest of my life on the river, I think." Ray picked a long piece of grass and stuck it between his teeth. "I'd be real happy, I reckon."

"Doesn't sound so bad." Daddy squinted as he dragged on his cigarette. "Sure would be an adventure."

Ray smiled but kept his eyes on the Mississippi.

"Was Red River ever this big?" I asked. "When it had water still?"

"No. It never was." Daddy took a pull of his cigarette. "This here's ten times as big. It goes on a couple thousand miles, I reckon."

Ray made a hum of agreement like he already knew so much, so I didn't let myself show how amazed I was.

"There's bridges all along it so folks can cross over whenever they want."

"How'd they get to the other side before the bridges?" I asked, imagining Indians on horseback, crossing with the river up to their knees.

"By raft," Daddy said. "That's what I'd guess at least. Wasn't the safest way, though. I imagine they'd sink pretty easy, especially when taking over a wagon or any kind of heavy load."

"Bridges are safer," Ray said. "Ain't they?"

"That's right." Daddy looked at his cigarette and took one last draw on it before tossing it in the grass. "They build them real strong. Put the legs of the bridges all the way into the river bottom, real deep, to support a lot of weight."

"How'd they do that?" I peered at the water and wondered how deep it was. Seemed to me it went all the way to the middle of the earth.

"Well, darlin', they had men swim all the way to the muddy floor."

"Didn't they have to breathe?"

"Nah. They'd just take a good breath before going down," Daddy said with a dead serious look on his face. "They'd take in air, filling up their arms and legs with enough to keep them going all day long."

"Is that true?" I asked, turning to Mama. She'd never lied once in all her life, far as I knew.

She shrugged and kept her eyes fixed on the water.

"Took them years to build even one of them. I read that whenever the river froze over, they'd have to stop working until it thawed all the way out. Sometimes the water would ice over so fast the men wouldn't get out in time."

"Did they die?"

"Not that I ever heard of. Didn't I say they were good at holding their breath?" He puffed out his cheeks and made his eyes cross.

I gave him my sideways, I-don't-know-if-I-believe-you look, but smiled anyway.

"Weren't they cold?" I asked.

"I'll bet anything they got half-froze themselves. Can't imagine how glad they were for a hot bath after they got out of all that ice."

Ray rolled to his side, watching Daddy tell the story and grinning like all get-out.

"I read another something that said once they got that bridge up nobody dared step foot on it." Daddy felt of his shirt pocket and pulled out a fresh cigarette. "Mary, I never did tell you thank you for that lunch. It was real good, sugar."

"Uh-huh," she said.

"See, folks were scared that bridge wouldn't hold up under them," Daddy went on after lighting his cigarette. "You wanna know how they got them to trust it?"

Ray and I both nodded.

"They hired themselves an elephant." Daddy raised his eyebrows and nodded his head. "You believe that?"

I told him I wasn't sure I did.

"If I could find that book I'd show it to you," he said. "They borrowed that elephant from a zoo not too far from here. Miss Jim was that elephant's name, if I remember right."

"Miss Jim?" I giggled.

"That's right. Miss Jim. Can't quite figure out if it was a male or female. Guess it doesn't matter too much." Daddy took a drag off his cigarette. "Anyhow, they put a collar and leash on Miss Jim and had him stomp across the bridge all the way to the Illinois side and back again."

Ray gave out the biggest laugh I'd heard from him in too long a time.

"It's true," Daddy said.

"Tom . . ." Mama shook her head and sighed.

"I'm telling you, this part is the God-honest truth."

"Did the bridge hold up?" I tilted my head, still not sure I believed him.

"It's still there, ain't it?" Ray said, still chuckling at the idea of it.

"Mama, is that a true story?" I asked.

"I don't know," she answered, getting up off the blanket. "I never know when it's your daddy telling the story."

"Well, I tell you, it's true. Most of it, at least." Daddy stood and brushed the crumbs and ash off his pants. "Sometimes the most true stories are the most ridiculous."

I helped Mama clean up the lunch things, all the time imagining Miss Jim the elephant walking heavy-footed across that bridge. And I pictured me riding along on its back with Daddy leading it by the leash.

I wouldn't have closed my eyes even to blink for fear I'd miss seeing something. Far as I could figure, it would take a full day to walk all the way across, especially on a slow-moving elephant. The river was just that wide.

I thought the God who'd carved out that river, scooping down in the earth with His own hand, must've been just as big as Meemaw had always said He was.

Just thinking of it made me feel small.

Daddy let me ride in the back with Ray. Mama sighed like she didn't approve of the idea one bit, but she didn't say a word of argument. I was sure glad for that. I didn't want to go over that bridge and see it all from behind a window.

When we made it about halfway across the river I got a feeling that sunk deep in me. If anybody'd asked me that day what it was I felt, I wouldn't have had any words for it. It was like nothing I'd ever had in my heart before. Akin to grief, but something different, too.

Part of the feeling was knowing how far we were from home. That river was a big, long, thick line, and once we were over it we couldn't go back.

Even if we did, it wouldn't ever be the same again. Not like it had been before.

I went ahead and let myself cry. Not a loud one or a messy one. A quiet cry.

When Ray asked me what was wrong, I told him I missed Millard.

It was the truth.

Once we crossed over to Illinois I settled in, using a soft quilt as a pillow, and let myself fall asleep with the open air and sunshine on my face.

I dreamed in black and gray and white.

Running, I kicked up sprays of black dust with my bare feet. My legs were strong again, my stride wide. It felt good, the air against my face and the way my hair fanned out behind me.

A swooshing, whooshing wind pushed at my back, forcing me to run faster and faster, the noise growing to a growl, to a roar. Turning, I saw a black duster lunging at me, its jaws open and spitting rocks and stones to sting at my heels, my legs, my back.

Try as I might, I couldn't see anything that looked familiar. Nothing that could lead me home.

The duster pawed at me, catching at me with a sharp claw and tossing me up into its swirling, twirling body. Arms waving wild, I tried to grab hold of something, anything, that might save me. Nothing but dirt and rock to catch in my hands.

Beanie stood on the ground, staring up at me, her hair standing on end and her skin tinged blue. She stepped right into the duster, her arms spread wide, letting it catch her up until she was spinning, spinning, spinning right along with me.

We fought the dust, the two of us, bleeding and bruised and scared. We fought to get to each other. Catching her, I grabbed tight and we flew round and round as one person.

Then she tore at my hands, forcing me to let go. She pushed me and pushed me again until I couldn't reach her anymore, until I was falling out of the duster and to the ground.

The black sucked her all the way in and carried her off to wherever it was headed next.

When I jolted awake it was dark and the truck had stopped. Ray sat beside me, his head leaned back against the truck, his eyes shut tight and chest rising and falling with asleep-breathing.

The truck moved on again and I rolled onto my back to watch the stars above me, trying to put the bad dream from my mind.

For the life of me, I couldn't get Beanie's face out of my head.

CHAPTER EIGHT

Mama made short work of getting us breakfast and heating up coffee for her and Daddy. She'd gotten real good at cooking over a fire. But when I told her I liked her camping-out food as well as her in-the-kitchen food, she just sighed and shook her head.

Daddy used his pinkie finger to trace the line on the map he said was our way to where we were headed. It angled and curved, crossing paths with other roads and running all by its lonesome in other places. He pointed to towns and cities we'd pass through. He tapped the map with his middle knuckle twice before lifting his head. He had a pleased look on his face.

"If I had to guess I'd say we'll be there before supper," he said.

"Where?" I asked.

"Gus's house." He let out a whooping sound and set to folding up the map. "It's our last day on the road."

"Thank the Lord," Mama sighed. "I'll be glad to sleep in a bed tonight."

"And I'll be glad to sleep in a bed beside you," Daddy said, winking up at her.

"Thomas," Mama said, sounding upset. "The kids."

"Sugar, you always have been mighty pretty when you blush."

Daddy was right about that.

Mama insisted on us finding a place with fresh water so we could scrub a little of the road off ourselves before we got to Gus's. Much as Daddy didn't want to stop, he did as she said. A nice man at a fill station let us clean up in the sink out back. The water was cold and smelled like bad eggs, but it sure felt good to be clean, even just a little.

The man even let us use the toilet. It was a nice change from doing my business in the bushes.

Mama had me change into a fresh dress and worked a braid into my still wet hair. She fretted about everything she could think of. Most of all, she worried over not being able to have hot water so we could get really clean. Daddy told her we'd done all we could.

"Besides," he said. "Gus isn't going to sniff us. He's got better manners than a hound dog."

Even Mama had to smile at that.

I'd hoped Mama would let me sit in the back with Ray, but she worried I'd get myself too worn-out. If I'd been a sass-mouthed girl I might have asked if she thought we were fixing to play baseball or hold a square dance back there. But I didn't say such a thing because I knew she'd get the soap back out of the box and have me taste it for my troubles.

I tried sleeping, thinking it might make the time go by faster. Excitement kept me awake, though, not allowing me to keep my eyes closed more than a minute or two. I couldn't hardly stand the waiting.

"You sure they know we're coming?" Mama asked. "Shouldn't we try calling?"

"They know," Daddy answered. "I can try to find a telephone once we get into town."

"I hate to put upon them." Mama folded and unfolded her hands over and over in her lap. "Maybe we should find someplace else to go for the night."

"Gus'll just insist we stay at his house," Daddy told her. "You know him. He wouldn't ever hear of us going to a hotel."

"Oh, I know," Mama said. "But what about his wife? I don't wanna put her out."

"Do you really think Gus'd marry somebody that got put out so easy?" Daddy winked at her. "She's put up with Gus nearly twenty years. She must be real patient." Mama touched her forehead and tapped her fingers against it real lightly. "Do we even know how to get to their house?"

"I've got the address in my billfold." Daddy pulled a cigarette from his shirt pocket and held it between two fingers, not lighting it just yet. "Might have to ask directions once we get to town."

Mama sighed and covered her face with both hands, rubbing at her forehead like her head hurt.

"You all right, Mama?" I asked her.

She shut her eyes and licked her lips. "I'm fine," she answered. "Just nervous is all."

We kept going, mile after mile, each one getting us closer to happy. Still, Mama looked more jittery and miserable by the minute.

Daddy let out a whistle and slapped his hand against the steering wheel. Then he reached around and scratched at his neck, letting his shoulders relax.

"Just got in Michigan," he said, a laugh in his voice. "Lord Almighty, we're just about there."

Mama touched the hollow spot at the bottom of her neck and breathed in deep. She blinked, her lids flitting up and down the way she did when she was trying hard not to cry. I reached for the hand she'd kept on her lap but she pulled it away before I could take it in my own.

I told myself she hadn't meant anything by it, still I felt a twinge of hurt.

Leaning forward, I rested my fingertips on the dashboard. The leftover grit from Oklahoma rubbed against my skin.

"Lean back, darlin'," Mama said, putting her hand on my shoulder. "It's not safe."

I did as she asked, glad for once to have her worry over me.

Smooth road gave way to bumpy, rutted dirt. Daddy had to slow down his driving, which was fine by me. It made watching the countryside pass that much easier. On Daddy's side of the truck were fields stubbled by green sprouts and on Mama's side were rows of stalks. Tractors rumbled over the land and men walked through the crop, hands stuffed in overall pockets.

Where the road curved to the right, Daddy pulled over and turned off the engine. He swung his door open and stepped out. He told us to come on and we followed him to an arrow-shaped sign.

"What's it say?" Ray asked, squinting like he was too nearsighted to make out the letters.

"Welcome to Bliss, Michigan," I read out loud to him.

"Bliss," he echoed. He stepped up to the sign and touched the letters as if he wished he could grab hold of them and make them stand still so he could read them without any trouble.

Daddy scooped me up, holding me close to his face and kissing my cheek. I worried I was getting too big for him to hold like that. But he didn't strain or grunt at picking me up.

"We've made it," he whispered in my ear. "We'll be happy here. Real happy."

I hoped more than anything that he was right about that.

He let me down and took my hand. The two of us looked up the curved road and squinted, trying to see a building or house or something. All we saw were thick trees and dirt road.

"Can't hardly see nothin'," Ray said.

"Guess we should get a closer look."

We loaded back into the truck, Mama telling me I should ride up front with her again so I wouldn't breathe in the dirt that got kicked up by the truck. I didn't argue or even let myself get sore about it. The excitement bubbled up so strong I couldn't hardly feel anything else at all.

Mama, though, had started crying. I couldn't figure out why. But I sure did hope they were happy tears.

❀

Not one of the buildings along the main street of Bliss was boarded up. They all had signs that said they were open for business. We drove along and saw a theater and diner and butcher and general store. It wasn't so big as Boise City, not by a long shot. Still, Bliss was alive and buzzing and I thought I'd like it well enough.

Folks walked up and down the street and a couple cars went past us from the other direction. A woman in a flowered dress watched us drive by. I didn't wave at her, still she smiled at me when she caught me looking at her.

Daddy parked the truck along the curb behind an old rusted-out jalopy. He sighed as he cut the engine and closed his eyes.

"I'd be glad to never drive another mile as long as I live," he said. Then he patted his stomach. "Sure am hungry. Bet y'all are too."

"I could get something together," Mama said. But the way she blinked slow and heavy, I thought feeding us was the last thing on her mind.

"I'll do it," I said.

She took my hand, squeezing it. "You don't have to do that."

"Hey, Ray," Daddy called out the window. "You hungry, son?"

"Yes, sir," Ray answered from the back of the truck.

"Looks like a good diner right there." Daddy nodded at a building along the side of the road. "Bet they've got good pie."

"Tom, we can't afford it," Mama said.

"Sure we can." He winked at her. "I put a little aside just in case something happened to the truck or we had to stay over someplace along the way. Still got every penny of it."

"I don't know."

"Bet they got a phone I could use to call Gus." Daddy opened his door. "You don't have to come in if you don't want to. But I sure would like a piece of pie and a cup of coffee. And I wouldn't mind having your company to enjoy, too."

"I'd like the kids to have some milk," Mama said. "They haven't had any in so long I can't even remember when."

"We're going to be all right, sugar," Daddy told her. "Life's going to be good again."

Mama nodded and touched her stomach like it ached, her fingers spread wide. "I want to hope it will be."

Every booth in the diner was empty. The only seat with a backside on it was a stool at the counter. The man sitting on it was the roundest person I'd ever seen. His short legs dangled from the stool and he let one of his feet sway with the music coming from the radio behind the counter. He was eating a sandwich that dripped with ketchup and grease. He turned toward us and gave us a nod of the head.

"Oh, Shirley," he called out after swallowing. "You've got customers."

A woman who I guessed was Shirley came through a door that swung shut behind her. She had on a nice blouse and a pair of slacks under her apron. I did my very best not to stare, but I'd never seen a woman in pants before. She smiled at me and winked like she knew how surprised I was.

I tried to think of a way to ask if I could have a pair of pants, just to play in. But the way Mama looked at me out of the corner of her eye, I knew she'd read my mind and the answer was never-in-my-lifetime.

"You folks go ahead and sit wherever you like," she told us. Then she cocked her thumb at the man on the stool. "I'll even kick this bum out of his seat if you want."

The man snorted a laugh out his nose and I wondered if he was some kind of hobo. By how rumpled his shirt looked, it wouldn't have surprised me one bit.

Daddy asked if we'd like to sit at the counter and helped me climb up on my stool. I could have done it all by myself, but knew Mama would've worried over me not acting ladylike. Seemed the right thing just then, minding my pleases and thank-yous. It was a small price to pay for a piece of pie.

"Just passing through?" the woman asked.

"Nope." Daddy got up on his own stool right beside Mama. "Just got into town. We're staying over to Gus's house."

"Gus Seegert?" Shirley smiled.

"That's the one."

"You must be the cousin he's been bragging about," she said. "I think the whole town has heard about you by now."

"Well, Gus has always been real good at telling stories." Daddy looked over at Mama. "Probably best if you don't believe all of what he says."

"I don't know about that," Shirley said. Then she took a pad of paper from her apron pocket. "What can I get you?"

"You should try the corned beef," the man at the end of the counter said, holding up his sandwich. "It's good."

"Well, we're looking for a couple slices of pie," Daddy said. "Maybe even a cup of coffee for my wife and me. Milk for the kids."

"All right." She put the pad back in her pocket. "Today I've got peach or blueberry."

I wasn't sure if I could ever choose, they both sounded real good to me, but I picked blueberry on account the crust looked extra sugary.

She served us before going back through the swinging door. The man at the counter got off his stool and poured himself a cup of coffee.

"Now, you came from Oklahoma," he said, leaning back against the wall. "Is that right?"

"Yup," Daddy answered. Then he reached his hand over the counter. "Tom Spence."

"Nice to meet you." The man shook hands. "Jacob Winston. But everybody around here just calls me Winston."

"Good to know you, Winston." Daddy sipped his coffee and flinched. "Good Lord."

"Strong, isn't it?" Winston slurped from his cup. "You get used to it after a while."

"Well, I don't know if I ever could," Daddy said. "That's something else."

"Yes indeedy." Winston nodded. "You need cream? Sugar?"

"Cream," Mama said. "Please."

He handed her a small pitcher and she poured a good amount of it into her coffee. The spoon made a swishing sound against the cup as she stirred.

"Have you lived in Bliss long?" Daddy asked, cutting into his pie. He'd picked peach and the fruit was a real pretty orange-pink.

"All my life," Winston told him. "I've never spent a single night outside this town."

"That so?"

The man nodded. "Yup. Never had a reason to leave."

"What is it you do here?"

"Well, I sit here and eat Shirley's grub most days." Winston finished off his coffee and poured himself more. "Other times I go around town spreading mischief."

"Sounds good to me," Daddy told him with a grin.

The two men went on talking about things that interested grown-ups. Mama slid her plate in front of Ray, the pie untouched, and sipped at her coffee. I could tell she was trying to get it down without making a face. After a minute or two Shirley came to the counter and asked Ray and me how we liked the pie.

We told her it was real good.

"I'm glad," she said.

"Shirley," Winston said. "How about you let me get their bill."

"You don't have to do that," Daddy said. "We've got money."

"This is my treat." Winston looked over the bill. "This isn't much at all."

"Thank you," Mama said. "It's real kind of you."

"I'm happy to do it." Winston smiled at her. "Just think of it as your welcome from the mayor of Bliss."

"Well, I should have known," Daddy said. "Gus said Bliss had a good old boy for a mayor."

"I'll take that as a compliment," Winston told him. "You know, Tom, I'd like to talk to you sometime."

"Is that so?"

"We're short a lawman here in town," the mayor said. "Chief O'Brien had a heart attack and Doctor Barnett told him he can't work anymore."

"How about that." Daddy nodded as if he knew the folks the mayor was talking about. "And there's nobody else in town wanting the job?"

"Nobody I'd trust." He raised his eyebrows. "I wonder if you'd think about taking the job?"

"You've never seen me before today. You don't know if I do good work."

"Gus said you're good. I take him at his word."

"Well, I'd like to talk about it, I guess," Daddy said. "Not today, though. I'd like to get us settled first."

"You think about it." Winston nodded. "It pays all right, if that'll sway you."

"I'll think on it."

"I'd be happy if you did."

"Say, I wonder if there's a telephone I could use," he said. "I'd like to give old Gus a call before getting to his place."

"Sure," Shirley said. "Jake, how about you show him where it is."

"Right this way," Winston said, nodding to the swinging door.

Daddy followed him, leaving us with Shirley. She leaned on the counter and gave Ray and me a pretty smile.

"You kids like gum?" she asked.

We told her we did and she handed us each a slice.

I thought of Mama's idea of entertaining angels and wondered if sometimes they saw fit to entertain right back.

If so, they'd serve up pie and glasses of milk and a stick of gum for good measure.

CHAPTER NINE

An old tan-colored dog sat among the green grass and yellow flowers that dotted every inch of Gus Seegert's front yard. It didn't bark, that hound didn't, it just panted hard, letting its tongue hang out the side of its mouth, and watched as we pulled up the drive toward the house. By the way it had its tail wagging I knew it wasn't much of a guard dog. I did hope, though, it might make a good friend.

"Guess this is it," Daddy said, parking the truck before turning to me and giving me a smile.

He didn't hop out of the truck or go running up the steps of the porch like I'd expected him to. Instead, Daddy blew out a deep breath and nodded before opening his door. In all my life I didn't think I could recall a time Daddy acted more nervous.

A woman stepped out onto the porch of the well-kept white house. She wiped her hands on her apron and smiled like she was the happiest woman in all the wide world. She stepped down to the walk and came toward the truck.

"Gus," she called. "They're here."

From around the house came a big man, just about the same age as Daddy and at least a head taller. He had on overalls that were so faded they almost looked white. And he had on a collared shirt with both sleeves rolled up to his elbows. Daddy pushed open his door and got out of the truck, laughing and clapping his hands.

"Lord have mercy, Gus," Daddy said, shaking his head. "As I live and breathe. Look at you."

"Tom," Gus called back, making long strides across the yard toward Daddy. "Still handsome as the devil."

I'd never in all my life seen a man pick Daddy right up off the ground the way Gus did that day. The two of them slapped each other on the back and laughed like one of them said something real funny.

It sure did my heart good to see Daddy smile so big.

Mama and I got out of the truck and Ray jumped out from the back. The tan-colored dog made his way to us and sniffed at our fingers and give them a lick like he wanted to make sure we knew we were welcome.

"Mary," Gus said, making his way to Mama. He took one of her hands in both of his. "It's real nice to have you here."

"I'm glad we made it." She let out a breath of air like she'd been holding it for days. "It's been so long."

"Sure has." He nodded at her. "Too long if you ask me."

"I don't think I've seen you since right after you came back from the war."

"I do believe you're right about that."

"You left so sudden . . ." Mama said, then shook her head.

"It took me a long time to get the nightmares to stop," he said. "Still can't think about a trench without gettin' nervous."

"Well, it's just nice to see you now."

"A lot's changed since then," he told her. "I'm not that same man anymore. I was young and foolish. Now I'm just old and foolish."

"You aren't old," she said.

"Turned forty beginning of the year. Sure feels old to me."

Mama smiled at him. "You seem happy."

"I am."

"Why didn't you come home?" Mama asked.

"Because I found home here." He nodded at his wife. "She's done me a lot of good. Just like you done for Tom."

Mama didn't say anything to that or smile even.

Gus went on to meet Ray and me and introduce his wife, Carrie. If I'd had to make a guess, I would have thought she was right around Mama's age, or maybe a little older. She stepped toward us and shook all our hands. That was when I noticed she wasn't wearing any shoes. When she caught me looking, she waggled her toes and gave me a wink. I liked her already.

"Gus, how about you show Tom and the kids around the farm." Carrie looked at both Ray and me. "One of our barn cats had a litter last night. I'll bet you'd like to see the kittens, wouldn't you?"

We both nodded. I hoped as hard as I could that Gus might let me hold one of them if I promised to be real gentle.

I tried not to hold out hope that he might let me keep a kitten for my very own. That might have been just too much good all in one day.

Mama decided to stay at the house with Carrie while the rest of us took a tour of the farm. That was fine with me. I didn't want her fretting about me getting overtired or climbing on a tractor or anything like that.

She wanted so bad for me to be a lady. It just wasn't my time for that yet. Being a lady seemed like it wasn't fun at all and I had plans to put it off as long as I could manage to.

First we walked out to the fields where Gus showed us how good the crops were coming in. He said they grew a little of everything. Corn in the north field and soybeans in the east. To the west was wheat and in the south he kept an apple orchard.

"Even got us a pumpkin patch," he told us. "Y'all like pumpkin pie?"

Ray and I looked at each other, neither of us sure what to say.

"Ain't you never had pumpkin pie before?" he asked.

"It's been awhile for things like that, Gus," Daddy said. "It isn't so easy to grow pumpkins in dust."

"Well, I'll tell you, you'll be glad to have one that Carrie makes come fall." Gus whistled. "Best part of Thanksgivin'."

"Can't hardly wait." Daddy touched his stomach.

"Even got a bunch that'll be good for carvin'," Gus said. "We have a

Halloween party here at the farm every year. Hayrides and doughnuts and all the works. You think you'd like that?"

"I've never been to a Halloween party before," I told him.

"Then you'll have to for sure come this year." Gus nodded once like it was settled. "You'll have a real good time. That is if your folks'll let ya."

I looked to Daddy, not sure if he'd be all right with a Halloween party on account we were Baptists.

"Sounds fine by me," Daddy told him.

I was sure glad for that.

"Over thataway," Gus went on, "Carrie's got her garden. Every kind of vegetable's growin' in there."

"It's a real nice place, Gus," Daddy said.

"Yup. We like it just fine." Gus breathed in through his nose. "What we lack in foldin' money we make up for with what we grow here. We got just about all we need right here. A good deal more, even."

"How you managing it?" Daddy asked. "You need money to pay the mortgage and your field hands."

"Tom, I'll tell ya. I never did trust no bank, not never." Gus turned his head and spit. "Never put a dollar in a bank in my whole life. Carrie said I was crazy, hiding it away here at the house. I always said, at least here I could keep a eye on it. Turned out I was right."

"I'm sure glad for that."

"Me, too," Gus said. "Can't imagine having to leave this place. Can't hardly think of it."

The two of them stood in silence the way men did sometimes. They squinted off over the land like they liked what they saw just fine.

"Well, I'm sure I'm forgettin' somethin'," Gus said. "What else y'all wanna see?"

"Mr. Seegert?" I asked.

"Oh, you don't gotta call me that, darlin'," he said. "It's either Gus or Uncle Gus. And I'll bet Carrie'll wanna be called Aunt Carrie. We're family. I can't have none of this Mr. and Mrs. Seegert stuff. Whatcha need, honey?"

"Well, Uncle Gus, I wondered if you had any chickens."

"Sure we do. Got the coop off to the other side of the house." He pointed. "You like hens?"

"Yes, sir, I do," I answered. "I know how to tend them."

"Ain't that somethin'?" He nodded like he was real impressed. I hoped he was.

"I don't break the eggs, either. I'm real careful."

"I bet if you asked nice, Carrie might let you visit them hens sometimes. Maybe even feed 'em if you give her a good smile."

"I'd like that," I told him.

"Wanna meet my goat?" Uncle Gus asked.

Ray told him he would.

We followed him to a pasture off the side of the barn. There stood an old goat with thick horns curling up out of his head. He had him a beard and chewed the cud, making that beard wiggle back and forth. The way that goat eyeballed us, I thought he'd take great pleasure in knocking us right off our feet.

"Fella over there? That's Squash," Uncle Gus told us. "He's a ornery old cuss. Stay outta his way if you wanna keep all your fingers."

"Why's he so ornery?" I asked.

"Just wait and see if *you* don't turn into an ornery cuss looking at Gus's mug every morning," Daddy said, laughter in his voice.

"It's sure a miracle Carrie ain't turned mean on me," Uncle Gus said. "Not yet, at least."

Clear to the other side of the pasture from Squash stood a pair of stout pack mules. They watched us, their eyes full of curiosity. Ray went right up to them and rubbed their noses.

"Come on, Pearl," he said to me. "They're soft."

I shook my head and stuck by Daddy, too nervous of their square teeth to touch them. I told myself maybe I'd try another time when I was more used to them.

"That's Molly and John," Uncle Gus told us. "Some mules ain't so nice. These ones, though, are good friends to me."

Uncle Gus made sure to show us his three dairy cows and the little calf that had just been born the week before. I wasn't so scared of that little fella and put my hands on either side of his sweet face. He blinked up at me and I couldn't help but love him right away.

We found the kittens in a stall of the barn. They were cuddled up against the mama cat, some of them feeding off her. She kept her eyes on us, that mother cat did, and I didn't dare get too close to her babies for fear she'd hiss at me.

I figured after a day or two she'd get to trusting me. She'd realize that I belonged there same as her.

Mama told Ray and me we needed to get baths before supper. She didn't get an argument, at least not from me. The warm water felt good on my skin. I scrubbed a good week's worth of filth off my arms and legs and from between my toes. I came up out of the tub feeling drowsy, like I could have slept the rest of the day away.

Ray did obey and got in the tub like Mama asked him to. But he didn't stay long enough, as far as she was concerned. She had to send him back more than once to scrub at his neck with a washcloth or under his fingernails with a brush.

I knew he was embarrassed by how red his face got and I wished she'd leave him be. Boys were part grime and it was like asking them to remove a thumb, having them scrub so hard. Then again, Mama never had been around boys too much and I wondered if she didn't know how they were.

"He doesn't know how," I told her after she sent him to get between his toes real good.

"Mrs. Jones had it hard, Pearl," Mama said, scolding me. "She did the best she could."

"Yes, ma'am," I said. "I was just—"

"You were just nothing. He's a good boy." Mama turned me so she could give my still-wet hair a good brushing. "I won't have you shaming him."

I was glad my back was to Mama just then. I wouldn't have wanted her to see how her words had stung me.

Aunt Carrie didn't let us help her cook supper or set the table even as much as Mama asked if we could. She just went ahead and did all the work herself which made Mama fidget and blush.

"You're my guests," Aunt Carrie said. "Just tonight, let me serve you."

She set out fine dishes with roses painted around the edges and silverware that sparkled in the light from the windows. A frilly white cloth covered the table. Just looking at it made me nervous.

"Carrie makes a nice table, don't she?" Uncle Gus asked, pulling out a chair for me to sit in. "Real fancy, huh?"

Ray took a seat across from mine, sitting slow and careful like he was afraid to bump something and cause it all to crash to the floor.

"Other day I dropped a whole dish of ketchup at dinner. Made a awful stain." He winked at Ray. "Believe it's right where you're sittin', son. Go on. Look under your plate."

Ray did as he was told. Sure enough, right there on the table cloth was a faded stain of dull red.

"She tried scrubbin' it out, but it just wouldn't budge," Uncle Gus said. "She wasn't mad at me for it or nothin'. These things happen. Carrie ain't never been one to get ruffled over something like that."

Ray put his plate down and his shoulders relaxed. Mine did, too.

I sure did like Uncle Gus.

The sky dimmed on that first day in Michigan and Daddy told us we'd best get ready for bed.

"Gus needs his beauty sleep," Daddy said. "He's gotta get up before the sun."

"Eh, couldn't sleep past five no more if I tried," Uncle Gus said, rubbing at his eyes and yawning real wide.

Daddy went to the truck to bring in a couple of our things. Just nightclothes and such. He called to Ray and me, saying we should come out with him. We did, thinking he needed help carrying a bag or two. Once we got on the porch, though, we saw him standing in the middle of the yard, staring at something in front of him.

"Look at them," Daddy said. "Pearlie, you have to see them."

I looked but all I could see was nighttime falling.

"See it?" he asked.

I didn't at first. But then I caught the blinking lights flashing bright here and there in the air. They faded only to flash bright again.

"Are they fairies?" I asked, awe and wonder making me feel as if I were in a dream.

"They're lightning bugs." Daddy reached for me, pulling me closer to himself. "Watch."

He cupped his hands around the air, catching one and holding it in front of my face. It crawled on Daddy's finger before glowing and taking to hovering near my face.

"Try to get one," Daddy said.

We stretched out our arms, Ray and Daddy and me, collecting the little critters. They tickled on my skin, moving up my fingers and hand to my wrist.

The way they glowed seemed pure magic. A good kind.

Aunt Carrie brought us a canning jar to put them in.

"Do you know why they do that?" she asked me, holding one of her own on an outstretched palm.

"No, ma'am."

"So they can find each other," she told me. "Isn't that nice?"

"It's the nicest thing I've ever heard," I said.

She smiled at me. "I think so, too."

Ray and I shared a room there in the farmhouse. Mama and Daddy were just across the hall. I was glad to be so close to them all. It made me feel safe.

Mama had made sure to tell me no less than three times as she tucked me in that she'd be just a handful of steps away from me in case I needed her or if I got up in the middle of the night with a bad dream.

I was so tired, though, I was sure I'd sleep clear into the next morning.

Laying in my bed, I heard Ray's gentle breathing, knowing he was already deep in sleep. And I could hear Mama and Daddy's low talking, their voices nothing more than a murmur.

It was enough just knowing they were there.

CHAPTER TEN

I woke to full sun on my face. Sitting up, I remembered I was in the room at the top of the stairs in Aunt Carrie and Uncle Gus's house. And I remembered we were in Bliss, Michigan. I about pinched myself, it seemed too good not to be a dream.

I got myself dressed, glad Ray was already up and out of the room so I had a little privacy. My work dress had the tiniest stain on it, right on the hem. If somebody didn't look for it, they might not even see it, but I knew it was there.

It was from just around Christmas time the year before. Beanie had knocked over Mama's coffee, the half-full cup spilling on me. Mostly it'd hit my legs but some splatters got on my dress. It hadn't been hot, but I'd been so mad at her I could've spit. There in that room in the Seegert's farmhouse fingering that remaining stain, I couldn't remember what it was I yelled at her. It wasn't nice, though, I knew that much.

Regret burned right in the center of my chest and I found it hard to pull in a good breath.

I sure hoped God would forgive me for the times I was so mean to my sister.

Trying to push away the thoughts and feelings and sadness of not having Beanie, I set to work making my bed the best I knew how. Then I looked across the room at where Ray had slept.

He'd tried making his bed. I could tell he'd put in a little effort at least. The blanket was pulled up to the pillow with at least a dozen lumps all the way to the foot of the bed. I fixed it, pulling the sheets and smoothing the quilt, fluffing the pillow so it didn't look slept on. Tugging and tucking and making it look nice.

My imagination tempted me with thoughts of being a grown-up woman and keeping house for my husband. For my kids, even. It poked at me, wanting me to see how happy I'd end up being some day.

Happy ever after.

Happy as a fairy tale.

But fairy tales weren't real. I remembered that as I finished up Ray's bed.

Aunt Carrie sat at the kitchen table, a cup of coffee beside her and a book in her hand. The clock on the wall told me it was after eight already. All the men would be out working the fields, making themselves useful. They'd have been at it for at least an hour already.

And there I was, just getting up. I felt like a lazybones.

Seeing Aunt Carrie there with her bare feet propped up on a chair made me feel a bit better, though.

"Good morning," I said.

She jumped, pulling the book to her chest and laughing at herself. She had the kind of laugh that was more a hooting sound than anything.

"Oh, goodness," she said. "Am I ever jumpy."

"I'm sorry, ma'am," I whispered, fearing she'd be upset at me for sneaking up on her even though I hadn't meant to.

"Don't be. I just got to the scary part of this book." She looked at the cover. "I should know better than to get so involved in a mystery. I sometimes forget that the world is still going on around me."

I knew exactly what she meant.

"Are you hungry?" she asked, getting up and putting a scrap of paper in her book to save her place. "I have some sausage I can warm up. Do you like toast?"

"Yes, ma'am," I answered. "Is my mama up?"

"She is," she told me. "She's out hanging some laundry from your trip."

Aunt Carrie bent and took a frypan out of a cupboard by her knees.

"I would offer you an egg or two, Pearl, but I'm afraid I've been too occupied with that silly book and have neglected my chicken coop duties." She put her pan on the stove and dropped a couple patties of sausage in. "If you want, I could gather a few. It wouldn't take but a minute."

"That's all right," I told her. "After I eat, I could get them for you."

"You're sure?" She lit the fire under the pan and soon the sausage sizzled against the heat.

"Yes, ma'am." I moved to stand beside her and watch the grease pop. "Mama had hens back in Oklahoma. I used to tend them sometimes. I don't mind them so much."

"That would be wonderful," Aunt Carrie said. "But first, I want you to eat. There's nothing worse than farmwork on an empty stomach."

Aunt Carrie handed me the bucket of scratch for the hens. She told me to put the eggs in one of the baskets she had on a shelf there in the coop.

"Watch out for Billina," she called after me when I walked away. "She pecks."

Her chicken coop was three times the size Mama's had been. And where our birds back home had been sickly and scrawny, Aunt Carrie's were round and active, wandering free all over the yard. Once they saw me with their breakfast in my bucket, they came clucking their good-mornings and pecking at what I scattered for them.

"Y'all must be hungry," I said to them.

The hens seemed real sweet and I was glad to feed them from the palm of my hand even. I knew it didn't take much, getting a chicken to like me. All it took was a little food and some soothing sounds. I sang to them soft and low the way Mama had when she took care of her hens.

Mama had a voice that sounded like a fresh, cool breeze. My singing was more like a rumbling engine, especially after being sick the way I'd been. The hens didn't seem to care too much, though.

Still, I wished I sounded like Mama when I sang.

Leaving the girls to their meal, I ducked into the coop for the eggs. I kept right on singing. It felt good and made the loneliness leave a little. I plucked the eggs up out of the nests, gentle as I could, placing them lightly into the basket.

Once my eyes got used to the dim light in the coop I realized I wasn't alone. One yellow hen sat on a nest, watching me as I collected the eggs. That girl didn't seem like she was fixing to move and I thought she must be the one Aunt Carrie had warned me about.

"Billina," I said, keeping my voice calm. "May I please have your egg?"

Slow and careful as could be, I reached toward her. Soon as I got close enough, though, she jabbed at me, trying to get me with her beak.

"Now, you don't scare me none," I told her.

I kept going after that egg of hers and she kept trying to guard it. I wasn't about to let a stubborn old chicken win over me. I had to get that egg. After half a dozen tries I did get my hand under her and grab the prize. I was careful as could be putting that one in the basket. It would've made me mad if after all that work I'd dropped it.

Putting the basket on the floor, I lowered my face close to Billina's.

"That wasn't so bad, now was it?" I said. "You're a tough bird, aren't you? But I think I like you most of all."

I reached out to give her a pat but she wasn't willing to make friends. Flapping her wings and jutting out her head, she opened her beak big as she could and screamed like the devil. It scared me so bad I jolted back and screamed myself.

Billina settled back on her roost, cackling like she was real pleased with herself for giving me such a fright.

"What'd you do that for?" I asked, holding both hands up to my chest, feeling my heart thud a hundred miles a minute. "You stupid hen."

I backed up from her, hitting against the wall of the coop which made me yelp. I slid down to my backside. My skirt was all hiked up on my legs, but I just did not care. And I started to cry.

It wasn't because of that hen or because I was alone. And it wasn't on account I'd gotten scared by a silly old bird. I cried because the sadness burst up out of me, an out-of-control blast of awful feelings. Everything I'd tucked down deep surged up and out like a bad coughing fit.

I cried so loud I thought sure somebody would hear me.

If they did, they didn't come, which was fine by me.

I made good and sure my face was dry before stepping out of the coop. My wailing must've bothered Billina enough to get her off her nest. She was nowhere in sight. While making my way to the house, a bird swooped low over my head. It wasn't a fancy one, that bird. Just brown of feather and chirping in little peeps. Still, I watched it dart up and down all the way to the trees.

She disappeared into a forest I hadn't noticed the day before. I wondered what it was a little bird might find in there. I imagined critters. Squirrels and deer and coyotes finding cover in those woods. I did believe if there were bears Uncle Gus would've warned us.

I figured a hundred years before that day Indians must've run among the trees, bow and arrow in hand, leather moccasins strapped to their feet, beads strung around their necks. They'd have used that as hunting ground, I was sure of it. At least they would have before the white man came and built their farms and towns and roads.

The weight of the egg basket grounded me, making me remember not to flitter off into my daydreams just then. I could've hovered over real life all day in my imagination if I wasn't careful.

Trying my best not to give the forest another thought, I turned toward Aunt Carrie's house. Much as I wanted to, I couldn't ignore the warning all my fairy tales had taught me—that the forest was a dark and wicked place where horrible things happened to children.

Even so, that old curiosity tugged at me, making me want to wander under the cover of all those trees.

Before opening the back door of the farmhouse I took one more look.

CHAPTER ELEVEN

Uncle Gus wouldn't hear one word of protest from Mama. He was just bound and determined that he'd throw a picnic to welcome us to Bliss. He couldn't hardly stand the idea that we'd been in town four days already without meeting every person who lived within five miles.

"It's too much fuss," Mama told him.

"Ain't neither, Mary," he said back to her. "You stop bein' so stubborn and let me do this for you and Tom. Kids, too. How else're they gonna make friends?"

Mama didn't have an answer for that, so she didn't say anything at all. What she did was cross her arms and jut out one hip the way she did when she was trying to show she was in charge. Didn't seem that worked on Uncle Gus so well.

I hoped real hard I might make a friend, maybe even two.

The picnic was to be that coming Saturday and I spent every single awake moment daydreaming about it. It'd be a bright day, the day of the picnic. The sun would shine on everybody, but not so hot that they'd sweat through their fine linen shirts or get red skin on their noses and cheeks.

All the folks would come and they'd play games in the yard like croquet or kick the bucket. None of the grown-ups would holler about the kids running around because Uncle Gus never minded that kind of thing. And Mama would let me play because she wanted me to make friends.

I imagined there would be at least one girl in the whole town who liked playing make-believe. Not in a baby-doll, playing-mama-of-the-house kind of way. But in the Indian princess and lady explorer kind of way.

In my prayers at bedtime I asked if God wouldn't mind giving me just one new friend. I told him I'd even settle for a girl who liked sitting around and talking if that was all He had to give. I made sure God understood I wasn't one to be picky.

In Jesus's holy name. Amen.

On the day of the picnic nearly all the folks from Bliss came out to the farm. Dishes and bowls and platters covered the table Aunt Carrie'd had Uncle Gus set up. Fried chicken and sliced tomatoes and potato salad had my mouth watering. There were cakes and pies and a jar of pickles near as tall as me.

Ray said he was fixing to try a bite of everything. I just shook my head and warned that he'd bust at the seams if he tried. He didn't listen to a word of it. That boy sure did love his food.

People sat at picnic tables and on the blankets and sheets Aunt Carrie'd spread out on the grass. They stood in clusters, holding plates of food or cups of lemonade. A gaggle of ladies stood around Mama. It seemed they squawked at her all at once. She kept her smiling face on the whole time.

It didn't matter where Mama was or what she was doing, she had a certain kind of brightness that drew all eyes to her. I sure was proud to call her mine.

Daddy stood out by the barn, a cigarette between his fingers. A couple other men stood beside him, including Uncle Gus. Every once in a while one of the men would say something and the others'd nod their heads or turn their heads to spit. A couple times they even smirked or let out a full laugh. Most of the time, though, they just stood together in silence, holding down the grass. They seemed happy enough to be doing just that.

A troop of boys had already stolen Ray from me, asking if he wanted to play a game of baseball out in a fallow field. They hadn't asked me and I did my very best not to pout about it. They didn't know me good enough yet. Soon they'd realize I liked playing catch just as much as any boy. And that I could throw a baseball just as hard, too. At least that was what I liked to think.

I went and sat on the back porch, watching everyone else enjoying the picnic. Slumping my shoulders, I allowed for a good old-fashioned pity party that only I was invited to.

Meemaw had always said that feeling sorry for oneself was like a pig rolling around in its own muck.

"You might like wallowin' around in it for a while," she'd said. "Might even feel good in a way. But it don't take long before you smell like manure and ain't nobody for miles wants to be around you."

Seemed to me, though, there wasn't anybody all too interested in being near me just then anyway.

In my lonely misery I watched Aunt Carrie flit from one group to another, touching arms and giving warm nods. She greeted newcomers and refilled the cups of folks who'd been there all along. In between landing among different swarms of buzzing and chattering people she checked on the food, making sure there was still plenty and swatting at hungry flies and thirsty bees.

She caught a glimpse of me and fluttered her way over, the light cotton of her dress dancing along with her movement.

"Are you feeling all right, dear?" she asked once she got near enough. "Have you had anything to eat?"

"I'm fine, ma'am," I told her. "I had some pie."

"What kind?" One of her eyebrows arched up for just a second.

"Apple." I licked my lips at the memory of the sweet fruit and spicy cinnamon. "It was good."

"I'm glad." She rolled her shoulders forward and leaned in closer to me. "Did you meet any of the girls yet?"

I hadn't and told her so.

All the girls I'd seen had been sitting in a circle that looked too tight for me to fit into. I'd had my eye on them and a couple of them had been watching me, too. We'd been checking to see if we'd like each other from all the way across the yard. Most of them had on dresses I guessed were made out of flour sacks just like mine were. Their shoes didn't look shiny new. Seemed to me they might make good friends. Most of them, that was.

The way one of the girls had squinted her eyes at me, I didn't think she'd like me if I was the only person in the world.

I felt the same about her even before hearing one word from her mouth.

"Would you like to go meet them?" Aunt Carrie asked.

"Yes, ma'am." It was a lie.

She held her hand out to me and I took it, letting her lead me off to where the girls sat. With each step I felt a thudding doom in my chest and a pulsing sickness in my stomach.

If she hadn't held my hand so tight I might have run off to see if the boys wouldn't lend me a ball glove. I would have even let them throw the baseball at me hard without complaining about how it stung my hand.

But when we got up close to the girls I knew it was too late. I prayed that at least one of them would like me even a little.

The girls made room for me in their circle and went around telling me their names. There was an Ethel and a Victoria, an Isabell who liked to be called Izzy and a Margaret who liked to be called Maggie. I knew as soon as those girls introduced themselves I'd get them all confused. I didn't think I'd ever be able to tell which was which.

The last girl, though, she was different. She sat stick straight with her legs folded like she was riding sidesaddle, holding her hands on her lap like a lady. Her copper-colored hair was curled just right with a red bow holding half of it in place pulled off her face. She was pretty and I thought she probably knew it.

I knew we'd never make friends.

"I'm Hazel Lee Wheeler," she told me, her words clipped and crisp and perfect. "My father owns the general store."

"Good to know you," I said.

"My family founded this town. My great-great-great-grandfather Bliss was the first to settle here." She puckered her lips and eyeballed me. "He's on my mother's side."

"Weren't there any Indians?" I asked.

"Well, yes. But he brought civilization when he came." She pursed her lips real tight and I wondered if she knew how much like a duck she looked just then. "My people came over on the Mayflower all the way from England."

"That must've been a long boat ride," I said.

She shot me a look that would've stabbed right through me if I'd let it. Good thing I'd decided not to care about what she thought of me.

"What's your name?" one of the girls asked.

"I'm Pearl Spence," I answered.

"You talk funny," she told me. "Are you a hillbilly?"

"There aren't any hillbillies in Oklahoma."

"Can you read?" another girl asked, saying her words slow so I could understand them.

"There're schools there," I answered, talking fast as I could.

Their questions went on like that for a good ten minutes. Much as I wanted to walk away from them, I obeyed the manners Mama'd taught me all my life and tried being polite enough not to tell them they sounded ignorant.

I did as Mama told me and tried to make a friend.

"I'm tired of this," Hazel said after a while. "Let's go watch the boys play ball."

I'd never been one for watching boys do anything. Back home in Red River I'd joined along in their play just so long as Mama wasn't nearby. But I did follow those girls that day.

The boys played in a field right beside the woods. We girls sat in a line and I yawned more than once I was so bored. Izzy or Maggie, I couldn't remember which, went on and on to me about her brother who was the biggest boy in the school. I repeated my ohs and reallys and uh-huhs, hoping she'd think I was listening.

After a while the boys noticed us and strutted over like they were some kind of big stuff. Not Ray, though. He wouldn't have known what to do with so many girls all in one place. After giving me a nod, he went back to get more food to eat.

I gave him a look like he best not leave me by myself with those kids, but he'd already put his back to me.

The other boys dropped to the ground, right there on the grass. They all had eyes for nobody but Hazel. It figured, I reckoned.

"Who's this?" the biggest boy asked, nodding at me. I figured he was Izzy or Maggie's brother.

"Her name is Pearl," Hazel told him.

"Well, hey there, Pearl," the big boy said. "Have you been in the woods yet?"

"Bob," the girl who'd claimed him as her brother said, her voice a whine. "What about the g-h-o-s-t?"

"What about it, Ethel?" Hazel asked. "You aren't scared of ghosts, are you?"

"It's just a story," another of the girls said. "Ghost stories aren't real, Ethel. They're just supposed to scare kids."

By how big Ethel's eyes were I figured that old story did the trick.

"Tell me," I said, sitting up straighter. "I wanna know the story."

"Are you sure?" The big boy smirked at me. "You won't get scared, will you?"

"Nothing scares me." It was a lie, but those kids didn't have to know that.

"Long ago, before the Civil War even, a whole bunch of slaves ran away from their owners down south," the big boy said.

"Did you have slaves back home in Oklahoma?" one of the girls asked.

I rolled my eyes and reminded her that slavery was against the law. I had half a mind to believe the school there in Bliss wasn't so good as I'd expected.

"Don't interrupt, Maggie," Hazel snapped.

"Well, some of those runaway slaves came all the way to Bliss," the big boy went on. "They hid out in those woods there until it was clear for them to keep going."

"Where'd they go next?" I asked.

"Up to Detroit, then they crossed over to Canada." The big boy shrugged. "If they made it that far, at least."

"Oh, Bob," another of the girls said. "Please don't. This story gives me the shivers."

"There was a woman who stayed out in these woods though, refusing to move along. She said she was waiting for her son to come, that he was going to meet her in the woods so they could go to freedom together." Big Boy Bob leaned forward and whispered. "But he never made it. He'd stolen a loaf of bread in Ottawa Lake and the store owner had him lynched."

One of the girls—Izzy, I thought—covered her mouth with a trembling hand.

"The woman still wouldn't leave the woods," Bob went on. "Her wails could be heard all over Bliss. When her crying finally stopped, someone went into the woods to see if she'd left. They found her in the hiding cabin deep in the forest where the runaways would stay the night sometimes. That cabin's right under the biggest tree in the forest. They found the woman there, dead. She didn't leave even then, though. Her ghost stayed behind, haunting the forest even all these years later. And still, on a quiet night you can hear her crying out for her son. They say that when she died the tree twisted in fright from her ghost screaming and wailing."

"I don't believe in ghosts," I said, keeping my voice steady even though it threatened to quake.

"So, you aren't scared?" Hazel moved her head so her hair flipped around her shoulders, for the big boy's benefit, I was sure. "Not even a little?"

"Nope."

I put both of my hands behind my back, hoping Hazel wouldn't see how the skin on my arms had turned to goose pimples.

"Then why don't you go have a look," she said. "If you really aren't scared, that is."

I turned toward the woods. I didn't give myself time to change my mind. Standing, I straightened my skirt and checked to be sure Mama didn't have her eyes on me just then.

"Where's that old twisted tree?" I asked.

"Right in the middle of the forest," Big Bob answered. "There's a trail that goes right up to it. See those two pine trees?"

My eyes followed where he pointed. "Yeah."

"That's where the trail begins."

Without another word I took off, running for the first time since the day of the big duster. My lungs ached and seized up, making me cough. I slowed, but I didn't stop until I got to the two pine trees and saw the opening into the woods.

CHAPTER TWELVE

Sunbeams pierced through gaps in the leaves. Green above me, in front of me, below me. The trees weren't one on top of the other like they'd seemed to be from far off. There was space between them full of fallen trunks that crumbled in rot and leftover leaves from years before.

The trail the big boy'd told me about wasn't so smooth and straight as I'd imagined it would be. It was more worn into a line that snaked between trees and around logs. Seemed to me it'd been there for years, maybe even before the white man came to claim the land from the Indians.

I imagined them, their moccasined feet barely touching the ground as they moved swiftly, bow and arrow in hand. Their only worry was stalking the deer or squirrel that would be their meal.

I pictured them coming upon me there in the woods and forcing me to go along with them to wherever their camp was. They didn't understand me on account I couldn't speak Indian and they didn't know so much as a word of English.

I'd be scared, not knowing what they meant to do with me. But I wouldn't struggle. Not too much, at least. There wouldn't be any use in fighting them. One thing I knew for sure about Indians was that they were strong.

Once they got me to their camp, I'd realize they weren't the scalping kind and they'd learn that I wasn't there to take anything away from them. They'd untie my hands and show me their wigwams or mud huts or whatever it was Indians in Michigan called home.

I'd only have time to teach them one word before I needed to get back for supper. I'd teach them "friend." They would smile like they understood and say the word over and over a hundred times before letting me loose to go back to Mama.

But they wouldn't let me go without an armload of gifts like beads and feathers and a squaw dress just for me made out of the softest leather they could find.

I sure would've made that Hazel's jaw drop then.

A cluster of flowers caught my eye. Right in the middle of a sunspot, they blazed up bright from the brown rotting wood around them. Purple and yellow and white and delicate, I stepped around a fallen-down branch, stooping low to smell them.

When I was smaller I'd have Meemaw tell me about when God created the heavens and the earth. He'd put sky and sea in place before He got busy putting in land and trees and grass and flowers. Then He made it all full up of birds and fish, animals, and people even.

He looked at all of it, every last bit, and called it good.

From where I stood, looking at those tall trees covered by moss and wrapped round with vines and hearing the chattering of the squirrels, I had to agree that He'd done a good work right there in Bliss.

It would have been a shame to pick those flowers. To take them from that quiet place might have been a sin even. Some things were best left where they'd been planted.

Standing, I meant to get back on the trail. But I couldn't see it. It was like it had disappeared while my back was turned. Had I wandered off farther than I'd meant to? Turning and turning and turning I tried to see something, anything, that looked familiar. Nothing did. Just trees and branches and leaves and crumbled stumps.

It was like the woods had grown thicker. Like all the terror I'd read about in my books had come to life. I was sure I'd worked myself into some kind of trap with no way out.

I'd been tricked.

"Dang fool," I whispered between quickening breaths. I cursed myself for being so stupid as to get myself into a mess like that.

Mama had told me many times my curiosity would only ever get me into trouble. Once again I'd gone and proved her right.

I kicked at a fallen tree trunk and screamed out a cuss. The only answer I got was a screeching of birds that flew off to some other place where there wasn't a silly little girl saying filthy words.

Slumping, I sat on the fallen tree, feeling the rough bark on the back of my bare legs and thinking it would serve me right if I never found my way back to the house.

A girl should learn a thing or two about wandering off.

I let myself have the kind of cry that takes a whole lot of shaking and choking and coughing. I went on until I was all worn-out, until I'd let go of all kinds of hurt. I figured I'd cried more since coming to Bliss than ever before in my life. I was getting real sick of boo-hooing all the time.

Nobody was around to tell me not to, so I used the skirt of my dress to dry my face and blow my nose. Eyes sore and swollen, I squinted to see what was around me, hoping I might be able to find something that could lead me back.

All the trees looked the same.

All the trees but one, that was.

Standing, I made careful steps to the tallest tree I'd ever seen. It stood beyond a thicket and a low-lying puddle. Once I got to it, I felt of its trunk. Thick and rough, it scratched against my palms. I noticed that the grain of the bark moved like a spiral, like it'd grown out of the ground spinning like a ballerina.

Then, just beyond it, I saw the cabin. The boy had called it the "hiding cabin." It looked as if somebody'd plucked it up right out of the sharecropper's row back in Red River and set it to rest there in the woods of Bliss. The glass was busted out of the one window and the wood was a rotted gray color. It leaned to the right as if it wanted to collapse but was too tired to make the effort.

A chill teased up my spine and I stood still as I could, waiting to see if the ghost would come.

I heard no moaning or groaning and I felt no whooshing past my face.

All I heard were birds calling out to each other and the rushing-water sound of the leaves in the wind.

Tipping my head back, I turned my face toward the sky. The tops of the trees swayed, their arms lifted high up, making me think of Mad Mabel waving that dingy old hanky over her head.

I wondered how those trees didn't break in the wind.

If ever I had to hide I thought that would be a nice and peaceful place to do it.

Seeing as how I'd made it all the way to the cabin, it only made sense for me to take a look inside. I promised myself I wouldn't step all the way in. All I wanted was a peek.

The wood of the steps whined and I reminded myself that there was no such thing as ghosts. The door screeched when I pushed it open. Not a ghost, I told myself.

I did step in. Just one step. The sun leaked through a gash in the roof, showing nothing but empty walls and cobweb-laced corners. Bits of dust hung in the air catching the light and sparkling as if they were made out of precious stuff.

Then I heard a shifting. Something dragged across the dirty floor and I turned to see what it was. There, in the corner and hidden in shadow, was a shape. Taller than me and a good deal wider. I made for the door, but the shape was quicker, blocking me from going out.

My first thought was that it wasn't a runaway slave haunting that cabin. It was Eddie DuPre.

Before I could have a second thought, I swung back and put my fist into the face then pushed past, rushing fast as I could to get away.

A bumped-up root caught the toe of my shoe, sending me splayed out on the ground, right at the base of the twisted tree.

"You're dead," I screamed. "You can't hurt me anymore."

Then I heard a very human-sounding voice cry, "What'd you do that for?"

Turning and sitting on my backside, my heart drumming hard, I saw a boy stumble out the cabin door, holding his nose while his eyes watered.

"It was just a goof," he said.

Panting to get my breath back, I pushed myself up off the ground. "I thought you were a ghost," I said.

"You did?" he asked, dabbing at his nostrils with his fingertips to check for blood. There wasn't any. I hadn't hit him near hard enough. "Really?"

"Sure I did." I put my hands on my hips trying real hard to hide how riled I still felt inside. "You scared me a little."

"Just a little?"

I nodded.

"You punch good for a girl," he said.

"Thanks." I shook out my hand the way I'd seen Ray do when he'd gotten in fights back in Red River. "I'm Pearl."

"I'm Caleb Carter," he said, putting out the hand he'd been using to wipe at his nose.

"Good to know you." Just to prove I wasn't squeamish, I took his hand.

I let Caleb lead the way back to the picnic. He was a big boy, just not as big as Bob. I figured he'd agreed to do the scaring to impress the bigger boy. That was the way of men.

As we neared the pines that stood guard at the tree line, I could hear all the folks still enjoying themselves at the picnic. Voices talking about this or that and a boy hollering, "I got it." Someone laughed, sounding for all the world like a rooting pig, and someone else let out a beefy burp.

I imagined Hazel and Big Bob and all the other kids standing at the edge of the woods, waiting for me to step out from between those trees. They'd be in awe, thinking I was the bravest girl in all of Lenawee County. And once they saw how swelled Caleb's nose already was, not a one of them would dare try and trick me again.

But it wasn't a kid at the end of the trail.

Mama stood with her arms crossed and wearing the angriest, most pinched-up face I'd ever seen on her. She'd never been one to give out a whupping, but she seemed to be fixing to change her ways just then.

"Mama, I—" I started.

"Not one word," she snapped.

Caleb slipped past us and rushed away. I thought he was more scared of Mama than any spirit that could've haunted the woods. He was right to be.

"The other kids—"

"I don't want to hear a single word out of your mouth." Mama whispered, but I knew if there'd been nobody around it would have been a powerful scream. "What in the world were you thinking?"

I kept my trap shut because I knew what was good for me.

"That girl Hazel came to me crying her eyes out over how you ran off into the woods." She shook her head. "She was scared for you."

"She wasn't, Mama—"

"Don't talk." She put her hand up to stop me. "Don't."

I shut my mouth, biting at the insides of my lips so I'd remember not to say another word. From how red Mama's face was, I could tell she wasn't in the mood for any kind of back talk.

"Good Lord, Pearl. How are you ever gonna make friends if you up and run away from them?" She blinked fast like she did when she was trying hard not to cry. "And did you ever think about what kind of maniac you could've met in those woods?"

"It's real pretty in there," I whispered.

"No. Don't you say anything." She pointed at the house. "You just go up to your room. I'll deal with you later."

She grabbed my arm and tugged me toward the back porch with her fingers digging into my skin so sharp I knew I'd have round bruises. Nobody seemed to pay us any mind and I didn't know if that was because they didn't notice or because they were too polite to stare.

Nobody, that was, except Hazel who stood next to the house, sipping a glass of lemonade and smiling like a mean old cat.

Back in Red River we had names for girls like her. Not a one of them was nice to say in mixed company, though, so I just thought them in my head and hoped for the day I might say them to her face without Mama there to hear.

Hazel wiggled her fingers in the air in a wave that made fun of me somehow and she made her smirk even bigger.

She looked uglier when she smiled than when she scowled, and I felt sorry for whatever fool would make the mistake of marrying her one day.

"I'm just so embarrassed," Mama told me once we were in the kitchen and she'd let go of my arm. "Here Mrs. Seegert put on the nicest picnic for us and you go and ruin it."

"But, Mama . . ."

"What?" She made her eyes meet mine and behind the green-brown of hers was fire that would burn through me if I looked too long.

"Nothing, ma'am."

Mama got right up close to my face. "If you ever do a thing like that again . . ."

She didn't finish and I half feared she'd say she would send me off. All of me feared she'd decide she didn't love me anymore. And I tried not to let myself think that maybe she saw too much of the DuPres in me. I wished I could get their blood out of my veins. If only there was a way.

"I'm sorry . . ." My voice crackled, threatening sobs.

"Not another word," she said, quiet like she'd been defeated. "Go up-stairs."

I didn't move right away. If I could see into her face, maybe there would still be a little love there. If it was gone, all was lost for me. I had nowhere else to go.

"Go on." She turned from me to go back outside.

Much as I wanted to stomp my feet hard against the stairs as I went up to the room, I didn't. I trod lightly, wishing I could just disappear.

I watched the rest of the picnic from out the bedroom window. After a bit, folks took their serving dishes and headed on home. Once they were all gone, Aunt Carrie and Mama started the work of cleaning up the plates and glasses and Uncle Gus folded up the tables and Ray got all the chairs.

Daddy stood off to one side of the yard with the man we'd met at the diner not a handful of days before. Winston, the mayor of Bliss. From what I could tell, those two men were talking business and I wished real hard I could hear what they were saying. I tried reading their lips, but both men had mustaches that made it next to impossible.

Daddy glanced up and, seeing me watching him, nodded his head once at me. I didn't smile at him or wave even. I didn't mind him seeing just how miserable I was right then.

I remembered reading about all the princesses in fairy tales that'd gotten locked up in towers by wicked stepmothers or witches or ogres. Difference between me and them, though, was they'd never done anything to deserve that punishment.

Winston left after a couple minutes, getting into an old jalopy that was so rusted it almost looked red. Daddy went about helping everybody finish picking up the yard.

I rolled over on my back and shut my eyes, not falling asleep but wishing I could. I stayed that way until I heard knuckles on the door. It was Daddy, I just knew it.

"Can I come in?" he asked.

I told him he could if he wanted to.

He stood in front of me, his hands on his hips and looking like the most handsome thing God ever did see fit to create. When God had knit Daddy in Meemaw's womb, He'd put extra time in to give him the kindest eyes and the warmest smile.

"How're you doing, Pearl?" He reached into his shirt pocket for a cigarette but, finding none, came to sit beside me on my bed.

"All right, I guess," I answered.

"Your mama was upset . . ." He didn't finish and I was glad because I was afraid of what he might say. "She got scared about you wandering off like that. It made her think of . . ."

Of Beanie, I thought. The way Daddy's eyebrows pushed together for just a second made me think that was exactly what he'd meant.

"Your mama was . . ." He paused and breathed in deep. "I guess we were just wanting you to make a few friends. Seems your mama was upset you didn't make nice with those girls."

What I didn't say was that I didn't need any friends besides Ray and that I never was one for playing dress up or house with the other girls. Never would be.

What I did say was that I wondered if Mama was still mad at me.

"Nah," he answered. "It's just, since Beanie . . . Since she died, your mama is scared to lose you, too."

"She is?"

"Course." He nodded. "We don't know what we'd do if anything happened to you. And when you were sick we were real afraid."

We stayed quiet a minute or two and I gnawed at the inside of my cheek, trying my very best not to start boo-hooing.

"I thought she was fixing to whup me," I said, shrugging.

"Well, maybe she was. But only because you mean a lot to her." He rubbed at his chin. "I'm not going to punish you. I think missing out on the picnic was enough."

I didn't tell him that I hadn't minded too much.

"What I wanna know, though, is why you did it." He turned and looked me full in the face. "Why'd you run off into the woods like that?"

"I wanted to show those kids how brave I was."

He mm-hmmed.

I nodded. "One of the girls asked if I was a hillbilly."

Daddy tossed his head back and gave a full laugh. When he'd finished he tsked his tongue. "Nah. We aren't hillbillies. Just Okies."

"Yes, sir," I said.

"Now," he said, squinting his eyes at me. "You wanted those kids to think you were brave, huh?"

"Yes, sir."

"Pearl, I don't know that I've ever known a girl as brave as you. Heck, you're even braver than some full-grown men I've met."

"I am?" I asked.

"Sure you are." He nodded. "But being brave isn't taking a foolish risk. Folks who are brave don't have to prove their courage to anybody."

He put his arm around me and pulled me closer to him.

"You wanna know who you remind me of?" Daddy asked.

"Who?"

"Meemaw. She never could pass on a dare." He smiled at a memory. "I heard one time she jumped on the back of a horse that wasn't broke yet just because someone called her chicken."

"Is that true?"

"Don't know." He put his hand on the back of my head. "Part of me hopes it is true. Even if it isn't, you get your grit from her, I do believe."

The whole rest of that Saturday evening I tried to picture Meemaw holding on for dear life to a wild horse just to prove she wasn't scared.

I got my grit from her. I did like the sound of that.

CHAPTER THIRTEEN

What I liked most about the church in Bliss was the way sunshine bled through the colored-glass windows, staining the white walls blue and red, green and yellow. What I liked almost as much was how the preacher didn't holler his sermons at us or call down God's wrath on our heads.

Instead he gave us the Word of the Lord with gentleness and a calm voice.

Meemaw might've thought he didn't have the Spirit or that he needed a little fire in his belly. But the way he kept his words smooth and his eyes smiling made me feel like God might be glad to give mercy after all.

I liked listening to that kind of teaching just fine.

The sermon that day was on the man named Hosea, how he'd married a "sinful woman." I knew he meant a woman who got paid to fornicate with men. Back home in Red River, Pastor Anderson would've used a harder word for that woman, one that growled up from the back of his throat.

But there in Bliss, the preacher didn't use harsh words for Gomer. He spoke of her like she'd been a real woman with struggles just like the rest of us.

Just like Winnie. I knew she'd been a "sinful woman." Pastor back in Red River had said so, more than once, right in the middle of his sermon.

That minister stood behind the pulpit and said how God had told Hosea that he best love that woman named Gomer. And He told him that he best take her back in his arms as many times as she returned to him after being with another man.

It was the way God welcomed sinners back to Himself.

Winnie and Gomer were sisters in my mind. Difference was nobody'd come along to rescue Winnie. Not like Gomer'd been rescued by Hosea. He'd come to save her on account he loved her. Didn't seem like anyone had ever loved Winnie, leastways not like that.

Every once in a while I pretended she wasn't dead. I never would've told Mama that, Daddy either. But I let myself think on that daydream sometimes.

I'd imagine she'd climbed up out of Eddie's cellar right along with me, her stomach whole, her eyes alive. That she'd gotten herself a train ticket to someplace pretty and green where she could start over and forget about all the bad that had been in her life. I just hoped she wouldn't have forgotten about me all the way.

I imagined her in a new dress, a nice blue one that matched her eyes. She'd wear her hair fresh curled and her face washed of all the paint she'd brushed on it. She'd look like herself.

She'd look like me.

The house she lived in would be a good one with flowers in the window boxes and a yard full of grass. Maybe she'd even have a cat sitting in the window, watching the birds that nested in the tree.

Winnie would wait by the door for her husband to come home from work. He'd be a clean-shaved man who wore a sharp suit and tie and had a kit that he kept in the hall closet to shine his shoes. He'd kiss her soft and tell her how glad he was to see her. Then he'd touch her stomach and ask how the baby was.

She'd keep that baby and raise it. She'd love it and watch it grow. He'd make for a good father and he'd teach that child all it needed to know about the world and family, and God even.

They'd never, ever leave that child.

Winnie would stay true to him and to that baby. At least that was how I pictured it in my mind. And for her great faithfulness, Winnie would have life brand-new.

Sitting there beside Mama in the church pew, the stained-glass window making a red puddle of light on my legs, I could've kicked myself. I'd gone and made a fairy tale.

All the wishing in the world for Winnie to be happy was nothing more than spitting into the wind. It was too late for her and I knew it full well.

After Sunday dinner Mama told me she'd like me to get a little rest. I asked if I could spread a blanket out in the yard to relax in the sun. She said that was fine just so long as I didn't wander off someplace. The way she raised her eyebrow told me she was still sore about me running off in the woods the day before.

I promised I'd stay put and I did intend to hold to it.

I lay on my back under the sky, squinting up and finding stories in the clouds. A marooned pirate crew on an island surrounded by man-eating sharks. A race between three horses and one giant rat. A mermaid twisting her way through the seawater to the surface, her hair billowing all around her head.

My eyes got lazy feeling and I let my lids close, feeling sleep gather me in its arms.

"It certainly is a nice day."

The voice woke me right up and I rolled to my side to see Aunt Carrie walking my way with a couple glasses of lemonade.

"I wondered if you would like a little company," she said.

"I'd like that," I told her, making room so she could sit beside me.

She handed me a glass. The lemonade was cold and sweet and tart. I took small sips hoping to make it last. I liked the way it stung the back of my tongue and how it cooled me all the way through.

Aunt Carrie tipped her head back, her eyes wandering the sky. I liked to think she was seeing pictures in the clouds, too. If she did, she didn't say so just then.

"Did you make a few friends yesterday?" she asked. "I saw you with the girls."

"I don't know." I shrugged. "I'm not sure they liked me so much."

"Some girls are that way." She took a sip from her glass. "Some girls are difficult to understand."

"One of them said she was real rich."

"Let me guess," Aunt Carrie said, turning her face toward me. "Hazel Wheeler."

I told her that was the one.

"I suppose they are comfortable. They come from what some of us would call 'old money.' They didn't end up losing so much in the crash as others." She leaned toward me and nudged me with her shoulder. "You aren't jealous of Hazel, are you?"

"No, ma'am," I answered even though I might've been just a little.

"I'm glad." She pointed at a puff of cloud. "It's a cat with a monkey riding its back."

"And that there's a turtle flying an airplane," I said, glad for her to play the game with me.

We traded cloud stories until we'd run out. Still, we sat in the nice day, our glasses empty on the grass beside us.

"Even rich people have troubles," she said after a few minutes of quiet. "You know that, don't you?"

"I guess so."

"They do. It's true." She smoothed her skirt and crossed her ankles. "No one makes it through life without some kind of trial."

I knew she was right even if I wished she wasn't.

"Soon enough you'll find that even the Wheelers have struggles," she said.

"I can't imagine they do."

"Believe me, Pearl. They've got more than their share."

She stood and offered me her hand and I took it, letting her pull me to my feet. She didn't let go as we walked back to the house.

Holding hands with her felt like coming home.

CHAPTER FOURTEEN

Ray's favorite place to be in all of Bliss, Michigan, was up in the old tree Aunt Carrie had told us was called a weeping willow. Ray would scurry up the trunk and relax into its branches. I would stay on the ground, hollering up about how unfair it was of him to go where I couldn't well follow.

"Come on then," Ray called to me between two branches.

We'd been in Bliss more than a week and I was gaining in strength. Still, pulling my full weight up a tree seemed impossible. I felt the bark, running my fingers along its grooves and ridges, working up my nerve to at least try climbing. But my nerve kept finding reason to stay away.

"You can see all the way into town from up here," Ray said.

"Can't either."

"See for yourself."

"I can't, Ray," I told him.

"You ain't tried." His face disappeared behind a branch thick as my thigh.

"I got a dress on."

"Don't matter."

"Does too." An ant crawled up the tree lugging something on its back. It changed route to avoid my finger. How lucky the little critter was, not having to worry about being ladylike.

"You need yourself a pair of pants," Ray told me. "I bet your mama'd make you a pair."

"Nuh-uh. She never would," I answered him. "If I so much as asked, she'd make me copy from the Bible where it says women shouldn't dress like men."

"It don't say that in the Bible."

"Sure it does."

"Where at?"

"Well, I don't know exactly, but God did say it." I picked at the bark, pulling a loose piece off between my fingers. "You don't see men wearing dresses, do ya? Mama isn't like to let me wear slacks."

"If you say so," Ray said.

The leaves rustled and I could tell it was because he was climbing higher and higher up. I pouted, even though I knew he'd never see it, and sat down at the bottom of the tree, leaning against it and closing my eyes. I sat like that for more than a couple minutes feeling sorry for myself.

"Hey, you awake?" Ray asked, his upside down face hovering near my head.

"Uh-huh," I told him, looking up to see how he was dangling from a branch by just his bent legs. "Be careful."

"I ain't gonna fall." He pulled himself up and swung down to the ground. "I been thinkin'."

"Yeah?"

"I been thinkin' about writin' a letter to my ma," he said. "I figure she might wanna hear from me."

"You need help?"

"Can't do it on my own."

"All right, then," I said, glad to be needed.

The two of us went inside and Aunt Carrie told us we could use a couple pieces of her good stationary. It was real pretty with sweet little daisies bordering all the way along the edge. She even let us use her ink pen. It wrote smooth, she told me, but I worried about making a mistake without a chance of erasing it.

Ray and I sat at the little table in Aunt Carrie's kitchen. He leaned back in his chair, rubbing at his chin and sticking his tongue out the side of his mouth. I didn't rush him. I knew he was thinking real hard.

"I ain't never wrote a letter to nobody before," he whispered, leaning forward and putting his elbows on the table.

"It's not too hard," I told him, smoothing the paper against the table-top. "You wanna start with 'Dear Mama'?"

"Write 'Dear Ma,'" he said, watching real close as I moved the pen over the page, nodding like he was giving me his approval.

I tried my best to keep my hand steady, to make the letters clear and neat. To keep the ink from splattering all over the place. It had been months since I'd written so much as my own name, though, what with the school closing down and me being sick. My hand started hurting before I got down even those two words.

"Tell her I'm happy here," he said. "Tell her there's green grass all over the place and that I ain't seen even a speck of dust. Not no dirt, neither."

"Sure there's dirt," I said, looking up at him. "How else would the grass grow?"

"You know what I mean." He pointed at the paper. "Write it down anyhow. Maybe she'll wanna come if she thinks there ain't dirt she's gotta clean up."

I wrote what he told me, sighing when I couldn't remember how a certain word was spelled. Then again, I didn't know that Mrs. Jones would mind so much if I misspelled a word or two. Probably she wouldn't even know the difference.

"And tell her she could maybe find a job up here," he told me, leaning over the page and watching me write. "Put down that if she comes we'll get a place all our own. Tell her I'll get a job, too, so we can make rent."

"Slow down," I said. "I don't wanna rush."

He waited, letting me catch up, but tapping his foot to let me know he was short on patience. I felt him watching and it made me nervous. Still, I wrote what he told me to. I didn't ask him where she'd get a job or if he'd stay out of school to work. All I did was write that letter as he said it.

"That it?" I asked once I'd caught up. "Anything else?"

"Tell her that I miss her somethin' awful." He waited a minute. "Got it?"

"Uh-huh," I answered. "You wanna sign it?"

He took the pen and slid the paper in front of himself. His whole hand wrapped around the pen. It took him near as long to write the three letters of his name as it had for me to write the whole thing.

I thought sure he'd rip through the paper, he pushed down so hard.

Once he was done he looked up at me like he was real proud.

I didn't have the heart to tell him he'd made his R backward.

Mama'd never been one for taking naps. Back in Red River she only sat down at meal times and when she had a radio show she wanted to listen to. Even then she kept her hands busy with mending. Meemaw had called her a "busy body," always moving around doing something.

But since we'd been in Bliss, Mama'd taken to resting more than I'd ever seen her do before. She'd sleep right in the middle of the afternoon, sometimes not even getting up to eat dinner. When she got up, she was no better than she'd been before.

Aunt Carrie told me she thought Mama needed all that rest, that she'd be better soon enough. Ray said she had the blues. Daddy, though, said she was going through an adjustment.

"It'll take some time," he'd told me. "She'll be back to herself before you know it."

As for me, I thought she was heartsick, missing Beanie and Red River and having her own house. I thought the very last thing she needed was to be by herself so much. Not if she was ever going to get better, that was.

So, about once a day I'd go into the room where Mama rested just to keep her company. She'd let me curl up beside her on top of the covers. I'd tell her about what I'd done that day or hum a song to her. She didn't seem to mind that I couldn't sing so pretty as she did.

After Ray and I folded up his letter and put his ma's new address on the envelope, I got to thinking about my own mama. I went to her room to tell her about the tree and the letter and a bird I'd seen early in the day. I was about to knock, but I noticed the door wasn't shut all the way. Peeping in I saw she was standing in front of a tall mirror, looking at herself in a dress I'd not seen before. She turned sideways and gathered the fabric at her back, pulling it tight on her too-flat stomach.

She turned her head toward the door and I pulled my head back so she wouldn't know I was peeking in at her.

"Might as well come in," she said, dropping the fabric so the dress hung like normal. "I can see you."

I pushed open the door and went to stand beside her. She put an arm around me and we looked at each other, at ourselves in that mirror. I'd grown to just below her shoulder. I wondered if I'd be tall as her some day. Maybe even taller.

I couldn't remember if Winnie had been short or tall. And I couldn't remember how her voice had sounded, not really. I'd never learned if she knew how to make a good supper or if she could sing sweet and pretty.

I did know all those things about Mama, and that'd have to be enough.

For about the hundredth time in the months since learning about how I was born, I regretted that Mama hadn't been the one to give birth to me. It was plenty, though, to know that she'd given me a life.

"You all right?" Mama asked, looking into the reflection of my eyes in the mirror.

"Yes, ma'am." I didn't want to tell her I'd been thinking about Winnie. She'd told me she wanted me to forget all about That Woman. "Is that a new dress?"

"New to me," she said. "Carrie told me to try them on, that they didn't fit her anymore. She said I could have any of them that suited me."

There on the bed she and Daddy shared were laid out dresses of all different colors and patterns.

"They're pretty," I told her.

"Aren't they?" She turned toward the pile, touching the fabric. "They're all fine dresses. Too fine, maybe."

"What do you mean?"

"I'm afraid I'd spoil them," she said, crossing her arms. "They're all store-bought. It's been years since I had a dress I didn't make myself."

"They'll look nice on you." I picked one up that had a green and blue plaid across it, handing it to her. "They'd just get wasted if you didn't wear them."

She held the dress against the front of her.

"Maybe I could wear them on Sundays," she said. "Maybe for special."

She smiled at the thought.

Ever since I could remember, I'd thought Mama the prettiest woman in all of Oklahoma. Her dark hair that held a spiral of curls, her creamy skin and warm eyes. The way her smile lifted her whole face when she laughed at something Daddy said. How soft and sweet her eyes were when she sang.

I didn't have so much as a drop of her blood in my veins, still I had hope that one day I'd glow the way she did. One day I'd be so nice a woman as my mama.

"I should hang these up," she said. "I'm just so tired today."

"I can do it," I told her. "You wanna lay down?"

"Thanks, darlin'." She let her shoulders slump and she hung her head like a rag doll. "Seems no matter how much I sleep I just can't get rid of this exhaustion."

"It's all right." I put my hand on her back, pushing her toward the bed. I pulled back the covers so she could climb in. Like she'd done for me most every night of my life, I tucked her in, pulling the sheet up to her chin.

"I'll be better soon," she whispered.

"I do hope so," I told her.

"Hope." She yawned. "I like how that word sounds."

"Me too, Mama."

After I got done hanging up all the new-to-Mama dresses, I left the room, making sure to turn the doorknob as I pulled it all the way closed. Mama was sleeping so good I didn't want anything to wake her.

It felt like something in my heart flickered, making it beat a little faster.

Hope sure was a pretty word.

CHAPTER FIFTEEN

I watched Ray and the tan-colored dog playing chase out in the front yard. Ray'd run one way and the dog would go after him, big slobbery tongue flapping out his mouth. Then Ray would jump and run the other way, teasing the poor critter to keep coming along.

The way that boy hooted and hollered made it seem like he was having the very best time of his life.

When I asked—even begged—Mama to let me go out, she just shook her head.

"You're sick," she said.

"I'm feeling fine now, Mama."

It was almost half-true. At least I felt better than I had the night before when a coughing fit near turned me inside out. They'd even sent for the doctor to come and give me medicine that made me feel all shaky and full of jitters.

He'd called it asthma. Said it was what happened sometimes after a bout of pneumonia. If somebody'd asked me I would've said too much was made about it no matter what name he called it.

"You can't spend the whole night coughing and gasping and tell me you're fine." Mama crossed her arms over her chest. "You're staying put for today."

"But Ray—" I started.

"I won't hear a word of it, missy," Mama said. "Just watch him out the window. That's fun enough."

Much as I wanted to, it wouldn't have done a thing for me to throw a snit fit over it. Staying inside and watching was nothing like running all over creation with Ray and that dog, but I didn't say that to her. Sassing Mama was a dangerous endeavor even if I was sick. Especially since Daddy usually took her side in the end.

I obeyed and stayed put.

Aunt Carrie told me she had a couple magazines I could look at if I wanted. I told her please and thank you and took the stack up to my room to read.

The famous lady airplane pilot Amelia Earhart was on the cover of one of them. I'd heard about her on the radio but hadn't ever seen what she looked like. Her hair was cropped like a man's, but she had curls that made it look pretty enough. Her leather jacket was open over a nice blouse and she leaned back against her airplane.

What made my eyes grow wide and my mouth drop was that she wasn't wearing a dress or a skirt. She had on a pair of slacks. I thought they sure looked smart on her even if Mama thought they were sinful on a woman.

I read the article about her quick the first time, then slow the second. I could hardly imagine it, a woman flying over oceans and mountains and fields. Seemed it would be real scary, especially flying all by her lonesome like she did. And at night, even.

I wondered what it had been like for her to jet through a cloud or look down from miles up in the air. What had the world below looked like from her airplane? I was sure it was real pretty.

Mama wouldn't allow it, me going up in an airplane like that. She liked me sticking to earth, staying in out of the sun and rain, and never having fun ever again. At least that was how I felt just then.

But if Miss Earhart came knocking, things might be different.

She'd stand on Aunt Carrie's porch, leaning back against the railing with her arms crossed. She'd have on her slacks and her leather hat with the goggles built in.

We would invite her in and she'd sit in the rocking chair, with Ray and me on the floor close to her feet so we wouldn't miss a single word.

She would tell about how she had learned to fly and how nervous she'd been that first time in the air. Then she'd go on about flying all the way across the sea. She'd have plenty of stories of adventures she'd met all because her mother hadn't told her to stay inside and be safe.

I'd wonder if she ever got lost, flying so much. When I'd get the chance, I would ask her. She would smile at me and get a faraway look in her eyes. Leaning forward, she'd make sure I was listening real close.

"Of course," she'd whisper just for me to hear. "Everybody gets lost sometimes. What matters is finding your way home."

Then she'd have Ray and me take turns riding in her airplane. She'd fly nice and low so Mama wouldn't be too nervous.

And all the kids in town—Big Bob and Hazel, too—would feel jealous of us. They'd want a ride, too. But there wasn't time for that. Amelia Earhart had come just for Ray and me.

When it was time for her to leave, she'd take off in her plane, doing a loop the loop that would get all of us to clap and cheer.

I'd wonder how she didn't fall right out of her seat, doing a thing like that. It didn't matter, I guessed. She'd go flying off to her next grand adventure, waving as she went.

And there I'd stay, on the ground, with the flying feeling still in my heart and stomach.

Man alive, did I ever hope one day I'd get the chance to fly.

For the better part of the afternoon, Daddy sat on the porch talking with Mayor Winston. Daddy smoked a couple cigarettes while Winston had his cigar. Both of them sipped at cups of black coffee and accepted cookies when Aunt Carrie offered them.

I was glad that Aunt Carrie offered me a cookie, too, even if I had to leave the sofa in the living room to eat it in the kitchen. I missed out on hearing all the two men were saying, but her cookies were worth it.

"Don't spoil your supper," Mama told me when she walked past, a basket of laundry balanced on her hip.

"I won't," I answered.

"Just one cookie, hear?"

"Yes, ma'am." I put the cookie on my napkin and took a drink of milk, feeling the cool of it touching my lip and making a mustache.

"Wipe your mouth," Mama said. "Don't drink so fast."

"Yes, ma'am," I said again. "Mama, what're Daddy and the mayor talking about?"

"None of your beeswax."

With that she stepped outside to hang the wet clothes on the line.

I finished my cookie and went back to the sofa in the living room. By then, though, the mayor was long gone and Daddy was putting out a cigarette in the dirt by the porch. When he straightened up, it seemed he stood taller than before.

That night I sat in the bedroom doorway listening to Mama and Daddy talk in their room. Their door was closed, but I could still make out what they were saying.

Ray stood behind me, his shoulder resting on the doorframe.

"We'll just be renting it," Daddy said. "Fella that owns it is giving us a good deal."

"That's fine," Mama said. "Just so long as it's got a roof and walls, I'll be happy."

"It's got a good deal more than that, darlin'," he said. "The kitchen's nice. Plenty of space. It's got an icebox even and a good cookstove."

"Don't get me worked up, Tom," Mama told him. "I won't be able to sleep."

"The porch isn't so big as ours was in Red River. Still, you can fit a swing on it if you want." Daddy went on and I closed my eyes, trying to picture a place so perfect as he described it.

It was a house painted a pretty shade of yellow with green shutters framing big windows that let in so much light we'd never have to turn on a lamp so long as it was daytime. There was a fireplace to keep us warm in the winter and plenty of shade trees to cool us in summer.

There'd be room enough for Ray and me to have our own rooms and even an extra if we had a guest come over. I thought we'd be able to have Millard come live with us if ever he made up his mind to move.

The yard would be big enough for us to have a garden. We'd grow all the tomatoes and peas and carrots we could eat. There'd be so much room that we'd have to put in flowers of every color in the rainbow. Every day we'd cut a different bunch of them to put in a vase on the dining-room table.

We four could be happy in a house like that. We'd be a family even if not a one of us shared so much as a drop of blood.

Blood didn't mean anything when it came to making a home.

I'd just about given over to the dream of that house when I heard Mama make a sound that was half sigh and half hum.

"It sounds real nice, honey," Mama said. "Real nice."

They didn't talk for a minute or two. Daddy's belt buckle clinked and Mama yawned.

"You sure you're happy taking that job?" she asked.

"I am. It'll pay just enough." His voice was firm and steady.

"Didn't you want to look for something else? Something different?"

"I'd miss it too much, darlin'," Daddy answered. "Keeping the peace is all I know how to do, Mary."

"It's not all you know," she told him. "Come to bed, Tom."

Ray and I went back to our beds real quick, but not before shutting our door. Somehow we both knew there were some things we didn't need to overhear.

CHAPTER SIXTEEN

The new house was on Magnolia Street. Mama told me that was the name of a flowering tree. One with bright pink-and-white petals. I asked if someday we might have one of those trees in our yard, maybe even just outside my bedroom window.

Mama said that would be nice.

It turned out to be a good house. The kitchen was just as nice as Daddy had promised Mama the night before. She touched every surface, calling them fine. Her eyes moving from cupboard to sink to floor to ceiling, she took it all in and nodded her approval.

Together, we walked through the house. Daddy told us the names of each space. Living room, study, dining room, root cellar. We went up the stairs to see the bedrooms, a whole hallway of them. Enough for Ray and me to have two each if we'd wanted.

My room looked out over the back yard, Ray's over the front. I thought that was fine. Standing at my very own window I hoped Mama would let me have my bed pushed right up against it so I could look out at the garden we were sure to plant. Beyond that were the thick woods that led all the way to Uncle Gus and Aunt Carrie's farm. The woods I'd wandered in on the day of the picnic.

"What do you think?" Daddy asked, crossing the room to stand by me.

"It's fine," I told him. "It's real nice."

"I'm glad you like it." He scratched at his head. "You want to go out in those woods again, don't you?"

I did and told him so. "It's real nice in there."

"Well, I guess that's fine, darlin'. I want you to be careful though, hear?" he warned. "I don't want you getting yourself lost."

"Yes, sir."

"You probably should take Ray with you." He winked at me. "I believe it would do him some good, too."

He patted my shoulder before leaving me in the room by myself.

I kept looking out at those woods, seeing the way the branches of ancient trees curved up to heaven like they were reaching for something.

Ray and I sat on the porch of the house on Magnolia Street. It'd turned out to be the kind of day that was as close to perfect as could be. I imagined heaven would be of blue skies and soft-looking clouds, gentle breezes carrying the sweet smell off of the flowering trees.

But instead of watching the birds flitter-flutter around, Ray and I were busy watching a yellow-headed boy crawling in and out of the bushes across the street.

"What's he doin'?" Ray asked.

"Don't know," I answered, wondering if children in the north were all a little touched in the head due to how it got so cold in the winter.

The boy crawled backward out of the shrubs with something in his hands. Careful as he could, he lowered it into a bucket and rubbed both palms on the legs of his pants. Standing, he caught us watching him and headed right our way, not even bothering to check for cars before crossing the road.

"Hi there," the boy said. He was a mite smaller than me and had the softest yellow-colored hair I thought I'd ever seen. "I'm Adelbert Barnett. You can call me Bert."

"Hi," I told him. "I'm Pearl Spence. This here is Ray Jones."

"Are you living here now?" Bert asked.

"Sure we are."

"My mother made cookies. She'll want to bring them herself later," Bert said. "She's helping my father. He's the doctor."

"I met him already." I sat up straighter and crossed my arms.

"All six of the Litchfield boys got into poison ivy," Bert told us. "Don't worry, they won't die."

"Glad to hear it," Ray said.

Bert turned to Ray. "You wanna see my frog?"

"I guess," Ray answered and shrugged like he didn't care either way, but followed the younger boy out the door anyhow.

It didn't bother me that they hadn't asked if I'd like to come along. What did I need to see a stupid old frog for?

I kept my spot on the porch keeping my eyes on Ray and Bert. They stood facing each other, Bert holding the frog on the palm of his hand and Ray with his arms crossed. They both jumped when that critter took a flying leap to the ground.

Served them both right.

Daddy and I sat on the front porch back at Aunt Carrie's farmhouse. We'd spent a good part of the day at the house on Magnolia Street and I was worn-out even if Mama hadn't let me lift a finger. He held a cigarette in his lips, fumbling in his shirt pocket, trying to find a match. I watched as bats flitted through the dimming sky. They darted and dove, black forms against darkening blue. If we were good and quiet we could hear them squeaking. Daddy said that was how they found their way.

Deeper and deeper the night sky turned. The moon came out as only a sliver of itself. It didn't give off much light that night, but the stars made up for it. Bright pricks in the sky numbered higher than I could count.

I thought of Abraham hearing God, so clear, telling him he'd be the father of more children than there were stars in the heavens. I wondered if the sky over Abraham had been the same as the one over me that night. Had there been more stars then or less?

And was he afraid, knowing he'd have that many kids to watch over? From all the Bible stories I'd heard between Meemaw and church, I'd learned his children ended up being a rebellious and stiff-necked people. They weren't ones to follow close or to listen up.

That must've vexed Abraham something awful.

"You see that there?" Daddy asked, pointing at a gathering of stars. "That's Cassiopeia's chair. And if you turn your head just right you'll see Ursa Major, the Big Dipper."

I tried making pictures out of the stars like I did the clouds but couldn't seem to make it work. Maybe if I'd tried harder I would've seen them but my eyes were tired.

"That bright star," he said. "See it?"

I told him I did.

"That's the north star. You ever get lost at night, you follow that star. It'll lead you home."

I nodded even though I didn't understand.

All the stars looked the same to me.

"Ray," I whispered across our borrowed bedroom. "You awake?"

"Nope," he answered.

"Don't be smart."

"Can't hardly help it."

It was too dark for me to see him real good, but I did imagine him grinning at his own joke.

"Ray?"

"Huh."

"You excited about the new house?"

"I guess so," he said. "It's sure nice."

"I'm gonna miss Aunt Carrie."

"It ain't that far, Pearl."

"I know."

Ray sat up on his bed, his outline dark against the white wall. "Wanna know what Bert told me?"

"Bert Barnett?"

"Yeah," he answered. "Wanna know?"

"Is it about his dumb old frog?"

"Nah, it ain't." He waved me over. "Come here and I'll tell ya."

I did as he said, careful to keep quiet so Mama wouldn't wake up. He made room so I could sit at the foot of his bed. I folded my legs up under me and faced him.

"You're sure you wanna know?" he asked. "I don't wanna give you night-mares."

"Oh, come on, Ray. Just tell me already."

He leaned forward. "Remember how the woods're haunted?"

I nodded. I'd told him about the cabin and the twisted tree and all Big Bob had said about the wailing ghost woman.

"You think it's true?" he asked.

"What I think is that it's the stupidest thing I ever heard," I told him. "I've been out there. I didn't see a single ghost."

"Ghosts don't never come out in the day, Pearl. Everybody knows that." Ray crossed his arms over his chest. "Ghosts is night creatures. Bert said them ghosts're callin' out for the souls that didn't find their freedom."

I swatted my hand at him, trying to make him think I didn't buy into any stories of ghosts and ghouls. From all the fairy tales I'd ever read, though, I'd learned that the forest was the place for ogres and witches and all kinds of evil. Still, I didn't want Ray thinking I was a fraidycat.

"I guess a handful of kids got lost out in the woods a couple of years back," Ray went on, whispering and leaning in. "Nobody found a one of 'em. Not a trace. They looked all over the county. All over the state, even. They thought they'd all disappeared into thin air."

I inched closer to Ray, knowing how big my eyes were just then and how I was holding my breath so I could hear his every word.

"But then one of them kids came back. A boy just about my age. He escaped in the night somehow and got himself all the way into town." Ray looked directly into my eyes. "The boy fell down right in the middle of the road, screaming about the ghosts and devils and the haints in the woods."

I gasped, putting my hands to my lips.

"Then what happened?" I asked, careful to keep my voice to a whisper.

"He died." Then Ray plopped right back down in bed, pulling the sheet up over his shoulders. "The end."

"Ray Jones," I said, shaking him by the arm to get him back up. "You can't just end a story like that."

He only responded by shutting his eyes even tighter. I knew he wasn't asleep, not the way he was fighting not to laugh at me.

"That story isn't real," I said, getting off his bed. "It's just a dumb old ghost story."

Going back to my side of the room, though, I just knew I was in for a night of bad dreams.

I pinched myself, trying to stay awake.

But the dreams won.

Ghosts swirled through my nightmare. They wove in and out of the trees, the birds and squirrels chattering and twittering away from them.

And in their hushed and shaking voices, they called out for me by name.

"Pearl, come be with us," they half sang. "Stay with us forever."

CHAPTER SEVENTEEN

Aunt Carrie sent us off the next morning with a couple dozen eggs and plenty of bottles full of fresh milk. She made Ray and me promise to come visit whenever we wanted. She made sure we knew there was no such thing as wearing out a welcome when it came to family.

"You know the way," she told us. "You are always wanted here."

Uncle Gus followed behind us, both his and Daddy's trucks loaded down with chairs and tables and bed frames. Each piece was something Aunt Carrie had insisted she had no use for anymore.

A couple field hands that worked for Uncle Gus rode along to the house on Magnolia Street. Mayor Winston was on the porch waiting for us to get there. They helped carry things in, waiting on Mama to tell them where it all belonged.

In the middle of the day we ate sandwiches Aunt Carrie had packed and drank coffee Mama perked on the stove in her brand-new kitchen. The men sat on the floor of the dining room since the table and chairs weren't unpacked yet. All but one of the men, at least.

He sat out on the back porch to eat on account he was a Negro and Mama had rules.

I thought about reminding Mama to be aware of entertaining angels, but I decided against it. She never would have allowed that an angel might come covered in brown skin and with wooly black hair on his head.

Mama wasn't prejudiced. She just had her ways. And those ways had been the ways of her parents and grandparents before her. But that didn't mean they had to be mine, too.

When I knew she wasn't looking I snuck an extra sandwich to the man. "Thank you, miss," he said, tipping his hat. "That's very kind of you."

"You're welcome," I told him, hoping he didn't notice how my voice shook.

I'd never been so close to a Negro before in my whole life.

Mama handed Ray and me a list of things to get from the general store. Things like flour and noodles and sugar and such. All the basics a kitchen should have, she said. It was like we were starting all over again, she told us, from scratch. I guessed that was pretty close to the truth.

Daddy gave a few folded bills to Ray and told him to hold it tight until we got to the store. I was in charge of the list.

All the way there I dragged my feet. I'd been to Wheeler's store a couple times with Aunt Carrie to get a thing or two. If anybody'd asked me, Mr. Wheeler's long fingers and sharp-angled face gave me the shivers.

"Come on," Ray said, grabbing my arm and pulling me along. "He ain't that bad."

We crossed the street and made our way to Mr. Wheeler's store. Ray opened the door, setting the bell to ring, and nodded for me to go in first.

Mr. Smalley's store back in Red River hadn't been half as big as Wheeler's. And the shelves there in Bliss were packed high with cans and boxes and bags of things to eat. Not so much as a spot was left bare, not that I could see at least.

I wondered if his shelves were full because he couldn't sell all the goods. Uncle Gus had told me that folks in Bliss had plenty by way of food they could grow themselves, but hardly anybody had two pennies to rub together. If they needed something, they'd make a trade. But from what I'd heard, Mr. Wheeler wasn't one to trade.

Mr. Wheeler watched us from behind the counter as we walked toward him and I wondered if he was worried that we'd steal something. He was the kind of man whose face was stuck in a frown, like he'd gotten himself frozen that way somehow. And his sharp eyebrows always stood at attention, more triangle than arch. Everything about him was sharp and pointy.

I wondered how many years of being ornery it'd taken to make his face look like that. Then again, he might just have been born that way. Hazel had angles and edges just like he did. But she was real mean, too. I guessed I'd never know for sure how they'd gotten that way.

Without so much as a hello or how-do, Mr. Wheeler cleared his throat and asked if we'd brought a list.

"Yes, sir," I said.

I put Mama's list on the counter and he took it in his long, slender fingers. Turning, he went about filling our order, leaving Ray and me waiting at the counter. Neither of us said a word for fear he'd turn and cock his eyebrows at us.

The bell over the door tinkled and I turned to see a girl come in. I thought from the looks of her she wasn't all that much older than fifteen or sixteen. She walked in, her head lowered and her hands still at her sides. She made it to the counter, standing right beside me, her fingers fidgeting with the fabric of her skirt.

I didn't mean to stare, but I almost couldn't help it. If I hadn't known any better I would've thought my sister had opened the store door and walked in so she could help Ray and me carry the groceries back home.

The girl had dark-as-night hair that came down in spiraled curls all over her head. She kept them tamed like Mama did with hers, though. Beanie's had been wild, fuzzing and frizzing and flyaway.

I tried to catch her eye so I could give her a smile. But that girl didn't turn her head or take her eyes off the points of her scuffed-up, beat-up, worn-down shoes.

She's not Beanie, I told myself. *She isn't.*

My mind knew the truth but my heart wanted to believe something altogether different. Seemed cruel how the heart could hold a hope that was dead as a stone.

Lifting my face, I saw Mr. Wheeler had gathered all the goods on our list and stood behind the counter, glowering over the girl beside me as if she belonged anywhere but right there in his store.

"Ahem," Mr. Wheeler faked a clearing of his throat to get her attention. "Are you planning on buying anything today, Miss Moon?"

She snapped her head up, breathing in sharp through her nose as if he'd frightened her. That was when I noticed her nose wasn't quite as pointy as Beanie's had been. Her skin was a bit darker, not creamy like my sister's. And her eyes were gray, not hazel.

See? I told myself. *It's not her.*

Still, I couldn't take my eyes from her face. I wanted to be extra sure.

"Mr. Wheeler, I'm still looking for w-work . . ." the girl started, her face turning red.

"You are, are you?" he asked, turning his back to the shelf and facing her full on. "Looking and working are two very different things you know, Miss Moon."

"I do realize that, sir." She swallowed hard. "But I'm sure I'll find something soon. It's just a matter of time."

"You've said all of this before," he said, lifting his chin so he had to look down his long nose at her. "And I still fail to see why any of this matters to me."

"I was hoping I could have just a little credit until I do find work," she said. "I don't need much."

I bit on my thumbnail trying to think of a way for Ray and me to leave the store. It didn't seem right, us hearing her beg that way. Mama would not have liked it one bit. Especially how rude Mr. Wheeler was talking to her.

But Mama would also be sore if we left without getting the groceries on her list, so I stayed and kept gnawing on my thumbnail.

"I wouldn't ask if I didn't think I could pay it back," Miss Moon said. "You know that."

Mr. Wheeler let his eyes flicker to the girl's face. "Miss Moon."

"Maybe a dollar or two is all I need." She lifted her hands so her fingers touched her chin. "And when I get some money I'll pay you back first thing."

"Miss Moon, you put me in a bad position." Mr. Wheeler turned and set to dusting an already clean shelf.

"I don't understand," she said.

"Excuse me, Mr. Wheeler, sir," I said, putting my hand up like I was in class waiting to be called on.

He turned his head, putting his eyes on me, and blinked once real slow-like. "Yes?"

"Sir, how much is the bacon?" I looked at the pile of groceries.

"Thirty-five cents," he answered.

"And the sugar?"

"Forty cents." He faced me, arms crossed over his chest.

"What about the coffee, sir?"

"A quarter."

"Can you please put those things back?"

"But they were on the list," he said, holding Mama's paper up and waving it.

"I know, sir." I crossed my arms over my chest. "But we don't need them just yet."

"All right. If you say so."

Mr. Wheeler slowly put away what I'd asked him to, giving me sideways looks with every item. Once he was done, he crossed his arms and pinched his lips together.

"Could you please tell us what we owe, sir?" I asked, trying to keep my tone polite as could be.

He figured our total and told us how much we needed to pay. I took the money from Ray and handed over enough to cover our bill. There were still two dollars in my hand. I knew even one dollar was a lot of money. Two seemed a small fortune. Still, we'd have more soon as Daddy got paid. Folding those bills once then twice, I pressed them into the girl's hand.

"This should get you by," I whispered, so Mr. Wheeler wouldn't hear.

She looked at her hand, tears gathering in her eyes. Opening her mouth, she made to say something but no sound came.

"My name is Pearl Spence. My daddy's the new police here," I said in a friendly, out-loud voice. "We live on Magnolia Street. Across from the doctor's house. We just moved in today. You come and see us. My mama would be glad to know you."

She nodded.

I whispered again. "I do believe you'll always be treated kind at my house."

Ray gathered most of the things we'd bought and I got the rest, trying not to look Mr. Wheeler in the eye to see how angry he might have been.

Ray worried all the way back to our brand-new house about how sore Mama would be at what I'd done.

The boy still had a thing or two to learn about my mama.

Our first night in the new house I heard every bump and squeak and creak. The way the light came in through my window made shadows on the walls of floating ghosts and strange-shaped monsters.

I waited until Mama had gone to bed for the night before I slipped out from under my sheet and made my way downstairs. Daddy would be up, I knew. He'd always been one for staying awake late into the night on account he didn't sleep well.

I found him reading the newspaper, sitting in a rocking chair in the living room, the soft glow of a lamp all around him. When he saw me he folded up that paper and snuffed out his cigarette in an ashtray that balanced on his knee. Doctor Barnett had told him the smoke was bad for me.

"You're getting stronger by the day, aren't you?" he asked, watching me walk his way. "I'm glad, darlin'. Real glad."

He dropped the newspaper on the floor and patted his thigh so I'd come and sit with him. When I sat on his knees it made me taller than him. It sure felt strange to be looking down on my daddy.

"Can I ask you something?" I asked.

"Hm?" He nodded.

"Are there poor people here?"

"In Bliss?" he asked. "Sure there are."

"Are there poor people everywhere?"

"Yes, miss." He scratched at his forehead. "Whole country's in a fix. I'd say there's more poor folks than rich these days."

"But not the same kind of poor as in Oklahoma, right?"

"No. I guess not." He pushed his eyebrows together. "Why? Are you worried about us?"

I told him I wasn't.

"Because we're all right, darlin'. This job's good. It pays enough."

"I know," I said.

"What is it then?" he asked.

I told him about Mr. Wheeler, the girl named Miss Moon, and the money I'd given her. He nodded as I went on.

"Ah, yup. Your mama told me about that," he said. He gave me a half smile. "She was real proud of you for it. I am too."

"You think she's going to be all right?"

"Who? That girl?" He squinted at me. "I think so."

"I think Mr. Wheeler's a mean man," I told him.

"You do, huh?"

"Yes." I shrugged my shoulders. "Mr. Smalley never would've talked to somebody like that. He'd have made sure she had something."

"Darlin', Mr. Wheeler isn't Mr. Smalley," Daddy said. "And this isn't Red River."

"Folks aren't so nice here as they were back home."

Daddy made a humming sound. "Well, I don't know about that. What I do know is that man has to be able to do business, Pearl. What if he had twenty people coming in, asking for credit and not a one of them paid him back a penny?"

"I guess he'd be in trouble."

"Sure would be."

"Did I do wrong?" I asked.

"No, darlin'. You did right." He took my hand. "Still, sometimes doing the right thing can get us into muddy water. Don't worry. He won't say anything cross to you."

"I hope not." Lifting a hand over my mouth, I covered a powerful and satisfying yawn. "Daddy, couldn't we find work for her? Here at the house?"

"Maybe. I'll talk to your mama about that in the morning," he answered. "That sound all right by you?"

"Yes, sir."

"How do you like having your own room?"

I told him I liked it fine. What I didn't say, though, was how lonely it was that night. How I wished my bed didn't feel so empty. How missing Beanie always hurt deeper when I was trying to fall asleep. And I didn't tell him how the Moon girl looked more like Beanie than not or how standing beside her made me feel the loss of my sister all over again.

Instead, I rested my head on his shoulder and asked him to tell me a story.

Not once in all my life did he decline. Not once.

CHAPTER EIGHTEEN

Millard had sent us a letter to tell us how things were back in Red River. "Still dry. Still dusty," he'd written. He wrote how a man had come to town wanting five hundred dollars to make it rain. Said he had a whole truck of dynamite he'd blow up that would bust open the clouds. Millard wrote that Pastor'd hollered in church, trying to get folks to dig into their pockets for the cash.

"I stood up right in church and told him I'd be surprised if we had five dollars between us there in Red River," Millard wrote. "I said if God wanted us to have rain so bad He'd just do the work Himself. Y'all should have seen Pastor's face."

He told us how he missed us something awful and how he was keeping an eye on the house just in case we ever found ourselves on the road back to Oklahoma.

I must have read that letter six times the day we got it and a couple more times after that. The paper was soft and had a little grit on it that came along in the mail. I rubbed that flour-soft Oklahoma dust between finger and thumb and wondered how much a sin it was that in a land so green and alive I desired nothing more than to go home to the dry and dead Red River.

It had taken some doing, but Mama found out that Miss Moon lived all by herself in an apartment above the newspaper. She'd been in town just over a year doing odd jobs here and there to make her way. Other than that, nobody knew anything else about her.

In her bold way, Mama climbed the steps to Miss Moon's apartment and asked if she wanted a job working at our house on Tuesdays and Thursdays.

The girl, Opal Moon, started that very afternoon.

Opal Moon took on the jobs of laundry and dusting and wiping down windows. She'd sweep the whole house from top to bottom and even help Mama bake bread. Some of the mornings when she'd knock on the back door I didn't know how Mama would manage to find anything for her to do. As far as I could see the house was already spotless.

With Opal doing so many things around the house, Mama fretted to Daddy that she wasn't needed so much anymore. She'd been used to the dust of Red River, how she was never done fighting it. But in Bliss our house stayed clean a good long time.

"How about you teach Ray to read," Daddy told her. "He'll need to go to school in the fall. Maybe you can help him out a little."

So Mama made up her mind that Ray would be able to read and write, at least a little, before the end of the summer. And when Mama got something in her mind she saw it through until the very end.

Each Tuesday and Thursday morning after she gave Opal a list of tasks, Mama set up the dining-room table with papers and pencils. She'd sit Ray down and have him copy out his letters.

During the first couple lessons I stood in the doorway and watched, amazed by how patient she was with him. How she corrected his mistakes with a kindness that went deeper than her heart, maybe right down to her soul, even. And he didn't get angry. He didn't let his frustration force him to quit. He'd stick his tongue out, just a little, focus his eyes, and try again.

It took courage, learning something so big as reading and writing. It took a brave person to sit in that straight-backed dining-room chair with a pencil resting against fingers and mind focused on A-B-C and so on.

I wondered if Ray knew he was changing his life, right there at the table with Mama looking on.

Ray Jones was real brave. That was sure.

A week or so into their work, Mama made me scoot out of the house. She told me I was distracting. I told her I'd stay out of the way, that she wouldn't even know I was there. She answered back that she didn't need me staring at Ray while he was working so hard.

"Go find some friends," she told me.

So I went to the library.

The library in Bliss was a grand old building all the way on the end of Main Street. If I hadn't known better, I would've thought it was a castle for a king and queen. It had a tower and pointed peaks. The doors had been carved with pictures of knights on the backs of horses with fairies hovering over the tops of trees and creatures of the woods stalking between tree trunks.

I imagined living there in that library, looking out at those below from my palace window, waving whenever one of the common folk caught my eye. They'd bow to me and I'd laugh and shake my head and wave my hand so they knew they didn't have to do such a thing for little old me.

If ever I was queen—or princess, even—I'd be a kind one and humble. Probably the humblest ever to exist.

Folks would say, "My, isn't she humble?" and I'd blush and tell them they were embarrassing me.

That was how humble I'd be.

I'd been inside the library all of three times and yet, on that fourth visit, I still felt a sense of awe about the place. I entered with reverence and careful, quiet steps just like I would've if it had been a church.

Mrs. Trask was the librarian. Had been since the library opened forty years before, at least that was what she'd told me. I was inclined to believe her. She had silver hair and a well-wrinkled face. And she stooped more than anybody I'd ever seen. If I'd had to guess her age I'd have put her at seventy-five. Maybe even seventy-six. I didn't ask if I was right though. Mama'd told me many times it wasn't nice to ask a lady her age.

She was real kind, Mrs. Trask was. Not once had I seen her scold somebody for returning a book late or make a nasty face when a book fell hard against the floor. She wasn't one to shush, either. Instead she offered gentle reminders of, "Do keep in mind you're in the library, my friend."

Mrs. Trask was nice.

Problem was, she didn't trust children to choose books for themselves and told me as much each time I stood at her desk. She insisted on having the final say on what I, or any child for that matter, checked out from the library.

"The world is full of dangerous books with dangerous ideas," she'd told me, pointing her fingers at her own head. "They have power. Words can be weapons and they can warp young minds. You wouldn't want your young mind warped, would you?"

I'd told her each time that I wanted no such thing. All I wanted was a book about adventure or exploration. Every time, though, I ended up with whichever book she thought to find for a girl my age.

Mostly what she picked for me were stories about fine ladies in hoopskirts, mending socks and waiting for their men to get back from some kind of war or from prospecting gold or from hunting grizzly bears.

The women in the books Mrs. Trask gave me to read stayed home while the men went off to have the adventures.

I sure did hate every single one of those books.

What I wanted were stories about Indians with tomahawks who went around and scalped the white man in revenge for settling on their land. Or a story about explorers tramping through unknown territory, seeing creatures nobody had so much as dreamed of before. I would have been happy to read a story of war or pirates or anything other than swishy skirts and elbow-length gloves.

I would've even been glad to read something about a nurse cleaning up after sick people all day long. At least she wouldn't be waiting around for adventures to happen for everybody else.

That day, my fourth visit to the library, I made my way to Mrs. Trask's desk, determined to get a book that might make my heart thump with delight. Even one that didn't make me nod off to sleep while I was in the middle of it would've been nice. I swallowed and put a real sweet and sincere smile on my face.

"Miss Spence, what a delight to see you yet again," she said in her just-above-a-whisper voice. "Are you interested in another book?"

"Yes, Mrs. Trask, ma'am," I said, trying to match the volume of my voice to hers. "I wondered if I might, please, be able to read a book about the Revolutionary War, ma'am, what with Independence Day coming up next month and all."

She sat still a moment and pressed a finger against her lips like she was trying to make sense of what I'd just said. Then she got up from her desk and walked quick as she was able toward the row of shelves she'd called "suitable for girls."

I knew right then I was doomed.

Using her bent-knuckled finger, she pointed at the spines of the books on a certain shelf until she found what she'd set out for. Pulling it down, she handed it to me.

When I saw the cover my heart about dropped.

It was a book about Betsy Ross making the American flag.

I made sure to thank Mrs. Trask and tried not to let on how sore I was.

Along one wall of the library were windows that let in good morning light. Each had a seat built into it and I chose the middle one that day. Leaning my back against the wide window frame, I pulled my legs up, stretching them out in front of me and opening the book across my thighs.

After reading that book for just five minutes I knew there wouldn't be anything more exciting in it than Betsy Ross poking her own finger with a sewing needle.

If I'd had a chance to write the story I would've made it so Miss Ross used dye laced with poison on the fabric so she might use it to kill off at least a couple of the red coats. Why they'd have their hands on the American flag, I didn't know. That was something I'd have to work out later.

And she'd have that old flag draped over her lap, rocking in her chair as she sewed the stars into the blue. What nobody would've known, though, was that she had her pistol under that flag, cradled in her lap, and she wasn't scared to use it if any of the British came charging into her house.

That sure would surprise them, I thought.

Then I imagined she had an Indian maid that carried a sharp knife in her belt. Her name would be Little Owl and she'd be just as brave as Betsy Ross. Maybe even more so because she'd seen battles all her life and was chomping at the bit to be right in the middle of one.

Because those two proved such brave and fierce warriors, I figured George Washington himself would reward them. He'd give Little Owl her freedom, of course, and promise not to disturb her tribal land since she'd proved what loyal friends the Indians could be.

As for Betsy Ross, he'd give her a medal of honor and a place in history right beside the men who fought in the Revolution. And, as a special reward, he'd make a law, too, that all girls in the good old U.S. of A. could forevermore read whatever books they darn well pleased.

I thought Betsy Ross herself would have preferred my story of her life over the one in the book I held on my lap. She'd have been upset by what a silly little girl that writer had made her out to be.

Maybe Betsy Ross and I could've made good friends.

"Oh, Carrie Seegert," I heard Mrs. Trask say. "What a nice surprise."

The old librarian rose from her desk, and from behind I could see she had a hump curving out from her back and I wondered if it gave her pain. If it did, she didn't treat folks ugly on account of it.

"Hello, Hannah," Aunt Carrie said, taking the librarian's hands in her own.

"How *are* you?" Mrs. Trask asked. "It seems I haven't seen you in years."

Aunt Carrie stood in front of her, smiling down into her face.

"Don't you remember?" she asked. "I was here just the other day."

"Of course you were." Mrs. Trask shook her head. "Silly me. I seem to forget things these days."

"It's no bother, Hannah. I understand."

"Seems to be the scourge of the old. Losing memory." She patted Aunt Carrie's arm a couple times before letting it rest there the way Meemaw did when she'd comfort somebody. "At least I can remember names still."

"That's very good."

"Now, I know you didn't come here to worry over an old woman." She clapped her hands together, but lightly, without making any sound. "You came for a book and I just got one in that I think you might enjoy."

Mrs. Trask picked a book from the stack on her desk and handed it to Aunt Carrie, reciting words that sounded more like a song than anything. When she was done, she breathed in through her nose like she was smelling something nice like flowers or baking bread.

Aunt Carrie thanked her and told her she'd like to borrow the book if she might. She wished Mrs. Trask a good day before coming my way. She sat beside me and we both said what a fine day it was turning out to be.

"What do you have there?" she asked, angling her head so she could see the cover of the book. "Betsy Ross, huh?"

I nodded, pulling my finger out from between the pages. I didn't care to keep my place anyway.

"I would have thought you were more of the kind to read about Davy Crockett or Lewis and Clark."

"Mrs. Trask only lets me read girl books," I told her.

"May I?" she asked, putting out her hand for the book.

I gave it to her and watched as she flipped it over like she was searching for something.

"Hm." She rifled through the pages and closed it again. "Funny. I guess I didn't realize there was such a thing as a girl book."

"If you ask Mrs. Trask she'll show you a whole bookcase full of them." I nodded in the direction of the shelf I meant.

She squinted up her eyes and said she knew exactly what I was saying.

"Ah, yes." She tapped her chin with her index finger. "Tell me, Pearl, do you like fairy tales?"

"I used to."

"Used to?" she asked. "You don't believe in them anymore?"

"No, ma'am," I answered.

"Ah. I suppose that happens to all of us at one point or another."

"It does?" I asked.

She nodded and told me it was indeed a common occurrence.

"One day you might start believing them again," she said. "Someday when you find that you need them."

"When will that happen?"

"Ah, but that's not for me to tell." She pointed a finger at me. "But you'll know when that day comes."

I hoped she was right. I sure did.

"Well, Miss Pearl, follow me. I believe I have just the book for you." She put the Betsy Ross book under her arm along with the one Mrs. Trask had given her. "Right this way."

I followed her and we ended up standing at a shelf in a part of the library I'd not been to before. She walked her fingertips across the shelf like two feet on a nice stroll. Her skin left marks in the gray dust like footprints. When she found the one she wanted she took it and rubbed her hand over the cover, smiling like she was looking face-to-face at a good friend.

"I think this might be the book for you," she said, handing it to me. "Instead of fairy tales, this is a wonder story."

Touching the cover, I read the title out loud. "*The Wonderful Wizard of Oz*?"

"You'll see." She held up the Betsy Ross book. "You'll enjoy it much better than this one, I promise."

I ran my fingers over the yellow and green and red cover. "I bet I will," I whispered.

"I'll be sure to ask Mrs. Trask to allow you to read whatever books catch your fancy from now on." She leaned in close and whispered. "She means well, truly. She just fears that some stories might damage young minds."

"She told me that."

"That's just because she knows the power of stories." She cleared her throat. "I'll be sure I'm careful with your young mind."

"Thank you."

"My pleasure." She nodded at the book in my hand. "Let me know what you think of that story, will you?"

I told her I would.

After she left, I stayed, reading the titles of the books that my aunt had decided were suitable for me. A hundred worlds written on paper occupied the shelves, waiting for when I'd be ready for them. I did plan to read every one of those stories.

Mrs. Trask peeked her head around the shelf, letting me know that the library would close in fifteen minutes for lunch. I wondered how long I'd stood there, dreaming about all the books in front of me.

I rushed to Mrs. Trask's desk to check out the Oz book. She didn't say a sideways word about me taking that one.

The good Carrie Seegert had kept her word.

I could hardly wait to read that book.

CHAPTER NINETEEN

Right from the start I knew I liked Dorothy Gale from the Oz book. She knew the Plains like I did and I wondered if they'd been dusty for her too, there in Kansas.

I sat on the front porch after lunch and tried to imagine what it was that had her living with her Auntie Em and Uncle Henry. Her real folks might've sent her out to live with them on the farm or maybe they'd both died of the dropsy. I wasn't sure. However it had gone, I could tell Auntie Em and Uncle Henry were good to her, that they loved her.

That was enough for me to know.

When I read the part about the cyclone, how it picked her house right up off the ground, tossing it about in the sky, I almost had to close the book. My heart started thudding and my lungs tightened. I got dizzy, light-headed, scared. It seemed the big duster was coming for me, reaching out from the pages of that book.

But I didn't stop reading, I had to keep on just to the place where I'd know Dorothy was all right. I had to know she was safe. It seemed she was, her house landing in a pretty place with kind folks to greet her.

When I pictured Dorothy Gale in my mind, she looked a lot like me.

I read, trying to keep my eyes from moving across the words too fast, knowing that I'd only get one chance to read that story for the first time. Every few minutes I'd force myself to stop, close my eyes, and really imagine the goings-on of the book.

I did wish Oz was real.

"Pearl?" Mama called from inside the house.

Her voice had a you'd-best-come-now edge to it, so I marked my place and went inside.

"Pearl Louise?"

"I'm coming, Mama," I called, stepping in the front door.

The house on Magnolia Street had a screen door that liked to slam shut if we weren't careful enough. Just that moment I forgot about that house-shaking slam until it was too late.

"Don't slam that door," Mama hollered at me from the other side of the living room, holding a hand to her chest like her heart was about to thump right out from her rib cage. "How many times have I gotta tell you?"

"I'm sorry, ma'am," I said.

On any usual day, Mama would've left it at that. But it wasn't a usual day. I could tell by the way Mama held her shoulders stiff and how she wore a scowl.

"You come running in and out of here all day long, letting that door slam behind you." She worked her face like she was trying to hold in a blazing hot anger. "You're about to knock all the pictures off my wall."

"I'm sorry," I told her again.

"Watch your tone, miss," she told me. "Go get washed up. And change your dress. The mayor's coming for supper and I need you to help me get the table set."

"Yes, ma'am," I said, rushing to the stairs that led to my bedroom so she wouldn't see the way my chin threatened to shake and the tears trying to work their way out of my eyes.

"Don't dillydally," she called after me. "We don't have time today."

Mama hadn't said anything mean to me and she hadn't whupped me, still I felt she was real mad at me. It made me so shaky I had a hard time working the buttons of my dress.

I tried hard as I could not to imagine there was some kind of yellow brick road that might lead me away from her and her cross face. But if I'd had a wish, those bricks would lead straight back to Red River.

I did what I could to help Mama and Opal get supper around, but I couldn't seem to get anything done right. After a while she sent me to the living room saying she needed me to get out from underfoot.

I told myself she was just feeling sick again, was all. She'd be fine once the spell passed. The last thing she'd have wanted was to hurt my feelings.

Mama was kind. Mama loved me. Mama took care of me. She never would do me harm, not on purpose, at least.

I tried to think on such things.

I saw out the living-room window that Opal Moon was leaving for the day. She always went in and out the back door because that was proper for the help. At least that was what Mama'd told me when I asked.

Opal had made her way around to the walk in front of our house and was headed toward Main Street. I rushed out onto the porch to tell her good night.

"I'll see you in a few days," she told me.

"Can't you stay for supper?" I asked her, my arm circled around the pillar by the porch steps. "I bet Mama'd love to have you."

Opal smiled and shook her head. "I don't think so."

"Why not?"

"People like me don't get to eat at a table with people like you."

She turned away from me, crossing over to the other side of the street, walking past the Barnett's house and straight toward town.

I worked real hard not to imagine her having supper all by herself. It sure did make me feel lonely.

When Daddy got home he sent Mama into even more of a tizzy than she'd been in before. All he did was ask if she couldn't set another plate on the table for a man named Abe Campbell.

"I don't even know who that man is," she said, her voice shrill.

"He's the newspaperman," Daddy told her. "Runs the whole operation himself."

"Well, why didn't you tell me before that he'd be coming? I won't have enough food," She moved around the table, working fast as she could to make room for one more. "That's fine, Tom. Just fine."

"I don't know what's got into you, darlin'," Daddy said, carrying a chair to slide under the table. "It's all right. We always have plenty."

"You could've at least let me know." She stopped moving and looked at him with eyes wide. "I wouldn't have let Opal go home early. I could've sent her to the store for more meat. I would've made more to serve."

"Well, I apologize." Daddy kept his voice even and calm. "I didn't know it would upset you so."

"Fine," she said. "It'll be fine. We'll make it stretch."

"You always make good suppers, sugar."

"I'm just anxious, is all. I get feeling like this sometimes," she said. "Like I'm about to jump right up out of my skin."

"It'll pass like it always does," Daddy said. "Just get a good breath."

"Lord, but do I think I'm losing my mind." Mama shook her head and touched a hand to her chest. "You'll have to send me to the loony bin before long."

"Nah," Daddy said. "You aren't all the way crazy."

She turned toward him and gave him a look that could've hurt like a slap.

"You're half-sane." He gave her a smile. "Almost half."

"Thomas . . ."

"Well, honey, I always did say you'd have to be half-crazy to stick with me all this time." He gave her a kiss on the forehead. "I should've let you know Abe was coming."

"It'll work out, I suppose." She wiped under her eye. "I haven't even done my hair."

"You're lovely, Mary."

Nobody could bring calm to Mama the way Daddy did.

Once our supper guests got to our house Mama was right as rain. She laughed at Mayor Winston's jokes and served up supper with grace and generosity just like she always had before, when we still lived in Red River. And we ended up having more than enough food, just like Daddy'd said we would. Mama smiled the whole evening through.

It seemed Mr. Campbell noticed Mama's smiles, too. I couldn't be sure, but I didn't think he looked away from her for more than a minute the whole time.

Meemaw would've said he was a string bean, Abe Campbell. And she wouldn't have approved of how his hair was overgrown, hanging all the way below his ears even. He had the kind of eyes that bulged just a little. She'd always said not to trust a man with bulging eyes, that he'd be one in possession of a terrible temper.

Still, he seemed all right by me.

Having company for a meal made for a full evening, especially when it was Mayor Winston who'd come over. He filled every last inch of that house with his booming voice and his thick laughter. I wished he'd come to supper every night.

Him sitting at our table made everything feel a little happier.

"My greatest regret is that I never managed to get myself married off," Mr. Winston said. "Tom, you don't know how good you've got it."

"Now," Daddy said. "I'm sure you've had plenty of chances. You just never got around to picking one yet."

"He's just too choosy," Mr. Campbell said. "He's always finding something wrong with whichever lady strikes an interest in him."

"Now," Mr. Winston said. "Nothing wrong with looking for the best."

"Well, it isn't too late," Mama said. "You might meet the right woman someday."

"Nah. I'm too old," the mayor said. "Any woman I find would be far too good for me, anyhow. Matter of fact, I think most women are far too good for the men they end up with."

"Isn't that the truth," Daddy said.

"Who would like some pie?" Mama asked, getting up from the table.

"That woman there, Tom," Abe Campbell said, nodding at Mama. "She's too good for you."

"Don't I know it."

Daddy smiled up at Mama and she rolled her eyes.

"Y'all stop it," she said before going to the kitchen door.

"Better watch out," Mr. Winston said. "Abe here is liable to steal her from under your nose."

The mayor and Daddy both laughed. As for Mr. Campbell, he kept his eyes on Mama.

From where I sat I could see her cheeks had turned the brightest red. Before she pushed open the door, she turned. It wasn't Daddy she peeked at, though.

The smile on Abe Campbell's face told me he didn't mind her looking at him. Not one bit.

After we finished off our dessert we didn't leave the table right away. The men each took turns sharing stories. Most of them made me laugh so hard my sides felt fit to bust.

Mr. Campbell broke into song more than once. Mama usually didn't allow singing at the table. Whistling or humming either. But that night she made an exception and I wondered if it was because Abe had a nice, smooth voice. She even joined him on a few of the songs, adding a sweet layer to them that made my ears happy.

Each time when the song ended I noticed how he had his eyes on her. I couldn't hardly blame him. Mama sure was pretty when she sang.

Daddy had Ray tell a couple of his jokes. He told the one about the parachuter having to dig his way through the dust just to get to the ground. Then he told one about prairie dogs and another about chickens laying hard-boiled eggs.

He didn't seem to mind the attention so much.

Mama walked around the table, refilling the men's cups and asking if they needed anything else. I knew what she served wasn't coffee. She'd run out the day before and fretted about it something awful, knowing company was coming. All she could manage was a can of ground-up chicory root.

She didn't say a word to me about it, but I knew she couldn't afford to get good coffee after I'd given the two dollars to Opal that day in Mr. Wheeler's store. She might not have blamed me, but I still felt guilty for it.

I was just glad all those men at our table were too polite to say even one word of complaint.

"Now, Gus was telling me how y'all got your roads paved," Daddy said, sipping at his chicory. "Just last summer, right?"

"Tom," Mr. Winston said, shaking his head. "you don't want to start this conversation with Abe around."

"You against Roosevelt's jobs programs?" Daddy crossed his arms and looked straight at Abe.

"I am," said Abe. "A man needs honest work, not a job handed to him by the government."

"Far as I know, it's honest enough," Daddy said. "Planting trees, putting up schools, building bridges. I hear they're even working on a zoo not an hour from here. All that seems as honest as it comes."

"Maybe." Abe leaned forward, putting his elbow on the table. "But where's this magic money coming from? Huh? How's old Roosevelt footing the bill to pay all these men?"

"Guess that doesn't concern me so much." Daddy reached into his shirt pocket for a cigarette. "Guess I'm more troubled by the folks that don't have enough to eat."

"Gentlemen," Mr. Winston said. "I tend to get awful indigestion when somebody talks politics right after supper."

"You're right," Daddy said. "Arguing over politics never changes minds about something. Just makes for sore feelings."

We sat at the table in quiet for more than a minute and I wished real hard that Mama might tell Ray and me that we could be excused. She didn't, so we just sat there suffering until the mayor clapped his hands.

"Now, I went and forgot to show you something." He winked at Ray and me. "You want to see it?"

"What is it?" I asked.

Mr. Winston held up his left hand and showed us where he'd lost one of his fingers to the first knuckle. Said a shark bit it off.

"Now, Jake," Abe Campbell said. "Always telling a big-fish story. You know it was nothing more than a lake trout."

"Sure," Mayor Winston said. "It never looks like a shark unless it's your finger being bitten off."

I was laughing so hard—even though I didn't think it was so funny, having a finger bit off—that I couldn't ask what really happened to his finger. I figured maybe it was the kind of story that would turn my stomach and make me have bad dreams. It was just as well that I didn't know.

That night was the kind that passed by too quick, far as I was concerned. If I could have, I would have made that time stretch so it would last longer than a couple hours. I'd have held it tighter, enjoyed it more. Maybe that was what memory was for, to keep hold of what we wished we got to live over again.

If only it could've come without the reminders of what we wished had never happened.

We all stood on the porch, watching the two men walking away into the still-light evening. Just before they turned down the road and out of our sight, Mr. Campbell turned and tipped his hat.

But it wasn't at me like I would have liked to imagine.

It was just for one person.

Mama turned and went inside, but not before I saw how she smiled and blushed.

CHAPTER TWENTY

Ray tossed an old baseball up and down, up and down. He'd throw it so high in the air he lost it in the sun and it'd come barreling down, usually closer to my head than I liked. I tried to stay to the other side of the back yard. The last thing I needed was for that ball to bash me in the face.

"Hey, Pearl," Ray called just before throwing that grimy old ball underhand at me. "Heads up."

I tried not to flinch too much when the ball slapped against my bare hand.

"Wanna go for a walk?" he asked, putting out his hand so I'd toss the ball back at him.

"I guess so," I answered, throwing it hard as I could.

"Let's go in the woods." He tossed the ball at me, softer that time. "I wanna see if I can't find a ghost."

"I told you, there's no ghost."

"Come on, Pearl. I ain't even been out there yet." He put out his hand. "Throw the ball if you're gonna play."

I did, throwing it harder than I'd meant to and sending it flying off wonky all the way to the far end of the yard. We both ran toward it, seeing who could get to it first. Of course Ray did. Then he lobbed it hard to another corner of the yard and we made chase again. Over and over, we threw and chased. Threw and chased. Until we found ourselves at the tree line.

"Come on," he said, nudging me toward the trees with his elbow. "Let's go see that ghost of yours."

"It's not my ghost," I said. "It's just an old tree and a falling-down cabin."

"Well, I wanna see it." He'd gotten taller that summer and had to tilt his head down just a little to look in my face. "I'll race ya."

He took off running, leaping over fallen trees and rocks, leaves crunching under his feet. As for me, I went slower, knowing I couldn't beat him, fast as he was. Besides, I didn't want to work my way into a coughing fit. My lungs were already sore from playing ball with him. I stuck to the trail, letting myself breathe in the clean air, hoping it could heal me somehow.

I made it to the twisted tree before he did, wondering how I could have beat him. Then I wondered if he hadn't gone off the wrong way. I called out for him more than a couple times, but he didn't answer.

"Ray Jones," I hollered. "Don't you try and scare me, hear? I'm not going to fall for it if you do."

All I heard in answer was the snapping and cracking of a branch from really far off. It made me jump and my heart thud. Sitting down at the base of the twisted tree, I tried calming myself and I listened for any sign of Ray.

Nothing.

Rain drip-dropped on my bare legs and arms. Not much of anything, really. Uncle Gus would've called it a spitting rain. It did surprise me, the rain. There hadn't been so much as a gray cloud in the sky when Ray and I stepped into the woods.

But just then the sun was blocked out by full-sky-covering clouds so I couldn't even guess what time it might've been.

"Don't worry," I whispered to myself. "Just don't."

So I opened my mouth and stuck out my tongue, trying to see how many drops of rain I could catch on it. One, two, three-four-five. I put my hands flat on the grassy ground and leaned back as I continued counting. Six-seven, eight-nine-ten-eleven.

I thought I'd never stop being amazed by rain for as long as I lived.

Then, just as my nerves eased and my shoulders relaxed, my blood turned cold. A rush of fear surged through my body and every inch tensed.

Ray was screaming.

"It's got me!"

I jumped up, sure my heart was about to drop all the way to my toes. Ray's voice came from deeper in the woods and I could just barely hear it. Over and over he screamed.

I ran toward him, not caring if I got scratched all up and down my legs or if I managed to get into a patch of poison ivy. I had to get to Ray. I had to help him. Save him. Ray.

"Help!" he screamed again. "Pearl!"

The fear made everything crisper, clearer. The greens and sounds of birds. The thud of my footfall on a branch here and there. The smell of rotting wood. The way my lungs groaned with every breath. Off to the side of me a good-sized branch, thick as a baseball bat, lay on the ground. Grabbing it, I let out as fierce a holler as I could manage. It came from some untouched part of me where I guessed a warrior lived just waiting to be released.

"You leave him be," I yelled, my voice more of a roar than it'd ever been.

Swinging the branch in front of me like a club, I realized there wasn't a weapon on earth that could work against a ghost. I held onto it anyhow, not sure what else to do.

I didn't see a ghost, or hear one either, for that matter.

All I saw was Ray. He was curled up in a ball on the ground three or four feet from me. He didn't move and I thought I'd lose my mind right there.

"Ray?" I whimpered, the brave warrior melting away from me.

For as strong as I'd felt just seconds before, I walked with weak footsteps, just seeing Ray. Ray on the ground. Ray broken. Ray unmoving. I held hope that I'd at least see his chest filling and emptying of breath, some sign that he was still alive. Anything. Finger twitching, voice groaning. Anything.

His body started shaking and I wondered if it was some kind of fit. I went to him, still holding that branch in case I needed to fight off the monster should he return for his prey. I just hoped if he did I'd be strong enough, brave enough.

With my free hand I grabbed Ray's shoulder, rolling him to his back.

I didn't see a bashed-in head or gashed-open face. And his eyes weren't rolled back in his head the way I figured they'd be if he'd got a demon in him. I didn't see a thing wrong with him. What I did see was Ray, laughing his fool head off, not so much as a bruise or scratch on him.

The greatest danger he found himself in just then was that I'd hit him over the head with that old branch in my hand.

"You aren't funny," I told him, dropping my weapon and walking away from him, trying hard to keep from wheezing too hard. "I'm never going to talk to you again."

"Oh, come on, Pearl," he called after me, still laughing. "It was a joke."

I kept on walking, not paying any mind to which way I was going. It didn't matter, anyhow. I'd started crying and couldn't see what was in front of me. I stopped, leaning against a tree. At least I could keep my sobbing in. I hated for Ray to see me cry as much as he hated for me to see him doing the same.

"I'm sorry," he said, coming up behind me. "Pearl, I didn't mean no harm."

He came around front of me.

"Aw, don't cry," he said. "I'm sorry."

"It's all right," I said, wiping at my face.

"I shouldn't tease you like that."

"I said it's all right."

"Sure?" He took a step closer to me. "You wanna hit me or somethin'?"

"No." That was a lie.

"You can if you wanna."

"I don't."

"I am sorry." From the look in his eyes I believed he was.

He turned away so I could dry my face all the way without him seeing. I was glad for that kindness.

Ray and I made it back to the house before the sprinkling rain turned to showers that turned to downpour. He said he wanted to sit on the porch and watch the storm roll in. As for me, I wanted to get out of my wet clothes. Before I went in the house, though, I wrung out my dress as best I could so Mama wouldn't scold me for dripping all over her kitchen floor.

I didn't find Mama in the kitchen. And she wasn't in her bedroom, either. I didn't think she'd have left the house without at least leaving a note for us to say where she'd gone. She had to be there somewhere.

I went upstairs to change into a fresh dress and to rest a little bit. My whole body felt sore and bruised from chasing through the woods.

That was when I found her.

Mama was on the floor in one of the spare rooms, her eyes closed and arms wrapped around a plain, regular old tan dress. She'd found the box of Beanie's things and unpacked every single rusty nail and busted plate and such that my sister'd had in her collection of junk.

"Mama?" I said, standing in the doorway. "You need me?"

She shook her head no, but did not open her eyes.

"Should I get Daddy?"

"No, no, no," she mumbled, rocking slightly on her behind.

"What can I do?" I took a step toward her.

"Nothing," she said, opening her eyes and looking right at me. "There's nothing you can do."

"I can try."

"Can you bring her back?" she hollered, spit darting from her mouth. "Because that's all that could make me better. All I want is my child."

Backing away slowly, like I was trying to get away from a rabid critter, I left Mama there on the floor and inched my way to my room. Even when I closed the door I could hear her wailing and sobbing. I nearly forgot to change out of my wet dress before sitting on my bed with my Oz book. I watched the rain blur my view of the yard through my window.

All I could hear was the rumble of coming thunder.

CHAPTER TWENTY-ONE

Our first month in the house on Magnolia Street passed so fast it made me dizzy.

With all the time Mama spent on lessons with Ray, he'd gotten better at putting words on a page. He couldn't write a whole letter to his mother by himself just yet, but he'd write a sentence or two. And he never needed help to spell. It seemed that came real easy for him.

His mother sent one letter and it wasn't very long. All it said was she liked her job, that the folks there in Arkansas were kind. She didn't say one word about coming to get him.

Ray, though, he didn't give up hoping.

He was sure any day we'd find her standing on the porch, all her earthly belongings stuffed in a bag. She'd have a little more meat on her bones, he reckoned, and her eyes would be clearer. They'd go off and find an apartment or a house even. Everything would turn out great for them.

"Just wait," he'd say to me. "You'll see."

Where Mrs. Jones had only sent one letter, Millard had sent four. I liked to think it was due to him missing us real hard. He told us how things were around Red River, who'd left and who'd come through. Nothing too exciting, really. Mostly a lot about hobos and drifters.

When he didn't have any news from back home, Millard would write stories about his life when he was a boy. Stories about walking through wheat up to his waist or about how his mother killed a rattlesnake one time with her frying pan. He even wrote about how his father had shot a coyote one day and they'd eaten it for dinner.

"We didn't have nothing else to eat," he wrote.

In each envelope Millard sprinkled in a pinch or two of red Oklahoma dust. I wondered if he hoped those soft dirt crumbs might lead us back to him the way I hoped the grass I mailed along with the letters I sent would bring him our way.

Just about once a week, sometimes twice, Ray and I would walk the half mile through the woods to Uncle Gus and Aunt Carrie's farm. The first couple times I had to take a rest once, maybe twice, along the way. But I got stronger every day, I could feel it. By mid June Ray and I were racing there.

He still beat me every time.

Uncle Gus let Ray and me wander in and out of the barns and fields and such. We'd visit all the critters, even Squash the goat who ended up being nicer than Uncle Gus had said he was. I'd sneak into the chicken coop to have a good talk with the hen called Billina. We'd become friends in a way. She'd sit still and listen just so long as I didn't try touching her.

Ray'd find good sticks to throw for the dog. Boaz, though, seemed more fond of licking our faces clean than chasing any old thing we tossed for him.

Every now and again Uncle Gus took us for rides on his tractor. He'd tell us where to hold on and always warned us not to touch the wheels while they were moving.

"You get pulled off and you could lose your hand," he told us. "I'd hate for that to happen to you."

I made sure to mind when I was on the tractor.

Sometimes, standing beside him, the rumble of engine filling my ears and rush of wind pulling at my hair, I'd look at Uncle Gus. I couldn't know for sure, but he seemed always to have a smile pulling up the corners of his lips. When I looked at him I saw he was happy being where he was, doing what he had in front of him.

Meemaw'd told me once that it did a body good to be content.

"It don't matter what state you're in," she'd told me. "Full or hungry, happy or sad. The good Lord God is a God of contentment, darlin'."

That was what I saw in Uncle Gus's face near all the time.

I meant to ask him how long it'd taken him before Bliss started feeling like home. I sure did hope it wouldn't take too long for me. Either that or I'd get to go back to Oklahoma.

Homesickness wasn't an easy ache to heal from.

When we didn't have anything else to do, Aunt Carrie paid Ray and me pennies to pick the ripe tomatoes from her garden. She always set a couple aside for us to take to Mama, too. I couldn't remember ever tasting a tomato that hadn't come out of a can Mama bought at Mr. Smalley's store. After having one fresh I swore I'd never touch one from a can again for the rest of my life.

I sure did like spending time in Aunt Carrie's garden. She had every kind of vegetable and they grew nice and plump. She'd point them out to me and I'd ask her when they'd be ready.

Aunt Carrie knew the answer to about every question I could think to ask. And she never made me feel like I was a bother when I had something I wanted to know. If I'd had to pick anybody in all the world to be an aunt to me—blood relation or not—I'd have chosen her.

"Next spring I'll let you help me plant," she told me. "Do you think you'd like that?"

I told her I would and felt the tug of nerves thinking we might still be there after a whole year had passed.

She had a bunch of rhubarb growing beside her house and Ray and I made a game of seeing who could eat a whole stalk without making a sour face. Aunt Carrie would watch us and laugh while our eyes watered and our faces turned red.

She never let us eat more than one stalk in a day, though, for fear we'd get the skitters.

On days when we stuck close to home, Ray and I would finish up our chores quick as we could and we'd take off running all through the neighborhood and all through the woods, staying out until Mama called for us or our stomachs started to rumble.

When she was having a good day, we'd have lunches at the kitchen table.

Daddy'd come home, too, and we'd have us a nice meal of sandwiches or chipped beef on toast. Sometimes Mama'd have a cookie for us and she wouldn't get sore if we dunked them in our milk.

But if she was having a bad day, we stayed away long as we could. On those days Aunt Carrie was glad to have us at her table.

I did my very best to put Mama's bad days right out of my mind. None of us said a word about those days to each other. We just endured them the best we could until the sadness passed and Mama was back to herself again.

Bert from across the street made a habit of bringing over whatever critter he'd managed to catch and telling us all about how he got it. It was always some different kind of creature like a field mouse or a garter snake. But, no matter what it was, Ray and I both knew Bert would end up killing it before the weekend. He never meant harm, he just wasn't so good at looking after the poor things.

I sure hoped his father was a better doctor than his son was a pet keeper.

Ray and I took part in no less than six animal funerals. Bert cried every single time.

Mrs. Barnett had herself the prettiest rose bushes in all of Bliss. Ray said it was thanks to Bert's critter cemetery.

When Mama was feeling especially generous, she'd give Ray and me a nickel and tell us to see a movie. The theater back home in Red River had shut down years before so we thought it was a treat to sit in those soft seats, completely silent, and watch whatever was playing. It didn't matter much to us. We just liked the magic of living in somebody else's story like we could do in the movies.

And we liked it when they played a reel of Will Rogers doing his lasso tricks. Ray tried doing those tricks at home, but Mama hollered for him to take the rope outside before he knocked everything off the shelf.

He never did get the hang of it.

Opal worked for Mama without so much as a complaint or an argument even on the bad days. In fact, she hardly said anything at all unless she was spoken to. I asked Mama most every week if we could have her stay for supper. Finally, after I'd nagged her too much, Mama told me we couldn't because white folks didn't eat with mulattos.

I had to ask Ray what that meant. His answer just made me feel even more confused. I couldn't see any way a body could be half white and half Negro. Ray said I'd understand when I was older.

I didn't mind reminding him he was only a year older than me.

"A year makes a lot of difference," he said, looking down his nose at me like a snooty grown-up.

What I couldn't figure was how Mama'd turn her away from our table. Sure, she never would've let a Negro take a meal with us; she had her rules. But not once in my memory had Mama ever turned away a white person who she could bless with a plate of good food. With Opal being a little of both, I would've thought Mama'd at least think of inviting her.

"For most folks, even a drop of Negro blood is too much," Ray told me.

Still, the Mama of Red River would've at least let her take a covered plate of supper home with her once in a while. Seemed the Mama of Bliss wasn't so inclined.

Daddy worked the days away. Not so much as when we lived in Red River, though, and I was glad. There wasn't much for him to do in Bliss, he told us.

"Not that I'm complaining," he said. "Not at all."

Things were peaceful there. At least they were that summer.

Just about once a week, Aunt Carrie would come over after she'd done her shopping at Wheeler's store. Mama'd make some fresh coffee or pour tall glasses of iced tea for the two of them to enjoy at the kitchen table. Aunt Carrie always did bring something special for Ray and me and we were sure to tell her thank you at least once for her kindness.

On those days Mama was kind and she smiled easy. She didn't get mad if the door slammed or if I had dirt under my nails. Those days Mama was her old self and it made me glad.

It seemed Aunt Carrie was a good dose of medicine for all of us.

I stayed on the porch under the awning on that rainy Monday, watching Ray splash in puddles with bare feet and the legs of his overalls rolled up as high as he could get them.

It didn't matter to him how many rainy days we'd seen, Ray never tired of them.

Mama, though, had been clear as glass about me staying out of the downpour that day. She'd fretted and worried over me getting sick again and wouldn't hear a single word of argument from me. I wasn't like to give her one, either. I wasn't the kind of girl who invited trouble, not so long as I could help it.

So, I stayed on the porch, pretending to read my book, and daydreaming about getting drenched.

Reaching, I put my hand out from under the awning, feeling the pat-pat-pat of the drops on my fingertips. I breathed in the smell of it, the rain, trying to figure out the right word to describe it so I could write to Millard about it. If I'd had the ability to capture that clean smell I would have sent it to him, folded up in my next letter. Surely that would be enough to get him to come to Michigan and in a hurry.

"Ray," I hollered at him from the porch. "What does the rain smell like?"

"Worms," he yelled back.

I shook my head at him. He might've been right. I'd never taken the time to smell a single worm and wasn't like to start just then. I had held them, though, letting them squirm in the palm of my hand. Ray'd told me he had even seen Bert eat one. Bert had said it'd wiggled all the way down and had left a sweet taste in his mouth. Mama had been sore that night when I couldn't stomach the noodles she served.

Pulling my hand back out of the rain, I wiped it on the skirt of my dress before opening the Oz book again. I'd already read through it three times and wanted to read it at least two more times before returning it to Mrs. Trask.

I wasn't ready to leave Dorothy yet. I knew I'd miss her a whole lot if I didn't read her into being anymore.

I still wondered what'd happened to her mama and daddy. My curiosity grew with each reading. Maybe they'd left her, not having the money to care for her anymore. Or they'd died in some kind of accident or from an illness when she was real small.

And I thought maybe her mother had tried protecting her from her father by wrapping her in a blanket just after she'd been born and laying her real gentle like on the steps of a church, watching from afar to be sure somebody picked her up.

Then I remembered that was no made-up story. That was me.

Ray ran up the porch steps and stood in front of me, water dripping off his nose and from his hair and fingertips even. That goofy smile of his made me want to shove him back off the porch.

But I didn't do that because I was a nice, God-fearing girl.

"Come on, Pearl," he said, putting his hand out for me to take. "It feels real good."

"I can't," I told him, trying hard as I could to resist the temptation.

"It ain't gonna hurt you." He looked over his shoulder. "Rain's kinda warm."

"Mama says it'll make me sick."

"Well, you take baths, don't ya?" He put his open hand even closer to me. "This ain't nothin' different."

"I gotta mind Mama."

"You can tell her I made ya."

He grabbed my hand and gave it a tug. Before I knew it, I was on my feet. I had just enough time to toss the book behind me on the rocking chair before I leaped off the porch.

Being out under the rain felt like a blessing. It soaked me through and through and I wouldn't have been surprised if my skin drank it right up. I was glad I hadn't bothered putting on my shoes that morning. The mud mushed up between my toes and made me laugh.

Cupping my hands, I caught the rain, tossing it into my face and at Ray. Face turned upward, I drank the water, liking the way it tapped on my tongue and cheeks.

I spun around and around, the skirt of my dress not flaring out like it usually would've. It was stuck against my thighs, plastered by the rain.

"Pearl Louise," Mama hollered at me from the porch, hands on hips. "Didn't I tell you to stay outta the rain?"

"Yes, ma'am," I called back, unable to keep the laughter out of my voice.

"I made her, ma'am," Ray called at her. "It's doin' her some good, don't ya think?"

He kicked at a puddle, sending a spray of brown water right at me.

"You'll spoil your dress," Mama said, taking a step away from the front door. "Come on, Pearl. Come outta that rain."

Ladies didn't play out in the rain. I knew that was what Mama would say once I came back to the house. But it was the last thing I wanted to hear just then. Being ladylike was as far from my mind as it could be.

"Mama, it's just like a bath," I said. "Just feels better."

She folded her arms, rubbing at them like she was cold.

"You'll catch your death," she said.

But I didn't know how that could be. Playing in the rain that day felt more like being alive than anything had in a real long time. If anything, it seemed like I was catching my life.

A whooping, hooting laugh came from inside our house. Aunt Carrie came out the front door and past Mama, making her barefooted way down the porch, her hands up in the air, her face holding the best, big-mouthed smile I'd ever seen. She got soaked right away, the rain making her hair hang in her face. She pushed it back before running toward Ray and me.

When she got to me, she grabbed both my hands and led me in a wild dance that about took my breath away. I didn't mind at all, though. I couldn't stop myself from laughing.

"Mary," Aunt Carrie called, letting go of one of my hands and waving for Mama to come. "When was the last time you played in the rain?"

"I never have," Mama answered, her eyebrows going up like she thought Aunt Carrie had lost her mind.

"Well, I can tell you it's been too long since I have." Aunt Carrie pulled me behind her to the steps. "You should join us. It's fun."

"Carrie . . ." Mama said, shaking her head. "We got canning to do."

"Oh, come on, Mary," Aunt Carrie said. "We can finish that up any time. Come on."

Just like Ray could get me to do about anything, Aunt Carrie seemed to have that same way with Mama.

Mama shook her head again, but I knew she'd be off that porch soon as she could get her feet out of her shoes.

Aunt Carrie took Mama's hand, making sure she got off the porch without slipping on the wet wood. Once her bare feet touched the ground, Mama shut her eyes, her lips pursed together and her shoulders tensed up next to her ears. It was as if she was trying to figure out if she liked it or not.

Then she lifted her hands, palms up, to feel the drops and a smile broke on her face.

Hair soaked, dress drenched, Mama opened her eyes and laughed.

She grabbed for Aunt Carrie's hand again, shaking it and squealing like she was ten years old.

"I can't believe you got me out here," she yelled.

"It's nice, isn't it?" Aunt Carrie asked.

Those two grown women stood in the grass and let the water fall all over them. I could have watched Mama standing out in the rain all day long.

God was the God of contentment. That was so.

But just then, with Mama smiling so wide, I thought He might just be the God of wild, out-of-control happiness, too.

It did me some good to think on that.

Ray showed me how to slide across the slick grass on my feet. I fell down more than once but it didn't hurt even a little. It was the best kind of good fun.

Booming thunder sent us all running for the porch. We stood there, huddled together, suddenly chilled by our soaked clothes.

Ray and I sat together, our backs against the house and the awning sheltering us, watching the cracks of lightning splinter the sky, and I forgot about anything sad happening in all the wide world. What I did think on was how out-of-my-mind happy I'd been, dancing in the rain.

While we ate ham sandwiches, still sitting on the porch, the storm eased. The sun found a break in the clouds and let in just enough shimmer to make a bow of many colors spread across the sky. It took my breath away.

Meemaw'd told me many a time that all the good gifts in any part of creation were from God Himself. The pretty sunsets and glad feelings were His good gifts. Whenever somebody did for somebody else, that was really a present from God.

"He don't change, neither," Meemaw'd said. "He don't shift like the sand."

She'd pointed out the window at the dust and said how it was different from one day to the next on account the wind moved it all over the place.

"He ain't like that a'tall," she'd said. "He's the same all the time. And He sure likes givin' to His children."

The rain that day had been a gift. Aunt Carrie and Uncle Gus, too. The library and letters from Millard. Ray and Daddy and Mama. Miss Shirley's good pie and the preacher's gentle sermons and the stained-glass windows. Mayor Winston's funny stories and Mr. Campbell's smooth singing voice. Even Opal and how she helped Mama.

All good gifts.

I didn't know how life could get any better. And I couldn't let myself think on how it might all fall to pieces at any minute.

From the kitchen came the sounds of Mama laughing at one of Aunt Carrie's jokes. Closing my eyes I pictured the way Mama must've been smiling all the way up to the corners of her eyes.

Just then, the gifts were good and perfect and plenty enough for me to feel like smiling all day long. And I asked if God might be pleased to keep life good just like it was in that very moment.

But a dark cloud moved over the sun, making the day dim again.

CHAPTER TWENTY-TWO

U ncle Gus sat out on the back porch of the farmhouse with Ray, the two of them whittling shapes into blocks of wood. It was a regular occurrence between the two of them, knives in hand and wood shavings flying out into the yard. They didn't talk when they were working, but that was how they liked it, I supposed.

Quiet between men was nothing more than a way of saying how comfortable they were together. That was one thing I was learning.

Uncle Gus had taught Ray all kinds of things about finding the shape of whatever he was carving. He told him how to use all the special instruments and how to be real careful so he wouldn't cut a finger off.

When they'd started whittling together I'd begged Mama to let me go out and watch. She'd told me I was to leave them be.

"I won't touch the knife," I'd promised. "And I swear I won't get in the way."

"Don't swear," she'd said. "And my answer is still no. It's something Ray needs for himself."

I hadn't understood what she'd meant by that. What I did know was that it sure made me sore to be left out. That was until Ray brought me the doll he'd carved for me.

"Gus helped me with the face," he told me. "The lips and nose mostly. But I did the rest. She's a Indian princess."

I told him I could tell because of the dress she wore, straight and without shape just like the squaw in one of the books Daddy'd left behind in Red River.

That evening, the day before the Fourth of July, Ray and Uncle Gus were out back of the farmhouse, working their knives into the wood. Ray'd told me he was going to make something for his mother.

"How'll you get it to her?" I'd asked.

"She can have it when she comes here to get me," he'd told me. "It'll be a bird. Might even paint it."

I told him I thought she'd like that a whole lot. I could only sit and wonder if she'd ever see it. Even if she did, she wouldn't be proud of him for making it.

She'd never been that kind of mother.

"Is there really gonna be a parade?" I asked for probably the fifth time that week.

We'd just sat down at Aunt Carrie's table for supper, waiting on her and Mama to bring out the pan of chicken and platters of fixings. I found it real hard to stay in my seat, my excitement made me restless.

"That's right, darlin'," Uncle Gus answered. "And your daddy's gonna be walkin' in it."

"Not of my own free will, though," Daddy answered, dropping his napkin onto one of his knees.

"It's part of the job, Tom." Uncle Gus worked at getting his napkin into the collar of his shirt. "I gotta walk, too, with the other veterans."

"What about Jake?" I asked, letting my feet swing back and forth under my chair.

"Don't let your mama hear you calling him that," Daddy warned me. "And, yes, Mayor Winston's walking alongside me."

"I'll wave at you," I said.

"I wish you would, darlin'."

"Who's hungry?" Aunt Carrie asked, coming into the dining room with a plate full of food.

"Be still my heart," Uncle Gus said. "My very favorite meal."

"You say that about everything I fix." Aunt Carrie reached over, putting the platter smack-dab in the middle of the table.

"And it's true every time." He winked at her. "It's even true that you're my favorite wife."

"I'd best be your only wife," Aunt Carrie said, giving him a pretend-angry look.

"You know you're the only gal for me," Uncle Gus said. "I'm too lazy a man to look after more than one woman."

Aunt Carrie shook her head and rolled her eyes as she took her seat. "You're something else, Gustav Seegert."

Mama walked in from the kitchen just then. I waited for Daddy to say something or other that might make her blush. He didn't say a word, though. Just watched her until she caught him looking. She pushed her lips together hard and put the bowl of mashed potatoes on the table and sat down.

I wasn't sure I'd be able to eat. It felt like I'd gotten a big old rock stuck in my throat. If I hadn't known any better I might've thought we'd left Mama back in Red River and picked up another woman along the way that was sour as a lime.

I never would have said a thing like that out loud. But I sure felt it deep down to my tippy-toes.

Once everybody'd settled into their seats, we all held hands and bowed our heads. Daddy said the blessing. Uncle Gus had my left hand in his right. His thick and heavy fingers covered over mine and after Daddy said "amen" Uncle Gus squeezed my hand so gentle before letting go.

The next morning Mama had to remind both Ray and me not to gobble our breakfasts. She told us we'd make ourselves sick if we weren't careful. I at least tried slowing down. It was just we were so excited about the parade, though, it was hard not to rush. Besides, we wanted to find good spots on the curb so we didn't miss a single thing.

Soon as our plates were clean Ray and I hurried to leave, Mama following behind us.

"Hold up," she hollered.

We turned, shoulder to shoulder, just inside the door. I tried not to let Mama see how impatient I felt.

"Now, you two stick together," she told us. "Don't get in anybody's way, hear?"

We told her "yes, ma'am."

"Find a good spot." She crossed her arms over her stomach. "And be sure there's room for Carrie. She's planning on sitting with you."

"Aren't you coming?" I asked.

"No. I've gotta get a cake in the oven for lunch. We're having folks over later on."

"Who?" I asked.

"Never you mind, snoopy." She made sure we met her eyes before she smiled. I could tell already, she was having a good day. "All right. Go on."

Ray and I bolted out the door. He jumped off the porch and was at the end of our walk in just a couple steps. I hurried but didn't run. I knew Mama was watching and would holler for me to slow down.

Folks were already lining the street when we got there. I was about cursing myself for being so slow, thinking sure we'd never find a place. But Ray didn't say a sideways thing to me about it.

We made our way through the crowd and saw there wasn't hardly a space left to sit.

"Looks like the whole county's here," Ray said, grabbing for my hand.

I gave it to him gladly. I sure didn't want to get lost.

A girl ran past us, one I recognized from Hazel Wheeler's group of friends. Old Caleb Carter chased after her, making to tug on her braids. When he went past us he flinched like he worried I might clobber him one for good measure. I would have if he'd tried pulling my hair.

That girl, though, giggled like she didn't want him to quit coming after her. Sometimes I thought girls were just plain silly. Some of them simply did not make any sense at all.

Ray pulled me past crowds and through clusters of people. Up ahead of us was Aunt Carrie, waving us over. It didn't take but half a minute for us to get to her and I was glad. Being in the middle of all those strangers was starting to make me feel antsy and cut off from fresh air.

"You got here just in time," she said, putting her hand on my back. "I managed to save us some seats."

The three of us sat right down on the curb with me between them. It felt safe being there and I could breathe easy again.

Aunt Carrie leaned over and whispered in my ear. "I always get so excited for parades," she told me. "There's nothing like them."

I thought that since I had no choice but to grow into a lady one day, I'd be happy to be the kind that Aunt Carrie was. The kind that wasn't afraid of sitting on curbs or laughing loud or walking around without shoes on.

Blasting, pounding, and trilling, the parade started with what Aunt Carrie told me was the high school band. They marched past us, playing a tune that made me wish I had a flag to wave. Their fresh-polished instruments flashed sunlight into the faces of the crowd.

"Bravo," Aunt Carrie called through her cupped hands.

Ray tapped his foot to the beat and clapped along with the song.

As for me, I couldn't hardly get over how the drums felt like they boomed all the way into my very own chest, like they thudded on behalf of my heart.

Next came a bunch of kids leading all different kinds of livestock through on leashes and ropes. Pigs and sheep and even a calf trod along the street behind their owners. One small girl pulled a wagon with the fattest rabbit I'd ever seen riding in it. A hand-painted sign declared it the "BIGGEST HARE IN ALL LENAWEE COUNTY." I didn't doubt that was true.

A boy trailed behind the rest, tugging on a lead tied around the neck of an old, ornery billy goat who didn't willingly take so much as a step.

That boy was red in the face, like a ripe tomato, and I could tell he was about to give up on trying to get that beast to mind him.

"Poor Jack," Aunt Carrie laughed. "Bless him."

The boy named Poor Jack stopped pulling and let the lead go slack. He wiped at his forehead with the back his hand.

Just then the goat let out a holler and took off running, dragging Poor Jack behind him, tripping over his own feet.

At least the boy got a good laugh out of everybody.

Lots more folks came down the street. Some driving tractors, streamers and flags tied to them and flickering in the wind as they rumbled by. A dozen or so ladies glided along with sashes that showed them to be the Daughters of the American Revolution. A man riding a one-wheeled contraption weeble-wobbled by and another rode a bicycle that was tall as a house. A juggler and a man on stilts and another dressed as a clown made their way past, too.

That parade was like nothing I'd ever seen before in my life. It made me think of all the stories Daddy had told about Jed Bozell and I wondered if he hadn't been real after all.

Ray tapped me on the shoulder long after the start of the parade. "There's your pa," he said.

Sure enough, Daddy walked right down the middle of the street. If anybody ever asked me if I had a hero I would've told them without batting an eye that it was Daddy. I felt sorry for anybody who didn't know him. My daddy was the best kind of man.

I kept my eyes on him, trying not to get choked from all the pride I felt.

Daddy wore his old rumpled hat, tipped back on his head so folks could see his face. Back in Red River he'd never worn a badge, not that I could remember. He'd said it made him stand out too much, made folks feel nervous. But there in the parade, he wore one. It was gold colored and gleamed, it was so new.

Daddy kept his eyes straight out in front of him, but he waved his hands back and forth over the crowd. Mayor Winston followed behind him, hollering out at all the folks, thanking them for coming to the parade. Everyone cheered as they passed by, hollering out their thanks and whistling.

"Daddy," I called, not expecting that he'd hear me through all the fuss.

But he did. He caught my voice out of the many and turned toward me, giving me a wink before moving on down the line.

I knew the parade was about to end when I saw folks all around me getting to their feet. I got up, too, and watched the handful of men who took up the tail end of the parade.

"These are the war veterans," Aunt Carrie whispered. "They're always the finale."

The men wore uniforms, some of them a funny green color and others of brown. One very old, very shrunken man had on a blue uniform that looked far too big on him. Aunt Carrie whispered that he'd fought in the Civil War.

Uncle Gus walked all the way in the back, carrying the American flag. Old Glory rippled in what little wind there was that morning. Still, I thought it looked real pretty.

I made to call out his name, hoping he'd see me and smile the way Daddy had. I was about to lift my arms and wave at him so he'd know we were there. But Aunt Carrie took my hand and, real gentle like, kept it held down.

"It's a time of quiet gratitude, dear," she whispered. "You can wave at him all you want later on. Now he needs the respect of hand to heart."

I did as she said, not feeling scolded. Instead I felt the thankfulness swell inside me. What for, I wasn't so sure. But I was just ten and war still didn't make so much sense to me.

My right hand on my chest, I felt the thump, thump, thump of my heart.

After they passed, Aunt Carrie nodded and asked if we'd like her to walk us home. I told her we'd manage just fine.

"We know the way," I said.

"I bet you do." She gave me a kind smile and a little wink. "Well, I'd best go find Uncle Gus. He'll be waiting for me at the end of the road."

"Are you coming to supper tonight?"

"Yes, we will. Your mama invited us," she said. "Isn't that nice?"

I told her it was.

We said we'd see her later and turned to go home. Along the way, Bert caught up to us. He walked with a strut like he was trying to show Ray how big and tough he was even if the top of his head barely reached Ray's shoulder.

"You like the parade?" he asked.

"Sure I did," Ray answered.

"Say, you wanna go down to the creek?" Bert asked. "Catch a couple turtles?"

Ray didn't give him an answer. He just took off running along with Bert toward the creek and I walked by my lonesome back home.

I tried real hard to believe it was fine by me, them leaving me out like that. It was a good day and the sun shone bright. Behind me, the band still played a bumping tune and folks around me were full of smiles.

They weren't smiles for me, though.

Mama, she'd be happy to have me near, I just knew it. She'd let me tell her all about the parade while I helped her do this or that in the kitchen. She'd laugh and smile and tell me how grateful she was to have a girl like me to help her get together dinner.

If there was one person in all the world I could count on it was Mama. The warmth that bloomed in my heart healed up my lonely feelings.

I walked along, my arms swinging at my sides and a bounce in my step. Glad was how I felt just then.

If only that glad feeling could have lasted more than the rest of that morning.

If only.

CHAPTER TWENTY-THREE

I could see through the big front window that Mama sat at the dining-room table. She touched her cheek and I thought she was wiping a tear out from under her eye. Her mouth was moving like she was telling somebody something.

Whatever it was she was saying made her sad. And here I'd held out hope for her to have a good day.

One of her hands was resting beside a coffee cup on the table, her fingers spreading and curling as she talked. I watched as her crying got stronger and she shook her head.

A hand covered hers, wrapped fingers around it. That hand belonged to a man. I wondered how Daddy'd made it home before me.

I opened the front door and walked in.

The chairs in the dining room pushed back fast, making a scrambling sound on the wood floor. Mr. Campbell turned and looked right at me, putting his hands in his pants pockets.

Mama held her hand to her chest, the hand he'd touched.

"Did you have fun?" she asked, using her other hand to wipe under her eyes.

"Yes, ma'am," I answered.

I forgot about asking for a cookie. It was just as well. I felt like I might be sick.

After supper the men went out back to play catch. Uncle Gus even brought an old wood bat and enough mitts for anybody who wanted one.

Mama gave me a look out the corner of her eye when I put one of those leather gloves on my hand. I made no show of taking it off and putting it back in the pile. What I really wanted to do was throw a fit. But I didn't want to ruin the day, so I held it in.

Aunt Carrie sat beside me on the back porch and together we watched the ball go back and forth, hearing it slap against the men's leather gloves. Every once in a while a stray ball rolled to my feet and I tossed it back to Daddy.

He always pretended like I'd whipped it so hard his hand stung under the mitt.

"It's nice and cool out here, don't you think?" Aunt Carrie asked, stretching her legs out in front of her. "Just right."

"Yes, ma'am," I answered, straightening my legs like she had and feeling the chill of early evening breeze brush over my skin.

"What was your favorite part of the day?" Aunt Carrie asked.

"Almost all of it," I answered, turning to look at her. "Especially the parade."

"What did you like most about the parade?"

"Seeing Daddy." I turned to her. "What was your favorite?"

"I liked seeing Uncle Gus in his uniform," she answered. "He looked handsome."

"Aunt Carrie," I said. "What war was Uncle Gus in?"

"The Great War, dear." She let her feet swing just above the ground. "He was in France. Same as my brother."

"I didn't know you had a brother."

"Well, I did." She sighed. "I suppose I don't talk about him much anymore."

"What happened to him?"

"He died," she said. "He never came home from the war."

"I'm sorry," I told her.

"I am, too."

"My sister died, too," I whispered. "It hurts real bad, doesn't it?"

"Yes." She nodded. "Yes, it does."

"Does it ever get better?"

"I don't know about better." She shifted, sitting up straighter, the palms of her hands pressed flat against the porch. "But the sadness changes."

I waited, not saying anything, hoping she'd explain what she meant.

"When my father was a boy he had an accident and he lost his arm," she said, shaking her head. "That happened a lot back in those days. Anyway, he said at first the pain was sharp, thudding, all through his body. Then, after he healed a bit, he still felt pain once in a while. As if the arm was still there, being torn off all over again. Other times it didn't hurt at all."

I felt of my own arm. The skin was smooth and whole. I tried imagining what it might be like to have it missing. Seemed it would've been hard to do about anything at all without it.

"Over time the pain of missing my brother became more and more dull. And then, after my folks died it hurt all over again," she went on. "But it's still there, pushing at me. Days like today I miss him a lot."

"Why today?" I asked.

"He would have loved to walk in the parade."

I thought of Beanie. She wouldn't have liked the marching band. It would have been too loud for her and she might have held her hands over her ears to dampen the sound. The animals might have caught her attention, leading her to want to ask a hundred questions even if she wouldn't even think of touching any of the critters. It sure would've bothered her to see them on leads like they were.

She would have liked seeing Daddy, though. That would have made her proud. She would have followed him out the corner of her eyes with her shy and quiet smile.

It would have tickled her to have him wave right at her.

Beanie'd sure loved Daddy.

And, boy, had he ever loved her.

I woke with a start, blinking away the last bits of a bad dream, and worked to free myself from the tangled up bedclothes. Sitting, I pushed my already-open window wider, letting in a nice breath of air. I was grateful for the breeze, lazy as it might be.

I rested my head on the window frame and closed my eyes. Just as I drifted back to sleep I jolted again, feeling like I'd fallen from a great height. Eyes wide open, I knew I'd never get back to sleep. Even if I did, the terrifying dream might come back and I didn't want to even think of that. The woods out on the other side of our back yard were quiet just then. I wondered if there were coons and possums wandering around, searching between fallen branches and under blankets of leaves for a little something to snack on. There'd be birds hunkered down in their nests, keeping chicks warm through the night.

I knew very well there weren't any ghosts out in those woods. Still, I could have sworn I heard the groaning of the runaway slave ghost and saw the shimmer of her floating just above the tree branches and hovering among the leaves.

Wrapping my arms around myself, I got an antsy, light-headed feeling. My heart beat so fast it made me afraid of it giving out. It was a lot like spinning out of control. I held on tighter reminding myself to feel the sheets on my legs, the mattress underneath me, the wall pressed against my shoulder, my face. I was there, in a house that was solid, unmoving.

"There's no such thing as ghosts," I whispered over and over, trying to convince myself it was true and not believing it one bit.

I couldn't get rid of the feeling that I was spiraling away from all I knew and into some strange darkness. The fear pulled on me, tugged at me, hoped to push me under so I wouldn't be able to breathe anymore.

When I kept my eyes open I thought for sure I saw the shadow of something wicked moving about in the yard. When I closed them I imagined ghosts with hollowed-out faces and demon-red eyes.

Spinning, spinning, spinning. I felt I was being lured away from the only place I'd ever wanted to be.

Home.

CHAPTER TWENTY-FOUR

I stepped off the back porch and took in the already-hot morning, knowing that by the end of the day it'd be blazing. It was a reading and writing lesson day for Ray, and Mama'd told me to scoot. I took my book and made for the woods. All I could think to do was find a spot under a nice shade tree to read where nobody'd come along.

Taking my time, I walked to the edge of our yard where the trees seemed to welcome me. Stooping down to smell the flowers that'd popped up on top of long stalks I told God He'd done a good job making that day. I wasn't sure He needed encouragement, but it felt real nice to be thankful.

Over my head a big old blackbird beat at the air with its wings, heading directly to the forest. I watched it until it disappeared into the thick trees. Even though I couldn't see the bird anymore, I could hear it cawing.

"One for sorrow," I whispered to myself, remembering an old nursery rhyme that'd been in one of Daddy's books. "Two for mirth."

Turning round and round I hoped to find another crow so I could break the spell of sorrow, but there were no more. Not out in the open anyhow. Maybe, I thought, there was just one more in the woods.

I decided I was sick of sorrow and wanted to be done with it. A good dose of mirth never did anybody any harm.

Quickening my steps, I walked into the woods, holding my breath when I remembered the spooky sounds I'd sworn I'd heard coming from there not two nights before. No ghouls swooped down at my head and I didn't hear the moaning of any ghosts. Still, I'd learned plenty enough about forests from all my reading.

Nightmares. That was what lived in the forest.

But the sunshine was kind that day, beaming down in glistening light-puddles on the ground. Dappled. That was what Aunt Carrie had called it. In her mind, she had a whole treasure chest of words that sounded like a poem all on their own.

"Dappled," I said out loud, not caring if anybody heard me.

Just the sound of that word lifted my spirits.

I couldn't think of a single bad thing that could happen just so long as the ground was covered in dappled sunlight.

I spent a good hour reading at the base of the twisted tree. Skipping along through the pages with my fingers, I read only the parts that I liked best. When Dorothy met the Scarecrow and when they entered the Emerald City. Flipping forward and back through the book, I ran fingertips over the smooth pictures, wishing they'd come alive like a movie.

Not far from my foot I saw something move across the ground and stop. Move and stop. I pulled my feet back and hollered at it before it slithered away, quick as lightning, under the porch of the cabin.

I didn't know if the snakes in Michigan were full of poison like the snakes in Oklahoma were, but I wasn't in the mood to find out.

Getting to my feet, I ran until I got to the opening of the woods guarded by the two tall pines.

I thought it only made sense to go visit with Aunt Carrie a bit, seeing's I was nearly to her house.

Besides, I was sure she'd have a cookie for me.

I found Aunt Carrie upstairs, sweeping the hallway floor. She stopped soon as she saw me and leaned the meat of her arm on the broom handle.

"Well, I was hoping you'd come today," she said.

"You were?" I asked.

"Yes, I was." She pushed her dust pile to one side and leaned the broom against the wall. "Come on."

I followed her into the room Ray and I had shared when we stayed there. On top of the dresser was a hair bow I hadn't known I was missing.

"It's yours, isn't it?" she asked.

"Yes, ma'am."

"When I saw it, I thought of you and smiled."

"Thank you," I said, letting her put the bow into my hand.

It was the kind that Mama'd thought was real pretty, one that was just about as big as my whole head. As for me, I'd never cared for it so much. I thought it made me look too little-girlish. I had every intention of dropping it along the way on my walk home.

"Now, if you can wait for me to finish sweeping the hallway, I have a cookie with your name on it," Aunt Carrie said. "Sound good?"

It did and I told her so.

I stood in the doorway of the room I'd borrowed and watched her finish up. When she was ready, I stooped and held the dustpan for her while she pushed the dirt into it. Once I stood upright, I saw a door at the end of the hall. Aunt Carrie turned and smiled.

"You're wondering what's behind that door, aren't you?" she asked.

"Yes, ma'am."

"Didn't you notice it before?"

I shook my head.

"You were too busy, weren't you?"

"I reckon I was."

"I'm happy to show you." She wiped her hands on her apron. "Go ahead and put that dustpan down, dear."

I did as she said and followed her to the far end of the hall.

"Ready?" Aunt Carrie asked, looking at me over her shoulder, her hand on the doorknob.

I told her I was, not sure what it was I needed to be ready for. Curiosity sparked in my mind, eager to see what was behind that door.

A spiral staircase filled the small room and Aunt Carrie told me to go ahead. I climbed, holding tight to the railing on account I felt nervous about falling.

"It's safe, Pearl," she said, following right behind me. "I've climbed up here a thousand times. Maybe more. And I have never fallen."

I did try to believe her even as my knees knocked together.

At the top of the stairs was a room that was glass window on all four sides. There was just enough space for the two of us to stand in there, side by side. It let in so much light it almost hurt my eyes.

"They call this a widow's watch," Aunt Carrie told me. She rested her fingertips on the sill of one window and looked out over the fields where Uncle Gus was sure to be working. "These rooms were popular long ago on houses that overlooked the ocean. Women would have them built so they could wait and watch when their sailors came home from months at sea."

Taking my time, I turned and looked out over the front yard and the fields of growing corn on the other side of the old dusty country road. Turning just a little more, I saw the chicken coop and the girls pecking away at the grass under the weeping willow. Then I moved and saw the apple orchard and the woods beyond. If I squinted just right I was sure I could see the tip-top of the twisted tree.

I wondered aloud why anybody'd call it a widow's watch.

"Because many of the men—the sailors—were lost at sea. They'd be declared dead." Aunt Carrie's eyes rested on me. "Widows would come to their watch even though their husbands were never coming home again. But they held onto hope, no matter how unlikely it proved to be. I think it may have been all they had left."

"That's sad," I told her.

"Isn't it?" A wrinkle of flesh formed between her eyebrows. "Yes. It is."

One for sorrow, I thought.

"I used to come here often when my brother Charlie was away at war," she said. "I'd pretend I could see him coming home to us."

"What do you pretend now?"

"The same thing," she said. She took in a breath and sighed it back out. Then she made her face brighter, less sad. She smiled even. "In the fall, when all the leaves drop from the trees, I'll be able to almost see the chimney of your house."

Lifting up on my toes I tried to see so far, but the green leaves blocked my view. I did plan on asking if I could come back after fall.

But then my eyes fell back to the twisted tree. Of all the trees in the forest, that one looked most desperate in its upward reaching. Its sparse leaves flickered in the soft blow of wind.

"What made that tree twisted?" I asked.

"Hmm. I don't know." Aunt Carrie crossed her arms. "It's been like that for ages. I wonder if that was just how it grew out of the ground. God must've wanted something a little different when He allowed it to grow."

"I heard it got twisted when the runaway slave's ghost screamed," I said. "The woman who'd lost her son."

"Who told you that?" she asked, pulling her head back.

"Bob," I said, not remembering if he'd ever told me his last name.

"He did, did he?" She laughed. "That surprises me not at all. Bobby has always been a creative boy. What story did he tell you?"

I tried remembering it as he'd told it. A runaway slave woman waiting for a son who never came because he was lynched. She cried until she died and turned into a haunting ghost. Aunt Carrie listened to every word even quick as I told it.

"So it isn't true?" I asked.

"No," she answered. "A good story? Sure. But not even close to the truth."

"Then what really happened?"

Aunt Carrie kept her eyes trained on the fingertips of the twisted tree.

"While it's true that runaway slaves hid in the woods, Ada was no slave," she said. "She wasn't born until right after the Civil War was won. And she was born free, here in Bliss."

Aunt Carrie said that Miss Ada and her family lived in the hiding cabin long after it wasn't needed for the runaways anymore. She stayed even after she got married herself and had a couple kids. Both boys.

"One of her sons works here on the farm," she told me.

I remembered the Negro man who'd taken his lunch on the back porch of the house on Magnolia Street. "What's his name?" I asked.

"Noah Jackson." She smiled. "He's a good man."

But Miss Ada's other son hadn't ended up so good. Where Noah was good, Ezra was mean. He'd been like that since a child, Aunt Carrie said.

"And when he got old enough, he went away," she said. "I'd let Miss Ada come and watch for him in this very room. It gave her some small comfort, the idea that she might see him come back."

"Did he?" I asked.

Aunt Carrie shook her head. "He did not. We never heard from him, not in all these years."

I turned my back toward the window that pointed at the twisted tree, leaning against the glass.

"Now, how her story turned into one about a ghost haunting the woods, I don't know." She gave me the kind of smile that looked more sad than happy. "But it is a sad story. A sad story for Miss Ada."

I nodded so she'd know that I felt the sting of sadness.

"Some prodigals don't come home," Aunt Carrie said.

"Why not?"

"Because it's just too hard."

We went down the spiral of stairs and out the door. The cooler air of the hall made me realize how warm the widow's watch had been. Aunt Carrie asked if an icy glass of milk would taste good with my cookie.

I did think it would.

But all the time I took small bites of oatmeal cookie and sips of milk, I thought of Miss Ada, there in the window, hoping for a look at her returning son. I imagined she'd readied herself to see him, to race down the stairs and out the door to grab hold of him, welcoming him home.

But he had never come down that path. Never returned to her.

One for sorrow.

CHAPTER TWENTY-FIVE

Mama had on a fine dress, one that Aunt Carrie had given her. It was of a dark purple cotton with a fancy bow flopping at the neckline. It was the kind of dress that hung on her just right, making her look like she belonged in a movie, dancing in the arms of Fred Astaire himself.

When I told Mama that, she said I sure had myself a good imagination. "It's just a church dress," she said.

Still, the way she admired herself in the mirror made me think she liked that dress just the same.

She had worked all afternoon at getting her hair to wave just so. Her lips even had a touch of color to them that she'd splurged on at the drugstore.

Mama and Daddy had been invited to dinner at the Wheelers' house. Daddy'd told Mama it wasn't anything special. Still, she'd insisted that he wear a clean shirt and tie. Daddy did all he could to try to get out of going.

But, as it often went, Mama got her way and Daddy put on his funeral suit. He did look awful handsome even standing stiff like he did.

I stayed beside Mama there in her bedroom, watching her touch up her lipstick in the mirror. She got up real close to her reflection and puckered her lips and rubbed them together.

"You look pretty, Mama," I said.

She moved her eyes so she could look at my face in the mirror. "You're too nice."

"You look like you belong in a magazine."

She raised her eyebrow at me and smiled. Then she looked back at the mirror and wiped at the corner of her lips to take care of a smudge.

"You want me to put some on you?" She turned to face me and held up the tube of lipstick. "Open your lips, just a little. Relax them."

She dabbed the color on my lips, making them feel sticky.

"Don't lick them," she said. "Now maybe a little rouge. Just a little."

The brush prickled against my cheeks and I had to fight the urge to scratch at my face. The powder tickled my nose and I was sure I'd sneeze.

Mama stood back and looked at my face, pushing my hair behind my shoulders. Crossing her arms she put her weight on one high-heeled foot and breathed in deep, blinking slowly.

"Oh," she whispered. "You look so grown."

Turning, I looked into the mirror. What I saw there wasn't my face but Winnie's. Her eyes and cheekbones and nose and lips. And I saw bright blue eyes the color of cornflowers.

"I look like her, don't I?" I said, a tear bubbling up out of my eye.

"Like who?" Mama asked, busying herself with clearing her brush and makeup off the top of her dresser.

"I hate that I look like That Woman." I lowered my chin so I wouldn't have to meet Mama's eyes. "I don't wanna look like her."

"You don't." She said it so sharp it surprised me. "You aren't like her, hear? Not even a little. I won't have you talking about her."

"Yes, ma'am."

She left me there in her room, staring into the mirror at the likeness of the mother who'd given me up.

We were meant to be asleep, Ray and me. Opal had told us Mama said we were to go to bed and not make one peep. We told her we'd stay in our rooms and fall asleep fast.

Neither of us had a mind to do that, though.

Instead we sat on Ray's bed, trying to scare the willies out of each other with every ghost story we could think of. For all the tales I came up with, Ray told spookier ones, bloodier and goose-pimple-raising.

He'd get going on some yarn of a headless man stumbling about through town or a tormented soul floating over the beds of children, looking for her lost love, and I'd be shaking with fright. I'd hold both my hands to my mouth, making tight fists, and I would be too afraid to so much as blink for fear I'd see a picture of the story in my mind.

I decided right then I'd do my very best to never ever sleep again. My mind got full up enough of nightmares to last a lifetime.

The sound of a woman's laugh caught my attention and I knew without even having to look out the window that it was Mama. I did look anyway and saw her walking down the street toward our house alongside a man.

A tall and lanky man. I could see his face by light of a streetlamp they'd both stopped under.

"Who's that with her?" Ray asked.

"Abe Campbell," I answered.

"What's he doin' walkin' her home?"

I just shrugged.

Mr. Campbell said something that made her cover her mouth so her laugh wouldn't wake the whole street. Then she swatted at his arm, letting her hand rest on him a second longer than I thought was proper. He looked at that hand and followed her arm with his eyes to shoulder to neck to face.

That sick feeling I'd gotten when I saw him touch her hand came back. What I wanted to do was holler out the half-open window for him to go on home and leave her alone. She had a family already and Daddy wouldn't like them walking and laughing together like that.

But I didn't yell. I didn't say anything at all. What I did was get up off Ray's bed and walk right to my room where I got in under the sheet and pulled it up to my chin. I knew Mama would check on me and I was going to make her think I was asleep.

When I shut my eyes all I could see was the way she'd smiled up at Abe Campbell.

It was the way she used to smile at Daddy.

Mama still smelled of her perfume when she leaned over and kissed my cheek. I stayed still as I could and tried breathing in slow and deep.

"I can tell you're faking," she whispered.

I opened one of my eyes a sliver to see if she was watching me. She was.

"How'd you know?" I asked, opening the other.

Mama was busy taking pins out of her hair. It fell to her shoulders, the curls wild, making her look like Beanie.

"A mama's got her secrets," she said. "Were you and Ray good for Opal?"

"Yes, ma'am."

"She give you supper?"

I told her she had.

"Did you have a good time?" I asked.

"Sure I did." She sat on the edge of my bed, crossing her legs and fingering through her mess of hair. "Half the town was there."

She went on to list all the folks that'd gotten all dolled up in the nicest clothes they had for the party at the Wheelers'. How they'd served deviled eggs and gelatin salad and little sausages. She said they even had a Negro fella there playing the piano and singing old songs.

"He wanted people to dance," she said with a wide smile. "Some did."

"Did you?"

"Well, no."

I asked her why not.

"Your daddy isn't so light on his feet, Pearl."

I thought of the times the two of them had danced to some song that came on the radio. Back in Red River, they'd put their bodies up close to each other, Mama's hand on Daddy's shoulder and his hand on her waist. They'd sway, shuffling their feet against the grit and making a crunching sound under the soles of their shoes.

Sometimes, if they didn't have any music playing, Mama would sing a song unlike anything we ever sang at church. Daddy would pull his head back so he could look at her face and she'd have to stop singing she'd be smiling so big.

"You've gone and made me forget the words," she'd sometimes say.

She'd finish, though, even if she had to hum.

Before letting her go, Daddy would always kiss her on the cheek or the forehead. She'd close her eyes like she was about to open them to the biggest surprise of her life.

If all that didn't make Daddy light on his feet I didn't know what did.

"What're you thinking about?" Mama asked, half turning to look down at me in my bed.

"I was just wondering where Daddy was," I told her.

Any bit of smile she'd had on her face dropped and she blinked twice before turning her eyes from my face.

"He got stuck talking to the mayor," she said, her voice gone chilly. "I got tired, so I came home."

"You walked by yourself?"

She nodded and hummed. "Yes."

CHAPTER TWENTY-SIX

Daddy didn't come home for lunch the day after the dinner party at the Wheelers'. Mama didn't say a word about his empty chair or the plate of food she'd placed at his spot that went untouched. All she did was push the cooked carrots around her own plate with a fork. Ray and I didn't do much talking, either. When we did, Mama didn't pay us any mind at all.

After I finished eating, I asked if Mama wanted me to take Daddy's lunch to him at his office. She nodded and went to the kitchen to put together a thermos of coffee. Even on a hot afternoon like that one Daddy would want his coffee.

"Take this right to him. And don't dawdle," she told me, handing me the plate and thermos. "Don't stay long if he's busy, hear? Your father has a very important job."

She said it like she wasn't all that convinced of her own words.

"And bring my plate back when he's done," she called after me.

July was turning out to be blazing hot. In Millard's last letter to us he said he couldn't hardly stand it and wondered if Red River had relocated to the surface of the sun when he wasn't paying attention. On the radio we heard there was a heat wave striking down the whole country. That afternoon as I walked to the police station with Daddy's plate of food I thought I was about to melt what with the heat beating down on me from the sky above, searing up from the pavement, and squeezing me in with the humid air.

Summers in Red River had been hotter than hot. But it had been a dry heat. Summer in Michigan was a whole lot of boil and simmer.

In church the Sunday before, the preacher had said, "In everything give thanks." He'd told us to give thanks in good and in trial and even in the days with nothing special going on. So, that day, I gave thanks to the Lord for the trees somebody had seen fit to plant all up and down Main Street that offered even the tiniest of shade.

I decided it felt good to give thanks and it passed the time just fine. A list of things I was thankful for grew in my head. Chirping birds and scampering squirrels. Ice cream from Miss Shirley's and nickel movies with Ray. Aunt Carrie's fried chicken and Uncle Gus's big laughs.

So many things grew in my mind like a garden of thanksgiving, blooming despite the gray clouds.

But when I stepped on a spit-out wad of chewing gum, it sticking to the sole of my shoe, I ran out of things to give thanks for. I wasn't sure a mess like that was on God's mind when He had that part of the Bible spelled out.

Daddy sat behind his desk in the police station. In one hand he held a lit cigarette and in the other a pen. His scribbling scratched across the paper. He'd set up a fan so it would point right at his face. Still, it didn't keep the sweat from beading up on his forehead.

When he saw me, Daddy put the pen down and stretched out his fingers like they were sore from writing all day.

"Lord, but are you a sight for sore eyes this afternoon," he said. "Did you bring me a little something to eat?"

"Yes, sir."

"That's a girl."

"And some coffee." I put the plate in front of him on the desk. "I can pour it for you."

"That's fine," he said. "Thanks kindly, darlin'."

Daddy took a cup from one of his drawers and told me it was clean. I filled it with coffee, making sure not to spill so much as one drop.

"What would I do without you?" he asked.

"I reckon you'd be hungry," I said.

"I think you're right about that."

Daddy got up and pulled over a chair for me so I could sit next to him with the fan doing its darnedest to cool the both of us. He handed me the newspaper to read while he ate.

"Might be funnies in there," he said.

I turned from one page to the other but all I found was a bunch of news. Trying to hide my disappointment, I folded it back up. That was when I saw a list of names. I ran my finger down it, smudging the ink and turning my skin gray.

It was real long, that list. And it had addresses printed right next to the names. Our name wasn't there and neither were Uncle Gus and Aunt Carrie. But I did read a whole bunch of names that had become familiar to me since coming to Bliss.

"Daddy, what is this?" I asked.

Daddy took the paper, shaking it to make it straighten in his hands. He shook his head and bit at his bottom lip.

"Why aren't we on that list?" I asked, looking over his shoulder at the names.

"This is all the folks in the county that are taking assistance," he said.

"We aren't?"

"No, darlin', we are not. Not yet, at least."

"Why'd they put that in the paper?"

"Don't know." He folded the paper and set it on the top of a stack of papers on the left-hand side of his desk. "Maybe out of meanness. Maybe because he wants to shame those folks. I know he's not fond of the government giving out assistance. Couldn't tell you why he'd do something so ugly, though."

I knew he was talking about Abe Campbell. After all, he was the one that wrote up and printed out the newspaper every morning.

Daddy made a sound that was half grunt and half growl. "Whatever it is made him print that, it's wrong if you ask me."

"Maybe he doesn't know it's wrong," I said.

"Maybe. I doubt that very much, though."

He pushed his empty plate to one side of his desk and set back to doing a little of his work. I watched him, seeing the way his handwriting slanted, especially with him rushing the way he was.

"There's some scratch paper in my drawer there," he said, not looking up from his paperwork. "And an ink pen you can use."

I sat beside him, my pen moving along the scraps of paper to make pictures of flowers and trees and a road that led to somewhere magical. Somewhere that had food aplenty and jobs for everybody. A place where lost little children found their homes and mamas weren't ever tempted to stray away.

When Daddy asked me what I was drawing, I didn't know what to say.

"It's just a picture," I said.

"It's a good one, darlin'," he said. "A real good one."

I stayed there with Daddy until he said it was time for him to make his rounds through town. I put the ink pen away and put all my pictures into a stack, tapping them against the desk so they'd be neat.

"You mind if I keep a couple of those here?" he asked. "I think I'd like to see something pretty every once in a while."

I told him he could have them all.

"Thanks kindly." Daddy put them on his desk right where he'd see them the next morning. "Now, you wanna go with me on my rounds?"

"Yes, sir," I answered.

"That's fine."

Daddy had let me go on rounds with him before, back in Red River. We'd go to the few stores still open, then out to the sharecropper cabins and the Hooverville to see the folks passing through. He'd get his hands dirty trying to help some fella dig out a tractor or he'd carry a heavy basket of laundry for a housewife.

He was a good man, my daddy.

There in Bliss, Daddy walked up and down the pavement in front of the post office and Wheeler's store and all the way to the library before turning back to pass the places on the other side of the street. We went past the movie theater and the little hardware store before ending up at Miss Shirley's diner where Daddy treated me to a dish of ice cream.

"Don't tell your mama," he whispered in my ear. "She'd be mad at me for spending the money."

I promised I wouldn't tell.

It felt good having a secret just between the two of us for a change.

Daddy wanted to go out to a farm clear to the other side of town. I asked if I could go with him, but he thought I'd better get back home.

"See if your mama's doing all right," he said. "She might just need your help."

I headed on home, but halfway there remembered I'd left Daddy's lunch plate at the station. Mama would sigh for the rest of the afternoon if I didn't bring it back the way she'd told me to. She might even holler and I didn't want more of that if I could avoid it. I turned back and took my own sweet time getting there.

The way the sun blazed its dragon-hot breath on me I didn't think it was a good idea to rush. As it was, the water-heavy air filled my lungs and made me cough every dozen steps or so. I thought maybe once I got to Daddy's desk I'd sit in front of that fan of his for a couple minutes to cool off before turning around and going back home.

I found Mama's plate right where Daddy'd left it and stood with my face inches from the fan. The air hit my face, but it wasn't near as cool as I'd hoped it would be, so I switched it off.

That was when I heard talking coming from down the hall where Mayor Winston's office was.

"People are talking, Abe." I knew that voice to belong to Mayor Winston. It was deep and full of gravel just then, not smooth like normal.

"Who is?" Mr. Campbell asked. "Wheeler? You know he's a bigger gossip than any woman in this town."

"So you're telling me it isn't true?" Mayor Winston paused before going on. "You didn't walk Mary Spence home last night and stand outside her front door for an hour chatting it up with her?"

Silence. Abe Campbell didn't answer. I got out from behind Daddy's desk and walked quiet as I could toward the hallway.

"You can't do that," Winston said. "It doesn't look good."

"I didn't do anything wrong."

"It looks bad, Abe." The mayor's voice was firm. "She's married. They've got kids."

"What do you want me to do?" Campbell asked.

"Stay away from her."

Neither of them said anything else for more than a couple minutes and I expected they were staring each other down like I'd seen men do in the movies. They had their eyes locked, not blinking, to prove who was stronger.

I wanted so bad to believe that Mayor Winston was the mightier man.

"Are you done?" Mr. Campbell asked.

"I guess I am."

"Good. I have work to do."

"Do the right thing, Abe," Mayor Winston said. "I hope you still know what that would be."

I rushed out the station door and to the street, walking fast as I could down the pavement in the direction of home.

When I passed the Wheelers' house I saw Hazel at their front gate, talking over the fence to one of the girls that followed her around. They stopped and watched me walk by. I stuck my tongue out at her before running fast as I could all the way back home.

I got to the front door of our house before I realized I'd forgotten the plate.

CHAPTER TWENTY-SEVEN

Gossip about Mama and Abe Campbell's walk only lasted a week and a half. But for those handful of days I thought I'd have liked to run off and never come back. At the store, the ladies would murmur to each other, thinking they weren't loud enough for me to hear. At church, we'd get stares. Worst of all was Hazel Wheeler and her side-eyed glances and stink-faced smirks.

I swore if she said one word—just one word—I'd knock the haughty look right off her face.

Daddy was the one to set folks right. He told them he asked Abe to walk Mama home that night to be sure she got there safe.

"Jake Winston and I had important town business to talk over," he'd told people more than once. "Fellas such as us can't make decisions lightly. Especially when it comes down to what kind of ice cream to have at the social next week."

The idea Daddy put into the minds of the people was that no harm was done.

At home, though, he couldn't hardly get Mama to sit down in a room with him. She'd get up and go or pretend she didn't hear him when he said something to her.

"An hour, Mary?" he'd asked when he thought Ray and I couldn't hear. "What could you have thought of to say to Abe for a full hour? I can't even get you to say hello to me anymore."

She never did give him an answer.

But after that week and a half passed, the folks in Bliss found something else to gossip about. News spread fast, sending all the ladies in town twittering and all the kids whispering from one to another.

The new schoolteacher had arrived in town all the way from the other side of the state. Word was she was getting paid by the government to come to town and teach. Some weren't too happy about that and I figured Abe Campbell was one of them. As for me, I was glad we'd have school to go to. I just hoped she'd be nice.

"Bert said she's pretty," Ray told me one day when we were walking out to the creek. He had his fishing pole leaned against his shoulder and an old coffee can full of worms.

I told him I'd go watch him fish, but I wasn't about to touch one of those worms. The way they wriggled and jiggled away from the end of the hook made me feel bad. Even when Ray hooked one, I made sure to shut my eyes real tight or look away altogether.

He thought it was babyish of me to shy away at that. I just did not care what he thought, though. He could think whatever he liked about me. I still wasn't going to murder one of those worms.

"When'd he see her?" I asked, meaning the schoolteacher.

Ray shrugged. "Don't know."

"Well, I don't care if she's pretty so long as she's nice," I said. "Teachers should be nice, not pretty."

"What's wrong with them bein' pretty?"

I didn't know how to answer that, so I took to running toward the creek. He chased after me, not liking to lose.

If ever I wanted to get Ray off one subject or another, I just had to challenge him to a race. That always got his mind off things.

It worked every time.

We got our first look at the new teacher at church the following Sunday. She sat in the very first pew with the preacher's wife.

All through the service the only part of her I could see was her long brown hair that she kept pulled back in a pretty ribbon that matched her dress. I wondered if she had a kind face and if she was quick to smile. I did hope so. And I hoped she had a pleasant voice, one that didn't give me the willies.

All during the sermon I kept my eyes on the preacher as if I was hanging onto every word out of his mouth. I nodded when I saw folks ahead of me nodding and I folded my hands and closed my eyes when it seemed like the rest of the church was praying.

But all I could think about was school starting in a little less than a month. It made me feel antsy and sick to my stomach. Still, I couldn't hardly wait for the first day.

Sitting there in the pew between Aunt Carrie and Daddy, I tried to imagine what our first day of school might be like.

Mama would make sure Ray and I had ourselves a good breakfast, one that would stick by us until lunchtime. She wouldn't pack us food to take since we'd come home for the noon meal because we lived so close.

She'd remind us to listen to the teacher and not to get in any sort of trouble. And she'd especially make sure I knew I wasn't to fight or cuss or daydream or spit even. If nothing else, she did know my weaknesses.

I would promise to try and that would seem good enough for her. And I would, try that was. I'd try hard as I could. As to if I'd succeed at any of it, I couldn't have promised that. But I would do my best just so long as nobody said anything to get me riled.

Ray and I would walk together, Ray even more nervous than me. He hadn't been to more than a day of school in a real long time. Much as he'd learned from Mama's lessons he still would have a hard time of it as far as reading went. He'd worry about how the letters leapfrogged each other all over the page.

He hadn't given up and wasn't like to. That Ray Jones could be stubborn when he needed to be.

Once we'd gotten to the school, I imagined us finding seats right beside each other. It would give him courage, knowing I was right there. He did have his friends, the ones he'd talk with after church or go off to play a game of catch with, still there was comfort for him in being by me. At least that was what I imagined.

In my daydream Hazel Wheeler wasn't even in the classroom. She'd gotten herself shipped off to a boarding school for mean and nasty girls with sour faces. All the friends she'd left behind would turn to me, asking if I'd like to be one of them. I wouldn't be so sure, but they'd ask so nice I couldn't say no.

The new schoolteacher would welcome us all to class and she'd call the roll. It'd take her a long time to get to my name seeing that Spence was near the end of the alphabet. But when she did get to me, she'd smile.

I just knew she'd be my friend even if she was my teacher.

When I imagined her voice she had an Oklahoma drawl even if she was from Michigan.

She wouldn't be the kind to slap palms with her yardstick or to put noses in a corner. She'd be one to throw the dunce cap in the trash and to laugh at jokes that were funny even if they were told at the wrong time.

The way I imagined it, she'd be the best kind of teacher there was.

CHAPTER TWENTY-EIGHT

On the morning I turned eleven I woke up feeling older. I got out of bed and stretched, sure I was taller than I'd been the day before. I wiggled my toes against the little rug by my bed, wondering if my feet had gotten longer. My best green dress even felt a little snugger. At least it seemed to fit tighter around my hips and shoulders. Not my chest, though, and that was all right by me. The last thing in the world I wanted was to grow in that way, not yet at least. I just thought I'd be embarrassed to have those things bumping out under the fabric of my dress.

I studied myself in the wood-framed mirror Daddy'd hung on my wall. Turning my head one direction and then the other, I studied my face, holding poses like the ones I'd seen women do in Mama's magazines. Pinching at my cheeks brought up the color just like biting did to my lips.

I wondered if now that I was eleven years old I'd be expected to look more grown, more dainty and refined. If I was, Mama would be sure to tell me.

If there was anything in the whole world Mama wished for me it was that I'd be polite and genteel.

I watched my reflection sigh and stoop her shoulders. What Mama wanted would surely take all the fun out of my days. Being a lady was a whole lot like work.

Stepping away from the mirror, I opened my door. Right away I smelled the baking cake and my heart fluttered with excitement.

"You'll have to figure out what you're going to wish for," Daddy had said the day before.

I didn't have to figure anything out at all. I knew what I was going to wish for already. I'd known for a good month.

As far as I knew, Millard had been to every one of my birthday dinners. He was every bit as much a part of our family as I was. He wasn't one to bring presents or to give a card, but that never mattered to me. It was enough for me to know that he'd be at my house, lending his scratchy singing voice to the happy birthday song, and that he'd want me to think long and hard about the wish I'd make when I blew out the candles.

"You don't wanna wish for somethin' piddly," he'd say. "Always try for the biggest wish you can think up. You never know what might happen."

I decided that my eleventh birthday wish would be for him. I'd wish that somehow he'd fold on his stubborn resolution to stay in Red River and pack his stuff, hopping on a train for Bliss that very day. It was the biggest and best wish I could think up.

He'd written us a letter just a couple days before, telling us the news from home, and I thought he was busier than ever with all the folks in and out of the Hooverville. He told of how they had better buildings for the people come to stay and how sometimes they'd have dances on a Friday night.

I bet Pastor didn't like that one bit.

"They even got a couple flush toilets down there now," he'd written. "Clean water out of the tap, too. Government's got some of their folks there to be sure it's all fine and good for the families. Real safe. Sometimes I wonder if that old Hooverville is the best place most of them ever lived in."

In that letter he didn't say so much as one word about leaving Red River.

I knew my wish would have to be mighty strong to pull him up out of the Oklahoma soil where he'd been rooted near all his life and bring him to us. I wasn't even sure it'd be right, having him leave.

But he'd always been the one to tell me to wish big, and I intended to do just that.

Mama shooed me out of the house. She said she had to get my cake frosted and chicken fried and that she and Opal had a lot of work ahead of them to get the house ready. We were to have company for supper.

That and Mama had a couple surprises to put together for me.

"And I don't need you sneaking peeks at me," she said. "I've worked too hard for you to spoil it."

I did as Mama said, not giving her one argument. I knew she'd scrimped and saved to have a good meal for my birthday. And she'd gone without sugar in her coffee for weeks so she had enough to bake a cake. It would have been the act of an ungrateful child to sass at Mama just then.

Besides, I liked surprises more than anything else, so I did as she said.

I went out back to see if Ray wanted to go into the woods with me. He sat out behind the shed on an overturned bucket. When he saw me, he turned quick, hiding something under his shirt.

"Don't look," he hollered.

"What are you hiding?" I asked, stepping closer.

"Don't ask questions on your birthday, Pearl."

"Is it a present for me?"

"I ain't sayin'. Don't ask me no more questions," he said. "Now shoo."

On any other day, his hollering at me like that would've hurt my feelings. Not on that day, though. I was happy to let him keep on carving on the piece of wood I saw peeking out from under the cotton of his white shirt. I turned right around and left him to it.

"Happy birthday, by the way," he yelled at me as I went.

"Thanks," I answered, not even looking over my shoulder at him.

I made my way to the library. It was a bright and sunny day and I was hoping to find another book to read. I'd read through the Oz book so many times I nearly had it committed to memory. I thought it might be good to find a different story for a change. Something from the shelf Aunt Carrie'd shown me.

As I went, a couple folks here and there called after me, wishing me a happy birthday. I wondered if Daddy'd told them to say that if they saw me. I didn't mind so much. It sure felt good to have that kind of attention.

Seemed every day Bliss got to feeling more and more like home.

Still, something nagged at me whenever I got to thinking I was some-where near happy. It made me think of a half-broken tooth Daddy had once. He'd forget it was sore until he chomped on something hard. Then it hurt him something awful.

After a week or two he had to get that tooth pulled so it'd stop paining him.

Making my way down the street to the library, I felt some kind of aching worry throbbing in the middle of my chest. It caught my breath and I gasped once, twice, and felt a flutter in my heart.

I put one foot in front of the other and kept moving forward. Bliss was home and I'd be happy there no matter how hard I had to try.

Mrs. Trask brightened up as soon as she saw me coming through the door. She eased herself up from her desk, moving slower than usual and wincing a little before she got straight as she was able.

"I have found just the book for you, Miss Spence," she told me. She pointed off to a row of shelves. "It's just over that way. Come along. We shall retrieve it together."

Following behind her I worried about what kind of book she'd picked for me. All I'd been reading for months was the Oz book and I had hoped to find a story just as good as that one. Sighing, I tried to have faith she'd chosen a book I would like.

When I saw the one she pulled off the shelf for me I couldn't help but smile. On the cover was an Indian man with a tomahawk in hand, his face stretched into a fierce battle cry.

Mrs. Trask winked at me and wished me a happy birthday.

I would have hugged her if I didn't worry I'd break her in two.

Sitting in the window seat, the light warming me, I read that book, my eyes not leaving the page except when I needed to blink. There weren't any battles, not in the first few chapters at least. But the words were such that I could about smell the Indian's deer-skin vest and hear his horse neighing.

Wanting to save some of that story for later, I closed it, putting it under my arm before checking it out and heading home.

"How do you like it so far?" Mrs. Trask asked as she stamped the inside of the book. "Are you enjoying it?"

"Oh, yes, ma'am," I answered. "I surely am."

"I am delighted to hear that, my dear."

I did believe she was.

If I could have been an Indian I would've wanted to be the kind that traveled all over. I'd be in the sort of tribe that planned according to the seasons and where the good hunting grounds were. A nomad, that's what I'd be. North in the summer and south in the winter. West when the buffalo were good and stout. East for fishing. I supposed I'd have followed the chief, trusting him to know the best way to go.

But if I couldn't have been born an Indian I might have been brought into the tribe somehow or another. With my light hair and eyes I wouldn't look like them. That could be all right, though, I reckoned. Somebody had to be able to go into town to deal with the white man. I'd be sure they got a fair shake for the animal skins they wanted to trade and I'd never allow them to get into the fire water.

I could teach the Indian children English, maybe even how to read and write. And maybe they'd teach me how to speak in whatever tongue it was they had. We'd learn each other's songs and stories and figure out that we were more the same than we'd ever realized before.

Turning the corner from Main to Magnolia I saw Daddy sitting on the front porch with Ray. They both leaned forward with elbows resting on knees, their faces serious. Daddy said a couple things to Ray and they both nodded.

Ray had his eyebrows pushed down over his eyes like he'd just heard bad news. He reached back and scratched at his neck. When he saw me coming he looked away fast.

I knew it wasn't the kind of talk I wanted to hear, not on that day at least, so I went around back to go in the kitchen door.

I didn't put my ear to the front door or sneak under an open window to eavesdrop on whatever it was they were talking about. I could already tell one thing. It was something I didn't want to hear.

A girl didn't want bad news on her birthday.

CHAPTER TWENTY-NINE

Ray asked if I wanted to go out in the woods with him. He stood in the doorway of my bedroom, grinding the toe of his worn-down shoe into the wood floor and keeping his hands shoved deep down in his overall pockets.

"I don't mind," I said, getting off my bed and marking my place in the Indian book.

We walked through the trees and over underbrush without saying so much as a word. His shoulders still slumped and when I looked at his face it seemed he was real bothered about something.

I knew we were going all the way to the twisted tree and the hiding cabin. And part of me guessed Ray would want to take off his shoes and climb up the tree like a monkey, his toes gripping at the bark and his fingers finding the grooves where the trunk curved up on itself like a spring.

But once we got there, he didn't go to the tree. Instead, he went to the crumbling porch of the cabin, sitting on the edge. I went to sit with him on the green-with-moss wood, hoping there wasn't a snake there waiting to give me a good fright.

A squirrel hopped along not too far away from us. For something so small, he sure did make a big noise of crunching leaves and rustling grass. Every now and again, he'd stop, that squirrel would, and get up on his hind legs, taking a good whiff of the air, his little head turning this way and that. Then he'd go back to his scampering about.

"My ma sent a letter," Ray said after the squirrel ran off into the woods. "Got here today."

"You want me to read it for you?" I asked.

"Your daddy already did."

"All right."

Much as I wanted to ask what his mother's letter had said, I didn't. I knew he'd tell me, but he'd want to do it in his own time. So I held my tongue.

He got to chipping away at the loose porch wood with his thumbnail. It didn't take too much because it was all rotted out. After yanking at one piece of it he flinched and looked at his thumb. A little blood formed a line of red under his nail. He whispered a cuss.

Ray Jones never had been one for harsh words unless he was telling a joke or a story to shock me. He did know all the cusses, though. I knew on account he was the one who had taught them all to me. He just didn't use them all that much. But that day he cursed in anger.

I hoped he didn't see the way I started at the hard sound of his voice.

He held up his hand. A thick sliver of wood had lodged itself under his nail. I took his wrist in my hand and used the thumb and finger of my other hand to pull the sliver out. He made a hissing sound when I did it and I felt sorry that it'd hurt him. But it needed to be done.

"You okay?" I asked him.

He nodded, putting out his hand so I'd drop the wood in his palm. Holding it this way and that, he got a good look at the sliver before flicking it to the ground.

"My ma left Arkansas. Said it wasn't workin' out so good for her there no more." He put his thumb in his mouth and sucked on it a second. "She's been staying in a Hooverville outside Boise City. Been cleanin' at a hotel there or somethin'."

He turned and spit off to the side of the porch.

"Guess she's thinkin' on headin' out west." His voice cracked. "Goin' to California to find some better work."

"How's she gonna get there?"

"Don't know," he said. "She never put that in the letter."

"You think you'll go?" I asked, my stomach feeling sick.

"Nope." He reached down, pulling at a tall weed beside the porch. "She told me I'd better stay put. For now, at least."

"That okay with you?"

"Yup."

Ray Jones wasn't one for lying. Never had been. He'd tell the truth even if a lie would get him out of trouble. But that day he did lie.

I didn't believe for one minute that he was okay with his mother going off to start a fresh new life without him. But I didn't say anything to him about it. I didn't think the lie had been for me anyhow.

I just wished he could've been happy.

Mama carried the cake from the kitchen, the eleven candles making a pretty orange glow on her face. Daddy had pulled the curtains to block out the still-sunny evening. Aunt Carrie and Uncle Gus had joined us for supper and they sang right along with everybody else.

I'd asked if Opal could stay, just for a piece of cake. Mama'd rolled her eyes and told me we'd wrap up a slice and save it for her to have the next time she came to work. I didn't argue, much as I wanted to. It might have been my birthday, but Mama still wouldn't suffer a defiant child.

Mama lowered the cake right in front of me to the table and I sucked in air, ready to make my wish for Millard to come to me. Ray sat in a chair across the table from me. He leaned forward, watching the candles flickering. There beside him was an empty chair. One Beanie could've sat in if she'd still been alive.

She'd have squinted at those eleven flickering flames, scowling even, as if they'd meant to do her some harm. She never had liked fire so much. And she wouldn't have sung along to the birthday song. She might have even pushed her fingers in her ears to keep the noise out.

But she would have turned her chin down and smiled with all her teeth showing when I blew the candles out. She'd have smacked her hands together over her head and laughed for delight.

I wanted her back harder than I'd wanted anything in all my life.

I let the breath out my nose, my shoulders lowering, my eyes still on the candles, still aflame and ready for my wish.

"Make a wish, darlin'," Daddy said.

I took in another big breath. Holding the air in my cheeks I watched the wax drip from the heat of the flickering fire, making puddles on the white frosting.

"You all right?" Daddy asked. "Pearlie?"

I told him I was and blew out my candles with what weak breath I could. Only a couple of them snuffed out, sending snakes of smoke slithering into the space in front of my eyes. It took me two more tries to get them all.

Worst thing was, I didn't make a wish.

After we ate our cake, we went to the living room where Mama'd put just a couple things out for me to open. A nice new bow for my hair that wasn't so big as my other one and a new dress she'd made for me to wear once school started. Ray had made me a carved-out dog to keep my Indian squaw company. Uncle Gus and Aunt Carrie got me a diary and a nice pen.

Then Daddy said he had one more gift for me.

"You do?" Mama asked.

"Sure I do. Now, it's not new," he told me, taking a box from his pants pocket. "It's used. I hope you don't mind."

I didn't mind and let him know as much.

"All right, then, close your eyes."

I did as he said and felt his fingers brushing against the back of my neck as he worked at something. A necklace, I thought. Eyes still shut, I reached up and touched a circle of cool metal that rested on my chest. I felt of the two small circles of tiny diamonds set into the gold. Before I even looked I knew what it was.

"Meemaw's locket?" I asked in a weak voice, feeling I'd cry right there in front of everybody. I missed Meemaw just as much as I missed Beanie.

"She'd have liked you to have it, I think," Daddy said. "You'll have to be real careful with it. You think you can do that?"

"Yes, Daddy."

I held that locket in my hand, seeing it for the first time since Meemaw had gone to sleep and never woke back up again. I knew if I opened it I'd see a picture of Beanie on one side and me on the other. I remembered Meemaw opening it on many occasions so I could have a look at our tiny faces.

"My girls," Meemaw would say. "My sweet blessin's from God Hisself."

Just the memory alone was worth more than any kind of present I could have opened that day.

"Thank you," I told Daddy.

"That's all right, darlin'." He cupped my cheek with his hand. "I'm glad you're happy."

And I was. Until I saw Mama's face at least. She looked at the back of Daddy's head like she would have found great pleasure in knocking him over.

It was then I realized. She'd wanted that locket for herself.

I slept with Meemaw's necklace strung around my neck. The locket had dropped down from my chest and lay heavy on the pillow beside my ear. Grabbing it, circling my fingers around the cool metal of it, I pulled it back to my chest, not letting it go.

Meemaw had worn it. Her skin had warmed it once; her eyes had looked at it. Her fingers had pried open the locket so she could look at the pictures inside. I wasn't one to believe in superstitions or lucky charms, but if I had been, I might have believed Meemaw's locket would keep me from harm.

I was eleven years old, though. I was far too old to believe things like that.

The sky wasn't quite dark yet and I wasn't even a little bit tired. Still, Mama'd sent Ray and me to bed before it got too late. Problem was, no matter how hard I held my eyes shut, I couldn't seem to force myself to sleep. Too many thoughts spun in my head and too much light bled through my eyelids. Even after the night got all the way dark and the rest of the house went quiet, I couldn't get myself to sleep.

I thought I might get sleepy after sipping at a cup of warm milk, so I got myself out of bed and opened my door and made my way step-by-step down the stairs.

A tiny puddle of orange light splattered against the wall at the end of the stairs. The light in the kitchen was on and I figured Daddy was getting himself a little something to eat. That was when I heard Mama's voice.

"I knew she'd do this," she said, an angry ribbon woven into her words. "She never meant to come and get him. You know that, don't you?"

"I know, Mary," Daddy said back to her. "If I'm honest, I hoped she wouldn't."

"So, do we just keep him with us then? What's she expecting us to do? Raise him with our big stack of money? We can't afford it, Tom. I bet it never crossed her mind to send us any money to help out."

"We'll keep him here. He's one of us now." Daddy's voice sounded lower than usual, like he was real tired. "If I thought he'd let me, I'd adopt him outright."

"Tom, don't be ridiculous," Mama said. "We can't just adopt any stray we come upon."

I sucked in breath and tried not to let her words cut me too deep.

"Mary . . ."

"I wonder what it's like."

"What's that?" Daddy asked.

"Just up and leaving like that," Mama said. "Sometimes I wonder about going off and starting all over without any link to the past."

"Mary, I don't like it when you talk like that." Daddy's voice had a warning to it. "Don't like it one bit."

"She abandoned him, Tom. Left him." Mama's voice had grown savage and shrill. "Just like That Woman did with Pearl. And we gotta take care of what they threw away."

"Enough, Mary," Daddy said. "You'll wake the kids and I won't have them hearing you talk crazy."

"What if I did that?" she asked. "What if I just up and left? What would you do?"

"I'd find you."

I walked real quiet across the dining room and to the kitchen door, peeking through the space between it and the doorjamb. Mama stood straight and tall, her arms crossed over her stomach, holding on tight like she worried she might fall all to pieces. Daddy leaned back against the counter, his face turned from Mama.

"I must sound crazy," Mama said, a strange lilting to her voice. "I don't know what's wrong with me."

"Nothing's wrong with you," Daddy whispered. "I know you'd never leave us like that."

"It's just since Beanie . . ." she started. Her voice grew thick and garbled. "I just don't know what I'm doing anymore. I feel like I'm losing my mind half the time."

"But you aren't, Mary. You're doing just fine."

"I miss my girl."

Mama's shoulders started the shaking first, then the rest of her body joined in. She covered her face with one of her hands. Still, she couldn't hold in the sobs.

Daddy didn't move. He didn't go to her like he would have not even half a year before. I wanted to holler out to him that she needed him to put his arms around her and tell her that it was all going to be all right.

But he didn't do that. It just seemed too much for him to handle. It was too much and he couldn't do a thing for her.

All he did was stand there and listen to her.

But written on his face was every bit of grief she cried out.

It didn't seem such a good start to my eleventh year.

CHAPTER THIRTY

In my dream Mama sat rocking back and forth in Meemaw's old chair, a bundled-up baby in a red blanket held tight in her arms. She hummed to it and patted its back the way mamas did when soothing little babies. Shushing and singing and whispering sweet words.

As for the baby, it cried out, screaming for all it was worth. Its little hands had broken free of the red blanket, reaching for Mama's face. She pulled back from it, avoiding its touch.

My shoes click-clacked as I walked nearer to Mama. It wasn't the noise my normal shoes made, so I looked down. I had on Mama's shoes, the ones with heels and a fine ribbon that laced up through holes all the way up the top. Somehow they fit even though my feet were much smaller than Mama's.

Click-clack, clack-click I went across the floor of yellow brick until I got close enough to touch Mama's hand. She started like she hadn't known I was there, like my touch burned.

"Can I hold the baby?" I asked. "I'll be real careful."

"It's not mine," she said. "This isn't my baby."

"I'll be careful," I said again. "I won't drop it."

"This baby isn't mine." She shook her head. "I'm not keeping her."

Taking another step forward, I looked down into the baby's face. "What's her name?"

"She doesn't have one."

"Where're her folks?"

"She doesn't have any."

Sighing, she took one last look at the baby's face before working her way to her feet. She moved so slow, like she worried she'd drop her or that the crying might get louder. The way she held the baby was as if it were made of glass.

I followed behind her as she walked out the front door. The yard wasn't green and there were no flowers growing pretty in the beds. Everything had been buried in dust. Mounds and piles of it.

Mama stepped off the porch, up to her ankles in the soft dirt, getting deeper and deeper into it as she went.

In a way that only happens in dreams, we walked for a long time that didn't last very long. We ended up at the hiding cabin in the woods, the one that was covered in vines and moss and rotting wood. It stood out, the emerald of it standing out against the tan and gray all around.

Without taking a second look at the baby, Mama stooped down, putting her, red blanket and all, on the dull gray porch. She walked away and I watched her until she turned into a mist that evaporated in the blazing hot day.

The baby kept on crying, wailing and bawling for her mama.

CHAPTER THIRTY-ONE

Aunt Carrie sat across the kitchen table from Mama. The percolator gasped and gurgled on the stove behind them. I stood at the sink, washing up the lunch dishes and rinsing them under the faucet. I kept working, careful not to pause too long in my sloshing and splashing so Mama wouldn't know I was eavesdropping. And I didn't peek over my shoulder more than a couple times in case they'd catch me spying.

Grown-ups didn't always have a sense of when a child was listening in and I was glad to take advantage of that as much as I could.

"Why didn't he ever get married?" Mama asked.

"Well, he was going to," Aunt Carrie told her, leaning a round elbow on the table and resting her cheek in her hand. "But she died. Just a year ago. He took it so hard."

I knew the "he" they were talking about was Abe Campbell. As for the "she," I was still trying to figure that out.

"What did she die of?" Mama rubbed at her earlobe with her finger and thumb.

"It was cancer. It spread through her so fast." Aunt Carrie shook her head. "It was awful."

"I'm sure it was." Mama shook her head. "That poor man."

"It's hard losing someone so young."

Mama got up and turned off the burner under the coffee.

Mama rarely used the telephone. She said it was because she didn't have anybody to call. Still, it sat in the living room on a table beside a couple framed pictures of our family and a music box she'd had since she was a young girl.

When Mama wasn't home, I liked winding up that old music box and watching the gold-colored roller spin and the tiny silver fingers plunking out the melody. It was a song Mama told me her father'd sing in the mornings when he'd come to wake her. No matter how much I asked, she wouldn't sing it to me.

She said it made her cry for how much it reminded her of her father.

We hadn't kept it out when we still lived in Red River. Mama'd left it wrapped up and in her closet so the dust wouldn't get in and destroy it. On the day we'd moved into the house on Magnolia Street, that old music box was one of the first things she unpacked.

After Aunt Carrie left that afternoon, I found Mama at the little table with the telephone receiver to her ear. She'd lifted the lid on the music box, running her fingertips over the velvety lining.

"We'd like to have you over for supper tonight," she said.

She smiled at whatever the person on the other end of the call said. Lowering the lid of the box, she rested her hand on the simple wood.

"Yes, I'm sure. All you need to bring is your appetite." Again, she smiled, closing her eyes. "All right. If you really want to. That's fine. We'll see you then."

When she hung up the telephone, she turned her back toward me and sighed. But it wasn't a sigh of being tired or sad. It was an altogether different kind of sigh.

"Who's coming to supper, Mama?" I asked.

"Mr. Campbell," she told me.

"Does Daddy know?"

She shot me a look that was all sharp and not even a hint of soft and she walked past me to her bedroom, shutting the door hard.

If I'd had my way, Abe Campbell wouldn't have come to supper that night or any other. Whenever he was around, Mama smiled and glowed and laughed. She was very nearly her old self again.

Still, I didn't like that it was somebody other than Daddy who brought that out in her.

It seemed my heart was about to break all to little bits.

If Daddy was upset about Abe Campbell sharing a meal with us, he didn't let on. He made nice, asking Abe about how the paper was going and if he had met the new schoolteacher yet.

"I haven't," Abe answered, spreading soft butter on his bread.

"Folks around town have been talking," Daddy said. "She's real pretty, you know."

Mama wiped at the corner of her mouth with a napkin, glaring at Daddy just long enough that I saw her do it.

"Abe brought dessert," she said, changing the course of conversation. "Isn't that nice, Thomas?"

Daddy's eyes narrowed. Mama only used his Christian name when she was upset with him about something or other.

"It is nice, sugar," he said back. "Real nice."

"Strawberry shortcake," Mr. Campbell said as if he didn't notice any kind of tense feelings floating between Mama and Daddy.

"I'm sure it's mighty good, Abe." Daddy nodded at him.

"It's in the kitchen." Mama got up from her seat so fast I was sure she'd knock her chair over into the wall. Daddy steadied it with his hand.

"Let me help," Mr. Campbell said, taking the napkin off his knee and putting it beside his plate before getting out of his seat. "It's no bother."

"Well, all right." Mama smiled at him and led him into the kitchen.

The two of them chatted and laughed while they were putting together the biscuits and strawberries and cream. Daddy turned his head toward the kitchen, tipping back in his chair so he could see them.

He watched the two of them in the kitchen until they came out with plates stacked high with shortcake and strawberries that looked so beautiful I thought they'd make the menu at any fancy restaurant.

Mama smiled the rest of supper.

Daddy barely touched his dessert.

After Abe Campbell left nobody said hardly a single word. Mama had me help her clean up. I stacked the plates too high, trying to only take one trip from the table to the sink. I didn't drop one of them, but I got awful close. Mama gave me a hard look and told me to be more careful.

"I don't need you breaking my good dishes," she said. "Do you have money to buy new?"

"No, ma'am," I answered.

"Then be more careful."

I did my very best even as my hands shook, she'd made me so nervous. Boy, was I ever glad when we got everything put away. I didn't need Mama hollering at me any more than she had to.

I sat beside Ray on the floor right in front of the radio, both of us watching it and imaging pictures to go along with whatever was going on in the program at the moment. Daddy sat on the davenport, smoking a cigarette, and Mama occupied the chair clear to the other side of the room from him where she kept herself busy filing her nails.

The warbled duet on the radio between a man and woman ended, the tinny-sounding instruments letting out one last *dah-dah*, and folks clapped their hands. I thought it might be fun one day to sit in the audience of a radio show. I wondered if any of the singers looked the way I imagined them in my head.

When I asked Mama about it, she said they were just regular people like us.

As pretty as Mama sang, I thought they might just steal her away from us if they ever did hear her voice. She could sing pretty as any of those women on the radio, maybe even a good deal better.

"Ray," Daddy said, leaning forward. "Turn that up, would ya, son?"

Ray leaned forward, turning a knob.

A man's voice garbled out of the speaker and I only picked out a word or two here and there.

"Regret" and "day of sadness." "Uncharted territory" and "flight." Then "a day our nation will not soon forget" and "incredible loss."

Daddy sank back into the cushions of the davenport and snuffed his cigarette out into an ashtray. Shaking his head, he let out a sigh.

"All were lost in the crash," the man on the radio said. "The pilot Eddie Rickenbacker, the aviator Wiley Post, and beloved humorist Will Rogers."

Ray's shoulders slumped.

"It's just a radio play," I said, hoping I was right. "It's not real. It isn't, is it?"

"I do believe it is, darlin'," Daddy answered, getting up out of his seat and switching the radio off. "What a day."

The house turned quiet and we all shared in it together.

CHAPTER THIRTY-TWO

Aunt Carrie sat on the top step of her front porch, working her fingers through my hair to give me what she'd called a "German braid." From what I could tell, it snaked all the way around my head like a crown or halo. It didn't matter much to me what it looked like. All I cared was that my hair was off my neck. I liked the way the breeze cooled my skin when my hair was pulled up.

She was gentle with my hair, Aunt Carrie was, never pulling harder than she had to when running a brush through or doing the over-under-over-under work of braiding.

"My hair was nice and smooth like this when I was young," she told me, pinning the last bits of hair so it would stay in place. "Mine wasn't this pretty shade of blond."

"I like your brown hair," I told her. "I always wanted my hair to be dark."

"Why's that?"

"So I'd look more like Mama."

Aunt Carrie put her hands on both my shoulders and gave them a kind squeeze.

"She's not my real mama," I told her, glancing at her over my shoulder. "Did you know that?"

"I did," Aunt Carrie answered. "Does it bother you that I know?"

"Not really."

"I promise I won't tell anyone."

"All right."

She told me I should come inside and look at my hair in the mirror in the room she shared with Uncle Gus. I did and thought she'd done a real nice job and I made sure to tell her so.

"Most girls wear their hair quite short these days," she said.

"Mama likes my hair long." I shrugged. "She'd be sore if I got it cut."

"Well, I think it's pretty."

"Thank you."

"You're welcome."

She touched my cheek and I thought what a good mama she would have made. But she never had any kids and it made me wonder why not. When I'd asked Mama, she'd just told me it was none of my business and barred me from asking Aunt Carrie.

But Mama was back at the house on Magnolia Street doing who knew what. I didn't figure she'd ever find out what Aunt Carrie and I talked about.

"Why didn't you ever have any children?" I asked, letting my words come out slowly and in a quiet voice. "Didn't you want any?"

"Oh, I did. I wanted ten. Twelve, even. Enough to fill this big old house." She reached out and pushed a stray strand of my hair into one of the hairpins. "It just never happened. I couldn't even have one. Sometimes that's just the way of things."

"Does it make you sad?"

"Every once in a while," she said. "It was harder at first, when we still thought it might happen. Now I know that I'm barren."

"What's that mean?"

"I'm not able to have babies," she answered. "You'll understand when you're older."

I thought I understood enough then. Aunt Carrie suffered from what Meemaw would have called a dried-up womb. According to Meemaw, that was the condition old Sarah from the Bible'd had and why she didn't give Abraham a son right away.

"Then, the Lord God done give her a boy even in her old age," Meemaw had said. "Praise Him!"

"Meemaw," I'd asked that day. "Do you think you might have a baby, then?"

"Oh, Lord no." She'd shook her head and cackled with her mouth open wide. Then she'd lifted both her hands toward heaven and looked up at the ceiling. "Please, God, no."

I'd laughed right along with her. I didn't understand what was so funny, but it sure had been nice to hear her laugh like she did.

"Aunt Carrie, do you ever think God might see fit to do a miracle on you?" I asked.

"To give me a child?" she asked back. "Oh, I don't know. I suppose if He wanted to, He could find a way."

"But miracles don't happen anymore, do they?"

"Well, I don't know about that." She joined her hands together in front of her, fingers laced together. "Do you think they do?"

"I don't know," I answered.

"Come with me," she said.

I followed her out of the bedroom and through the kitchen where Aunt Carrie handed me a basket. She took one too. Then, out to the garden we went to gather the ripest and freshest tomatoes I'd ever seen. We pulled full-formed carrots from the dark soil and cut zucchini at the stem.

It wasn't a half hour later and both our baskets were full to overflowing of good food. I had to tuck a couple cucumbers under my arm since they wouldn't fit in the basket.

"Looks like I'll have a good canning year," Aunt Carrie said. "Gus will get sick of all the stewed tomatoes halfway through winter."

She loaded a wagon full of gifts from her garden. Once Ray came in from working the fields with Uncle Gus she told us we should go ahead and take that wagon with us back home to Mama.

"She'll like all this, don't you think?" Aunt Carrie asked.

"Yes, ma'am," I answered.

She put both her hands on her hips and let out a contented sigh. I did the same, hoping the more I echoed her the better chance I had of growing up to be like her.

I imagined, for the smallest of moments, how it might be if Aunt Carrie was my mama. Then I lowered my hands off my hips and did my best to put the idea right out of my mind. It would've broke Mama's heart to know I entertained such a thought.

"It's been such a treat to have you with me today," she said. "I hope you feel at home here."

I nodded, wanting so bad to tell her how it was the homiest place in all of Bliss but not knowing how to get the words out right.

As Ray and I walked away, trying to keep the wagon steady on the rutted dirt road, I was quiet, thinking about what she'd said.

The whole way back home I asked God if He wouldn't think on making Mama be her normal self by the time we got back to the house on Magnolia Street. I sure did miss the Red River Mama.

Seemed to me the God who hung the stars and spread the waters over the earth could do something so small as that.

Ray and I got the wagon pulled around to the back porch and carried in all that we'd brought home from the farm. Mama did put me right to work setting the table for supper, but not before I washed my hands real good. And she did send Ray to scrub in a bath.

"I do believe you found all the dirt on that farm," she said to him.

I thought sure my prayer had worked. She wore a real nice smile on her face when she said that.

Ray got himself to the tub and I heard the water running and then a sloshing sound when he got in. I imagined he'd gotten half the bathroom floor good and wet in the process. The way Ray splished and splashed made me think he'd grown to enjoy a good soak in the tub.

Mama came to the dining room to check on me. She rested her hands on the back of one of the chairs and told me I was doing a fine job. That made me stand up a little taller.

"Oh, just three plates, though," she said. "Your father's working all night, I guess."

She gathered the extra plate and napkin and silver, taking them back into the kitchen, humming the whole time.

Something in my heart felt dry and barren.

CHAPTER THIRTY-THREE

On nights when Daddy worked, I couldn't sleep so well. When I closed my eyes I'd think of all the worst things that could come to be. A thief could come in to steal from us, hurting Mama or taking her away. If I let myself sleep, I might not hear her cry out for help. I might not be able to save her.

Something could catch on fire—a washrag in the kitchen or a forgotten coal on the fire—and we might sleep right through until it was too late to get out. If I stayed awake, I'd smell the smoke. I could get everyone out of the house.

Daddy could get hurt while he was away from us. He could get caught in the line of a bullet from the gun of a thief or be driving down a dark country road when his truck would flip, making him stuck inside. My being awake could do nothing to save him, but my prayer said over and over might.

"Dear God, please protect my daddy," I'd mouth. "Keep him safe because we need him so bad. Don't let anything happen to him. In Jesus's sweet, sweet name, amen."

Soon as I'd finished praying that, I'd go around and say it again for good measure. Just in case.

I'd read in the Bible that we weren't to babble on and on in our prayers like the pagans did. So I only let myself say that prayer for Daddy four times, asking God if He would forgive me for asking more than once.

Somehow I thought He didn't mind too much.

I watched out my window hoping maybe I'd spy a fat raccoon wobbling his way across the yard or a skunk rooting around in Mama's flower bed. Those critters didn't bother me at all, just so long as the raccoon didn't overturn the trash or the skunk didn't let out any stink. What I didn't like seeing, though, were possums. They made my skin crawl.

The only creature I saw wandering about that night was tall and walking on two legs. I knew from the lanky shadow he cast that it was Abe Campbell. It was in the way he swung his arms, lazy, at his sides. How his shoulders were broad and square. The way he reached up to run his fingers through the front of his hair. It was him all right.

I would have preferred a possum just then, rat tail and all.

What was Abe Campbell doing in our back yard in the middle of the night? I didn't know the answer to that and I didn't care. I just wished he would turn right around and go back to whatever hole he had come up out of.

But he did not. He stepped right up to the back porch and held his fist up a moment before letting it rap-tap-tap on the door.

Sitting up in bed, I waited, wondering if Mama'd even heard the knocking. And if she had, would she answer it? I hoped she'd send him away, reminding him of the time of night and letting him know that Daddy wasn't to home.

The door did open, and through my screened window I heard Mama tell him to come in.

He did.

I held my breath and counted to a hundred, sure he'd leave by then. He didn't. I counted to a hundred again and again. Still, Mr. Campbell hadn't left. Getting out of bed, I got on my knees and lowered my ear to the vent. I heard their voices as a mumbled, jumbled murmur of sound.

If I wanted to know what they were saying, I had to get closer.

I left my room and snuck down the steps. They hadn't turned on so much as one light.

"Evildoers do hate the light, you know," Meemaw'd told me long before. "They do their evil deeds in the dark so as not to get themselfs caught."

Once I was at the bottom of the steps, I peeked around the wall, trying with all my might not to make so much as a single sound.

Mama and Mr. Campbell stood on the other side of the dining-room table, closer to each other than I thought was proper. They were so close they almost touched. I was sure they could feel each other's breath. Mama had to tip her chin up so she could look him full in the face.

Both of them kept their hands to their sides.

They spoke in soft voices like they meant to keep their words a secret held between the two of them. But if I listened real close, I could just make out what they were saying.

"You shouldn't come here," Mama whispered to him. "I thought we agreed."

"I know." He shook his head. "But I figured . . ."

"People still find things out even in the middle of the night," Mama said. "You can't come like this again. Somebody could've seen you."

"We aren't doing anything wrong."

"Abe"—Mama's voice was full of scolding—"this needs to stop. I'm a married woman."

"I haven't been so happy in a long time, Mary."

She crossed her arms and turned her face from him.

"You're happy, too," he said. "When I'm around at least. I know it."

"I don't remember what it feels like," she said. "I'm tired, Abe. It's so hard being sad all the time."

He took her hand. She left the other arm wrapped around her waist and she still didn't look at him.

"I hate seeing you like this." He stooped down so he could look into her face. "You don't have to live like this anymore, Mary. We could go—"

"Tom used to make me happy," she said, interrupting him. "He was all I wanted."

"He doesn't anymore, though." It wasn't a question.

Mama started crying. Abe Campbell put his arms around her and she let him. She didn't pull away like she should have and she didn't tell him to let her go. What she did was rest her head against his chest the way she would have if he'd been Daddy.

He only let go after the heaviest of her crying had passed.

Then he lifted his hand, putting his fingers along Mama's jawline, tracing it all the way to her chin. She reached up and put her fingers around his wrist. But she didn't force his hand away; she didn't push him back. She held him and leaned her face into his touch.

Bending, he drew near her, putting his lips against hers. She let go of his wrist and put her hand on his chest, resting her fingers on his shirt, but not forcing him from her.

It didn't last but a moment, but it was long enough to knock the breath right out of me, leaving me feeling like I might fall all to pieces right there on the floor.

I decided right then that I could never forgive her for that.

I never would.

Somehow I got myself up the stairs and back to my room without making any sound. At least not so far as I knew. I didn't know if it would have mattered one bit to either of them if they had heard me. They were too busy keeping their eyes stuck on each other.

When I got to my room my legs nearly gave out. I felt so weak all of a sudden and the air wheezed in and out so that I had to think real hard about every breath I took in. If I hadn't known better I might have thought I was going to die right there.

I sat on my bed, staring out the window to see when he'd leave. When he did, Mama held the door open and told him to have a good night. He turned and kissed his fingertips.

I didn't move, not so much as an inch, all night long. I didn't know that I could have even if I'd wanted to. I stayed put until the dawn blossomed as the sun rose inch by inch in the sky.

By then Mama was stirring out of her room and setting the coffee on the stove to perk. Her singing filled the house as if she just could not help herself.

For the very first time in all my life, I wished she'd just shut up.

CHAPTER THIRTY-FOUR

Getting out of my bed, I saw my reflection in the mirror on the wall. Half circles of purple showed under my eyes and my mouth was turned down. My hair was still in the German braid Aunt Carrie'd put it in the day before. Feeling around with my fingers, I took out all the pins, dropping them on top of my dresser. It didn't take long for my hair to come undone around my shoulders, waved from being in the braid all night like it'd been.

Ladies kept their hair long. That was what Mama had always told me. She'd said it was a lady's glory, her long hair. The Bible even said as much.

Ladies were kind and gentle. They were slow to get angry and quick to smile. Ladies didn't run or burp or pass gas or forget to say their prayers before taking a bite of dinner. They kept their knees together when sitting and didn't slurp their soup. Ladies never, ever cursed or took so much as a sip of booze.

Being a lady was as important to Mama as saying the sinner's prayer and following the Ten Commandments.

As for me, I was done trying to be ladylike.

I gathered all my hair into one hand, pulling it in front of my shoulder and letting it hang down my still-flat chest. Not thinking of anything at all, I opened the top drawer of my dresser where I kept odds and ends that didn't have a place anywhere else. I felt all through that drawer until my fingers wrapped around cool metal.

I turned away from the mirror.

It took just a few good snips and a whole foot of hair was freed. I let it all fall to the floor at my feet. What remained swept against my jaw and tickled against the back of my neck.

When I gazed back into the mirror, I cried.

No matter how much I tried, I couldn't think of a way to hide what I'd done. Mama would be upset with me for sure. I cussed under my breath, wishing there was some kind of magic that might put my hair back together again.

But all the king's horses and men couldn't help me out of that pickle.

"What am I gonna do?" I whispered through my ground-together teeth.

Pacing around my room, I stepped over the fistful of hair on the floor, wishing I was smart enough to think up something to do.

Nothing.

Shutting my eyes, I decided to be brave. I'd go down the steps and hope Mama would show mercy just like I meant to show her even after what I'd seen the night before.

She'd forgive me and I'd forgive her.

On tiptoe I went down the steps and crossed to the kitchen, pushing the door open and taking in a good breath. She stopped her singing when she heard me coming.

"Well, I wondered if you'd ever get up," she said, her back to me. She had something in her stew pot to boil. "Just get a slice of bread for breakfast, hear?"

"Mama?" I said.

"Don't make me get it for you, darlin'. I'm up to my elbows . . ."

She looked at me over her shoulder. Her face was beaded up with sweat and her hair had formed tiny ringlets around her face from the steam that clouded up from the stove.

Mama turned toward me, her hand on the counter like she needed its support to keep her from falling over. Her mouth dropped open and her eyes went dull like she was fixing to get good and angry.

"What did you do to your hair?" she asked. "Where is it?"

Trying to explain to Mama what I'd done was like trying to swim with lead weights for shoes. I was drowning in her stare. All I managed to get out were stammering noises that didn't mean anything at all.

"But why?" she asked over and again. "Why would you do that to your beautiful hair?"

I told her I didn't know, which was a lie.

Mama always could sniff out an untruth just like she was an old bloodhound.

"You'll tell me," she said.

"I saw you," I said back.

It was only a whisper, but its weight hung heavy in the air between us.

"Saw me what?"

"I saw you with Abe Campbell."

"You didn't see a darn thing, missy." She crossed her arms.

"He kissed you." I felt a hot tear make a trail of wet down my cheek. "And you didn't make him stop."

Mama took a step toward me and shook her head. "You saw no such thing, girl. It was a dream."

"It was real," I hollered, letting my voice fill with wild anger, making it out of my control. "I saw it and I'm going to tell Daddy."

The back of Mama's hand hit one side of my face and then the palm struck the other. I stepped back to get away from her but she grabbed my arm, digging her nails into my skin. Using my free hand, I tried fighting her off, tried prying her fingers loose.

"Let go of me," I cried. "You're hurting me."

"You won't tell your father anything, you hear me?" She pulled me toward her so our faces were close. "It never happened. You're lying."

"But I'm not," I whimpered. "I saw it."

"You'll do as I say. I'm your mother."

"No, you're not."

She shoved me from her. I fell backward, stumbling until I came crashing down to the floor, my head hitting the kitchen table.

A glass mixing bowl, one that'd belonged to Meemaw, smashed on the floor, one side of it shattering into so many pieces I'd never be able to count them.

"Don't you ever say that to me again," Mama screamed. "Never."

Ray must've heard all the carrying on. He came running into the kitchen, a look of alarm on his face. His eyes went from Mama to me and back again.

"What happened here?" he asked, standing between us.

Mama opened her mouth like she wanted to give an answer, but none came. Looking at me, but careful not to meet my eyes, she shook her head like she wanted to deny that she was the reason I was there on the floor. She turned back to the stove and stirred what was stewing in the pot.

Ray helped me get to my feet and told me to go up to my room.

"I'll take care of everything," he whispered. "Just wait for me."

I did as he said, not feeling anything as I climbed the steps or went into my room. There on the floor was my hair. I left it be and went to the other side of the room.

I made my bed the very best I could even though every inch of me trembled. I thought it would've made Mama proud.

CHAPTER THIRTY-FIVE

Hard-heeled shoes clipped up the steps, followed by the padding of bare feet. My bedroom door opened and I tensed my body, expecting to see Mama walk through.

Instead, Opal came in with Ray at her heels. She had him close the door behind them and came right to me, touching my face. Her hands felt cool against my aching cheeks.

"Are you all right?" She looked me all over from my eyes to my arm and then rested on my hair. "Are you hurt?"

"I'm okay," I answered. I wasn't sure if it was a lie or not.

"Do you have any shears?" she asked.

I told her I did and pointed at the dresser. She nodded and told Ray to get them for her.

"Is my mama still here?" I asked.

Ray shook his head, handing the shears to Opal. He said he wasn't sure where she'd gone.

"Probably just the store," Opal said. "But she could be back any minute. We'd best hurry."

"How did you know to come?"

"Ray came to get me." She touched the jagged and uneven ends of my hair. "I can fix this. Do you want me to?"

I nodded.

She had me stand upright and still in my bedroom as she used the shears to clip the ends of my hair, straightening it, making it even. Hers were gentle hands and warm. She worked quickly but well. The hair fell, covering my dress and the floor. Opal said she'd help me clean it up soon as she was done.

"Who did this to you?" she asked, standing in front of me and checking to be sure she'd made it even.

I shrugged. "I did," I answered, whispering.

"Why?" she asked, looking me right in the eye.

I didn't want to tell her and told her so.

"All right." She used her hands to brush the hair off my shoulders. "You'll have to change dresses."

When she was done, she and Ray left me alone so I could get changed. Then I let them back in and Opal used one of my clips to hold back the one side of hair that wanted to cover over my eye. Ray made himself busy cleaning up all the yellow hair clippings off the floor with a broom and dustpan.

"Thank you," I said, touching the ends of my hair, feeling how even she'd managed to get it. "That was real nice of you."

"It was nothing." She stood behind me, tilting her head so her reflection joined mine in the mirror, making me look like I had a second head sprouting from my skull. On any normal day that might have made me laugh.

She brought me a piece of bread on a plate and a half cup of milk.

"You can't start your day without a little breakfast," she said.

I told her I did appreciate it.

"I'd best go," she said. "Before Mrs. Spence gets home. I don't need to lose my job today."

"I won't tell her you came," I said.

Before she stepped out the door, she turned toward me and smiled.

"Your hair looks nice like that," she said. "It suits you."

I didn't even get to tell her thank you before she shut the door behind her.

I asked Ray if I could borrow a pair of his overalls. He looked at me like I was half out of my mind, but still went to his room for some he'd outgrown over the summer.

"Your mama's gonna be sore," he said.

"I don't care," I told him, taking the soft denim pants from him. "I'll tell her I stole them from you if you want."

"You don't gotta do that."

"What you saw today, what Mama did—"

"Pearl," he interrupted me. "You didn't deserve it."

I turned away from him. He'd made me cry and I didn't want him feeling pity for me.

"Thanks," I said.

I shut the door after he left and put those overalls on over an everyday blouse I had. I asked Ray to show me how to work the buckles on the shoulders. Other than that, I thought they were easier than putting on a dress.

Mama was home by then and I decided to walk right past her wearing those overalls. She gave me a don't-you-dare kind of look when I reached out for the doorknob.

"What're you doing?" she asked. "You're not leaving this house like that."

I set my jaw, tucking all my fear into my cheek like I did when I was making a poker face. Turning the doorknob, I pulled and stepped out on the back porch. Ray followed behind me.

"You come right back in here," she hollered, her shoes clacking across the floor like she meant to chase us. "Pearl Louise, I said come back."

I'd never once in all my life disobeyed Mama on purpose. It surprised me how easy it was. And how sad it made me.

It had me feeling lost.

I leaned my back against the twisted tree, the bark of it rubbing against me as I shook with crying. Ray stood beside me, holding one of my hands and not saying anything because he knew it wouldn't make anything better. Not really.

What I needed most of all was just to know he was standing right there. Somehow, he knew that.

"I can't go home," I said. "I never wanna see her face again."

"You don't mean that."

"I sure do." I sniffled. "I gotta run away."

"You ain't neither," he said.

I knew he was right. It would've taken more strength than I had to do a thing like that.

He tugged on my hand. "Come on," he said. "Let's go see Carrie. She'll know what to do."

I followed behind him, making my way between trees and stepping over whatever lay in our path. By the time we got to the end of the trail we were running, our hands still held together.

For once, he wasn't trying to race me.

Once we got to the farmhouse my tears had dried. There was something about running through an apple orchard that cheered me up. Having Ray there with me helped, too.

I was glad. I didn't need Aunt Carrie worried about me or asking questions I didn't know how to answer. The last thing I wanted was for her to think anything bad about Mama.

When Aunt Carrie saw me, she clapped her hands and laughed. "Look at you," she cried. "A pretty haircut and overalls? What's next? You running for president?"

I told her I might just do that someday. She laughed and told me she didn't doubt it for a minute.

"Wait right here," she said.

She went inside her house and came out in a pair of pants to match me. They belonged to Uncle Gus and she'd had to fold the legs up more than a couple times. She cinched a belt around her waist to keep them from falling off.

She said it was all right just so long as we kept it our secret.

"Half the town would think I'd lost my mind if they saw me in these," she said. "I'm surprised your mama let you out of the house in those."

I just kept my mouth shut and gave her a smile. Then I nudged Ray with my elbow to remind him he best not say a thing.

He said he was going to find Uncle Gus and took off running into the field.

"I have never worn slacks before," Aunt Carrie said, looking down at her legs.

"They feel funny," I said, feeling of my thighs, not used to having so much material between them like that.

But, oh, what freedom, being able to run and climb and play without fear of my underthings showing or the need to sit like a lady.

I'd kicked off my shoes soon as I got to the farm, letting my feet shuffle in the dewy grass. My soles were far from tough the way they'd been in Red River. It would take more than a couple shoeless days to rebuild the thickness of skin.

I hadn't felt wild and free like that in too long.

"Have you ever climbed a tree?" Aunt Carrie asked.

"No, ma'am," I answered.

"Would you like to learn how?"

I told her that I would like that just fine.

She went inside for a couple books before taking me out to the old weeping willow tree. Aunt Carrie told me where to grab hold of the branches and showed me the best way to work my feet to get a good grip while I was climbing. It wasn't so hard as I'd expected and I didn't mind being so far off the ground, just so long as I had a good stout branch under me.

Up in that old tree, I sat and read one of Aunt Carrie's books about a girl named Alice who fell down a long tunnel into a strange world of talking animals and magic food that made her change size. I didn't care for that story quite so much as the Oz book. At least in Oz Dorothy had found a handful of friends. There in Wonderland Alice was wandering about all by herself. Seemed the only thing that even half helped her out was a cat that kept disappearing. Reading that story just made me feel lonesome.

Aunt Carrie had a book of poetry and every once in a while she'd read me a line or two. I'd close my eyes to listen, letting the words form pictures in my mind the way she'd taught me to.

When I did that, the watercolored butterflies or starry nights or yellow daffodils took shape in my imagination, leaving less and less room for the bad pictures of what had happened just that morning. That was the magic of poetry.

One thing I'd learned from my aunt was that poetry was best when shared out loud, with a good friend. Another was that beautiful words strung together had the power to heal.

Aunt Carrie turned a page and sighed, holding the book to her chest and closing her own eyes.

"'Hope is the thing with feathers,'" she began, not even having to look at the page. "'That perches in the soul.'"

She went on, reading of a little bird that sang without stopping through a terrible storm, giving hope to any who heard her. And in return, that sweet bird didn't ask for anything, not even so much as a crumb.

I pictured that bird in my mind. She was a buttery color of yellow with feathers fine and wispy. She wasn't fancy as a peacock or a parrot, but she was pretty enough just the way she was. Her voice wasn't shrill as some birds sang. No, hers was smooth and trilling. And she sang for no other reason than to lighten the load off the hearts of the burdened. Hers was a song of hope.

"Do you understand the poem?" Aunt Carrie asked after she'd finished reading through it a second time.

"I think I do," I answered, finally opening my eyes.

"I read this poem often when Charlie was away at war," she said. "It's one of my very favorites."

"Mine, too."

She leaned back against a steady and strong branch and wrinkled her forehead.

"It's nice to think on," I said. "Hope is a real nice word."

"Indeed, Pearl." She smiled at me. "Some storms rage so loud that it's hard to hear the sweet song of hope. But it's always there."

Hope was a feathered critter. And sometimes it fluttered just out of reach.

Aunt Carrie said she had some things to attend to before the field hands came in for dinner. I asked if she would mind if I stayed there in the tree for a little bit longer. She told me that was all right by her.

"You stay as long as you need to," she told me. "Make yourself at home."

I wished I had the nerve to ask if I could stay there forever.

The Alice book open on my lap, I tried reading about her drinking from the little bottle. Every time I got to the end of the page I'd have to go back and read it all over again. My mind was just too distracted.

I shut my eyes and leaned my head back on the branch behind me.

I listened for the song of birds.

Long as I waited, I only heard one bird. But she wasn't singing. She screeched, her voice scratchy and sharp.

Hers wasn't a song of hope.

CHAPTER THIRTY-SIX

Daddy had never been one to raise his voice at Mama. Even when he was angry with her, he kept calm and quiet, measuring each word. He'd grit his teeth together, working to hold onto his self-control.

Even when Mama'd scream or stomp her foot, Daddy stayed even.

So when I heard him holler at her, I grabbed hold of the sheets on my bed, clutching them in both my fists so hard my knuckles hurt.

"What is this?" Daddy yelled.

"It's nothing," Mama answered. She didn't yell but her voice was icy.

"It doesn't look like nothing to me, Mary."

"Were you going through my things?"

"Why do you have a letter from Abe in your jewelry box? Tell me why."

Neither of them made a sound. Then Daddy let his voice quiet a little.

"Are you having a love affair with him?"

"It's just a note," Mama said. "That's all."

"I don't want you seeing him," Daddy said. "I want you staying away from him. Don't invite him to supper anymore. No more going for walks or calling him on the telephone. You hear me?"

She didn't say she would do as he said. She didn't say anything at all.

"You see him on the street, you're to turn and walk away," he said. "I won't have you tearing this family apart."

"It's already torn, Thomas," she said. "Don't you see that?"

I felt my arm, resting my fingers on the scratches Mama'd made there just that morning. They were still sore.

"Why, Mary?" Daddy asked. "Just tell me why you're doing this."

"He cares," she said.

"I do, too, Mary. I love you dearly."

I wanted Mama to tell him that she loved him, too. To say that she'd never so much as look twice at Abe Campbell ever again. I wished so hard that she'd fall into Daddy and beg him to forgive her for letting her heart stray.

But she didn't.

Instead, she went on and on, her voice shrill. She yelled about how Beanie would've still been alive if Daddy'd moved us away from Red River like she'd begged him to. She screamed on and on about how if he'd cared he would have never let Eddie DuPre into our home. I mashed the pillow on my head, holding it tight on my ear so I wouldn't hear her anymore.

I started humming, my eyes clamped shut as hard as I could force them. Humming and singing anything I could think of. Hymns and radio songs and little ditties I'd learned at school.

My voice crackled and choked with my crying, still I kept on.

It was all I could think to do.

Ray and I were the only ones home the next morning. I went in every room of the house, calling for Mama, but she wasn't anywhere I looked.

"She ain't here, Pearl," Ray said.

His eyes were red rimmed and for having been outside all summer long, he looked awful pale. I didn't think he'd slept much more than I had the night before.

"He'd never hurt her, you know," I told him.

"I know," he answered.

I went to the bedroom she shared with Daddy, thinking maybe she was still in bed. Pushing open the door, I stepped inside, my heart beating so hard I could hear its rushing in my ears.

I let out a relieved sigh when I saw she wasn't there.

Mama never liked me to be in her bedroom unless she'd invited me. She didn't want me snooping in her things. Still, I didn't leave. I stepped in and closed the door behind me.

Hanging on the wall was a gold-colored frame with a picture inside it, the kind of photograph made special in a studio. It was of the four of us. Daddy, Mama, Beanie, and me. Daddy and Mama sat side by side on a bench. Beanie was on Daddy's knee and I was on Mama's lap. Mama had her arm around my waist, her hand resting on my stomach.

She'd kept me safe then.

I couldn't hardly stand looking at that picture for the way it reminded me how good it'd been once upon a time.

A fairy tale that had a very unhappy ending.

I saw a shoe in one corner of the room. It was a shoe with worn soles and a buckle that was polished just enough to shimmer. It lay, abandoned, on its side. I squatted beside it, my finger tracing the shape of a scuffed-up spot on the black leather near the heel.

It had happened, that scuff, when she was carrying a basket of dirty clothes out back before scrubbing them on the washboard. She'd tripped just enough that she stumbled, turning her ankle and rubbing part of her shoe against the wood of the porch.

Daddy'd offered to buff it out with some of his shoe polish. Mama'd said it was fine, though. Not to worry. They were old shoes anyhow.

Turning, I saw her basket of mending full of hose that needed stitching up. She'd worn those stockings so long they'd tear if she so much as looked at them.

Daddy'd told her to go buy a new pair. Maybe a couple pair, even. We had the money for it if she needed. But Mama'd said it was fine. Not to worry. She'd never been one to buy new when she could fix the old.

On her dresser was the gold band Daddy'd given her on their wedding day. It didn't shine the way I imagined it had those years before.

He'd promised to get her another, one with a bigger diamond and smooth gold. But Mama'd said it was fine. Not to worry. She said it had good memories in every scratch and dull spot. The promise she'd made to him on their wedding day held still, no matter how fine the ring.

I slid it on my finger, bending my knuckles to be sure it didn't slip off.

There on the dresser, propped against an old glass ashtray, was an envelope with Daddy's name written on it in Mama's neat penmanship. I traced the T-H-O-M-A-S with my fingertip. I'd never liked it when Mama used Daddy's given name.

I remembered to take the ring off my finger, careful to set it back on the dresser right where I'd found it. Mama would've been real mad at me if I lost it. She'd have been sore that I'd been in her room in the first place.

I made sure to close the bedroom door behind me and to hold the letter with firm but gentle fingers.

I looked out the window to our back yard. All I saw of Ray were his bare feet dangling from the branch of the tree. That was fine by me.

The way I figured it, I needed to take that letter to Daddy and I needed to go all by myself.

I thought about leaving a note for Ray, but wasn't sure he'd be able to read it on his own. Besides, I did believe I'd be back before he even knew I was gone.

Soon as I stepped foot out of the house, a feeling a lot like dread settled into my heart. Much as I wanted to, I didn't look in that envelope.

Walking down Main Street with that letter in my hand, I moved my feet like I would have any other day. I smiled at folks passing by. When they said "hello" I said it back to them.

What I'd learned about hard times was that no matter how bad things got I could force a smile like nothing was wrong at all.

CHAPTER THIRTY-SEVEN

After Daddy read the letter he leaned forward, putting his elbows on his desk to read it again. Then another time. With his fingers he rubbed at his forehead.

"Daddy?" I asked. "Are you okay?"

He lifted his face like he'd forgotten I was sitting right there on the other side of the desk from him. Standing, he turned his head one way, then the next, feeling of his shirt pocket like he'd misplaced something. Then he looked down at the letter and folded it once, twice, pressing the creases between his fingers like he wanted to keep it sealed like that forever.

"We gotta go home, darlin'," he said. "Come on."

He walked his normal pace and I trotted along to keep up. Every couple steps I looked up at his face to see if he'd broken yet or if he was near to it. I wasn't sure why, but he'd seemed close to tears when he read that letter. But he kept his face firm and strong. If anybody'd been walking by, they wouldn't have known anything was wrong at all.

I wasn't watching where I was going and tripped over my own two feet, falling down on my knees and feeling the sting of where the pavement tore at my skin.

"You all right, darlin'?" Daddy asked, taking a knee beside me and getting a look at my bloody legs. "Oh, honey. You got it good. You think you can walk?"

I told him I could and he helped me to my feet. But once I was standing the pain started throbbing in my knees, my head, my heart. I thought if I opened my mouth to tell him how it hurt I'd get to wailing and moaning and all the town would hear my very heart breaking.

I still didn't know why.

When we got home we found Opal standing out on the front walk, waiting to be let in to start work for the day. Soon as she saw us coming, saw my roughed-up knees, she rushed to meet us and took my hand in hers and put her arm around my shoulders.

"I'll take care of this," she told Daddy.

He didn't put up a fight.

She made to walk us all the way around to the back door, but Daddy stopped her.

"Go on in the front," he said.

"Yes, sir." She led me up the porch steps and right inside to the bathroom.

"Now, sit on the edge of the tub. I've got to put something on those knees," she told me. "What happened?"

"I fell on the pavement," I said. "I wasn't looking where I was going."

"That happens sometimes, huh?" she asked, taking a little brown bottle out of the bathroom cupboard. "I've still got the scars from when I was a girl."

She poured the ointment on a washrag and dabbed my knees. It stung something awful and I breathed in a hissing sound through my tight-clenched teeth.

"Sorry," she said. "Just a little more."

When she'd cleaned them out as much as she could, she put bandages on them, saying I should take it easy for the rest of the day.

"Maybe just stay inside so they don't get infected or anything." She jiggled the bottle of ointment. Only a few more drops sloshed in the bottom. "I'll make sure your mother knows you need more ointment."

"But she's gone," I whispered.

"I don't understand," Opal said back to me.

I didn't understand, either.

Daddy told Opal she could go home for the day. He told her we'd need her tomorrow and maybe the rest of the mornings that week.

"I'll pay you extra if you'll do a little cooking, too," he told her. "Mrs. Spence had to leave town unexpectedly."

"Is everything okay, sir?" Opal asked, her eyes wide.

"Sure. Yes." He nodded and folded his arms. "Just family business is all. I don't know when she'll be coming back."

"Yes, sir." And with that Opal turned for the back door.

"Opal?" Daddy said, stopping her. "From now on you'll use the front door when you come and go."

"Yes, sir."

Once she got to the front door she hesitated a moment before turning the knob.

CHAPTER THIRTY-EIGHT

D addy had Ray and me get into the truck. Neither of us asked where we were going or why. It didn't seem the time to ask Daddy anything just then. I sat between them in the front. Daddy on my left, one hand on the steering wheel and the other rubbing at the back of his neck. Ray on my right, his elbow propped up on the open window and his hand riding the air that rushed at us as we rode along.

The good dog Boaz met us where the farmhouse drive met the road. He ran alongside the truck until we got all the way up to the house. Ray got out of the truck and squatted so the dog's face was right in his own and he rubbed at the mutt's jowls. Bo whined for happiness.

"Oh, poor Boaz," Aunt Carrie called, stepping down from the porch. "Are you telling Ray how neglected you are?"

The dog paid her no mind at all. Far as I could tell, he didn't need anybody else just so long as Ray was there.

"Carrie," Daddy said. "I'm sorry I didn't call you first . . ."

"What is it?" Aunt Carrie pulled at the collar of her dress and the color drained right out of her face at the sound of Daddy's voice. "Did something happen?"

"We're all right." His eyebrows twitched together and he licked at his lips. "I just . . . well, I need some help with the kids today. Wondered if they could stay here for an hour or so."

"Of course," she told him. "They can stay as long as you need them to."

"I do appreciate it," Daddy said, turning toward the truck then changing his mind and facing Aunt Carrie again, like he didn't know what to do with himself. He slapped his thigh so it made a clapping sound that got the dog's attention. "It's real nice of you."

"Tom?" She took a step forward. "Can I do anything for you?"

"Nah." He nodded at her once. "I'm just . . ."

"Mama left town," I said.

Both Aunt Carrie and Daddy looked at me and I felt the full weight of their stares.

"She'll be back, darlin'," Daddy said. "I'll bring her back, hear?"

I nodded, trying with all my strength to force hope.

Aunt Carrie and I sat at the table in her kitchen. Her cup of coffee steamed and my cup of hot cocoa hadn't lasted nearly long enough. She didn't ask about Mama and I didn't tell her, either. If she had wanted to know, I wasn't sure what I would've said that wouldn't have made Mama out to be a bad woman.

She wasn't a bad woman. She was good. Mama was good through and through. I had to think it over and over so I remembered.

"There's something I wanted to show you," Aunt Carrie said, getting up from the table. "Wait here."

She left the room and came back with an old photo album. She put it on the table before sitting back in her seat.

"Go ahead," she told me. "Take a look."

Careful as I could, I opened the cover of the album. Black pages held pasted on photos of folks from long before. In the pictures were faces I could have sworn I knew, just they looked younger.

"What is this?" I asked.

"It's Gus's," she answered, pointing at a picture of a tall boy with a big, goofy smile plastered on his face. He wore his war uniform and stood straight as he could. "That's him."

In the next picture he stood between two small women, his arms resting on their shoulders. One of them looked straight into the camera.

"Meemaw?" I whispered, half expecting her to laugh and say something to me. I nearly choked for how missing her set like a rock in my throat.

"I believe so." Aunt Carrie put her finger under the face of the other woman. "And that's Gus's mother. She'd be your great-aunt Lettie."

Old Aunt Lettie had her face turned up to look at Uncle Gus. "She looks proud," I said.

"I believe she was."

Turning the page, I saw a photo of the main street in Red River all decked out with banners I imagined were red, white, and blue. Folks lined up and down the street wearing their Sunday best for the occasion.

There were no mounds of dust piled against the buildings and the streets were clean and tidy. All the shops were open without so much as a single board nailed over a window.

"Gus said that when he got home from the war they threw him a parade," she said. "It was quite the celebration, I guess."

I pictured in my mind that the band played "Over There" all the way through at least twenty times, maybe even more, and everybody sang along with every word, welcoming their own Johnnie back again.

He'd ridden on the seat of a wagon pulled by a pack of thick horses. I asked who was driving the horses, but Aunt Carrie said she didn't know. It didn't matter much, really.

I flipped through more and more of the pictures. It seemed all the folks of Red River had wanted to have their picture taken with him. In one Mad Mable had her arm linked with his. She'd turned her face toward him, saying something that made him half smile. She looked plenty sane then, pretty even. In another was Millard, not near as wrinkled and gray as I knew him to be, still a good deal older than Uncle Gus, though. They stood side by side, both straight as possible like they were trying to prove who was taller. But of all of those, I liked the one with him and Daddy most. Whoever had taken that picture caught the two of them in the middle of a laugh.

The last picture in the album was of Uncle Gus alone. He stood against a building, a cigarette between his lips and his head turned from whoever had the camera. His shoulders weren't held straight like they had been in all the other photos and his mouth wasn't turned up in any kind of a smile.

There he stood, home from so far away. But I wondered if he'd felt like he had returned to something just as unfamiliar as the foxholes he'd left behind.

Once you go you can't never come back, Beanie had said to me so many months before, sitting right next to me on the porch of our house in Red River, Oklahoma.

I wanted to believe that wasn't true.

It was after dark when Daddy came to get us, his truck lights blaring through the night. I was half-asleep by them, cuddled up on the sofa, my head resting on Aunt Carrie's lap. Daddy scooped me up and carried me to the truck. Ray followed behind us, dragging his feet so that I thought he was just as tired as me.

"Where's Mama?" I asked once Daddy pulled back out of the drive.

"She's in Adrian, darlin'," Daddy answered.

"Where's that?"

"Not too far away."

"Can I go see her?" I waited for him to answer. He didn't. "Can I?"

"I don't think you better," he said. "No more questions for tonight, darlin', hear?"

"Yes, sir."

When we pulled up to the house on Magnolia Street, it was dark. If I hadn't known any better, I would've thought nobody lived there anymore.

CHAPTER THIRTY-NINE

The next morning I rolled over in my bed, listening for the sounds of
Mama moving about the kitchen. I expected to smell the perking coffee and frying bacon.

But then I remembered she wasn't there.

Without allowing a single thought of missing her, I got myself up and
to the kitchen. Making breakfast would be my job.

Daddy and Ray sat at the kitchen table to plates of scrambled eggs and
sausage and toast. Daddy said he hadn't had anything that tasted so good
in a real long time.

That surprised me. It seemed he had to force every single bite down.

Bert came by, wanting Ray to help him build a wood cage for some
poor, unfortunate critter he'd come across.

"You wanna come see it, Pearl?" he asked.

I knew he was asking only because he felt sorry for me. Ray must've told
him about Mama. It didn't matter to me, really, Bert knowing. Most the
town couldn't hardly talk about anything else.

I told him I wasn't feeling so good. It was mostly true.

Stacking the dishes, I managed to get them all the way to the kitchen
before dropping the lot of them. They made a great crack and smack against
the floor, just missing my bare toes, sharp breaks in each of Mama's good
china plates.

Dropping to my knees I did what I could to fit the pieces back together,
wishing I had the power to un-break them.

"Pearl?" Daddy said, walking toward me fast.

"I'm sorry," I whispered. "I didn't mean to . . ."

"What happened?"

"They were too heavy." I held up a shard of plate in each hand. "I can fix them."

"Are you hurt?"

I shook my head and bit at my bottom lip. "I'm sorry."

"It's all right, darlin'," he said, his voice soft. "I'm not mad at you."

My eyes blurred and I couldn't keep hold of myself anymore. Daddy didn't shush me and he didn't tell me everything would be all right. We both knew that might not be true.

What he did do was wrap his arms all the way around me and pick me up from the smashed plates. He let me sob from the deepest part of my aching heart.

When I'd calmed a little, Daddy had me sit on the davenport. He pulled the rocking chair up close so our knees almost touched. He breathed in and out of his mouth and bit at the inside of his cheek. More than once he shifted in his seat like he couldn't seem to get comfortable.

"Is it my fault?" I asked before he got the chance to say anything.

"What do you mean?" he asked.

"It's my fault she left, isn't it?"

"Darlin' . . ."

"I made her upset."

"Pearl, if she was so upset she'd leave, it was her own fault." He leaned his elbows on his legs and let his hands hang between his knees. "She's a grown woman, honey. She's smart enough to watch after her own feelings."

"But she is gone, isn't she?"

"It's just, your mama . . ." He pushed his lips together so hard his mustache almost reached clear to his chin. "Yes. She is."

"Isn't she ever coming back?"

"I don't know," he said. "I do hope so."

"What if she doesn't?" I folded my hands and held them on my lap. "What if she stays gone forever?"

My shoulders sunk into the back of the davenport and I let my head drop so I was looking at my hands. Tears drip-dropped onto my lap. Daddy moved forward in his chair so he could get closer to me.

"Go on, darlin'. Say what it is you're thinking," he said. "It's all right."

I didn't have words to ask what was so bad about me that both my mothers'd had to leave. And there wasn't a way for me to tell him how scared I was that he'd catch on and take off, too.

"Why would she leave?" was all I could manage.

"Now, I don't know." He kissed my cheek and used his thumb to wipe away a couple tears from under my eye. "But there's always a chance she will come home."

"How do you know that?"

Daddy shut his eyes hard like he was trying with all his might to hold together. Then he sat back in his chair and turned his head so he could cough a little into his fist.

I half expected him to tell me a story from the Bible the way Meemaw would've. I thought she'd have told about how Peter turned away from Jesus but came back later on, full of sorrow. She would've said how Jesus forgave him. Part of me wished Daddy would say something like that just then.

But Daddy'd never been one for preaching.

"I ever tell you about the time my pa was sick?" he asked.

"No, sir," I answered.

Daddy had only ever mentioned his pa a handful of times, if that. And when he did it was a quick word about him doing this or that to make Meemaw go out of her mind with his teasing her. I'd always liked hearing about him. Daddy'd told me if I'd ever met him I might have called him "Pawpaw."

I missed him. Or maybe I missed the idea of having a grandfather. Even Mama's father hadn't lived to see her wedding day. I guessed that was just the way of things.

I leaned forward, careful not to touch the bandages on my knees for fear they'd rub my sores and hurt something awful. I didn't want anything distracting me from Daddy's story about his pa.

"Guess it's about time I got around to telling you more about him, then," Daddy said, his eyes on the floor at his feet. "He was a good man. Real good. Born and raised in Red River."

"Did he know Millard?" I asked.

"Course he did." Daddy smiled with the far-off look in his eyes he got when he was telling a true story. "They got into lots of trouble together when they were younger. At least that's what I understand."

Using his hand, he wiped under his nose.

"He loved Meemaw, my pa did. Did all he could to show her." He nodded. "I don't know that he ever said the words to her. He wasn't a talker, my pa wasn't. He did show her every day. I do believe she understood."

Daddy reached into his shirt pocket and took out a cigarette, holding it between his fingers.

"I was right around sixteen when he took sick. It was summer. Wouldn't let us send for a doctor. He had too much pride." Daddy licked his lips. "Went to work every day no matter how sick he was feeling. He said that's what a man did. Said he had to provide for his family."

He held that cigarette between thumb and finger, rolling it one way and then the other.

"He got so skinny. Lord, I thought Meemaw'd go crazy with all the times she had to make his clothes tighter. I punched the extra holes in his belt myself. He just wasted."

I sat, staying quiet so Daddy could tell his story without me interrupting him.

"He got so he couldn't get himself outta bed. There wasn't hardly anything left of him." Daddy cleared his throat again. I didn't think it was from being hoarse. "Right before Christmas that year Meemaw told me I oughta go tell him good-bye. I tried to be a man and be strong. Couldn't, though. Just could not."

I reached for the hand that wasn't holding the cigarette and held it in mine. One thing I'd learned was that holding hands was safe-making. It gave courage. The way Daddy squeezed my fingers real gently told me he thought so, too.

"My pa let me cry and he patted my knee. Must've took it all out of him to do that patting. He couldn't hardly keep his eyes open." Daddy shook his head. "When I was all cried out, he told me he was proud of me. Said he wished he'd get to see me as a man. I promised I'd do my best to make him proud."

He put that unlit cigarette back into his pocket and put both his hands on mine.

"It was real hard on Meemaw, having Pa die like that, watching him waste away to nothing the way he did." He scratched at his stubbled cheek. "It took her a real long time to be herself again. Lord, do I ever miss him. Both of them."

"Daddy, is Mama going to be all right?" I asked.

He sighed and nodded.

"She's not dying, if that's what you're asking." He shook his head. "I guess what I'm trying to say is there's hope. Just so long as she's still breathing, there's hope she'll make her way back home."

"Why did she leave us?" I asked, my voice sounding small and thin.

"She just did," he answered. "Sometimes folks just do things for no good reason."

I cried and he held my head to his chest and I heard his heart pounding.

CHAPTER FORTY

Nighttime was when I missed Mama most. The quiet of the house on Magnolia Street set to ringing in my ears until the roof settled, popping and creaking and making me still with fear. I rolled this way and that, getting my bedclothes all twisted and tangled around me. The pillow wasn't right so I flipped it over and punched it back into shape. My feet were too warm so I kicked the blanket off them. I just could not seem to get comfortable no matter what I tried.

I gave it up and got out of bed.

If I'd had so much as an ounce of courage, I might have gone right out the back door and walked all the way to the twisted tree in the middle of the woods so I could cry my eyes out over losing Mama the way Miss Ada had for her boy. It wasn't the thought of raccoons and possums and coyotes that kept me from so much as touching the doorknob. It was knowing that Miss Ada's son hadn't ever come back. It made me remember that Mama could stay gone forever, too.

Instead, I sat at the kitchen table with the lights off and imagined that Mama was on her way back home. I pictured her making her way right then. That she'd gotten to missing us real bad and meant to be with us first thing in the morning.

I shut my eyes and pictured our house with its orange and yellow marigolds making sunny dots along the walk to the porch. Daddy'd stand beside me in the green grass yard that he'd cut fresh so it would look nice when Mama turned the corner to our street.

She'd come walking, her suitcase hanging from one hand and handbag slung over her shoulder. Her body would move slow, weary from traveling from so great a distance. Her face would be wet with fresh tears.

I'd see that her mouth was moving with silent words, rehearsing, no doubt, her begging-for-forgiveness speech. She'd be ready to beg us to take her back, even if just so that she could work as our maid until she'd proven she wouldn't stray again.

I'd hesitate just a moment, feeling the weight of missing her one last time and the hurt she'd done when she left me behind.

But I wouldn't be able to hold back long. Not even as hard as I tried. I'd run, fast as I could, not caring how unladylike it was. I'd get to her and wrap both my arms around her waist, holding her so tight she'd never be able to leave us again.

There'd be no fattened calf or fine garments for us to give. Not even a parade with all the folks in town singing along with the booming band.

But Daddy would come down the path, Mama's wedding ring in his hand. He'd slide it back on her finger where it belonged.

All would be set to right.

The end.

But doubt had wriggled like a worm into my heart. Even if she did come back, we'd never be back to how we'd been.

In the morning I made a list of all the things we needed from Wheeler's general store. Flour and sugar and canned things. We needed some meats and dry goods, too. Opal told me she'd go, but I told her I didn't mind. Ray went along with me to help pull the wagon back to the house.

Mama hadn't been gone three days and already we were running out of everything, it seemed.

The door of the store was propped open and we walked in without the bell dinging to announce we were there. Mr. Wheeler stood off behind one of the shelves with a woman I recognized from here and there. I couldn't remember her name just then, and that didn't matter much at all to me.

The two of them spoke in hushed tones, just between them. But they weren't hushed enough that Ray and I didn't hear what they were saying.

"I haven't gotten a paper delivered in days," the woman said. "I went by Abe's office and the door was locked."

"He's left town," Mr. Wheeler said.

"You don't say."

"I do." Mr. Wheeler moved closer to her. "Mrs. Spence is gone, too."

"The policeman's wife?" she asked.

"A little strange, don't you think?" Mr. Wheeler said. "They both end up being gone at the same time?"

"Very strange," the woman said, her voice almost more manly than Mr. Wheeler's. "I'd say there's something funny going on."

"I wondered about her from the first she walked into this store." Mr. Wheeler cleared his throat. "Something was off about her."

"Maybe that's the way down there," the woman said. "I hear they're real backwoods down south."

I stood at the counter holding my list. It shook and my grip crumpled it up all along the one side.

"I never would have guessed it of Abe, you know," Mr. Wheeler went on. "I've known him all my life. Never would have guessed he'd go after a married woman."

I let go of the list, letting it flutter to the floor. And I went right out the door making sure I stomped hard with every step so they'd know I'd heard them. There was nothing I needed so bad that I couldn't ask Opal to get it for me.

It felt like Mama'd slapped me all over again.

CHAPTER FORTY-ONE

The morning of the first day of school I wore a new dress that Mama'd sewed out of a flour sack for me over the summer. I had five new dresses that she'd made, one for each school day of the week, and each was a different color. One was yellow and another blue, one had green plaid and another had polka dots of many colors. The one I liked best of all, the one I put on that morning, was black with a thousand little yellow and white daisies all over it.

Facing the mirror in my room, I watched my reflection as I pushed the buttons into their holes. Mama'd never seen me wear any of the dresses. She hadn't even gotten around to having me try them on.

Boy, was I ever glad they fit anyhow.

I wished so hard that I could just be angry with her for leaving. That I could rage and spit and steam over what she'd done to us. But the sadness was sharper than the anger. At least it was then. And whenever I let myself get all worked up over Mama I'd just end up crying for how hard I missed her.

I wanted her back.

Shaking my head, I decided I couldn't boo-hoo over her that morning. I tucked the feelings into the corner of my mouth, biting on the inside of my cheek to remind myself to forget her, at least for a little bit.

Opal had bleached my socks real good so they wouldn't look dingy under my new, spit-shined black shoes. I even wore Meemaw's locket, careful to drop it under the cotton of my dress so it wouldn't get snagged on anything that might break the chain.

After a couple failed tries at getting my hair into a bow, I asked Opal if she wouldn't mind helping me. She made quick work of pulling back half my hair so it would stay out of my face.

I sure was glad Daddy'd asked her to help us get ready for school.

Before I went downstairs for breakfast, I tried to imagine what Mama was doing just then. Maybe she'd found herself a job there in Adrian. Cooking at a restaurant or cleaning a hotel. Maybe she was taking in laundry or watching kids for some rich folks. She might've even found herself a job working at a hospital. She'd always said that was what she'd have done if she hadn't married Daddy.

Whatever it was she'd found to do, I wondered if she remembered it was the first day of school. I wondered if she worried over me having a good day and making friends.

Again, I told myself to forget her and pushed aside any feelings I had for her.

I put away my hairbrush and went downstairs where Daddy stood waiting for me. He gave me a nice grin and told me how pretty I looked.

"My girl Pearl," he said. "Now, you be sure not to break too many hearts today, hear?"

It was the first I'd smiled since Mama left.

Bert Barnett walked with Ray and me to school. Both of those boys walked stiff in their fresh-starched shirts that I knew would be nice and loose by the end of that day. Ray had even used a little of Daddy's pomade to sweep the hair off his forehead. It sure made him look grown. And handsome, but I wasn't about to tell him that.

"Know what I found?" Bert asked as we made our way down Main Street. "A baby raccoon out in the woods."

"You shouldn't be going out there by yourself," Ray told him.

"I was careful," Bert said. "Wanna hear about the baby raccoon?"

He went on and on about how small it was and how it had liked the piece of bread he fed it. He'd brought it home all cradled in his arms and tried to convince his mother to let him keep it.

"She made me take it back, though." He sighed and let his shoulders slump. "She was worried it would scratch me."

"I heard of a fella that caught a baby raccoon down in Ohio someplace," Ray said, working at rolling up his shirtsleeves. "He raised that coon from birth. Once it got full-grown, that critter got mean. One day he got some kind of wild hair in him and bit off the man's thumbs."

"Both of them?" Bert asked, stopping right in the middle of the walkway.

"Yes, sir," Ray answered. "Come on. We'll be late."

Bert looked like he might faint, thinking on such a thing as that. I had half a mind to tell him that most of Ray's stories were just tall tales and to pay him no mind. But, then again, I thought Bert should be more careful about the critters he came upon in the woods.

"So you touched it?" I asked.

"Of course I did," Bert said. "I let it crawl all over me. It liked it."

"I read somewhere that if a mama raccoon smells human on its baby she'll leave it," I said.

"Well, I don't think that's true." Bert went on and on about raccoons and I didn't hear a single word of it.

The rest of the way to school I was trying not to think of that baby raccoon left all by itself in the woods.

One thing I'd learned was that mothers weren't always good at sticking around.

We got to the schoolyard just as the sound of a clanking handbell rang through the clusters of kids. They made their way into a line by the school steps and Ray and I did the same. The schoolteacher, Miss De Weese, stood at the door, calling for our attention. She warned us all against running through the hall and instructed that we should keep our hands to ourselves.

"Everyone should take a seat in the classroom," she said, her voice nice and clear. "Younger children in the front, older in the back."

We filed in and the teacher smiled at me as I walked past her. It relieved at least a tiny bit of my nerves.

Bert had to sit in a row in front of Ray and me with the younger and smaller children. Ray and I sat together just as I'd hoped we would and I thought he was plenty anxious about the starting of that day. He hadn't been in a classroom since he was six years old. He'd turned twelve over the summer. But he'd worked hard. Mama had, too. I did have faith their lessons would help.

If nothing else, he'd learned to read just enough to show that he was smart. And he could write a whole bunch of words. Mama had tried to start in on fixing his grammar, but found that was a battle he'd hold firm against.

Even if they'd missed their last few lessons, he was still ready for school, I just knew it.

All the chitchatting in the room came to a stop when Miss De Weese stood at the front of the desks, a clipboard in her hand with, I imagined, a list of all our names. She said when she called our names we were to answer with the word "present" loud enough that she could hear it, but not so loud that it was a yell.

That room was overfull of kids and roll call seemed to take half of eternity to get through. Knowing my name would be all the way to the end of the list, I got to daydreaming about what I'd like to do just as soon as school let out for the afternoon. I thought of making fresh-baked cookies with Opal and reading under the tree and watching Ray whittle on the horse he was making for me. I'd gotten myself so distracted I didn't hear Miss De Weese when she called my name. Ray had to elbow me in the ribs so I'd pay attention.

"Pearl Spence?" Miss De Weese called.

"Sorry, ma'am," I said after clearing my throat. "Present."

More than a couple kids laughed quietly at me.

So embarrassed, I blinked at my desk, working at not crying. What made it worse was that when the teacher called out Hazel Wheeler's name, the girl announced she was present without so much as a hint of a stutter.

When I turned to see where she was sitting, straight as a rod, Hazel scowled right at me from just one row behind. I wondered if that wasn't her very best smile on account she was such a sour and mean human being.

I didn't doubt that at all.

We went about our lessons all morning long, not taking a break from working out arithmetic or from searching maps in geography. We wrote our hands sore when practicing our penmanship and read quietly at our desks until Miss De Weese told us to stop.

It took Ray a long time to finish his work, longer than everybody else in the class, as a matter of fact. And I was sure he didn't get all his answers right. He didn't seem to care, though. He was doing what he could and I thought he was proud of himself.

Besides, other than Big Boy Bob, he was one of the larger boys in the room. It would have been a fool that poked fun at him.

We were real close to the noontime dinner bell and I was looking forward to running wild outside after sitting still and quiet for so long. I'd even managed not to daydream so much as one time since the teacher called the roll. I checked the clock on the wall, seeing we didn't have more than thirty minutes left in the morning, and I started getting antsy.

Just then a girl shuffled her way into the classroom. Even from where I sat I could tell she was the kind who would have benefited from a long, hot-water bath with a strong bar of soap and a scrub brush. A couple kids behind me snickered at her as she stood there, waiting for Miss De Weese to tell her to come in.

"Did anyone think to bring clothespins?" Hazel asked. "My fingers are going to get tired of holding my nose."

I flashed with anger at Hazel for saying such a thing and turned to glare at her. Too bad she didn't notice. She was too busy seeing who else was laughing at her little joke besides just her.

I remembered Meemaw telling me that in times of temptation the good Lord would always provide a way of escape. I got to praying that God would give me some way to flee the temptation of flattening Hazel Wheeler's nose.

In Jesus's holy name, amen.

Turning to face the front of the room I saw that the late-coming girl hadn't moved so much as an inch. Dirt smudges soiled her overalls and the shirt she wore under them was yellowed and stained. I figured those were all the clothes she had to wear and wondered if they'd been handed down from an older brother. Wherever she'd gotten those clothes, they were bad. So bad they made all the rest of us in our feed-sack dresses look dressed to the nines. Her hair hung in greasy threads against her neck and her cheeks, and in her eyes. It wouldn't have surprised me to find out that her shoes had holes in the soles and that they were more than a couple sizes too small. The way she walked made me think they hurt her something awful.

Making her way past all the taken desks she bounced her lunch pail against her leg. It made a hollow sound, that tin pail, and I wished she'd stop letting it hit her thigh. All the kids in the class were watching her, hearing her. It made me sad, knowing they were thinking less of her than themselves.

If I could've made a bet, it would've been on her family being on Abe Campbell's list of folks taking assistance. Just thinking of him made my stomach sour.

The only empty seat was on the left-hand side of me and that was where the girl was headed.

"Don't get too close to her," a boy near me whispered loud enough for the class to hear. "Delores gots cooties."

When she stopped and slipped into her seat I half turned toward her. I didn't see any bugs crawling around in her hair, but I did understand how there could've been some. The girl was filthy as could be and sure smelled the part.

"Delores Fitzpatrick?" Miss De Weese asked, still sitting at her desk. "Is that your name?"

The girl nodded but didn't look up at the teacher.

"I'm glad you made it today."

The girl bent down and slid her pail under her seat.

"Did Uncle Frankie Roosevelt pack that lunch for you?" a boy asked, reaching out his foot and nudging the pail with his toe.

"Excuse me," Miss De Weese said to the boy. "Did you say something you'd like to share with the class?"

"No, ma'am," he mumbled.

"Then kindly keep your mouth shut until I ring the lunch bell."

"Yes, ma'am."

I knew he was making fun of that Delores girl for being poor. He was teasing her for needing the relief. I clenched my fists so hard my fingernails dug into my palms.

As mean as some kids in Red River got about Beanie or anybody that was different from them, not a one of them—not a single one—had ever made fun of somebody for being poor. We'd all been poor. Ray was one of the worst off, even. And we'd never said so much as a single word about it to him. We just plain knew not to.

When the lunch bell did ring I was glad. But I waited in my seat until everybody else cleared out and it was just me and the teacher and Delores Fitzpatrick in the room. Last thing I wanted was to get in a knock-down, drag-out fight on the very first day of school. I thought I'd let all the other kids, especially that Hazel Wheeler, get a head start on going home.

Delores took her pail and pulled out what little lunch she did have inside. Just a slice of bread folded in half that I'd have guessed had only a dot or two of ketchup inside it and an old, wrinkled-up apple that looked like it had seen better days more than five years before. I tried not to stare so I wouldn't embarrass her.

"Miss Spence?" Miss De Weese said from her desk where she'd begun unpacking her own meal. "Are you staying or going home?"

"Going home, ma'am," I answered, sliding out of my seat. "I'm sorry."

"You don't need to be sorry."

That Miss De Weese certainly was a kind lady. I was glad.

Just as I stepped outside the classroom door, I heard the teacher say something to Delores. I stopped and listened.

"Would you believe I packed two cookies today?" she asked. "Would you like one, Delores? It's oatmeal raisin."

Hearing shuffling steps I peeked in to see the girl grab the cookie and rush back to her seat before taking even one nibble. She hadn't said thank you, but I didn't think that mattered so much to Miss De Weese.

I turned and left, stepping outside, glad to find Daddy and Ray waiting for me in the schoolyard.

"You having a good day?" Daddy asked once I made my way to him.

"I guess so," I answered, not wanting him to worry about me too much. He had plenty on his mind as it was.

"That's fine," he said. "How about we get a bite to eat at Shirley's today? She's got meatloaf sandwiches."

Ray and I both told him that sounded real good.

My brand-new shoes made a clipping sound on the pavement as we made our way to the diner. The shoes I'd worn before never had made anything but a clunking. I thought of those shoes, stowed away in the bottom of my closet.

"Daddy," I said. "Do you think it's all right if I give my old shoes to Delores?"

"Who's Delores, darlin'?" he asked.

"A girl in my class." I took a look at him out of the corner of my eye. Then I made a point of whispering, "I think she's poor."

"Well, I don't mind." He nodded at me. "You best ask your—"

Mama. He was about to tell me I best ask Mama.

Not one of us said anything to each other until we got to the diner.

CHAPTER FORTY-TWO

Hazel Wheeler busied herself with talking behind her hand into some girl's ear. Both sets of eyes followed me all the way from the gate of the schoolyard to an old tree not three feet from the steps. It was only the second day of school and already I felt a fight coming on.

"Don't you pay her no mind," Ray told me. "She's just tryin' to get your goat."

"Well, she's already got it," I muttered. "I hate everything about her."

"You don't hardly know her." Ray stayed standing and shoved his hands in his pockets. "Don't borrow trouble, Pearl."

That'd been something Meemaw had said when she was still alive. Somehow it hadn't irked me near as much when she'd said it.

"I'm telling you what, if that girl says one sideways thing to me . . ."

"You'll turn around and walk away from her," he told me. "She ain't worth gettin' in trouble over."

"Maybe she is," I said under my breath.

Ray sat on the stump beside me and leaned forward so his elbows rested on his thighs.

"Pearl, that girl will never be half as good as you," he said. "You know that?"

I didn't know that but I kept it to myself. Good girls didn't drive off both their mamas before they'd reached the age of twelve.

"Don't let her get to you. That'd just be givin' her what she wants."

I wanted to ask Ray when it was he'd started talking just like Daddy, but Miss De Weese came out the school door, ringing her bell as the kids

284

hustled to get in line. I hung back so I was right behind Hazel and the girl she'd been whispering with.

The part of me that was full of evil wanted to yank on her perfectly bouncy sausage curl until it straightened right out.

Then I remembered what Meemaw'd told me time and again when somebody treated me mean back in Red River. She'd dry my eyes with the hem of her apron and pat my cheek with her crooked-fingered hand.

"You gotta find a way to bless 'em, honey," she'd said. "When somebody treats you bad, you gotta think of somethin' good to do to 'em. They might hit you again and again, but you gotta come back with blessin's every time."

Some days I wished I could stop remembering things Meemaw'd told me. Seemed easier just to smack Hazel across the face and be done with it.

Walking behind her and watching her silky and shiny ginger-colored hair sway back and forth across her shoulders, I couldn't think of one thing to do to bless Hazel. She already had everything she needed and I sure didn't want to tell her she was pretty.

Pretty is as pretty does, I thought.

Right before we walked in the school she peered at me over her shoulder, giving me a look that told me she thought I was worse than worthless.

"Good morning, Hazel," I said in the very sweetest voice I could make. "I do hope you have a nice day."

Her eyes grew wide before she narrowed them at me.

My kindness took her by surprise. It felt better than punching her in the mouth would've. Besides, kindness wasn't near as hard on my knuckles.

I held my shoulders back and felt a smile creep up on my face.

Miss De Weese held me after class to wash the chalkboards and clap the erasers. The fine powder that puffed in the air in front of my face reminded me of Red River. It was fine and silky just like the Oklahoma dust. It also made me cough something awful when I breathed it in too deep.

I deserved the punishment and I knew it. Still, I'd felt justified in trip-ping a boy in class after I heard the nasty word he'd called my mama.

When the teacher had asked me why I'd done it, I just looked her in the eye and told her I didn't know for sure. That wasn't the whole truth but the last thing I needed was for her to know our family business, even if the whole rest of the town seemed to know more about it than I did.

Ray had waited for me on the stump, gnawing away at his fingernails that could've used a good clipping. His hair was growing out dangerously close to his collar and it seemed his pants had shrunk a good inch in the legs.

Mama never would've let those things go. And she wouldn't have toler-ated the grime that'd taken up housekeeping in his ears, either. I thought I'd have to see what Opal could do to help him.

"Ready?" Ray asked once he saw me walking down the school steps. "Wanna cut through the woods?"

"Nah," I told him. "I'm too tired."

He kicked at a pebble that was loose on the pavement. I could tell just by the way he half shuffled his feet that he was disappointed.

"You go on if you wanna," I told him. "You don't need me holding your hand."

"You sure?" he asked.

"Sure I am." I shook my head. "I know the way home without you."

He didn't wait for me to tell him twice. He took off running toward the woods fast as he could. I imagined him one day with a big old woolly beard that grew all the way down to the middle of his chest and hair so long it curled up around his ears and at the nape of his neck. He'd have a cabin all his own where he'd live in the woods, trees growing all the way around so he wouldn't even need a fence.

Ray wouldn't be a hermit. He wasn't that kind. But he would like to keep to himself sometimes. He'd always let me come and sit to visit just so long as I brought him food enough to last a month.

And if I'd ask real nice he might even let me live out there with him.

I dreamed of all we'd have out in our cozy cabin in the woods until I got to the front porch. Opening the door, I saw that Opal was there waiting for me.

"May I please have something to eat?" I asked.

She nodded and walked to the kitchen without saying so much as a word. It seemed odd to me that she hadn't asked how school was or why I was so late getting home. She hadn't even asked what I'd like to eat.

That was when I realized something about the house felt wrong. A little bit emptier.

The portrait of President Roosevelt still hung on the wall above the radio and the rocking chair was still in the corner with Daddy's ashtray on the table beside it. The photos of our family were there, still where Mama'd placed them on our first day in the house. The telephone and the few books Daddy'd brought from Red River and Meemaw's old Bible all stayed where they lived on the table.

Mama's music box was gone, though. And the lacy doily she'd kept under it. Her mending basket was missing from beside the chair she'd liked to sit in.

I went to the bedroom my parents had once shared, the one Daddy had avoided since Mama left. Anything that had been hers was gone. Dresses and shoes and even the quilt from the bed. Checking the dresser, I saw that her wedding ring was gone, too.

"Pearl," Opal said, standing in the doorway with a piece of bread and jelly on a plate. "Come on out of there."

"Were we robbed?" I asked.

"Your mother . . ." She sighed. "Mrs. Spence. She came for a few things."

As an act of instinct, I felt for Meemaw's locket where it would've been on my neck had I put it on. But that morning I'd left it in my dresser up in my room. I'd worried about it getting lost or broken. It was my most prized possession and all I had left from Meemaw and Beanie.

I'd wanted to protected it, so I'd left it home, safe in my top drawer.

Racing up the stairs, I crashed into my room, the door banging on the wall behind it. All was normal, just the way I'd left it that morning.

If only I hadn't gotten myself held over after school I might've seen her.

I'd have begged her to stay. I would have done anything.

I put my hand on the cool metal knob of the top drawer and pulled. Without looking, I felt around for the chain of my necklace, for the gold with tiny chips of diamonds. It wasn't there.

I opened the drawer wider, leaning over it to inspect. My eyes only caught a glint of light on my shears and a stack of folded-up letters from Millard.

I slid the drawer closed gentle as I could and rested my fingertips on the top of the dresser. Mama's fingers had just touched that same metal and wood. Her feet had been in the same spot that mine were in just then.

My chest felt squeezed by some large and unseen hand that wanted to crush me to dust. I tried to breathe deep. I shut my eyes and gritted my teeth.

I never did tell Daddy that Mama'd stolen my locket from me. To speak it would have been to make it true. It would have made me admit that Mama'd done something so low. That she'd hurt me once again.

What I did do was imagine how I'd be if ever I did see her again. Every time I thought on it, I pictured Mama walking my way, her sorry eyes fixed right on me. As far as I was concerned she could just keep on walking.

I would just turn my back on her.

CHAPTER FORTY-THREE

We'd been in school a full month already and Opal sent us off each morning wearing thick jackets. I wasn't sure I had ever been so cold as I was walking with Ray and Bert to the schoolyard. The whole way we'd purse our lips and blow into the crisp air, pretending we were smoking cigarettes. Mama'd said long ago that it wasn't nice pretending like that. It didn't matter anymore, though, what Mama said. She wasn't there to get sore or sigh or give me a sideways look.

When we stepped out of the house that morning, the air had a different kind of smell to it. As we walked and puffed out our mouths, I tried thinking of what the air smelled like. It was brand-new to me, that smell, and it was like nothing I'd ever breathed in before.

"Look at them trees," Ray said, nodding out behind the house at the woods. "Ain't that somethin' else?"

It sure was. Orange and yellow and red, the trees seemed to have all changed colors over night while we were sleeping. They were so bright, so startling, I would have thought they weren't real if I hadn't known any better. If I squinted my eyes just right it looked like the whole forest was ablaze.

Seemed the entire world was changing right before my eyes. The air blew colder and grass poked out of the earth a duller shade of green. Fields that'd been full of growing things were harvested to stubble; the remaining stalks had gone a hay color. Geese flew south in their practiced formation.

Where Mama was, she saw it, too. I imagined her stopping in the middle of her morning to look up at a tree or to see a squirrel darting across her path with a mouth full of food for storing up. She'd put a hand to her heart, in quiet awe of the colors and the way the air smelled like spice and warmth.

And I imagined—I hoped—she maybe thought of me doing the same thing. I did hope Mama still gave me a thought every once in a while, even if it was small as a crumb.

A crumb might just lead her back to me.

After school on a Friday toward the end of October, Ray and I opened the front door of our house to the finest and sweetest smell I could have imagined. If warm had a smell, that would've been it. The smells of baking apple and cinnamon and sugar filled the whole house and made my mouth water.

Aunt Carrie stood in the kitchen with Opal, the two of them wearing aprons with beads of sweat on their foreheads even though the day outside was so cold. Canning jars lined the counter, most of them filled to the brim with applesauce.

"Oh, good," Aunt Carrie said when she saw us. "Just in time. We need someone to make sure this tastes good."

She gave each of us a spoon with a bite of the applesauce on it. It was nice and warm and tasted like autumn. I said it was real good, that I liked it a whole lot. Ray, though, said he might have to taste a little more of it.

"Maybe I'd need a whole bowl of it," he said, shrugging. "Can't hardly tell if somethin's good unless I eat more'n a bite or two."

"You sound just like your Uncle Gus," Aunt Carrie said, laughing.

She did give Ray a good ladleful of the applesauce in a bowl. When I asked real nice she gave me one, too.

Opal told us we should sit at the dining-room table. We did as she said and ate our applesauce with the kitchen sounds of jars clomping on the countertops and the rings spinning around the glass to hold down the lids.

After we finished I went to my room and wrote a letter to Millard, telling him about leaves and applesauce and how cold it got when the sun wasn't warming the sky. I put a pretty orange leaf in the envelope, hoping it wouldn't crush to powder on its journey down to Red River.

In all the letters I'd written him that October I hadn't said one thing about Mama. I was sure he knew about her leaving though, on account each of his letters ended with him asking, "You all right?"

In my letters I made sure not to give him an answer.

My envelope sealed and addressed, I walked down to the kitchen, wishing I could capture the goodness of that canning day somehow in the folds of paper so Millard could smell it. I thought he would have packed his bag right away if he could've caught a whiff of that applesauce.

"Can I take this to the post office?" I asked Opal. "It's for Millard."

"Go ahead," she told me. "I've got a stamp there in the drawer. You know the one."

I told her thank you and headed for the front door.

"Come right home when you're done," she told me. "And button up that coat."

It was a fine day. Even cold as it was, the sun was kind and my coat kept me warm enough. Not too many people were on the street that day. All the shops had their doors closed to keep the heat in. It was as if I had the whole town to myself and I liked that.

The post office was toasty and the postmaster snoozed at the counter. I let him sleep and slid Millard's letter in through a slot in the desk and snuck out, careful not to let the door slam behind me. If ever there was a good day for napping, I thought that was it. Besides, if I'd woken him, that postmaster would have wanted to talk my ear off about the price of stamps going up or this or that and I wanted to get back to the house before Aunt Carrie left for the day. I hoped maybe she'd even give me another taste of that applesauce.

The Wheelers' house was right across the street from the post office.

Where it'd seemed fine and grand in the glow of summer, the dim light of that October day made it dark and wicked looking. Even under the warmth of my coat I got goose pimples. I would've sworn that house was haunted.

I gave a start and let out a small yelp when I saw what looked to me like a ghost standing right in one of the full-length windows on the second floor of the house. Wrapping my arms around myself, I took a second look and realized it was Mrs. Wheeler standing there, staring out.

I'd hardly seen her more than a handful of times in all the months I'd lived in Bliss. She wasn't one for coming to church and she didn't lower herself to walk along the street with the common folk in the town. From the way Hazel talked, Mrs. Wheeler was too important and too busy to do something so regular as running errands or sitting at a friend's kitchen table for a cup of coffee.

Far as I knew Hazel wanted nothing more in life than to grow up to be just like her mother.

She didn't see me, Mrs. Wheeler didn't. As a matter of fact, it seemed she didn't see anything at all. Her eyes were fixed way down the road, in the direction that led north out of Bliss and toward places I'd never been. One of her hands was held over her mouth and by the way her body moved in jerks and how her eyes closed every once in a while I wondered if she was crying.

And I wondered what it was she was missing, what it was that made her so sad.

I couldn't help but think on what Aunt Carrie'd said. That everybody had a hurt in their heart. Maybe even two or three. Everybody was missing something whether they liked to admit it or not.

As much as I didn't want to, I felt sorry for Mrs. Wheeler because I'd seen that same look of pain on Mama's face.

Grief can do terrible things to a person, Aunt Carrie had said.

How true that was. How terrible and true.

I didn't hurry back to the house on Magnolia Street. As it was, every step made me miss Mama more and more.

CHAPTER FORTY-FOUR

Back in Red River we'd never celebrated Halloween. Pastor had told us it was the devil's holiday with kids dressed up as ghosts and witches, running from door to door and begging strangers for candy. Never mind that everybody in town knew each other and would gladly give a sweet to a child that asked nice.

Each year in my memory Pastor Ezra Anderson had devoted a whole sermon to the evils of Halloween.

"Witchcraft and demon possession," he'd screamed. "That's all that'll come from such pagan holidays."

Meemaw would sit in the pew, rocking back and forth the way she did when the Spirit grabbed hold of her, calling out amens as Pastor ranted.

So when Aunt Carrie asked if we'd come to a Halloween party on the farm, I was surprised when Daddy told her we wouldn't miss it for all the world.

Had Mama been around she'd have made sure we didn't go.

It was just one more thing on a long list that made life without Mama different.

If I could have, I would've traded that party to have Mama back even if just for one day. I wouldn't care if I missed out on the treats or the costumes. None of that would matter if I had Mama. I'd gladly sit beside her on the davenport, content to be quiet along with her.

Instead, I made myself pretend that I couldn't wait for Halloween to come along.

The party was the talk of Bliss for a whole week. Miss De Weese had to disallow all discussion of it during school on account none of us could keep our focus on our work. All anybody wanted to think on was what they'd wear for a costume or who they might sit with on the hayride. A couple boys even tried guessing who might win the pumpkin-carving contest.

Opal told me she'd help me with my costume just so long as I didn't go as anything scary. She said she could help me make an angel costume if I thought I'd like that. Far as I remembered from reading the angel stories in the Bible, they'd been scary enough to the folks that'd seen them. If they hadn't been I didn't know why they'd had to say "fear not" so much.

When I told her that she just smiled and told me I was something else.

I asked if I could go as Sacagawea.

"I don't even know who that is," she told me.

I showed her in the book Mrs. Trask had let me borrow from the library how Sacagawea was an Indian woman who helped the explorers Lewis and Clark. Opal just looked at me like I was speaking German or some such strange tongue.

"You want to be an Indian?" she asked.

"Yes, ma'am," I answered with a smile.

When she told me I could, I about fell over with surprise.

I added that costume to the list of things Mama would have said no to if she'd still been at home.

I thought when she came back someday she'd be real surprised by all that'd changed.

Of all the things to do at that Halloween party—bobbing for apples and square dancing and jack-o'-lantern carving—the very best fun I had that night was sitting on a bale of hay on the wagon pulled around by Uncle Gus's pack mules.

The hay prickled my skin through the brown-colored fabric of my Indian squaw costume, but I did not care even a little. The cool breeze blew through my still-short hair making me wish I'd brought along a warm sweater like Opal'd told me to. But the full-of-stars sky twinkled down at me making me forget the goose pimples on my arms and the way my teeth chattered. An almost full moon lit up the trees and the stubble of harvested cornstalks and the smile that had been on Ray's face all night long. Anything that could've haunted me that night was pushed far from my mind.

Uncle Gus took us over fields and along the edge of the woods. He wove us between rows of apple trees that had been picked clean of their sweet apples to make pies and cider. Oh, how I wished I'd had a cup of warm cider just then.

The sounds of the party—the bouncing music and hooting laughter—seemed far gone from us as we rode along. All I wanted to hear were the clip-clopping of mule hooves along the ground and the light clicking of their harnesses.

If he'd offered, I would have let Uncle Gus drive me around like that all the rest of the night. Cold as I was, I didn't want the free and easy feeling of the bumping ride to end. I imagined a warm arm wrapped around my shoulders, pulling me to her soft side. She'd hum a happy tune, stopping every now and again to wonder over all we saw.

"Did you see that shooting star?" she'd ask. "Make a wish, darlin'."

Or she'd plant a kiss on the top of my head, healing every hurt part of my soul.

But when I imagined her sighing before sounding out the words of a poem, I realized it wasn't Mama I was imagining but Aunt Carrie.

Mama never would've done something so unladylike as ride around on a bale of hay.

The ride was over, I could tell by how Uncle Gus slowed the mules, pulling up on the reins as we neared the barn and clucking his tongue at them. One of them let out a ghostly sound. It wasn't a whinny and it wasn't a bray. It sounded more like a witch's cackle and I tried not to let it spook me too much.

Ray and Bert climbed over the side railings and took off running toward the table piled high with doughnuts. Uncle Gus swung his legs down from his seat and set to freeing the mules from the wagon, leading them one at a time back to the stables where I knew he'd have fresh feed for them to nibble. Once he finished that, he came around by where I had stayed on the old wagon. He rested his arm on the side of the wood right behind me.

"You all right?" he asked.

"Yes, sir," I told him. "Thanks for the ride. It was real nice."

"I'm glad you liked it." He nudged me with his elbow. "We'll go again this winter sometime. It's real pretty out here after it snows."

"I'd like that."

"Tell you what, I'd even let you sit up front if you'd like," he said. "You could steer the mules wherever you wanted to wander. You think you'd like that?"

"Yes, sir," I told him.

A thought passed through my mind. Just a flicker of imagining. I pictured Beanie riding along beside me on that wagon, not daring to so much as touch the reins, a shy and happy smile stretched across her face.

The spark set a slow burn of longing deep in my gut. I sure missed my sister.

"Well, I think you'll wanna come along." Uncle Gus patted me on the back. "It's just about time for the ghost story."

"Is it real scary?" I let him take my hand and help me off the trailer, hay still clinging to my Indian squaw clothes, thoughts of my sister still in the center of my mind. "Will it give me nightmares?"

"Nah. You'll see." He leaned down and whispered in my ear. "Don't tell nobody else, but I got a funny one this year."

Uncle Gus didn't let go of my hand as we walked to where Daddy was busy building up a big campfire. Other men carried over logs and stumps for all the kids to sit on.

Ray had saved a spot for me right beside him and I took it, glad for the warmth of the fire but even more glad to be near him. The flames were hot, almost too hot, but I wasn't about to move away from them. I hadn't realized how cold I'd gotten on the hayride.

Uncle Gus sat on the tallest stump so we could all see his face, yellow and orange in the flickering firelight. Nobody said so much as a word, or moved or cleared their throats, even. We all leaned in, our eyes on the man, waiting for him to begin.

"Y'all ready for a scary story?" he asked, his voice just above a whisper. We nodded our heads, still silent.

"Well, then, I'll tell ya one." He rested his hands on his knees, elbows pointed outward, and looked at all of us sitting there, his face not showing one hint of a smile. "There was once a man here in Bliss . . ."

Uncle Gus went on a long time telling his story and all the kids laughed and shrieked and listened close as they could. Seemed it was a powerful good story. When I looked around I saw the adults standing by to hear it, too.

As for me, I couldn't keep my mind still to follow along. All I could think of was Mama. Hard as I tried to push the idea of her away, I couldn't. I just wasn't strong enough.

The story ended and all the folks clapped. The kids around me clamored for another story and Uncle Gus said he had just one more. He started in on one about a dark and foggy night that wasn't scary at all. I was real glad for that.

Once the fire started to die down, mothers gathered their children, wiping their faces of sticky-sweet and putting an arm around their shoulders to guide them to their cars. They followed, sleepy children full of doughnuts and apple cider and memories that might last them a good many years.

I rode in the back of Daddy's truck alongside Ray, not saying a word. We were too tired, I thought, for talking. Arms folded on the side of the truck bed, I rested my head on my hands, watching the dark farmland rush past me.

In my heart was a longing I'd grown tired of. A wanting I wished so hard I could shake off myself.

Even when we got to the house on Magnolia Street and Daddy half carried me up to my room, putting me to bed, costume and all, the feeling stayed.

I wanted Mama.

CHAPTER FORTY-FIVE

The night before Thanksgiving I dreamed of Beanie. She ran off like she always did, faster than I could go. Chasing far behind, I called for her to stop, to come back to me. Her feet moved across the grass, dew wetting her shoes and making her slide along between the apple trees. If I listened close I could have sworn I heard her laughing.

It was a good sound.

How she ended up there in Uncle Gus's apple orchard I couldn't figure out. In life she'd never left Oklahoma, let alone made it all the way to Michigan. It didn't matter really, I guessed. It was a dream and Beanie visited me with a smile and a laugh. It made me glad.

"Come get me," she called over her shoulder, still darting here and there, getting herself lost among the apple-heavy branches.

Reaching the end of the line she stopped, a breeze lifting her hair. Her wild curls spiraled up from her head and she leaned back so the sun would warm her face.

The wind picked up, making a pinwheel of green grass and fresh-fallen leaves of orange and yellow and red right in front of my sister. She lifted her hands and I thought it was her way of wondering at the glory of such beauty.

"Where's Mama?" she called to me, her eyes closed.

"I don't know," I answered. "She went away."

"But not how I went away?"

"No."

"She got lost?"

"No, Beanie," I called to her, having to talk louder because of the wind-swirl filling our ears. "She left us."

"Then she'll come home again."

The flowers turned to dirt, the blades of grass to dust. They gathered together into a dark-as-ink cloud, roaring all around Beanie and me.

"Don't be scared," Beanie hollered at me. "Mama'll come back."

I tried standing still, but the storm around us pushed at me, knocked me to my knees. I curled into a ball on the ground.

But it was then I heard Beanie singing. Not with a girl's voice and not with words. She sang like a bird that wasn't afraid. A bird that wouldn't ask for so much as a crumb.

Aunt Carrie let me help in the kitchen. She put me to work peeling potatoes and cutting them up for boiling. I was real proud that I didn't cut myself once and I only sent two slippery potatoes flying across the room as I worked the peeler over them.

But each time that happened Aunt Carrie let out a hooting laugh, clapping her flour-covered hands so they sent a cloud of white puffing up around her face.

"You're doing well, my dear," she said. "You're a good help to me."

Women's work was hard. And Thanksgiving food was forever-long work. At least that was how it seemed to me.

But as much as Aunt Carrie laughed, she made it a lot more fun.

Before it was time for us to eat our meal, Uncle Gus packed a load of food into his car. Pies and breads and a whole basket of eggs. He even took a whole turkey, roaster and all, putting it in the trunk.

"Where are you taking all that?" I asked after he carried out the last of it.

"Well, I'm fixin' to take it out to the Fitzpatricks," he said. "I do believe they could use them a little feast today, too."

I thought about Delores and her small lunches, her dirty hair, and her worn-out clothes. Then I imagined her sitting at a table with a plate of food in front of her. More than she'd be able to eat. The picture in my mind was of her smiling with every bite she took. It seemed as pretty a sight as any I could see.

"Can I go?" I asked, hoping maybe I'd get to see Delores even for a minute.

"Just so long's it's all right with your daddy," Uncle Gus said.

Daddy said it was fine by him, so I climbed into the seat next to Uncle Gus, smelling all the good food and trying not to let my tummy rumble.

Hungry as I was, I knew the Fitzpatricks were even hungrier. I imagined standing beside Uncle Gus while he carved up that turkey at their table, dishing it up and passing it out. The family'd be so grateful they wouldn't know what to say. Delores would smile at me shyly and I'd nod back at her, to let her know that I was right happy to see her enjoying the food we'd brought.

It didn't take us ten minutes and we were pulling up to where Delores and her family lived.

I'd heard the kids at school tease about the Fitzpatricks' home more than once, how it'd been a chicken coop before they moved in. I thought they were just making fun until I saw it with my own eyes on that Thanksgiving morning.

Aunt Carrie's hens had a bigger coop than the Fitzpatricks did.

Uncle Gus pulled up real close to the door and cut the engine.

"We'll just put the food right there," he told me, pointing to where a porch would've been on any other house. "We're gonna leave it there and drive right on back home."

"Why?" I asked. "Can't we say hi?"

"No, miss. They'd be too embarrassed." He nodded. "We'll just let them hold a little of their pride."

I helped Uncle Gus place the food in front of the door, worrying the whole time that it would be cold before they could get to it. And sorry that I wouldn't see how happy it made them. I wished so hard that I could've heard them say thank you for the kindness we'd shown them. I didn't say a word about it, though. We moved quiet as we could and quick, too.

We climbed back into the car and drove away from the chicken coop house. Just before we turned down onto the road, I looked back.

The food was already gone.

We sat around Aunt Carrie's table, our plates full to the edges with turkey and mashed potatoes and cranberry sauce. I tried eating dainty-like, the way Mama had taught me. Ray, though, shoveled it in like he hadn't taken a bite of food in a month.

Between him and Mayor Winston, we weren't like to have anything left over.

"Now, Carrie, I gotta say I ain't never had such good mashed potatoes," Uncle Gus said. "I'd sure like some more if I might. Please and thank you."

"I'm happy to say I didn't make them this year." Aunt Carrie handed him the dish with a pretty silver serving spoon sticking up out of the yellowy mound. "Our Pearl made them. From peeling to mashing. She did all of it."

"Well"—Uncle Gus put two helpings on his plate—"must be why they taste so good."

"I guess it couldn't hurt me to have a little more of them," Winston said, reaching for the bowl. "Pearl, some day you'll make a man real happy."

"Hold on there," Daddy said, pretending to be upset. "She's not allowed to get married until she's thirty. At least."

I pretended to be embarrassed because it seemed the ladylike thing to do. Really, though, I was right proud. I was glad nobody said a thing about any of the big lumps of potato I hadn't managed to smooth all the way.

"I ever tell you about the time old Jed Bozell came for Thanksgiving?" Daddy asked, winking right at me.

I couldn't help but smile and real big, too. I thought sure Daddy had run out of Jed Bozell stories soon as we left Oklahoma.

"Now," Uncle Gus said, lowering his fork to his plate and sitting back in his chair, "that's a name I ain't heard in years."

"You know about Jed Bozell?" I asked, leaning forward.

"Course I do." Uncle Gus grinned at me. "Fella came to Red River every single year."

"And he was real?"

"Real as you or me." He shoved a big forkful of potatoes in his mouth. He had to give them a good chew, still he made a humming sound like they tasted real good. "Tom, go on with your story, would ya?"

And Daddy did go on. He told a story about Meemaw making Thanksgiving dinner and how Jed Bozell's human dragon had helped cook the turkey all the way through by spitting fire on it. And he told of the cats that did acrobatics in the living room and the woman who sang opera in a voice so high all the dogs in Red River came running.

Ray slapped at his leg under the table he got to laughing so hard, and Uncle Gus backed Daddy up that every word of the story was true. Winston took quick breaks between bites to chuckle at the ridiculousness of it all. Aunt Carrie listened with one eyebrow raised the whole time like she wasn't sure what to think. Still, she had a smile on her face that made me believe she was right delighted.

As for me, I gave thanks for lumpy potatoes and kind uncles. For pretty tablecloths and aunts who smiled easy. For stories that made pictures in my head and books that drew me to wondering. I gave thanks for the folks who shared that very table and for Delores and her family, too. And I gave thanks for the one who was somewhere else.

And for Jed Bozell. I gave double thanks for him.

CHAPTER FORTY-SIX

It wasn't the first snow. That had happened weeks before. But it was the first that left a good blanket of white over everything. I stood at the back door of the house on Magnolia Street and waited for Ray to find a saw. I thought I might sweat to death before we made it out the door for all the warm things Opal insisted on me wearing.

Ray and I stepped off the back porch and let our booted feet sink into the three inches of snow. As soon as we were far enough away from the house so Opal wouldn't see, I lowered my scarf, shoving a gloveful of snow into my mouth.

All it tasted like was water, still there was something magical about it.

"You ready?" Ray asked once we reached the tree line.

I told him I'd been ready near half an hour.

We walked in together, the forest seeming different with the leaves all fallen off and the snow dusting the branches. It was quieter, even, as if the cold had made all the birds shy. Winter seemed a season of stillness.

We reached the clearing near where the twisted tree stood, tall and bare. Its many arms reached up to the God who'd made it and I wondered what it could be that it needed from Him. I imagined the woman, Miss Ada, standing beside that tree not so many years before, missing her son the way I missed Mama. I pictured her standing beside that tree, her arms lifted same as the branches, asking God if He'd be so pleased as to send her boy back home.

I thought about raising my hands over my head, too. I thought if I begged Him for Mama one more time maybe that would do the trick.

Trouble was, she was the one who had to do the returning. God wasn't one for forcing. He was one for gentle nudges. How I hoped she'd let herself feel His elbow.

"You comin'?" Ray asked.

I told him I was and followed him to a clearing where the evergreens grew to just the right height. Where he'd stepped I stepped, my feet in the holes he'd made in the snow.

We walked past the cabin, the one window like an eye. I imagined Miss Ada standing in that window, staring out.

Watching and waiting for the part of her that was lost.

Waiting and watching, an untrue hope all she had to keep her from crumbling.

She couldn't hardly help herself, I didn't think, from checking in between kneading dough and hanging laundry on the line. She would peek out, just in case, before turning down the lights for the night. And every morning she'd pass by that window, a hand on her heart, allowing a quick look out the corner of her eye.

Just in case.

Ray and I picked our tree and he dragged it until we stepped out of the forest and made it all the way to the house on Magnolia Street. He leaned it against the back porch and put a hand to his chin, examining it to see if it would be right.

"I think it'll be just fine," he said.

"It's a good tree," I told him. "I like it."

We stood admiring it for a couple minutes as if it were a fine painting hanging in a museum somewhere.

"Hey, Pearl," Ray said after a moment.

"What?" I asked.

"Heads up," he hollered.

When I turned toward him I ended up with a faceful of cold and wet.

We ran all over that back yard, our footprints scuffing up the fresh snow. We threw handfuls of it at each other until Opal hollered out for me to pull my scarf back up over my mouth.

Then Ray found a good untouched spot. He fell backward onto the ground, his arms stretched out at his sides.

He lay there real still with his eyes closed, taking in deep breaths like he meant to fill up on the good feelings of that very moment.

Opening one eye, he caught me looking at him and I hoped he'd think the red in my cheeks was from the cold air.

"I know what you're thinkin'," he said, lifting himself up on his elbow and grinning at me.

"Oh yeah?" I crossed my arms and stuck out one of my hips. "What am I thinking?"

"You're thinkin', 'My, my, but that Ray Jones is a handsome young man.'"

I bent over at the waist and laughed so hard I thought my sides would split.

I didn't dare tell him he was right.

CHAPTER FORTY-SEVEN

Miss De Weese had me playing Mary the mother of Jesus in the school Christmas pageant. She told me I didn't have to do much more than hold the baby doll Jesus in my arms and keep a peaceful look on my face as the shepherds came to see the sweet Christ child.

"I've never held a baby before," I told her, hoping that would lose me the part. "I don't know how to. I'd probably drop it."

"Didn't you ever play with dolls?" Miss De Weese asked.

I guessed she didn't know all that much about me yet.

"Why don't you get Hazel Wheeler to do it?" I asked.

Miss De Weese said that Hazel had played Mary the year before, it said so in the program somebody'd saved in a file. And Ethel the year before that. She told me that it was time for somebody else to take a turn.

I just did not know why it had to be me.

From what I remembered, Mary of the Bible was about as perfect as any girl could be. I didn't imagine she'd ever sassed her folks or took something that didn't belong to her. She was God's pick for Jesus's mother due to the fact that she was so good.

As for me, I was anything but good. It would take either a miracle or mighty good acting for me to play that part.

On the day of the pageant I knelt at the manger, the swaddled baby doll Jesus in my arms. Like Miss De Weese had told me, I didn't look at all the folks sitting in the pews watching me. Instead, I kept my eyes on the face of the fair-skinned, blue-eyed newborn Lord.

The cattle lowed and the sheep bleated. The shepherds shook with fright.

Angels gloried and wise men gave gifts. Joseph stood off to the side like he might just get sick.

I kept all those things and pondered them in my heart.

When I'd been smaller I'd thought Mary and Joseph and the baby Jesus had stayed there, taking up housekeeping right in that Bethlehem stable. From the watercolor picture of the first Christmas in my Bible, it hadn't looked any worse than some of the cabins the sharecroppers stayed in back in Red River. Maybe even a good deal better.

I'd learned since then that it wasn't so.

But for that night, that short time, it had sheltered that holy family. I wondered if God hadn't seen fit to clear away the animal smells and plug up the drafty gaps in the stable walls. If He'd let a little of the angel's glory song stick around until it turned to a lullaby for His sweet baby Son.

And I hoped that, in His greatness, He'd looked at all He'd done on that night in that humble and dim stable and saw that it was good.

Daddy kept the fire going all day on Christmas. Aunt Carrie made sure we stayed full up with cookies and ham and potatoes and such. Ray beat me no less than five times at chess on the set he'd gotten under the tree that morning.

All those funny-shaped pieces did nothing but confound me.

Uncle Gus told us stories of Christmases past. He sure did have a lot of them to share on account he'd seen so many in his life. At least that was what he told us.

I took to sitting on the davenport, my brand new book of fairy tales open on my lap. It wasn't the same as the one I'd had before. The pictures were different, darker. But the stories were more or less the same.

I read them slow, those stories, letting them sink back into that familiar part of my soul that knew them each by heart. Princesses turned to slaves and fairy godmothers saving the day. Three little pigs and bears and blind mice. A girl in red gone to call on her grandmother.

Fairy tales with happily-ever-after endings that I needed right about then.

Right smack-dab in the middle of that storybook was the one of the boy and girl, them being taken from the home where they'd not been wanted, not been loved. They'd found danger and struggle and darkness along the journey. But they'd found their way to a new family and a new life.

They'd gotten home.

And not a trail of crumbs could have led them away.

```
┌─────────────────────────────────┐
│ TELL THE WORLD THIS BOOK WAS     │
│                                   │
│  GOOD   │   BAD   │   SO-SO      │
│         │         │              │
│         │         │              │
│         │         │              │
│         │         │              │
└─────────────────────────────────┘
```

Discussion Questions

1. At the beginning of the story, Pearl and Ray discuss leaving Red River. Have you ever been in a situation where leaving a place/job/church was the logical decision, but emotionally it seemed impossible? How did you work out that tension?

2. What did you think of Ray's mother's request that Daddy take her son with them? Was this a selfish or selfless act? What might have been her motivation? Should Daddy have agreed to take Ray? Did your perspective on this change as the story unfolded?

3. Many families from the Dust Bowl region relocated to California where there was the promise of work and good pay. The Spence family goes north to be with a cousin Daddy hadn't seen in over a decade. What do you think of their choice? How might the story have been different if they'd gone to California?

4. In an agriculturally healthy place such as Bliss, the people weren't as hard-pressed to find food during the Great Depression. However, they felt the pinch of the financial crisis in other ways. How might they have experienced the Depression differently than those living in the Dust Bowl region? From those living in a major city?

5. It was common for local newspapers to publish the names of those who took assistance from the government during the Great Depression. Why do you think this was a common practice? What purpose could it have served? What was your reaction to that part of the story?

6. From Pearl's perspective, Mama's behavior in Michigan is out of character. What are some changes Pearl sees? What caused these changes? Is Mama being internally or externally motivated, especially in her interactions with Abe Campbell? Have you seen this kind of transformation in someone you know? What was it like?

7. For Pearl, stories are a way to process her life as well as escape from it. What role do stories play in your life? What childhood book was your favorite or made the strongest impression on you?

8. To help the nation recover from the Depression, President Roosevelt established many government programs in the New Deal. One was the Works Progress Administration, which hired people to build national infrastructure, document the era through newspapers and photography, and teach in rural communities that could not afford a teacher (like Miss De Weese). Some chaffed at this program while others praised it. What do you think of such government programs? Could people have survived the Depression without those jobs or food assistance? What might the reaction to such programs be today?

9. What types of prejudice are evident in this novel? How does Pearl largely manage to observe them and not participate in them? What has shaped her view of others who are different from herself?

10. Near the end, Pearl feels the tension between anger and sadness and the desire to forgive Mama. This is a complex emotional state and can be confusing for adults, let alone children. Have you felt this type of emotional tension before? Were you able to resolve it? How?

11. Pearl's story continues in *A Song of Home: A Novel of the Swing Era.* What do you think will happen to her in the completion of her story? What would you like to see happen? If you could wish one thing for her life, what would it be?

Afterword

I based the town of Bliss on a southeastern Michigan farming community called Blissfield. As a child I visited the family farm there once or twice a year. I have rich and happy memories of wandering around the barns, cartwheeling my way across the vast yard, and riding on an old tractor with my Grandma Pearl's cousin Gerald Seegert.

For this city girl, my days on that farm were magical and I look back on those visits as some of my favorite memories.

Someone else lives in the house now, the land parceled out long ago. Grandma Pearl and her cousin Gerald have been gone for a long time. But what I have are those memories. This novel recaptures part of my childhood.

ALSO AVAILABLE FROM
SUSIE FINKBEINER

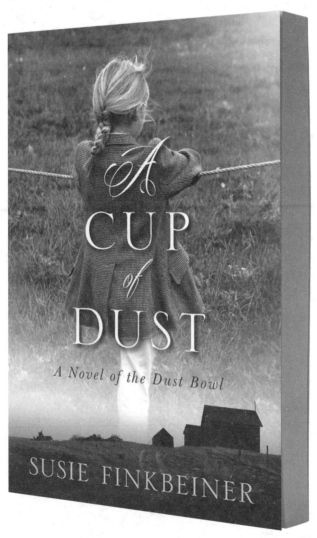

And don't miss *A Song of Home,*
coming February 2018!